What the critics are saying…

"The attraction between Nerin and Karinna is blazing hot...Together they just about go up in flames. Run...do not walk, to experience the story of Karinna and Nerin, and to find out where the necklace ends up." ~ *Maggie Ryan, Sensual Romance/The Best Reviews*

"This anthology titillates, teases and captivates its audience. *Myra Nour, Sahara Kelly* and *Ann Jacobs* are three powerful authors who know what readers desire, fantasize about and need. This anthology is a MUST read and I can't help but wonder....will the magical necklace reappear someday?" ~ *Tracey West, The Road To Romance*

"...Having the necklace tie these stories together is wonderful...Watching it as it goes through time, and not lose its magic. Watching each of these very different couples find happiness, love, and sexual fulfillment." ~ *Lisa Wine, The Romance Studio*

"...Grab a tall glass of cold water and hold onto your seat because *Sahara Kelly* will take you on a hot and exciting ride with her wonderful story *Visions*...I highly recommend *Mystic Visions* written by some of today's very talented authors." ~ *Lisa Lambrecht,* In The Library Reviews

"...a trio of talented authors, three tales of destiny, and the magical necklace that binds them together...A fun way to pass the time with three very unique voices penning the timeless tale of love's destiny!" ~ *A Romance Review*

"An emotional story, *Zayed's Gift* still maintains it's eroticism while Brian sorts through his own demons, with the help of some unlikely characters, and others that are familiar...a wonderful anthology..." ~ *Romance Reviews Today*

"*Zayed's Gift* is a tale of release from captivity -- from the bonds of custom and habit, of the mind and of the body. Jacobs has a gift with words...a powerful story and Jacobs handled it well...an enjoyable, satisfying conclusion to a well-written anthology." ~ *Ann Leveille, Sensual Romance*

"...a very heartfelt and romantic tale with *Zayed's Gift*. While this was a short story, the plot was one you instantly got into and the characters felt like old friends...and the sex scenes... oh my... were very hot." ~ *Lisa Lambrecht, In The Library*

"...a heat-seeking tale of ecstasy and love. The necklace proved *Zayed's Gift* to be true."~ *Brenda Ramsbacher, Women on Writing*

4 *stars* "The erotic novellas in *Mystic Visions* are held together by an extraordinary necklace that brings lovers together and reveals their love. Readers will enjoy the variety of sexual encounters and lovers in these stories and the unique gifts that sexual chemistry brings to passion. -- *Cindy Whitesel for Romantic Times*

"A fun way to pass the time with three very unique voices penning the timeless tale of love destiny!" ~ *Connie for A Romance Review.*

"This magical, mythical story tells of the creation of the magical necklace that wends its way through the rest of the stories in the anthology." ~ *Ann Leveille for Sensual Romance*

Ann Jacobs
Sahara Kelly
Myra Nour

MYSTIC VISIONS

ELLORA'S CAVE
ROMANTICA PUBLISHING

An Ellora's Cave Romantica Publication

www.ellorascave.com

Mystic Visions

ISBN # 141995265X
ALL RIGHTS RESERVED.
Dragon Fire Copyright © Myra Nour, 2003.
Visions Copyright © Sahara Kelly, 2003.
Zayed's Gift Copyright © Ann Jacobs, 2003
Cover art by: Syneca

Electronic book Publication: March, 2003
Trade paperback Publication: October, 2005

Excerpt from *As You Wish* Copyright © Myra Nour, 2004
Excerpt from *A Kink in Her Tails* Copyright © Sahara Kelly, 2003

Warning:

The following material contains graphic sexual content meant for mature readers. *Mystic Visions* has been rated *E-rotic* by a minimum of three independent reviewers.

Ellora's Cave Publishing offers three levels of Romantica™ reading entertainment: S (S-ensuous), E (E-rotic), and X (X-treme).

S-*ensuous* love scenes are explicit and leave nothing to the imagination.

E-*rotic* love scenes are explicit, leave nothing to the imagination, and are high in volume per the overall word count. In addition, some E-rated titles might contain fantasy material that some readers find objectionable, such as bondage, submission, same sex encounters, forced seductions, etc. E-rated titles are the most graphic titles we carry; it is common, for instance, for an author to use words such as "fucking", "cock", "pussy", etc., within their work of literature.

X-*treme* titles differ from E-rated titles only in plot premise and storyline execution. Unlike E-rated titles, stories designated with the letter X tend to contain controversial subject matter not for the faint of heart.

Contents:

Dragon Fire

Myra Nour

Chapter One

Knowing he had but moments left to him in this transitory state, he concentrated on the slender form he could barely distinguish in the gloom of the darkened room. His eyesight was not very effective in this astral plane. Reaching down, he stroked one hand over her face, liking the delicateness of its features. If she awoke, she would think ghostly hands played with her. Grinning, Xandor placed a hand on either side of her breasts, caressed her body all the way down, to the top of her thighs.

He couldn't really feel the softness of her flesh. His senses were dull. But he could imagine. His mind could very well fill in the gaps of his cloudy long-distance senses. Even in his ethereal form, he found her tremendously exciting.

She groaned in her sleep and he wondered if she'd felt his touch. The soft moan stirred him even more, encouraged him to stroke her flat abdomen. He realized then that she was totally nude; that stimulated his interest even further. Flouncing restlessly, she mumbled in some unknown tongue. He pressed down harder with his transparent hands, kneading her breasts, and she moaned loudly.

Abruptly, he sensed his time was at an end. In frustration, he ran one hand through her soft-looking tresses while he slowly withdrew. She sat straight up, staring as if she could see him. Xandor knew this was impossible, even for one trained in the magical arts, but she seemed to sense him floating above her.

"*Sinar biur.*"

Even her words haunted him with their singsong beauty. Both hands reached for him in entreaty, and somehow he knew she whispered, "Don't go." His energy was dissipating fast, her face fading; the last image he had was a single tear tracking down her formless face.

While his spirit traveled super-fast, back to his physical body, he thought about that tear. How odd it was that something as insubstantial and impermanent as a tear should be the only thing clearly visible to him in that dim room.

Xandor's mind and spirit returned with full force to his body, which shivered violently. His pulse raced and he had trouble breathing. He seemed to be on overload. He'd never cut it so close before when thought-searching. Breathing deeply, he calmed his frazzled senses.

His thoughts went to the mysterious woman, who called to him again and again. She'd been awake the last journey. Today, when he found her, she was deep asleep. He had floated over her form, only a dim outline to his astral senses. But it caught his interest and fired his imagination with its slender lines. What was it about this particular female that drew him two galaxies across the stars?

He didn't know but intended to find out.

Her thoughts had been unshielded. *Curious. She is not psychic, nor does she practice magic of any kind.* Xandor found this puzzling. He would have guessed only a creature of immense power could have drawn his attention and pulled him, as she had done.

Xandor shook free of his musings. His body's biorhythms had returned to normal. Glancing around, he thought about the method by which he thought-searched.

He sat cross-legged in the center of his room softly lit by four fat red candles strategically positioned in a semi-circle in front of him. Each foot-high candle represented his level of magic power. Fourth level was attained by a limited few, he among them. Xandor frowned in frustration when he momentarily considered the fifth level. A place reached by even fewer students—never, as yet, by an Earthling, among whom it was rare to attain even the third level. Hence, as a fourth class wizard from Earth, he was already seen as strange by some. To others, he was an inspiration, especially young Thorras, the only other sorcerer from Earth. For three years now Xandor had been studying and practicing fervently, but felt no closer to his goal of attaining the fifth level.

The room was set up to further such studies—it was circular to channel psychic energy toward the room's central area. The walls were green granite; the speckled and swirled patterns in the heavy stones were beautiful, but decoration was not their purpose. The stones' thick, absorbent nature created a room of solitude, undisturbed by the noisy life outside its walls. For his stature as a fourth class wizard, Xandor had earned a room with a large window overlooking one of the few lush courtyards contained in the busy hub.

While preparing for meditation, he closed the heavy, luxurious gold velvet drapes, which adorned the window frame. His favorite form of meditation and self-teaching in the arts was thought-searching. It took only a few moments of intense concentration before his inner spirit soared to spaces beyond this planet, often, even beyond the confines of this galaxy. Many nights he practiced this searching activity.

Connecting with minds of sapient aliens was thrilling and educational. One never knew what new tidbit of information he would pick up from a humanoid inhabiting another world. Most beings were not even aware of his superficial infringement on their thoughts. But some, who had mystical powers, had become friends over the years, pen pals of the mind.

Once he'd crossed paths with an Aki witch, something he'd been warned against. He'd returned to his body with a splitting headache that lasted for several days. He'd been lucky. The mental blow she'd dealt him easily could have resulted in insanity.

During one of his thought travels, he'd encountered a race of beings that were whispered about in dusky corners; no one ever knew by what name they called themselves, for it was rumored to invoke their name was to invite them into your soul.

A few sorcerers who'd turned to the dark forces for their power source were thought to have given allegiance to this demon race. While on his short sojourn to their world, he'd noticed the very air was laden with stygian evil. He'd withdrawn immediately, but not before the cold red glare of one creature's eyes lit upon him. Returning to his room shaken, he was convinced he'd barely escaped with his soul intact. It'd been weeks before he attempted another journey.

On his next search after the horrible incident with the grim creatures he found the *Taweeg*. The planet was filled with magic; it danced on the wind, sighed through the trees, sparkled in the air and lakes like rainbows.

Today's journey had been different, though. Today he had sought her. Last week he'd been in the middle of a search when he was drawn to a particular planet on the far fringes of the galaxy. The distance by ship would be astronomical, but to his trained wizard mind, it was but a moment's flight. It'd taken him a few minutes to wander among the stars, following the singsong voice of some unknown being, before he'd located the right planet. By the time he'd connected with her mind, it was time to return.

Thought-searching throughout the galaxy took much energy. His body let him know to reconnect with his physical form, before he was on the verge of collapse. He'd touched her unique mind—let her surprise and curiosity, at his intrusion zing through his nerve endings, before having to depart.

She was not a magical being. She shouldn't be able to call to him like the Taweeg do. Xandor found this confusing. At least she was not frightening like the Aki witch. He smiled at that thought. Still, why was she able to contact him?

Shrugging mentally, he went over the details he learned in delving into the fringes of her open mind. Her thoughts were filled with happenstances of her daily life: romps through forests so lovely as to take a man's breath away, some strange rite where she splayed her body among thick leaves of low growing flowers, and singing to a funny-looking creature perched on her hand.

Her singing was ethereal, ghostly in its beauty, angelic. He had never been a religious man, unlike some of his peers. He never seemed to have time to even consider his options. But if one could truly hear angels sing, he'd wager this petite female would outshine them. Her siren song spoke to his very soul. Listening to her, he'd been as spellbound as any youthful sorcerer caught up in a *Zardak's* web spell. As he thought, he realized it had to be her singing that drew him to her.

Uncertainty rioted through him. Was she filled with an alien magic he knew nothing about? Was she going to pull him under a wicked spell, destroy him somehow? Perhaps drain his magic through her singing? Such things had been known to happen, but he still couldn't reconcile the fact that he sensed no mystical powers on her. Only the witch and demon race had stirred his reactions as much as his brief encounters with the mysterious, siren female.

His thoughts returned to her slim figure and soft skin. A throb in his groin drew his attention from his musings about the girl. He was rock hard, his cock pulsing madly, like it did when he was a teenager and spied some attractive girl. Idly, he wondered if her flesh would be as velvety smooth as it seemed.

Closing his eyes, he tried to remember how it felt when he caressed her. It was delicious, almost real. In his mind, he continued to stroke her breasts, then his mouth descended on one hardened nipple. It was only in his mind he suckled on it, but his body reacted as if he really pulled the nipple into his mouth. Each time he sucked on the nub, his cock twitched. Continuing his oral assault on her breast, his hand slid down and stroked her pussy. *Delicious.* Then his finger slipped inside her wet silken walls. He replaced his finger with his cock, pausing at the entrance to her vagina. It was super-hot and seemed to suck him in, a wet invitation.

Xandor's daydreams had made him horny. Should he relieve himself? He grinned ruefully. Most men, even sorcerers, wouldn't hesitate. But he was different. Engaging in sexual activity, even masturbation, sucked energy from the body in great quantities, so that the magic was less effective—at least for that particular day.

Shrugging philosophically, he stretched out full length upon the soft *crituun* fur throw beneath him. The downiest fur known to this galaxy. He was already nude, since thought-searching was done without clothes to cut down on encumbrances.

Circling his right hand in an "o" position, he pushed his cock back and forth between his clenched fingers, while he brought back the image of thrusting it into her soft pussy. Running one hand through the luxurious pile while the other stroked his cock created a delicious double sensation. His breathing became ragged when he contemplated each stroke he'd love to give his siren. In his imagination, her hands caressed his cock, making the sensation more gut-wrenching. Fondling his balls with his left hand, he continued his fucking motions, the invisible girl at the receiving end of his strong stabbing movements.

Even in his mind, he wanted to satisfy her as well. So, he levitated his imaginary siren in front of him, and then stretched her body in a horizontal position. With a wave of his hand, he spread her legs wide and up. Her lovely pussy, called to him as strongly as any legendary vamp.

Wet, pink lips, luscious and inviting, pulled him forward. He sank into her warm flesh, his nose and lips soaking up her essence. Only after he had smelled and tasted her to his heart and cock's content did he lick her clit. She tasted of woman and desire. *Wonderful.* His tongue picked up speed, flicked her hard nub at a frenzied pace. His siren groaned loudly. Her orgasm flowed over his tongue and he sucked it up greedily.

He wanted her. Needed her beneath him. Switching his fantasy again, he positioned his cock at her pussy. She was still suspended in the air, very open and amenable to his thrusts. Gripping her hips, he shoved into her with ease, the levitation making it a silken glide. Her hot pussy gripped like a hand, snug and smooth. Each plunge of his cock moistened the passage more. He was slick with her juices and they ran down into his pubic hair.

His desire settled, centered in his groin and set fire to his blood. Moving his hand and cock in synch, he moaned low while he thrust fast and furious, incorporating circular gyrations into his imagined fucking. A pressure was building in his balls, threatening to burst. Changing his inner scenery around, he watched while she placed soft, full lips upon the head of his cock, looking up at him with dark eyes.

That was it. It felt as though his cock were filled with too much fluid, as a balloon filled to over capacity, threatening to burst at any moment. His blood was boiling hot when he shoved into her, pouring his seed in several large spurts into her greedy, sucking mouth. It was wonderful, this sudden release.

Afterwards, Xandor was more relaxed than he'd been in quite a while. He knew he'd neglected his body's demands many times, having wished to save energy for his conjuring. But, at the same time, a flash of frustration at his own weakness filled him.

Shrugging at his guilt over losing valuable energy, he prepared for bed, then fell heavily to the mattress. Sleep overtook him quickly.

Chapter Two

The next day, Xandor decided it was time to consult Master Talorg, the most powerful sorcerer at the school and their leader. Perhaps he'd have the wisdom to know why this mysterious woman affected him so.

Master's straight-faced assistants eyeballed him when he made his request. One nodded, then slipped silently through the huge double doors of Talorg's chambers. Xandor examined the portal while he waited—nothing else to do, unless he wanted to get in a staring contest with the *Gegli* wizards guarding the Master's sanctuary. Not something he counted among fun things to do, since these aliens had large slit-shaped green eyes that reminded him of a snake's. Of course their eyes would appear like a snake's, Xandor laughed inwardly. The *Gegli* were descended from reptiles.

The entrance to Talorg's chambers was a grand affair. The green stone facing was carved with symbols, the language of the ancient *Rithroll*, the first of the wizard races on this planet, who had created this school where those magically gifted could come to learn. No one knew how to read the etchings anymore, except the Master, who passed this knowledge to whatever being inherited the leadership.

The ten-foot tall doors, made from durable wood found on Tokalis Four—a planet in this very solar system—could withstand strenuous chopping or an attempt to pound them open. They must weigh several hundred pounds each. Such protection was not needed. No invading army had shown interest in the wizard planet, as it was known, except a demon race eons ago. The doors' powerful construction simply symbolized the Master's commanding presence.

A short-lived relief flashed through Xandor when the other *Gegli* waved him through the entrance. Not that he was nervous around the Master, who was kind-hearted and as easy to talk to as a best friend. But now he questioned his own motives. Why should he bother the busy Master Talorg with a slip of a girl, one he'd never truly met?

The chamber was huge and it took a few seconds to reach the head wizard, time in which Xandor made a quick scan of the room, as he always did. He loved this room, and he loved Master Talorg. The chambers but reflected his scholarly nature. The walls, like Xandor's, were composed of the green granite, yet whereas Xandor's bedroom was sparsely furnished, the Master's was crammed with objects.

A large alcove extended from the sleeping chambers, its stone walls lined with bookshelves, each packed with volume after volume of ancient texts. The leather-bound, priceless tomes were lined up neatly on the shelves, but stacks of volumes also had been jammed horizontally on top of the others when no more room could be found. What he wouldn't do to get his hands on these sacred texts, some so old the pages crumbled even when they were carefully turned.

Only Master Talorg and fifth level wizards had access to their secrets. Of course students had computers, which held vast reserves of knowledge from the universe. But, he felt a love for the old ways, thumbing through archaic volumes. As did the Master.

"Come in," Master Talorg said quietly, nevertheless his voice carried amazingly well in the large chamber.

It came as no surprise to find the leader hunched over an open book, a bright lamp made from *raglo* worms the only illumination in the otherwise gloomy alcove. Master's desk sat exactly in the center of all the surrounding shelves. Xandor bowed slightly when he reached the desk.

"Be seated, my boy." He waved at a thickly upholstered leather recliner, twin of the chair the Master sat in.

Despite the desk between them, the old wizard's aura was still crystal clear. Deep blue, powerful and deadly should he wish it so.

Clearing his throat, Xandor made a bad start. "I'm here about..." He paused and stared at Master.

His long, milk-white hair splayed out upon his black robe when Talorg nodded. "It's about a girl."

Surprise flashed through him, although he should be used to Talorg's ability to "read" troubled apprentices by now.

"Yes, I dreamed about this female. She drew me to her while I was thought-searching, but I could sense no power on her."

"I have been waiting for you to come to me about just such a situation."

Bending forward, he tried to discern the old man's expression. "You knew she would sing to me, pull me to her?"

Talorg laughed, a deep, startlingly pleasant sound. "No, but I knew you would eventually start to realize there is something you lack. That you must have if you are to ever reach the fifth level."

Confusion pulled his brow into wrinkles. "I don't understand."

"What I'm about to share with you must not be told to others." Master stared at him, waiting for a response it seemed.

"Not a word, Master."

"To attain the fifth level, a wizard must fulfill a certain destiny. He must secure his soulmate."

He peered back at the ancient sorcerer. Marriage? Was this what he meant? How ridiculous! He, and other wizards, *needed* a woman to complete their power?

Ignoring his turmoil, Talorg continued, "Sometimes, wizards find their enlightenment without aid. They may come here already paired with a partner, or fall in love while in training." He examined Xandor thoughtfully. "If not, the sorcerer must discover on his own the secret to his power."

"But, Master, a female is needed for me to attain the fifth level?!" He knew not just his words, but his whole face expressed his disbelief.

The Master's dark brown eyes never left Xandor's face. His eyes were captured by Talorg's intensity. "Have you never wondered why we have no women wizards?"

Xandor frowned, thinking back over the years. "I do remember considering it when I was a very young sorcerer."

"Do you ever sense power on females?"

He felt astonished. "Yes, I have. Please continue."

"Women have their own innate energy source. Some alien species become witches and other wielders of magic power. Yet, no woman of distinctly humanoid appearance has ever shown such ability as to become a wizard."

Xandor just sat, fascinated by this revelation, and waited for Talorg to continue.

"Yet, the power is still there—untapped, you might say."

He was becoming even more perplexed. "Please, Master, tell me what this all means?"

"Even females who have no overt magical aptitude have abilities endowed to womenkind: their power over men and mastery of the birthing process." Clearly noting his bewilderment, Talorg waved one hand gracefully and conjured a glass from the molecules in the air. Stretching his arm, he held the container beneath the light. "What do you see?"

"A finely cut crystal goblet, with what appears to be wine in it."

"Correct." He took a sip of the deep, burgundy liquid, a pleasantness coming over his heavily wrinkled face. "Not just any wine, but *Hargarian*."

Xandor couldn't help it, his mouth watered. He'd only had the privilege of tasting this heavenly ambrosia once, when he was young and splurged much of his hard-won earnings on a cupful.

Waving his free hand, Talorg brought forth another glass, which appeared unexpectedly in Xandor's hand lying in his lap. Xandor gripped it quickly, almost dropping it in his surprise.

"Drink."

Needing no further urging, he did, quashing the delighted moan that threatened to escape.

"Taste delicious?"

"Yes." He raised the glass, but Master snapped his fingers and it disappeared. Xandor couldn't stop the disappointment that flashed through him.

Talorg's drink had vanished as well, but the next instant he waved again, conjuring strange cups for each of their hands. Xandor turned the vessel this way and that, noting the crudeness of its construction; it appeared to be carved from grey rock.

"From the planet Ito," Master said softly.

"I've heard they are barbaric primitives."

"Just so." Talorg smiled at him. "Now drink."

Sipping the fluid, he glanced up at his host. Master seemed to expect a response. "Tastes better than the wine served here with dinner, but I can't place it."

Nodding sagely, a mischievous smile lit Talorg's face. "It too, is Hargarian."

"No." Holding the primitive cup away from him, he examined it minutely, and then took another sip. Hard to believe it was the same wine.

With another snap and wave from the Master, the heavy cup dissolved and another took its place. Xandor whistled in appreciation. "Is this made by the troll-like aliens on Brakstar One?"

"Yes. Lovely, isn't it?"

"Exquisite." He held the tall, thin wine glass toward the light, admiring the way the beams shot through the many faceted cuts.

"Carved from a single *rrai* stone." Talorg turned his hand, examining each side as well. "Takes them several months to carve each one, as the rrai is extremely hard, similar to Earth's diamonds."

Xandor observed the flickering rainbow colors wash over the surface, just as the Master did. "Renowned artisans," he muttered thoughtfully.

"To think, such clumsy looking creatures produce such priceless objects." Catching Xandor's eyes once more, Master commanded, "Drink."

Almost reverently, Xandor took a minute sip. Heavenly. Closing his eyes, he took a larger sip. This time, he didn't even try to stop the sigh that escaped his grateful lips.

"The true secret of the Hargarian wine's unique flavor is in the vessel in which it is served."

He frowned. "I'm still not sure—"

The Master interrupted, "You are the wine. Your soulmate the vessel."

Xandor's brow cleared. "You mean my power will increase if I find my true mate?"

"Just so." Talorg nodded, smiling happily. "Without your soul match, you will never attain the fifth level."

Oh great! All these years of hard work and his final accomplishment rested on some female who he'd never even met?

"How do I find her, Master?"

"You already found her through your thought-searching. Now, you must make a soul kin to draw you to her physical form."

"That will take powerful magic."

"Yes, all you can muster." Talorg smiled at him kindly. "To aid your quest, I give you permission to draw upon the Dragon Fire."

"Master." Xandor's voice quivered slightly. "Thank you." He stood and bowed respectfully, knowing instinctively his audience was at an end.

On his way back to his apartment, he thought about what Talorg had said. First, he must consider the soul kin and how he would compose such a talisman. Only when he knew what he must make would he allow himself to go into the Dragon Fire's presence.

The Dragon Fire. The most sacred object in this universe to the sorcerers who attended this prestigious institution. Normally, only the Master and fifth level wizards might be permitted to tap into its power. And only once had he seen it. As a new initiate he had been taken on a tour, like all were offered during their first month. Xandor knew he was being accorded a rare privilege, one that made him sweat just thinking of the task ahead.

His chambers seemed too confining. Without thinking, he headed toward the lush courtyard. Strolling along the winding maze-like trails, he came upon his favorite spot for contemplation, a tiny laid-brick circle with a splashing fountain set in the center. The fountain had no statue to distract his thoughts, simply a hole for water to shoot upward. But through several varying layers of rock, the water danced upon on its way down, creating a most pleasing sound, one made for meditation and relaxation.

Making a conscious effort, he disconnected his thoughts, letting them free float. Only the vague form of his mystery maid and the task of creating a soul kin occupied his mind.

An image began to emerge, one he found somewhat surprising: a necklace.

Xandor awoke from his self-imposed trance, knowing now the task set before him.

Chapter Three

Preparing himself the next day for his entry into the Dragon Fire's sacred realm didn't take much time: a quick shower, and then he simply slipped into a ceremonial robe he kept for special celebrations.

Xandor ran one hand ruefully down his black leather pants and matching vest, his normal apparel, which he'd had to leave hanging in his closet. He was more comfortable, both in body and spirit when he wore these. Some wizards had arched eyebrows at him when he first arrived at the school, but they said nothing. It was an individual decision what one chose to wear.

Many alien sorcerers did wear flowing robes, clothes of the office, so to speak. But some dressed in outlandish outfits from their worlds. The primitive *Jarsutak*, who produced awe-inspiring shamans, wore loincloths with multiple layers of beads strung around their necks, while the highly technological *Cograths* simply donned form-fitting spacesuit-type uniforms. He thought the bird species of *Akra* the most spectacular, sporting only their natural plumage.

Blame it on his rebellious youth when he zoomed around new Chicago on his skycycle, but he felt at home in biker clothes. Xandor chuckled to himself. A wizard's outward appearance was as important as his magic ability for frightening a potential enemy or impressing a suppliant for his services. His ruffian apparel did the trick, more often than not, in gaining him instant respect, or at least a wary approach. The ceremonial robes were encouraged, but not enforced. On the few occasions when they were called for, he wore them out of respect for the order and Master Talorg.

No jewelry draped his body; he didn't personally care for it. But, he picked up his wizard ring from the small box kept just for it. He slipped it onto his fourth finger. Its red *cortakian* gem sparkled like fire, set off beautifully by the raised gold engraving of the Varzkar dragon, caught in flight on the stone's surface. The priceless ring had been given to him when he reached the third level. And now he wore it only when making a trip offworld or when, as now, he had some magical task of great import. Those around him well knew his fourth level status; no need to impress them.

The necklace he'd conjured in his mind earlier edged back into his thoughts. He knew he was a study in contrasts when it came to jewelry. He didn't like to wear it, yet always made petitioners talismans to wear. His mother loved jewelry and was always buying some exquisite piece or other when he was growing up. His father grumbled, but couldn't really complain since mom had her own inherited wealth. Still too young to fully understand that boys and men didn't wear jewelry—according to his father's philosophy—he'd loved watching his mother's joy and allowed her to drape necklaces and bracelets on him.

One day, she'd brought home a large collection of beaded necklaces and they both looked like primitive natives by the time she finished ringing their necks and arms with the jewelry. They'd been giggling and jumping around the room to her favorite song, one with a drumming beat, when father walked in.

That was the end of his personal excursion into wearing jewelry. After that day, any time he showed interest in anything his father construed as unmanly, he'd be yelled at for being a "sissy boy". He'd signed up for an art class, one of the ancient arts of painting with oils but withdrawn after the first day, tired of his father's belittling attitude.

Not that his father was a total jerk. He had his good points. He was a good provider. He loved mom dearly, even though the two got into many heated arguments. Especially when his father started his sissy boy chant. Often, even though he was tired after work, his dad would play football and baseball with him. They'd even gone fishing a few times—memories he treasured.

His mom on the other hand, he could find no fault with. She was always loving, a brilliant thinker, and eccentric in her tastes in clothes and vacation destinations. He loved his mom and often felt guilty because he didn't visit her more often. *Maybe when I finish my fifth level of training?*

But it'd been his father's tough guy attitude that had driven him out of the house many a night as a teenager, and perhaps it influenced his decision to hang out with boys who loved trouble. He remembered thinking, if I robbed a bank, maybe dad would think I'm manly.

Xandor shook his head. What an idiot he'd been, barely skimming real trouble for years.

Until that day he had gone with two friends and robbed a convenience store. It landed him in juvenile jail—the place where his life turned around completely.

Shaking off thoughts of his youth, Xandor smoothed the silky material of the robe over his wrist. He smiled at the one frivolity the wizards granted themselves in purchasing the costly silk spun by the konkols of Volarn. He admired the embroidered symbols along the cuff; more silver decorations edged the bottom of the black robe. Not merely decorations though, but the lost language of the ancient Varzkar.

Xandor frowned when he stared in the mirror. He had to admit he looked impressive, in a very different way than usual. But still, to him, he looked more like a sheik than a sorcerer. Oh man, wouldn't his father yell "sissy boy" if he could see him now?

He laughed out loud. His dad's chants no longer bothered him, although it'd taken him many years to get to that point.

*   *   *   *   *

The trip to the Dragon Fire's chamber didn't take long, mere minutes, but getting through the entrance took longer.

27

Four wizards guarded this sacred room. Two held fifth level status; the other two were only third level wizards, but being Dizopon gave them an edge.

These aliens were famous throughout this galaxy as hired soldiers. Their bodies bristled with tiny, pointed spines from which they could shoot sharp barbs. Their natural weapons inflicted a temporary paralysis, making the Dizopon much sought after. But it was rare to see any dedicated to sorcery, the pay being vastly higher for their services as warriors. The two guarding the chamber were exceptional among their peers and took their duties as seriously as did the fiercest mercenaries.

One fifth level wizard checked a log-in sheet carefully, while the other meditated. Xandor knew the wizard checked the flow of his mental emanations. The two dangerous Dizopons examined him minutely as well, their eyes crawling over him as if searching for hidden weapons. Breathing slowly, he tried to manage his frustration at the stringent entry requirements, but the staring, spiny-tipped sorcerer-soldiers made it a difficult task at best.

Finally, the two higher-class wizards glanced at each other, then waved him toward the immense doors.

This portal made the Master's look small by comparison. The doors were at least twenty feet high and composed of a mysterious substance he was unfamiliar with, a shiny black wood that was both beautiful and very substantial. Carvings along the stone facing were so heavily entwined, he couldn't make out where one letter started and another ended. They almost looked like leaves and vines twisted about each other.

He was surprised when the sturdy door slid open with ease. Must have a mammoth spring system.

Xandor made sure the door closed completely before pausing in awe before the Dragon Fire. He didn't want to share even an inkling of his emotional excitement with those outside.

It was all his, at least for the duration of his visit.

He barely glanced at the background, which consisted of heavy red velvet drapes, covering all the stone walls. Someone, many years ago had decided a simple setting for the brilliant Dragon Fire was best, and no one had thought to disagree through the years, or question the decision. The sacred Fire captured any petitioner's full attention, so he noticed little else.

Dragon Fire was held within a spherical glass container, which hung suspended in the center of the small room by magic spells. For the most part it consisted of red flames with swirls of yellow flowing outward from its center. But the pattern never stayed the same; it moved constantly, as if a gentle wind blew upon its fiery mass. Yet nothing eddied within the circle of glass except the fire from one of Varzkar's sacred dragons.

Ancient beasts, creatures of legend. Said to be powerful both physically and magically. The myths were so old — they'd been handed down countless generations, until not much real truth remained of their being.

One truth held fast though, that the dragons had existed. The wizards of this institution guarded the final enchanted breath from the last of their line.

The ancient scrolls told of the dragons and Rithroll sorcerers connection at that time, how they fought together against an unnamed evil enemy, which threatened the whole universe. Not much was left of the archaic tale, except the knowledge that the dark forces had been defeated and sent back into the foul dimension from whence they'd come. No one knew what caused the great dragons to start dying off, but some speculated the underlings of the stygian realm cursed the beasts before departing. The scrolls reported that the last dragon lay dying, and with its final exhalation, gifted its magic to a powerful, wise wizard. This ancient practitioner of the arts grasped the fire with his own magic and bound it together until he could seal it within the glass container.

Coming out of his contemplation, Xandor considered his task. Once he had reached the fourth level, Xandor was trained in how to tap into the Dragon Fire's potency. All who reached this stature were schooled thus, even though some would never attain the fifth level.

Treading reverently forward, he paused in front of the orb. Placing his hands in the power position, crooked fingers grasping each opposing digit, he concentrated, centering his energy between his clasped hands. When his hands warmed to an almost uncomfortable heat, he was ready.

Releasing his grip, his right hand stretched forth slowly, but he never hesitated, even when his hand slid through the glass like it was water. Xandor breathed deeply, a self-imposed trance holding his natural trepidation at bay.

He didn't stop until his hand reached the center of the swirling mass. The fire, amazingly cool, washed over his hand and lower arm. Tiny pricks of electric sparks danced along his flesh, feeling pleasant, not painful.

While his arm received power from the Dragon Fire, he repeated a short chant over and over; one slanted toward his present need. One never requested anything other than the aid required at the precise time.

The fiery dragon breath flicking along his skin grew warm and would soon turn scorching.

It was time to withdraw.

Xandor drew his hand through the glass as easily as he had slid it in, and then clasped his hands in a prayerful attitude, repeating the ancient Varzkar words he'd been taught. Words thanking the Dragon Fire for its gift. He hated to leave the sacred presence, but knew he must.

Slipping out quietly, he nodded to each of the guards, gratified to note their eyes were lively with interest instead of suspicion when he exited.

* * * * *

Returning to his chambers, he spent some time simply sitting and staring at his hand, enjoying the sensation of great power flowing from it that tickled his other senses with rivulets of energy.

Then, sighing, he quickly changed clothes. The ancient magic wouldn't last past this day and he had much to do before it left him.

The large, primitive desk set against one wall already held all he figured he'd need to make the necklace. Drawing near, he stared down at the collection of items many a craftsman would envy. Gold to accent jewelry, various sizes of rainbow-hued gemstones, none priceless, but pretty. Also a large handful of stones from diverse planets, each with their own unique quality. He ran his eyes over his tools—some made for shaping, others for cutting or punching holes.

Xandor laughed aloud. He had a wonderful collection, from which he could make almost any piece of adornment. Usually, his charms were twists of metal with perhaps a few gemstones entwined in the cool grasp of the material to give them an artful appearance. For women, he sometimes composed flower-like pieces; they seemed to enjoy them so. But one thing he always did was to kiss each talisman with enchantment. Such a small gesture gave the seekers of magical alms a sense of control over their bleak lives. Xandor would never infuse a love potion or curse within the metal shapes, but instead touched them with a well-being spell. Thus, the wearers had a sense of peace when they wore the talismans around their neck.

His habit of making a necklace for petitioners came about by chance. The first suppliant he'd ever treated for sickness had been wearing a simple silver chain. The young woman had been so fearful when it came time to leave that he wanted to give her something for assurance. Touching the necklace, he'd put a well-being spell on it. It'd taken him three days to find a space ship going back to Varzkar. During those three days he frequented the small town, he ran into the woman more than once. She glowed with beauty and happiness. So, he saw that necklaces blessed with well-being spells would be a wondrous gift. Something suppliants would treasure all their days.

And now he made a different kind of charm. For himself this time.

He picked up a misshapen *bylar* stone, his choice for the base of the soul kin necklace. It looked nondescript now, but once shaped and polished, would shine like a pearl. Most important, the stone had the ability to hold a magic spell for an indefinite time period. No bylar stone had yet lost a spell cast upon it.

Using his forefinger, Xandor formed it into an oblong shape, only slightly smaller than his palm. It would have taken hours to fashion it thus with his tools; the stone was almost indestructible.

But with magic, especially enhanced with the Dragon Fire, it took him only minutes.

Next, he removed his paint box from the drawer. Thoughts of the goddess *Virsa* had come to his mind earlier when thinking of the necklace. The goddess who watched over lovers. The goddess's eyes were said to place blessings on those in love. Recently, he'd vacationed on the lovely planet named for her. Certainly, the people of Virsa believed in her powers. And there had been an abundance of lovers walking arm and arm wherever he strolled. The paintbrush dipped into the paint idly while he considered what he wished to create on the stone's smooth surface.

He was a decent artist, but it'd never been an interest he pursued strongly as he wished. He decorated his room with a few scenes he favored—a seascape, an ancient ruin almost hidden among thickly leafed trees, and a bowl of tasty fruit. Pretty mediocre subjects as far as art went, but ones he enjoyed.

This time he couldn't blame his father. While in juvenile detention, he'd been sent to the occupational teacher, Mr. Diggers. Xandor smiled fondly. Sometimes during those years, he swore the man named himself Diggers, because he loved to *dig* at his students. The young, angry Xandor had only half-heartedly put together model ships or sloppily hammered wood projects together. That was, until Mr. Diggers insisted he tried painting. Or hounded him, more like it, until he did pick up a paintbrush and give it a go.

He'd fallen in love with painting, but hadn't practiced it enough over the years to be really good. It was Mr. Diggers who had directed his future as well. His teacher was not magically inclined, but later, Xandor found out Mr. Diggers did have the ability to sense magic in others. It'd been he who contacted the institution on Varzkar. The school had been interested enough in an earthling with potential to send a fourth level wizard to question and examine him.

He didn't know exactly how it happened, but when he reached his sixteenth birthday and two years shy of his release, he was paroled to the custody of the most prestigious sorcerers' institution in the known universe. He thought perhaps Mr. Diggers had put in a good word for him, but was sure it would never have come about until he was eighteen, if not for the intervention of someone powerful on Varzkar. Xandor never found out who was behind his early release. But something inside him told him it was Master Talorg. Which was only the start of his vast love for the head wizard.

Shaking his head at his memories, he concentrated on the soul kin. The paintbrush swished quickly while he created one of the goddess's eyes upon the bylar stone's finished plane.

Afterwards, he held it at arms-length, satisfied with the composition. The eye was the brilliant cornflower blue of legend. He frowned when he noted that the white had dripped in one corner of the eye, forming a snowy teardrop just below the tear duct.

He could have left the background a pearly white, it was close enough in coloration, but the artist in him wanted the duller white of an eyeball.

Taking a soft cloth, he rubbed the tear away and repaired the lower eye. Using magic, he efficiently punched two holes in the hard stone and then he attached the gold chain he'd laid out for this purpose. Holding the necklace by the chain, he was happy with his work, until he saw the tear had reappeared.

Rubbing gently, he erased the tear again, and then examined the area. He could see no indentation on the stone, nor could his finger rubbing along its smooth surface, detect any depression. Even as he watched, the tear began to reform.

Frowning, he stared at it, trying to fathom the mystery. There was no reason he could discern for the tear forming.

Finally, with a laugh, Xandor realized magic was afoot here. Whether it was the Dragon Fire trying to assert itself, or his own inability to "get it right", he didn't know.

Staring at the half-finished necklace, it came to him. He needed something from the mysterious female, in order to draw him across the galaxy to her side. Something physical. Last time he'd visited, she'd cried when he left. Was the Dragon Fire trying to show him the way? He wasn't sure.

Certainly, he didn't have the power to accomplish the feat of gathering a tear from her and bringing it to this planet under normal circumstances, but maybe bathed in the Dragon Fire, he could.

Placing the necklace carefully on the desk, he prepared himself for thought-searching. Would she be asleep this time? He hoped so; he liked the image of waking her to his presence.

Setting up the candles and stripping naked didn't take long. Relaxing so he could drop into a deep trance took longer than usual; his mind kept wandering back to her form and how excited it made him. Shaking his head, Xandor clamped down hard on his physical reactions, which included a hard-on. Breathing deeply and repeating the school's chant fueled his meditation.

Chapter Four

It seemed he zipped across the vast emptiness of space in record time, pulled to her presence immediately upon arriving at the planet.

Satisfaction ripped through him. She was asleep. He did not plan on approaching her defenseless body in an aggressive manner, but the thought of awakening her was exciting.

Tenderly, he stroked one hand through her locks, shivering at the sensation. Soft as baby hair. Amazingly, his sense of touch was stronger. Desiring to explore this further, he caressed her uncovered abdomen as before, entranced by the muscularity just beneath the satiny skin. She moaned and flinched restlessly. Slowly, his right hand, the one that had received the gift of sacred fire, slid across her silky skin. *Wonderfully tactile.*

Astonishment and pleasure fought for dominance within him. The Dragon Fire's influence was strong. He would be able to get what he had come for.

Without warning her eyes popped open. Even in the dusky room, he could see her peering curiously upward at him.

"You came?"

Xandor had conjured a spell before leaving, in case she spoke. Now he was glad for that forethought. He understood her perfectly. Any words he emitted she would hear in her language, rendering a translation machine unnecessary. They were quirky pieces of technology anyway, not always translating correctly, and had been the cause of friction between planets more than once.

"How could I resist your call?" He made his tone playful.

"Call?"

"Your singing."

A soft giggle erupted into the silence, startling him. "What are you?"

"That remains to be seen," he replied mysteriously, not yet ready to tell her.

"Why have you come, then?"

"To make your acquaintance...and to give you pleasure, if you allow it." He waited with bated breath for her response.

She exhaled a soft sigh. "I thought you'd never ask. I have dreamed of you, ever since you made yourself known to me."

"Have you?" Reaching down with both hands, he stroked her sides, the least intrusive sexual gesture he could make, while awaiting her answer.

She raised both her arms in response. Xandor lowered his body, levitating just above hers. Placing his hands against her cheeks, he rubbed her velvety skin gently with his thumbs and stared into midnight blue eyes he could barely distinguish from the blue-black shadows enveloping them. When his lips touched hers, he was dissatisfied with the sensation. It was as if he used the slightest pressure, when in reality he pushed down hard to gain even this feeling.

Neither taste nor smell were involved in the exchange. He could tell nothing of her flavor or scent, whether they were sweet or exotic. Quashing his frustration, he put more effort into his embrace, wrapping his arms about her slim form at the same time. It was surprisingly easy to wriggle his arms underneath her in his present state. Although he would have preferred full body stimulation, as one would normally receive in such a situation, enough filtered through that he became hard while they continued to kiss. She wiggled her lower body against his cock and he groaned into her mouth.

Breaking from her abruptly, he moved lower, licking the tiny buds atop her small breasts. He could tell her skin was silky smooth, but that was all. Would her flesh taste different than a human female's? Would she give off a heavy musky odor, or something totally different?

She moaned softly when he laved her breasts, and he was satisfied that she too was receiving at least partial sensations. Next, he caressed her slender thighs, kneading and circling, moving at a snail's pace toward her pussy. Excitement lanced through him. Would she be built like an Earth woman, or would her composition be something new and unusual? He wished the darkness would evaporate so he could see her beauty. Normally, he could cast a spell to light the gloom, but he couldn't in his present form and maintain contact.

Sliding his right hand up her thigh, he inserted one finger gently into the folds that felt like human labia. He'd also touched a fine thatch of hair before slipping his finger forward. He'd planned on exploring those lips with his finger, but she surged upward suddenly, grasping him with her wetness. Complying, he pushed his finger deeper into her soft warmth. Gently, he slipped a second finger inside, gratified by the very human feel of her pussy, but wishing he could receive the full impact of touching her.

Wriggling her hips, she moaned softly and ran one hand up and down his arm. "Oh, yes."

The excitement in her voice made his cock throb.

Abruptly, she stopped all movement and peered up at him intently, perhaps trying to discern the planes of his face. "That feels so nice, but I want you inside me."

Xandor didn't stop to think if he could or not. He quickly placed his cock at her opening and slipped it slowly inside. He groaned. *If it felt this wonderful, what would the real thing be like?* Soft, wet, and hot. Perfect.

"Yes, my dream lover." She moved her hips in rhythm with him.

Unexpectedly, he sensed a drop in his energy level and shivered violently. His activity had apparently distracted his mind, for he was dangerously close to losing contact with his physical body. Would, unless he rushed back across space immediately.

Withdrawing fast, he levitated upward, throwing his words toward her as he departed. "I will come to you again."

While he gathered his power about him like a shield before thrusting himself into the vastness, her last, tearful distress-laden cry tore at his heart. "Don't leave me."

A sudden sinking hit his semi-transparent stomach when he realized he'd almost forgotten his mission.

Zooming quickly back to her room, he reached down and caught a tear that trailed forlornly down one cheek. No time to dawdle. Xandor left with no backward glance or further words. He didn't have enough power in his astral body to cast a spell to protect the tear while in transit. Hopefully, the Dragon Fire would be enough.

When he returned to his body, he fell weakly to his side, clutching himself with both arms as cold ripped through his system. It took a few minutes before the rough shivers left him.

Sitting up with strenuous effort, Xandor carefully unclenched his fist and sighed in relief. A single drop rested in his palm.

Xandor drew energy from the objects around him, aiding his normal strength to return in minutes. Immediately upon rising to his feet, he walked carefully to the desk and held his hand over the necklace.

Using a whiff of magic, he directed the tear. It rolled down his palm to his forefinger, and then dripped in one plop onto the necklace. It hit the jewelry exactly where the stubborn teardrop had reappeared twice. Quivering slightly, it settled, looking like it had always belonged in that spot.

Xandor waved his hand over the necklace, which held the drop securely in place with a spell, while he repainted the eyeball and lower eyelid.

Once it dried, he picked up the piece by the chain. Everything held in place. The tear stayed where it should and the paint didn't drip.

Breathing a sigh of relief, he examined the necklace. It still needed something.

After a moment, a thought came to him. His dear mother had been a world traveler, and on returning from a trip to the Middle East, she'd brought back one souvenir he'd thought was intriguing. It was similar to the necklace he'd created, minus the teardrop. A common piece sold in the region to ward off the evil eye. Only that exotic necklace had sported dangles along the bottom.

Taking out his tools, Xandor first magically burned holes along the bottom, and then attached three pieces taken from earrings he'd bought from the local bazaar. He'd liked the rich red color of the *cortakian* stones, similar to Earth's ruby.

After attaching the ear drops, he decided to go all out and lined the stone's edge with gold chain. Holding it up, he grinned. It certainly looked exotic now. Whether he'd wear it remained to be seen. Rather fancy for a man's chest, he thought. Maybe he'd give it to his siren.

He placed a powerful spell over the necklace to protect the fragile paint and tear. Now nothing would rub them off throughout many millennium.

Finally, he gathered the last of the Dragon Fire, which was quickly fading from his system. Waving his hand over the jewelry, he infused it with magic. The tear would draw him to her across the galaxy's vastness, a directional finder of sorts.

Being somewhat of a romantic at heart, Xandor also created a general spell, which would affect anyone who held the piece. After all, he would not survive thousands of years. Thus, if two star-crossed lovers met, the necklace would recognize them as soulmates.

Turning whimsical, he added the finishing touch with a puff of breath over the piece. When these lovers embraced, the tear would vanish, reappearing when they were not locked in each other's arms.

After he examined it as a whole, he had to admit the tear finished off the piece nicely. The drop of water actually looked like a priceless diamond with its shimmering iridescent beauty.

* * * * *

After completing the necklace, Xandor became busy with more practical matters, like informing friends and professors of his impending journey.

Stopping by the bazaar, he purchased the items he needed for the trip, then returned to his quarters, where packing went quickly. Having kept things to a minimum, he stared with satisfaction at the bag sitting on his bed. If he needed much else, he could conjure it with magic or buy it in port.

He tucked gold coins and *tizorsan* crystals into his baggage. Both were widely accepted as exchange units and should cover any unexpected needs. Xandor had more than enough of both monetary units; he'd gained much wealth traveling offworld throughout the years, helping planets with different problems. The institution encouraged fulfilling suppliants' requests. But he also enjoyed aiding others, because it gave him good practical experience in using his magical skills. The last task he did, was slip the necklace over his head—it now rested in the safest place he knew while traveling.

* * * * *

Finding a ship the next day was not difficult. Spaceships were always coming and going. Ferrying wizards and petitioners was a healthy business in these parts. Plus, the huge bazaar hosted by the nearby town offered the wealthy sorcerers anything their hearts desired—any herb, potion, sacred objects, and so on, that might be needed for a spell.

Also, there was a hefty trade in the wizards' services in fueling ships. Though the Volarnian crystals could be recharged by technicians, the more powerful *rydarda* crystals needed Varzkar wizards to repower them. Only Varzkar wizards of the fourth and fifth level could do it. A few fifth status sorcerers were scattered across the universe, so not all buyers came to Varzkar, but the spaceport always had a thriving business going on around it.

Finding a ship going in the direction he wished took a little more effort. At first, Xandor wasn't sure how the process was going to work. But he soon found that when he talked to a ship's captain about a certain sector, the necklace turned cool. He'd secured it under his vest, where it nestled warm against his skin. Each time he tried a different sector the jewelry would chill against his chest. But, when he paused to speak to a captain heading toward the *Vortar* sector, the necklace warmed, almost to an uncomfortable level. He chuckled to himself, amused at the hot-cold game the necklace imitated.

Chapter Five

Xandor traveled on that first ship for a week, enjoying the new acquaintances. It was the first true break he'd had in a long time.

After that, his journey took on a routine of searching for a new ship once the one he currently flew in took a turn in a different direction than the one he sought. Seeking out the captain's assistance ahead of time helped. He was then informed, before putting into port, if the next navigational course would not be in the direction he needed to go.

Sometimes he found a ship immediately upon arriving at a spaceport, at other times he had to wait a few days, up to a few weeks, to catch just the right ship. Not that he minded the waiting, at first. Xandor had always enjoyed investigating new worlds, even though landing ports rarely put a planet's best assets forward.

On the few occasions when he had to stay past a few days, he ventured into the worlds' interiors, exploring to his heart's content. Otherwise, he steeped himself in the bars, clubs, and entertainment that were offered around the ports, which ranged from seedy to ostentatious.

He was restless and the frequent stops, in exotic spaceports were boring.

Finally, at the far reaches of the next galaxy, his ship stopped on a small planet called *Sertosh*. The port could barely lay claim to that name, with only one landing pod and a tiny round building through which passed infrequent visitors. No clubs or bars were in sight—which Xandor actually found refreshing. Instead, a massive growth of huge trees surrounded the area. It being nighttime when he arrived, Xandor could tell no more about the place.

One thing rang clear though: this was her world. The evidence sang along his nerve endings, while the necklace turned a toasty warm.

The gregarious blue-skinned alien at the information desk quickly called a taxi over to take him to the Wild Zort, a local inn. Surprise and pleasure flashed through him when a one-man coach, drawn by a strange beast—kind of a cross between a burro and a dog—stopped outside. A hunched over elderly man sat atop the piece, in front of the customer's cushioned seat. He was as friendly as the desk clerk had been. In the twenty minutes it took to arrive at the quaint inn, Xandor learned much of this world.

The blue-skinned Sertoshians were the only people occupying this planet. Nothing spectacular like *tizorsan* crystals had ever been discovered here, so offworlders usually steered clear of it. Plus, it was out of the way, even for most deep space routes. Only the occasional weary traveler or person seeking a peaceful environment in which to vacation stayed any length of time on Sertosh.

The whole idea of such an untrammeled place appealed to him. His siren would be unspoiled by technology or alien influences. And she would be blue-skinned, a difference he wished to explore further, very soon.

The inn reminded him of something straight out of his history lessons about ancient Earth. It was primitive but held everything he really needed.

The servant who showed him to the room quickly threw a powdery substance over a pile of rocks in the small fireplace, and then lit it with a primitive instrument. It cast a cheery glow within the cool, but cozy bedroom. Based on the warmth he'd felt from the fireplace of the main room downstairs, he knew this room would soon lose its icy chill.

* * * * *

Sleep that night was deep and dreamless, leaving him astonishingly refreshed the next morning. Starting his investigations in the dining area downstairs, Xandor struck up conversations with any talkative person around, which included everyone but the cook in the kitchen. The Sertoshians were fascinated with his wizard status, and though awed, didn't draw back from him like some aliens had on past journeys. In turn, the Sertoshians were enthralling to him.

While he itched to hunt down his future wife, he took his time in asking questions about the culture, especially those revolving around courtship and marriage rites. Some of their traditions were bizarre and erotic in nature, though logically derived from the Sertoshians' biological makeup. The females could not release eggs from their ovaries unless compatible males made them experience orgasms for three days in a row. Only after the third orgasm would the woman's body release an ovum, which would be fertilized. The ritual that had evolved was called the Jekar, like the orgasm itself.

If the man trying for the maid's hand failed to fulfill the three day Jekar, he could not marry her. Actually, Xandor realized from the discussions, the woman could choose to marry a man in such a case, but it was rarely done, because that meant no children would be produced.

He couldn't wait to explore the limits of the three courtship days required before any given couple was allowed to seal the union with vows. Three days of him trying to make his mystery girl climax. Recalling the slim beauty of her body, he ached to perform the Jekar with her. His masturbation had given him but short-lived relief. Almost every night his thoughts returned to her half-seen, partially felt form.

His balls hurt from his frequent hard-ons with no release. But he refused to masturbate again. He wanted to plunge his cock into her pussy, not his hand.

He was rock hard just thinking about her. It was sheer torture.

Seeking to turn his thoughts to more restful subjects, he strolled outside. He trod the winding trails around the Wild Zort for several hours, soaking up the natural beauty and thinking about how to proceed in finding his mystery girl.

* * * * *

Upon returning to the inn, he secured the services of the elderly taxi driver who seemed to have permanent residence in the hotel. Several guests had already informed him of the nearest town and he was anxious to explore it. Perhaps his future wife resided there.

The town was small; probably no more than ten thousand people lived within its borders. That fit in, of course, with the descriptions he'd received earlier from the inn patrons. Sertosh was comprised of villages and towns, with scatterings of individual dwellings nestled in the vast woods.

The natives' appearance intrigued Xandor; he wondered if the older patrons of the inn presented a true picture. He wondered if silver hair crowned all the peoples' heads. Every Sertoshian he'd run into so far had sported silver tresses, but they'd also been older.

Once the carriage halted in the center of the bustling town, he saw that his guess had been correct; men, women and children all were silver-haired. He thought their pointed ears a charming addition, giving them an elfin look.

The Sertoshians were also short people. The men averaged five foot five, while the women only hit about five foot in height, some shorter. Their forms were slender. Between the height and slim shapes, the illusion of elfin heritage was stronger. But, as with his siren, he smelled no magic on anyone. Thus, in appearance only, did they fit the traditional elf image.

The town folk seemed thrilled to see him. They were a curious lot. He was barraged on every side with questions. He was invited into a local pub and gratefully sipped several small glasses of the delicious beer. Soon, the pub turned raucous and he slipped out unseen, walking the streets, looking at the strange sights that abounded.

Much later, he rested on a bench set between vibrant bushes, which reminded him of roses. No odor came from the lovely flowers, but they were easy on the eyes and soothing to the senses. It was strange; the whole place was invaded with flowery scents, yet the rose-like flowers, which were most prolific, had no smell.

He chatted with the Sertoshians who strolled by, but not once did he get a clue about the girl who'd drawn him here. Xandor concluded she didn't live in the immediate vicinity, or else the necklace would have alerted him to her presence. Yet, he also knew she was not clear across the planet, but nearby. How he knew this, he didn't have the foggiest idea.

Getting up to leave, he saw a *Dava* coming toward him, smiling. He was the first alien Xandor had seen in town; this alone made him pause and wait for the elder to reach him. The *Dava's* bulbous head and six limbs always made him think of an octopus. They were highly respected though, renowned as teachers and truth-seekers.

Quickly throwing a shroud over his thoughts, against the skills of mind reading some *Dava* boasted, he smiled at the approaching alien. Xandor knew without asking what he wanted; it was evident in his painfully crooked gait. The *Dava* were also known to have agonizing arthritic conditions due to their four lower limbs.

"Elder, may I be of assistance?" he asked when the alien stopped in front of him.

"Most honored wizard, I mean not to bother you with such trivial things as personal pain." Smiling, his kind eyes spoke the truth of his statement. "I was simply excited to see a Varzkar sorcerer so far from home."

Placing his right hand across his chest, Xandor bowed slightly. "It would honor my sect if I could be of service." Sure he was right in his thoughts about the alien's arthritis, he fished in his pants pocket and brought forth a talisman. He handed it to the *Dava*.

"Is this a charm of well-being?" At his nod, the elder placed it around his neck with quivering hands. "Thank you, most honored sir."

"That is not all." Xandor gave the old man a list of ingredients to mix in a potion that would soothe his limbs. Two herbs he might not find on this isolated planet, but could secure readily once he returned to more common space routes.

Reaching into his voluminous robe, the *Dava* fetched forth a handful of valuable gold coins.

Waving his hands, Xandor tried to reject payment, but the elder insisted, grabbing his nearer hand and folding his fingers around the money. Finally, Xandor accepted the coins, knowing to refuse further would insult the old *Dava*.

"Goodbye." He bowed again.

The old *Dava* inclined his heavy head slightly and crossed his arms.

Xandor realized something intriguing—the old *Dava* brought it to mind: not one person he'd met seemed to be afflicted with illness, nor did any Sertosh native appear disabled. They were an astonishingly healthy bunch of people. Never before had he walked through a town and not been accosted for assistance with health or love needs. This was an interesting puzzle. He intended to delve further into the mystery, once he found his soulmate.

It'd been only several miles between the inn and town, though the old driver clopped along at an agonizing pace. Now, he decided to walk back and enjoy the lovely forests surrounding the primitive road. Xandor had never seen trees like those growing on this planet. Some were tall and slender with leaves clutched close to their trunks. Others were immense giants, easily topping those around them, spreading their twisted limbs wide, while the leaves splayed in far-flung splendor from each tiny branch.

Remarkably, the most prominent trait, shared by them all, was the color. No matter if the trunk sported a width greater than a man's body length, or was thin and willowy; the bark of each was a gray hue. The delicate, birch-like trees' bark was patterned in soft stripes, composed of lighter grays and darker, almost black, shadings, while the giants' bark shone with a silver-gray wash.

The leaves were the most amazing, running the gamut from bright silver atop the sapling trees, to a pale grayish-beige filling the wide spaces between the mammoth trees. Other creamy beige- to dark gray-leaved trees abounded, although the other two were most prevalent. Standing back and surveying his surroundings, Xandor realized everything looked surreal. How could it be so achingly beautiful, like something out of a fairy tale?

By the time he'd almost reached the inn, Xandor was quite relaxed. His mind wandered freely. Unexpectedly, the necklace warmed and he would swear it hummed against his chest. Not sure which way to turn, he continued down the road and the soul kin cooled immediately. Retracing his steps, he noted the necklace warmed again after a dozen feet. He turned in all directions and the charm heated further when he faced the east.

Spying a winding trail, almost covered by thick growths of bushes on either side, Xandor took off down it, holding the necklace in his hand. It did hum. He could feel a slight vibration against his palm. This directional sensing continued for some time, and then once again the necklace went cold. Turning different directions, Xandor discovered the piece now wanted him to head south. Luckily, he found another path, this one slightly less overgrown.

He'd paused in a flower-bedecked meadow to get his bearings and search for another trail, when two things happened at once. The necklace thrummed harder against his skin and he heard the loveliest song floating on the wind.

It was her.

Chapter Six

Following the angelic voice led him to the far corner of the meadow. A girl knelt among a mass of colorful flowers, singing to them and gently caressing their leaves with one hand. It was a strange act, but then maybe it was a religious ritual her people practiced.

"Hello," he called softly, stopping a dozen feet away.

Her face turned upward, clearly startled. What a sweet face it was too. A perfect, slim oval. It fit well with the slender lines of her body, or what he could see of it.

She sprang to her feet. Ah, yes, a very slim figure and nicely proportioned. But he couldn't squelch his disappointment when he saw the tiny breasts beneath the cloth of her tunic. Not that he desired huge breasts, but something beyond prepubescent mounds would have been nice. Xandor felt like slapping himself. He was being a cad toward the woman his soul was mated to. He was sure he would grow to love them.

Of course she shared the common traits of Sertoshians: pale blue skin and silken, silver hair. Her tresses fell in a straight shiny cut to the tops of her slender shoulders, while pointed ears peeked from her hair on either side. With satisfaction he noted the lush curves of her lips and large eyes, dark from this distance, so he couldn't say for sure what shade of blue they were. He'd already noticed that all the Sertoshians had various hues of blue for eye coloring.

"Do you like what you see?" Along with her statement, she pushed her hands into either side of her tiny waist, aggravation clear in her tone.

"As a matter of fact, I do." Laughter edged his voice and brought a hesitant smile from her, making her face slip from elfin bewitching to womanly beautiful.

"Who are you?" she demanded, looking a bit nervous.

"Don't you know me?"

"How could I?" She paused and her hands slid to her sides. "You are an alien...but something does seem familiar about you." Frowning, she said, "Perhaps if I read your aura, that would help."

Xandor was surprised when she started singing again, staring at him the whole time. Unexpectedly, she stopped in the middle of a line, it seemed.

"You are a sorcerer."

It almost sounded accusatory. "Is that a problem?" He wondered if she had a dislike of magic or wizards.

Biting her lower lip, she shook her head no. Her fine hair flying about partially hid her confused expression.

"Maybe if you'd explain why a wizard is such a frightening proposition?" None of the other Sertoshians had reacted so. Why her?

Sighing, she said, "It's not your sorcery, it's you." Her eyes slid downwards. She peered at the earth, as if seeking answers.

"You were expecting someone else?"

"Yes!" Her eyes came back to his face, her countenance cleared.

"Perhaps a lover?" After seeing her beauty, the thought of being her lover was even more exciting.

Nodding, she stared over his shoulder at the woods. "A lover...and more."

"A mate?" *Me*, he wanted to shout.

Cocking her head, she smiled up at him. "How do you know so much?"

"Am I not a wizard?"

She laughed. "Then tell me, sorcerer, where is he who is to be my husband?" She ran one hand through the ends of her hair. "I dreamed of him."

"And do you draw this mate to you by your dreams, or maybe your singing?" Was she a siren after all? Though he concentrated on her being, he still could detect no magic in her emanations.

"What an odd thing to say. We have no magic in our essence." Her eyes twinkled mischievously. "But, sometimes, when one dreams of her true love, she meets him soon afterward."

"Sounds more like a superstition." How charming. She believed in portents in dreams.

"Mmm, it is." She nodded. Propping one bent elbow at her waist, she stroked her chin and stared at him. "But, some of us believe it to be true."

"*Sinar biur*," he said softly, never taking his eyes from her face. Just saying those words to her made his cock hard.

"Wh...what?" She shivered, her eyes became huge, a mixture of fright and hope mingled in their core. "It cannot be you," she whispered.

"Why, because I am a wizard?" He lowered his voice, made it a verbal caress.

"Yes, and an offworlder."

"Has no one from your planet ever married an alien?" He grinned, but her eyes were hooded in thought and she didn't notice.

She nodded. "It is rare, though."

"But not unheard of?"

"Why do you wish such a union, wizard? Would not one of your own kind be more fitting?" Her eyes flitted up and down his form, as if delving into the secrets of what seemed to her an insane wish.

He laughed. "I would have thought so before, that is, if I ever considered marriage in the first place."

"You speak strange words. There are puzzles and mysteries in them, I think."

Stepping a few feet closer, he was gratified when she didn't pull away. The lovely navy blue of her eyes, tipped with long, thick fringes of blue-black lashes, excited him. "You have been a mystery to me ever since I first met you. But, I think you are my true love." Did she realize how badly he wanted to hold her? That at long last, he was but moments from stroking her velvety skin and feeling the texture of her lustrous hair?

"Think?" She cocked her head at him, curiosity shining from her magnificent eyes.

Fumbling beneath his vest, Xandor brought the necklace into view. Her eyes widened in excitement. He spent the next few minutes explaining the jewelry to her and what his Master had said.

"Then, you used your magic to find me?"

Her elfin face was most curious. *Good.*

"No, not the first time. It was an accidental encounter…but apparently fated to be."

He could tell by the gleam in her eye, she believed in such things as destiny and fate. "I only know one thing. Ever since our first meeting, I can't get you out of my thoughts." If she only knew how *hard* she'd made sleep for him.

"You spoke of the necklace." She pointed at it lying on the outside of his vest. "And how it found me." Tapping the side of her cheek, she asked, "Now, how do you prove I am your chosen one?"

"Easy." He grinned and told her the secret. He hoped his explanation wouldn't frighten her off.

"A simple embrace?" Her eyes twinkled with held-in laughter and disbelief. Shrugging, she moved to within arms-length and peered up at him.

Her acceptance was a bit disconcerting. But he wrapped his arms about her and leaned down to kiss her. She suddenly squeezed him around the waist, about as sexy as a hug from a sister. Then, ducking her head beneath his arm, she slipped away and turned to look at him, pointing at the necklace.

Xandor pulled the necklace up and peered at its surface. No change.

"Let me see?" She stood on tiptoe.

Exhaling in exasperation, he turned it so she could look. *Great!*

"Your talisman doesn't work." She sucked one side of her bottom lip inside her mouth. It was not particularly an attractive habit, but it made his cock twitch anyway. *Such full, lovely lips.*

"I don't think that's the kind of embrace it calls for."

"Really?" Her tone was playful with a hint of sensuality that intrigued him. He wanted to rip her clothes off, strip the pretense from their flirtatious game.

"Shall we try again?" This time when she stepped into his embrace, he tightened his grip around her waist and latched onto her lips in case she should try and slip away again. Her lush lower lip gave beneath his pressure, exciting him and his cock. Her mouth opened at his tongue's urging. The taste of her wet inner skin was sweet, like honey, and inflamed his senses further.

He twirled his tongue and was pleased when she met his efforts with a dance of her own. Their tongues slid against one another, over and under. He rimmed her lower lip, sucked on it gently, and then caressed it with gentle licks while he continued to apply suction. She moaned. Satisfaction flashed through him at her response. When he released her lip, she imitated his sucking and licking, and his cock throbbed in response.

Abruptly, she pulled back, gazed at him with passion and curiosity combined. Stepping from his grasp, she fingered the necklace and then turned it toward her before flipping it up toward his face.

"The tear is gone," he whispered, filled with wonder.

"You doubted your own spell?" Amusement was in her voice again.

"No." He shrugged, and then added, "I don't know. I've never conjured such magic before."

"It is considered powerful on your world?"

"Yes." He peered down at her, wondering what her thoughts were. He wanted her. Down on the ground—dirty didn't matter. Could he wait for her acceptance?

Of course, he sighed inwardly in frustration.

Letting the necklace fall back onto his chest, she said, "There is a more powerful way in which we know when our chosen has come."

"The Jekar?" *Would she consent to the sexually intense ceremony with him?*

"You know of this ceremony?" Her eyes probed him.

"Just what some of your fellow Sertoshians told me." She seemed to be waiting for him to continue, so he did. "A man who seeks to be known as your true mate must make you orgasm for three days in a row." He smiled sensually. "Sounds like a nice tradition to me." *When do we start?* he wanted to shout.

She giggled, and then broke into a full belly laugh. "Oh, there is so much more than that."

Watching her wipe a tear from the corner of her eye, he was almost afraid to ask. "What else?"

"For one thing, the orgasm is not an *ordinary* pleasure response, but must be a full-body orgasm."

"Full-body?" He was intrigued, but a touch of unease washed through him.

"It is easier to demonstrate than explain, but we Sertoshian women experience an orgasm that effects our whole system." She seemed pleased by his astonished look. "And only the woman's true love, he who is meant for her heart and spirit, can make her erupt into body orgasms three days straight."

"Why three days?" *By the sacred Dragon Fire, that had to be a challenge!*

"Because it takes three body orgasms to release our egg for reproduction. Thus, only our true mate can give us children."

Right. He'd forgotten. "Sounds like a pretty foolproof method of contraception...that is, if you're allowed to have normal sex?" Good contraception all right, but it made a suitor's job very difficult.

Giggling again, she said, "Of course we can engage in regular sex and have normal orgasms."

"That's a relief." He frowned, deep in thought. What had the elderly men at the inn told him about the ritual? "Isn't there a ritual to get ready for the orgasm ceremony?"

"Yes." Placing a hand on his arm, she stroked it lightly. "But, first a couple normally tries every day ordinary sex, to see if they're even compatible."

When she caressed his arm, his cock twitched and his balls tightened. *I'm as hot and horny as a teenager.*

"What if they're not compatible?" He groaned inside even as those words shot out. *No!* He couldn't be defeated now, not when he was so close.

"I have never heard of such an occurrence." Her eyes seemed to turn darker. Was that desire deepening their lovely hue?

He cleared his throat, then asked, putting humor into his voice, "Don't you think we should exchange names before exchanging bodily fluids?"

"Zira."

"Xandor."

Chapter Seven

When the stranger had first hailed her, Zira was truly astonished. She'd never spoken to an alien before and never would have considered doing so alone and isolated as she was when he approached. His appearance was really odd. Tall, he wore black clothing she was unfamiliar with which, coupled with his ebony hair, gave him an almost threatening air. But his pleasant demeanor kept her from bolting, in spite of his physical menace.

Of course his golden brown skin had given him away as an alien right off; yet she found it to be an attractive color. She became more curious while they spoke and intrigued by his image. True, he was much taller than her people, towering over her by a foot, but after they had talked for a bit, the height difference seemed to matter little.

His physique was broader, more muscularly defined than the slimmer proportions of Sertoshian males. While they spoke, her eyes wandered those bulges, curious about what lay beneath the black material he wore. His hair seemed heavier and thicker than her own, and the inky locks, which caressed the tops of his wide shoulders, invited exploration.

When she'd read his aura, she'd been shocked. A wizard. Here on Sertosh? Not only that, he had come seeking her as his mate?

She'd waited for many weeks for her true love to make himself known, and finally, this exotic stranger appeared. Though she'd had several boyfriends over the years, never had one held enough attraction for her to consider as a husband. And now this alien wizard appeared, claiming they were meant for one another.

After he pulled the necklace from beneath his clothing and shared the extraordinary tale with her, she was both excited and cautious. She knew nothing about him. He'd just literally materialized from the stars.

Were they truly fated lovers?

The Jekar came to mind and she breathed a sigh of relief inside. If he were truly the heart for her heart, the Jekar would prove it to be so. And if not, at least she could enjoy sexual explorations with this sorcerer-man from another world.

Her suggestion of a "compatibility test" was not really necessary. Oftentimes, couples went straight into the Jekar ceremony. But, while speaking with him, she had decided that he was handsome in his own way, regardless of his outlandish appearance. Zira wanted to scrutinize the magnificent body, test his manly and wizard powers to their fullest. To delve beneath his midnight black eyes, probe their mysteries and truths.

Once she'd made her mind up, her quandaries ceased. Zira unclasped the belt at her waist and untied the tunic's shoulder straps. The dress dropped, pooling at her feet. She kicked the material away and stood with arms at her sides, awaiting his response. Would he still desire her, once he saw her nude? She knew she was considered lovely on Sertosh, but would Xandor also think so? How would she rate against the exotic beauties of other planets?

It surprised and delighted him, when her dress dropped with no coyness or pretense, simply: *here I am*. A long courtship was not something he wanted; the sooner he returned to Varzkar with a bride, the quicker he could attain the fifth level. He'd been relieved to discover Sertoshians open-minded views toward sex, but still found her candor startling.

Her lovely, slender body pleased him greatly. Everything from her shapely legs to her curving waist, was nicely proportioned. Everything, that is, except her breasts. They were tiny, what Earthmen termed "mosquito bites". Guilt flashed through him at his callous thoughts; this woman was fated to be his true love.

Even so the dark blue nipples intrigued him. Would they taste like blueberries? Xandor laughed inwardly at his own silliness, perhaps a nervous reaction to his less than kind thoughts about her breast size.

His eyes dipped downward, fixating on her groin. A thin strip of silver hair topped the dark blue line nestled between her pussy lips. *What would her lips taste like?* Annoyed at his stray thoughts, Xandor pushed blueberries again from his conscious mind. His body wouldn't cooperate though, and his mouth watered in anticipation.

"You're so beautiful."

She simply smiled at his remark.

Following her lead, he slid out of his vest and then pants, standing quietly for her inspection. Was it his imagination? Heat seemed to lash across his chest, flit around his biceps, and then play about his belly button for an agonizingly slow moment, before moving lower. Xandor sucked in his breath; his cock stood to full attention at her perusal. Probably it was his crazy, horny imagination running rampant.

"You are also beautiful, wizard." Her voice was breathy, excited.

"And you," he stepped closer, running his hand down her hair, "are bewitching."

"Are you going to bewitch *me* with your magic?" Her blue eyes danced with mischief.

"I plan to." Placing both hands on her face like he'd done during his thought-search, he caressed her skin, his cock twitching at the velvety softness. If her outer skin was so silky, what would her pussy feel like?

The kiss started out slow and sensual, but then deepened into a scorching play of lips and tongues. After a few heated moments, he kissed his way down and licked her neck; she groaned in reaction. Clearly her swan throat was sensitive. Her breath came faster and her hands went wild across his chest, stroking and squeezing. His nipples tingled from her touch.

Her skin tasted of flowers. Tasted like violets and some other exotic flavor. Her flesh must be saturated with it, for each time his tongue stroked her skin a fresh burst of the wondrous substance welled forth. She smelled of the rosy odor that had pervaded the village. Was it the people themselves that sent off the wondrous smell?

As if by mutual agreement, their entwined bodies sank slowly downward, until they knelt facing each other. Xandor ran one hand through her silken tresses, and then gently tipped her head backward. Attacking beneath her jaw with fresh vigor, he soon had her moaning, her hands rubbing frantically through his hair. By the time he moved down to her breasts, her body seemed fired with desire.

She moaned. "Oh, that feels nice."

Licking one nipple with a long stroke, he grew excited by the taste. Not blueberry, but something earthy. He placed his mouth full over the hardened nub and suckled gently. Then, he alternately ran his tongue around the areola and flicked the nipple. Definitely tasted of flower blossoms, probably the same lotion flavored liquid he'd tasted on her neck. She must coat her skin with it. When he sucked harder, she moaned and flounced restlessly in his arms.

"I want you."

She giggled.

This position didn't give him the freedom he wanted, so he lowered her body to the ground and knelt above her while his hands roamed her breasts as he desired. One hand kneaded her right mound while his mouth and other hand caressed the other. He wanted all her flesh inside his mouth and he sucked in as much as he could, but still some of her firm flesh was denied entrance. Surprisingly, her breasts felt fuller; perhaps her excitement had plumped up the flesh somewhat.

Still sucking on her breasts, he slid his hand slowly down her flat stomach, circling her belly button with fluid strokes, then squeezing and massaging the tender skin at her waist.

Velvet. The thought of pushing a finger into her sweet pussy made his cock throb. Next, his hand tickled the hair at her mons and she arched upward, begging for his entrance. Not one to refuse a lady's request, Xandor slipped his hand between her thighs, holding it there. He liked the way her thighs clasped him in a tight embrace. Moist heat met his hand when he slid one finger into her pussy. Her flowery scent enveloped them. It was as if they'd stepped into a hot house filled with exotic orchids.

She bucked, moaned and shoved against his hand. "Yes…" She sighed.

Setting a rhythm that alternated slow and fast finger-fucking, he soon had her aroused to a fever pitch. Satisfaction flashed through him when her vagina gripped his finger in a tight spasm while an orgasm ripped through her. Releasing the nipple he'd sucked to a hard peak, he glanced upward. Her face was ecstatic, but he didn't see any spasms in her body like she'd described to him.

As if sensing his perusal, she opened her eyes and smiled at him. "That was nice." Her tone was throaty.

"Not a full-body orgasm, I assume?" She was so beautiful, her response so hot—he hoped it wasn't the Jekar. He wanted to continue.

Giggling, she stroked his face. "There will be no doubt when it occurs." Glancing down his arm to his hand between her thighs, her gaze turned heated again. "That feels so good," she wiggled her hips in a rotating motion, "but I want you inside me, like when you were my dream lover."

"Wouldn't you like me to taste you?" His voice came out rough-edged.

"You have given my breasts wondrous attention, but it is time to move our relationship deeper."

Xandor smiled. He appreciated her humor, but she had misunderstood his wish to taste her. Perhaps they didn't practice oral sex here; that thought excited him inordinately. *Good.* Initiating her into the pleasures of genitals and oral expertise, would give him the edge he might need during the Jekar, in order to push her into a full-body climax.

Withdrawing his finger, he replaced it with his cock. He paused for a few seconds, enjoying the sultry look that overcame her face when she noticed his slight nudge at her vagina. Her brilliant eyes had been closed, but she opened them and stared at him, invitation flaring within them as plainly as spoken language. Xandor slid in an inch at a time, watching her expressive face when he eased all the way in.

By the sacred Dragon Fire, she was a tight fit. He was hungry, starved for her pussy.

He set a slow rhythm, sometimes thrusting his cock in with one long stroke, sometimes bobbing in and out—withdrawing all but the last few inches of his length and shoving it back and forth into the mouth of her pussy. This action worked her into a fervent pitch, her body moved in conjunction with his while her head moved restlessly upon the soft grass beneath her. Her soft sighs pleased him immensely.

"Oh, oh." Her head thrashed as she moaned.

Wanting to keep the sexual heat as high as possible in order to move her closer to Jekar, he sat up. He kept his legs together and his cock within her and positioned her in the dominant position atop him. Her bent legs were spread on either side of his lower body while her hands grasped his shoulders. At first her expression was perplexed, but then he shifted her lovely derriere upon his cock and her face showed appreciative understanding.

Taking up the movements on her own, she slid back and forth in a rocking motion, an ecstatic expression flushing her face. "Mmm, your *vunu* is so hard," she said breathily.

Bracing his hands behind him, he watched, encouraging her to take over and guide the action. Perhaps to attain Jekar the female had to be in control? He wasn't sure, but wanted to discover all the parameters of the experience. He loved the way his cock was sheathed to the hilt in her moist heat. She leaned in toward him and grabbed his face, bringing it forward.

Her tongue plunged into his mouth while she continued her frenzied dance upon his cock. While she moved in her sliding rhythm, he slipped his tongue in and out of her mouth. He groaned when she changed her movements, gliding her pussy in a circular motion upon him, her slick juices drenching his cock and pubic hair. When she did this, he stroked her tongue with small circles, and she realized what he wanted. Matching the spherical movements of his tongue, she rotated around his cock wildly.

She pulled up, the release causing a suction that made his cock ache. Shoving downward quickly, she jammed herself to the hilt upon him. Repeating the motion, up and down, they both jabbed tongues into each other's mouths, replicating the stabbing movements she made upon his cock. Gripping her hips to aid her, he thrust savagely upward into her pussy. His groans mingled with hers.

"Yes!" She wiggled upon his cock for emphasis.

Her soft sighs turned into a longer, drawn out whimper, one he caught in his mouth, sucked it in like sweet nectar.

His cock was swelling; he couldn't hold off a climax much longer. Her pussy moved in slow swirls upon him and then her vaginal ring gripped him in a tight clasp.

Pulling back from her lush lips, he bellowed, grasping her waist while he released his sperm. Never taking her eyes from him, she continued her movements, slowing to a sensual rotation as his seed spurted inside. Her pussy pulsed several times in a matching greedy rhythm.

They collapsed slowly to the ground after her body sagged in final release. He cuddled her in his arms, soothing the velvety skin on one arm. Their sex had been wild and wonderful, but he knew she'd not achieved Jekar.

Why didn't that really disappoint him?

Chapter Eight

"You are a very powerful lover." Her breath fanned his chest hair. It tickled.

"And you are a dream come true." Never, though, had he dreamed of such a steamy encounter.

She giggled at his double entendre.

A loud squawking sound interrupted anything else she might have been going to say. Rolling over to her back beside him, she glanced at the sky with annoyance, and then spoke loudly, "Can't you give a girl a few minutes alone with her handsome wizard?"

A flutter of leaves in the small branch above their heads drew his eyes. Something like a brilliant royal blue bird perched on a sprig of branch that appeared too fragile for it, even though the creature could fit in his palm. Silvery leaves covered most of its form and he found himself curious about it. *Why had Zira spoken to it like it could understand?*

"Well, you'd better come down if you want to be introduced," she said with a laugh.

Wings fluttered madly — the animal had lost its balance and pitched downward in a fast, awkward spiral, bouncing once at their feet. *Astonishing.* A tiny dragon, not a bird, sprawled in an untidy heap. Its miniscule, clawed feet stuck straight up, while the force of its fall had crimped its leathery wings into what looked like a very uncomfortable position.

"Is it dead?"

Giggling, she said, "Of course not, he's too hard-headed for that."

The small beast sat up, a groggy look on its funny, dragony face. "Yeep, yeep," it yelped loudly, gazing at Xandor's companion with an accusatory look.

"It's not my fault you still don't know how to gauge your own weight." She shook one finger at the silly thing.

Changing tactics suddenly, the dragon fluffed its wings outward, glancing skyward quickly. With a flurry it shot upward. It flew a dazzling display of spiraling swoops, squawking out "yeep" the whole time.

"What was that?"

"Ak, my pet."

"Oh." He watched its crazy dance upon the wind. "What's it doing?"

"Trying to catch dinner."

Now Xandor saw the tiny bee-sized, winged bugs the little dragon pursued so enthusiastically. Nearing one Ak opened his mouth and scooped it up while he flew by.

Taking one of her hands, he kissed it gently. "It's getting late, I should be going." He glanced upward. "Besides, I have the feeling it...he is not very happy with my company."

Laughing merrily, she nodded. "He is a jealous little lout." Her gaze slid sideways. "If you still wish to perform the Jekar, you may come to my house tomorrow."

"I wouldn't dream of being anywhere else." He smiled deeply, feeling truly happy and at peace. Sex today had been great. What would the Jekar be like?

Giving him a confusing mix of directions to a house nestled far into the woods, he nodded as if it were a simple matter. In reality, he memorized her words, knowing he'd still have to use a spell tomorrow to help guide him to her.

* * * * *

The walk back to the inn was very pleasant. The silver-cream toned woods were filled with strange wildlife. None he spotted physically, but lively choruses of bird-like and insect songs vied for his attention. Closer to the inn, he did see a few more of the funny dragons flitting between the large trees.

Now, he recalled that some of the townspeople had sported what he had taken to be brilliant birds atop one shoulder. But since none had drawn near at the time, he didn't get a good view of them. In any event, the Sertoshian dragon was a far cry from the legendary beasts of Varzkar — dragons to be proud of.

His room had grown chilly by the time he reached the inn, but he didn't care since he stripped immediately and dove beneath the thick covers.

* * * * *

The next morning he bathed and dressed with care, feeling a little nervous. Just what would the ceremony entail? And just how hard was it to get a Sertoshian maid to achieve a full-body orgasm? He was her true mate, but would he be able to do the deed? It hit him that perhaps he should approach her seduction with more than the usual sexual foreplay. Perhaps something more unique would throw her into Jekar.

Outside, he called a local bird and whispered instructions to the tiny red thing, no bigger then his thumb. He would have preferred one of the large purple species he'd seen fly overhead, since they'd be easier to see. But they were resistant to his magic, while the red bird flew down immediately. At least he shouldn't have trouble tracking its bright color among the foliage.

Keeping up with the bird was harder than he first thought. Its size made it difficult to see in the forest and it flew as fast as a bee. But luckily, it kept flying back to him every few minutes, drawn by his spell, before flitting off ahead. After an hour of hiking fast down small trails and pushing his way through heavy undergrowth, he burst through clinging vines into a large clearing.

A small, but well-kept cottage sat in the center, its thatched roof reminding him of pictures from old England. The sides were smooth, perhaps made from an earthen mixture, painted white, with several green-shuttered windows brightening its exterior. Around the cottage were flowers so profuse he couldn't have walked without stepping on them, if not for the pathway of beige stones winding through them.

Past the house, gardens spread out in wondrous display of husbandry. He'd already sampled some of the local fare and his mouth watered just thinking about the delicious vegetables and fruit offered here. Although, now it also hit him he'd not seen his fellow guests at the inn partake of anything except a syrupy looking drink and slices of fruit.

Once he stopped in the cleared area directly in front of the house, the door opened wide and a group of people flowed out. Zira was front and center, looking somewhat anxious. Grabbing his hand, she introduced him first to her father, a man in his fifties. Then every relative was named and each nodded to him in respect. He'd never remember all the names and didn't even try; thirty-some individuals was too overwhelming. After introductions, he spent almost an hour answering questions about sorcery. Although the Sertoshians had no magical powers and therefore no wizards, they were well-informed of the art and treated it with awe.

After everyone seemed to be satisfied about his background, they filtered outward, strolling in the flower gardens and chatting among themselves. They left him totally alone with Zira, except for her father, Wythoth. Giving each of them a solemn look, Wythoth held out his hands. When Zira placed her right hand in her father's nearest hand, Xandor received the message from her eyes to do the same. Wythoth brought their hands together, palms flat against each other, then fished a piece of beige twine from his pocket and wound it around their wrists.

"May the Jekar be successful," he intoned in a deep voice.

"Jekar," Zira repeated softly and then looked at him.

Xandor echoed her. Her father nodded and then walked away without another word. A strange ceremony. But he was thankful for its brevity. Some cultures had marriage ceremonies that stretched into days. Of course this ceremony would be more comparable to an engagement, he guessed. Though of a temporary nature, if they didn't achieve Jekar.

Taking his hand, she led him inside. Later, Xandor had vague recollections of a simply furnished cottage, something that passed his conscious mind at the time. His attention was centered on the huge task ahead of him. Zira opened a green door to a bedroom, hers he assumed. A soft, fully-stuffed mattress covered in a patchwork quilt took up most of the cozy room. His eyes barely flitted over a primitive dresser with feminine items scattered on top, returning instead to the simply-made four poster bed.

Through the walls, he heard the chatter of all her relatives. The thought of them listening dampened his ardor a bit. And who knew how much noise Zira might make if she reached Jekar?

"Are your relatives going to stay outside the whole time?" He couldn't keep the discomfort from shining through his words.

She giggled. "Yes, but don't worry. They won't hear anything."

Not sure what to make of that remark, Xandor heard the very next instant a strange mix of clanging and squeaks from the yard. Zira ignored the sounds, staring at him with a sultry look, while he cocked his head, trying to discern what her relatives were up to. Suddenly, a mixture of instruments started playing. He recognized a flute-like instrument and a softly beating drum. He wasn't sure of the other instruments. Probably they were unique to this world. Whatever the source, her relatives did a very good job. The slow sensual music would cover any noise they might make.

Without ado, Zira untied her tunic and let it slide slowly down her slender form. Just that simple act excited him. He undressed quickly. Watching her face, he noted with interest the hazy look that came into her eyes, almost like she had put herself into a self-induced trance. Climbing into the bed, she spread her limbs and nodded toward silky scarves tied to the posts near her hands.

Standing with his legs grazing the quilt, he looked down at her slim form, his cock already engorged. "Do I need to tie you? Is this part of the Jekar?"

Her eyes grew large with inner excitement and that drug-like enhanced glow. "Yes. I must not touch you until Jekar is near. Only then may I grip you in passion's embrace."

Her words had a ceremonial ring to them. Xandor shrugged mentally and reached over, to tie her hands in a loose knot she could easily escape from. Then he climbed in at the foot of the bed, settling himself between her splayed thighs. It was a singularly difficult spot for him. Her lovely, alien pussy was right there in front of him, and he wanted nothing more than to plunge his cock into it immediately. But the Jekar demanded more restraint.

Her breathing became heavier the longer he stared at her. Good. Gave him more time to do something he'd been dying to do all along. The silver curls ran in a thin line along her labia, the dark blue color shining through the pale hue of her hair. He wanted to see all of her hidden charms.

"May I look at your *flakora*?" He purposefully used the Sertoshian word for the female genitals. His questions yesterday to the old codgers at the inn and their subsequent telling him more than he asked had paid off.

"Yes. Oh yes, please." Her legs trembled.

Unexpectedly, she drew her legs upward until her heels rested just below her hips and then spread her thighs wider.

A much better view.

Gently, he pulled her labia apart. She had no inner folds like human females, only smooth blue flesh all the way to her vaginal channel topped by a nubbin of skin in approximately the same location as a clit would be. A sweet blueberry, just waiting to be eaten. She was already moist. He watched as her small vaginal entrance pulsed once, like an exquisite flower opening and closing. Purposefully, he didn't touch her. He wanted her to squirm and beg him to fondle her before he would allow himself to do so. At the same time he felt like begging her to let him plunge his cock into her soft flesh.

Xandor glanced upward. Zira stared down at him, her face washed with sexual desire, while her hands clutched the silky scarves for dear life. Her breathing was ragged and her stomach quivered. *Not yet, my lovely.* With that thought, he eased the lips closed, holding his hand cupped over her mons. Her groan flashed through him like a physical touch.

He actually felt her pussy grow warmer beneath his touch. His little finger nestled in her slit and it became soaked with her juices. He brought his hand up, letting her see her fluids coating his finger. Slowly, he licked the thick liquid from his finger. Her breath hitched.

"Do you dare guess what I'm going to do to you?"

"No—don't tell me."

"Only that I am going to make you desire me as you have no other man before."

Her delicate eyelids fluttered closed and she moaned. "I already do."

Kneeling now, he clasped his hands briefly, calling forth a spell, one that caused a long feather to grow in quicksilver speed from the tips of each forefinger. Then, leaning over her body, he stroked each feather down her body. Beginning with her sensitive neck, he ran them down her sides, all the way to her toes.

He repeated this several times, without coming any nearer her other erogenous zones, pausing only when a ticklish reaction overcame her features. For the most part, she just gazed at him sultrily and arched her body to meet the softness of the pleasure instruments. His fingers brushed her flesh as well, and he was astounded by the downiness of her body hair. Even the short, silvery hairs covering her legs, were silken.

"Your skin is so soft."

While he spoke, he slithered the downy quills down her middle, again avoiding her breasts and stopping just short of the curls atop her mons. Moving around her groin, he stroked the feathers up and down her legs, slipping them to her inner thighs. His cock ached to plunge into her softest flesh. Her eyes, darkened with lust, stayed on his movements. Her breath caught when he played around her thighs.

The light caresses came back up her body, this time centering on her swollen breasts, around and around, until she bit her lower lip. Only then did he flick her hardened nipples, adding them into the play around her breasts. His nipples ached in sympathy, desired to be played with. Would she suckle him, give his sensitive nipples the attention he planned on giving hers?

Sliding the quills ultra-slowly, he edged straight toward her pussy, watching the heat flicker across her face. She held her breath when the feathers fluffed her curls, and then dipped to the outside of her lips, tickling and massaging gently. She gave a loud groan, then flounced restlessly.

It pleased him to see moisture gathering in the line of her lips. So he breathed deeply, enticed by the heady, flowery odor of her desire. His cock surged at the thought of thrusting first his tongue then his shaft deep into her tight pussy.

"You are torturing me." Her words shoved past a moan.

"Do you wish me to stop?" His face was serious, but he wasn't.

"No!" Her answer shot out swift and loud.

"Good, then I think you're ready for the more extreme foreplay." He just hoped it'd be enough to plunge her into the Jekar.

She trembled, her gaze eager.

Chapter Nine

Again Xandor rocked back on his heels and clasped his hands, concentrating with all his power on the spell. First, he withdrew the quills into his fingers. Then, even while he bowed his head over his hands, they were rendered into a putty softness by his chant and short, downy feathers sprouted over all the flesh.

Zira's eyes widened, a touch of fear flickering in their depths while she watched the process. Repeating the performance with the two quills, he started at her neck, but this time the jelly-like quality of his hands both massaged and stroked when they followed the prior pathway.

By the time he reached her breasts again, she was arching to meet his caresses and moaning little "ohs" of pleasure. Working over her breasts in his present state was most pleasant. The softness of his hands created a unique sensation for him, as well for her. Jelly softness met firm flesh. He wondered what her soft, wet pussy would feel like on his engorged cock.

Those tiny breasts were certainly responding, plumping up nicely beneath his massage, like they were actually growing larger. He wanted to suckle them so badly, his mouth watered, but he restrained himself.

With surprise, he realized each tit filled the whole of each hand. Rearing back a bit, he stared at them, shock riveting through him. They'd grown from an undersized "A" to at least a good sized "B" cup. Perhaps it was something that occurred during intense sexual stimulus, but didn't want to break the mood by asking.

His teasing and kneading, his double-edged assault—the downy feathers and jelly quality of his flesh, drove her mad with desire. He saw it in her tense face, the trembling of tiny muscles beneath her skin, and the increasingly rapid breathy moans.

"Oh, Xandor, what are you doing to me?"

He stroked the baby soft flesh at the joining of her thighs and then circled her curls, moving at a snail's pace toward the center of her pleasure. At long last, he flitted gently over her mons, alternating the feather light touches with firmer pressure on her lips. Her butt rose off the bed, begging him to enter her. His cock was so hard with that same urge he felt ready to explode.

The legs pressed to either side of him trembled. Satisfied she surely must be near an orgasmic state, he slid his right hand into her folds, rubbing it up and down. Rotating her hips, she thrust against his hand.

Wet heat. He wanted to taste her hot, rose-scented juices so badly. But he clamped down on that desire. His seduction had design and purpose.

Concentrating briefly, he magically re-firmed his fingers. By the time he decided to slip a feathered finger inside, it was already slick with her juices. He rammed the finger in swiftly, taking a different tack than the gentle strokes earlier. Gasping loudly, she bucked upward. He'd been right. She was ready for something harder, something to drive her over the edge. Finger fucking her hard, he got the reaction he wanted. She came swiftly, grasping his finger tight with her inner muscles.

His cock ached for her, but he wanted her to make the first move toward their joining. Instead of withdrawing, he continued to stroke her insides with a gentle gliding motion. Her moans had ceased and he dared a glance upward. Those dark eyes were lit with a fiery need. She fumbled with the scarves, and then reached for him. He slipped his hand from between her thighs and slid slowly up her body.

"I'm going to fuck you until you scream."

"Quit talking and *fuck* me then!"

His cock slid inside her pussy as he descended on her delectable lips. He plunged full length into her softness. It took all his self-control not to climax as her tight sheath clamped around him. The inside of her mouth was hot and so was her tight pussy, wrapping around him with a steamy snugness. Plunging into both warm, wet orifices at the same time, gave him double pleasure.

Releasing her lips, he licked swiftly down her chest. He concentrated on a plump breast, even though he had to twist his body slightly due to the height difference and squeeze the breast upward.

Sucking hard on her nipple sent a charge of heat to his already sensitive cock. He suckled greedily. Couldn't get enough of that wondrous taste. Continuing his fierce assault on her breast, he thrust into her hard as well, enjoying Zira's moaned responses. Loosing her breasts, he grasped her thighs and brought them upward, draping her legs over his shoulders. Stretching his body out like he was going to do pushups, he balanced on his toes. The contact between pussy and cock was intense and deep.

Her muscles tightened around him, and glancing at her face, he saw it had deepened to a dark blue. She had squeezed her eyes tightly shut. In this position he would easily see if she went into Jekar or not. Slamming into her forcefully, he thrust his cock all the way home, eliciting a string of gasping moans.

"Yes, harder. Harder!" she cried, then her whole body went rigid, and he had to clasp her hips tight to keep the genital contact.

He never stopped his strokes, watching in fascination when the flesh all over her body quivered. Reaching between their bodies, he kneaded one breast hard, and then rubbed the nipple between his fingers just as harshly.

The quivers rippled into a body spasm, as if she were epileptic. Zira screamed. Not a gentle lover's yelp, but a full-throated cry that pierced his eardrums. "Aw yeee!"

Without losing his rhythm, he continued plunging into her hot wetness, riding her orgasm with a huge one of his own. He tensed, shuddered, then released his seed and a rough yell of his own, although his couldn't match hers in volume.

"Zira." He exhaled, as he pumped out the last of his sperm. Only when her body lost its rigidity and she collapsed in a loose-limbed heap did he stop his movements, which had slowed to gentle thrusts.

Easing down, he rolled to the side, wrapping his arms about her to bring her along. After a few minutes, she glanced up at him.

"You did it."

"We did it." He kissed her cute nose. "What now?"

She took a deep breath, letting it out slowly. "We rest here a bit, regain some strength." She smiled at his responding laugh. "Then we can…I don't know, do whatever you wish for the rest of the day."

"I'd like to spend it with you, preferably somewhere else though."

Giggling softly, she snuggled down into his arms and they drifted off to sleep.

* * * * *

Awakening later, Xandor glanced at his solar watch. They'd only napped about half an hour. He wanted to spend as much time as possible getting to know his sweet alien love. After all, they barely knew anything about each other.

A chuck under his chin got his attention, and he looked down. Zira was awake and smiling, a very pleased expression on her face. But upon meeting his eyes her expression clouded. "Wizard, if we attain full Jekar, what then?"

He sighed. "First, please call me Xandor." He paused. "We must return to Varzkar, so I can try to attain the fifth level."

Her gaze flitted to his chest. "Yes, I remember you explaining that." Chewing her lower lip, she turned her lovely blue eyes upward once more. They were full of doubt. "But, Xandor, I do not wish to leave my home. I love my father. I have many dear friends...and," she waved an arm at the room at large, "this planet is special. Even you must sense this."

"I do, but there are wonders I wish to show you, why—"

She placed a finger over his lips. "Not now, please." Her eyelashes fluttered down against her velvety skin.

Something in that simple gesture told him she was feeling fragile at this moment, that he shouldn't push it. Giving her nose a peck, he said, "Then, let's just go enjoy the rest of the day." With that, he jumped up and dressed, pretending not to examine her countenance while she did the same.

His sweet siren had every reason to be concerned. She had been raised on one world and had never traveled outside its limits. She loved her people and this planet and she saw no reason to go beyond what it offered. His task then had been doubled.

Not only must he attain Jekar with her, but he must also convince her that going with him would be a fabulous experience. Xandor mulled things over swiftly. He knew he could introduce her to many wonders, at least verbally. But he thought it would also be a good idea to make steps toward friendship. If she liked him, as well as desired his lovemaking, leaving Sertosh wouldn't be as hard a choice to make.

Once they exited the cottage, the crowd of relatives all shouted "Jekar" in unison. He and Zira were surrounded by jovial Sertoshians who clapped them on their backs, wishing them well with the other two Jekar days. They must have heard the sonic scream Zira had emitted, otherwise, how would they know Jekar had been achieved?

Relatives served them refreshments and slices of delicious fruits. After a while, he whispered, "Are you ready to go?" At her nod, he grasped her hand. They waved goodbye when they headed for the woods.

"Where do you wish to go?"

"Just for a walk with my girl."

She smiled only slightly; a worried look still creased her brow. He wanted to smooth her worries away, but had no idea how. "Why don't we go back to the spot where we met? It's a lovely place," he said finally.

It didn't take long to reach their destination. They found a grassy knoll and he sat with his back against a tree while Zira sat cross-legged a few feet away. Xandor remembered being surprised at the softness of the grass when they first made love. It almost felt like carpeting.

Zira stared at the flowers next to her and gently caressed their leaves, but her thoughts were obviously elsewhere. Clearing his throat, he drew her attention to him, and then asked about her life and friends. At first she was hesitant, but soon enthusiasm overcame her while she told him little tidbits from her childhood. He laughed along with her, entertained in spite of himself. One trait he was known for was his seriousness. Some wizards claimed he never laughed, but that wasn't true.

His laughter was simply meagerly meted out. He took his schooling too seriously and had little time for frivolity. But while they talked, he found it easy to joke and laugh with the lovely Zira. Getting into the spirit of the conversation, she started asking him questions about his homeland and youth, clearly skirting his wizard training or life on Varzkar.

* * * * *

Xandor confused her a little, but mainly fascinated her. On the one hand, he was a powerful wizard, on the other, as a youngster, he'd led a reckless, carefree life. A bold contrast. She'd definitely decided he was very handsome, after she'd gotten used to his differences. Especially after seeing him nude.

Muscles rippled along his body—not huge in girth like *Debothor* wrestlers, more like his body had been formed by years of constant activity. Asking him just that question, she was not surprised by his answer—he swam everyday in the pool at his wizard school. Just the mention of his institution made her edgy, so she changed subjects again, asking him more questions about his mother, who he seemed very fond of.

Xandor appeared so solemn most of the time, she was happy to find she could make him laugh. He seemed much younger when he relaxed. She thought he took himself and his studies too seriously. He needed to live more, love more. A smile flickered at that thought; he certainly was doing just that now, here on Sertosh. Maybe she was a good influence on him.

But those considerations brought back his comment of needing to return immediately to Varzkar. How could she? It was true her life was simple, but she was very content. She had needed nothing, until she started dreaming of her mate to come, and even then it never crossed her mind he would be anything but a fellow Sertoshian.

Then, this powerful, handsomely exotic stranger slipped out of my dreams and walked into my life.

She slid her eyes sideways to examine Xandor while he told her some tale of childhood pranks. He had a brilliant mind, schooled in many subjects, and his magic was awesome in its might. He could be a ruler of a planet if he wished, but somehow Zira sensed he would not pursue such a power-driven goal. He'd mentioned aiding planets; she was dying to question him further, but at the same time, didn't want to bring up his sorcery and his homeworld.

How could she leave this place she loved and go off into a strange, frightening environment she knew nothing of, except that which he explained? He was someone who counted in this universe; she was a simple maid with only ten years of schooling. She pictured herself standing next to him, surrounded by wizards flinging magic spells around until the very air filled up with dancing sparkles. While she watched in fascination, she began to shrink, until she was no bigger than Xandor's hand.

A squawk shook her from the silly reverie. Ak landed awkwardly on her dress. Here was an individual who really was the size of her hand and it didn't seem to faze him one iota. Not liking the direction of her musings, she turned to her companion.

When he spied Ak perched on her shoulder, he said, smiling at them both, "You never did introduce us."

"Ak, this is Xandor, a powerful wizard."

"Yeep."

"Pleased to meet you," he said politely.

Zira was sure he didn't think Ak could understand him.

"Pleased," Ak chirped.

Xandor's shock was plain. His whole expression said, *Did I just hear a dragon speak?*

Chapter Ten

"You'd better close your mouth before a *vaqi* flies into it." Zira chuckled.

"*Vaqi*—where?" the yeep asked and looked around with swift, jerky movements of its tiny head.

Zira tickled Ak's underbelly. "Nowhere, you silly."

"I...I had no idea he could talk."

She giggled. "Of course not. Only rudimentary words and he understands about the same level too."

Staring at the blue figure perched atop her shoulder, he said, "I'm very pleased to meet you, Ak."

The dragon blinked its brilliant ruby red eyes at him, and then yawned. Without further ado its head drooped and snores erupted in occasional snorting fits.

"Tell me about these wondrous creatures?" The tiny dragon fascinated him.

"It is a yeep...so named for its strange call." She stroked the dragon's chest. "They are favored as pets."

Xandor nodded. "I can see why. Do the yeeps have any magic abilities?"

"No. They are simply cute, entertaining animals."

He found that somewhat disappointing. A dragon was not always a dragon, he guessed.

Suddenly, Ak snorted loudly and then unceremoniously flopped forward onto Zira's chest, claws still clutching her dress. His snorts were muffled against her tunic but she went on talking, not paying the slightest attention to her pet.

"Um," he pointed, "aren't you going to do anything about him?" The yeep presented a most undignified picture.

She cranked her neck down and sideways. "He's all right."

"Looks uncomfortable." What he really wanted to say was that he looked totally ridiculous.

She shrugged. "If it bothers you." With that she wiggled her hand beneath Ak and shoved upward. He blinked, half-awake now, and he resettled on her shoulder in a proper position.

"Food!" he squeaked loudly and took off in an abrupt burst of energy, causing Zira's hair to fluff out wildly.

Xandor watched the little dragon scoop up several *vaqi*. He had to admire the little guy's flying ability, but so far, other than the language skills, he was rather disappointing. He had hoped when seeing the tiny dragon, it would be a magical being like the legendary Varzkar dragon, but the little yeep simply wasn't made of the same material.

Landing again on his mistress's shoulder wide-eyed and alert, Ak looked around—probably searching out more food sources.

"*Ezlor!*" The yeep jumped off Zira's shoulder onto her lap, then hopped and skidded onto the earth, crawling with clumsy shambling movements towards a low growing bush. His walk resembled a bat using its wings like a second pair of legs. Creepy.

"No, you don't." Zira reached for the tiny beast, but missed him. In spite of his awkward locomotion, he was fast even on the ground.

Ak's head reappeared from the bush, a wiggling white caterpillar grasped in his beak-like mouth. He looked at them like he'd done something fascinating, and then made a gulping motion, trying to swallow the insect down like a snake would.

"I said no." Zira's voice was very frustrated. She grabbed the dragon by the neck and turned toward Xandor. "Can you help me please?"

"What do you want me to do?"

Placing her fingers on either side of Ak's beak, she pulled up and down at the same time. "Grab the ezlor and gently pull him out."

"Why?" He frowned. "It's just a caterpillar, and you let Ak eat those flying bugs."

"Please, just do it, then I'll explain."

Shrugging, somewhat tired of the silliness, Xandor gingerly grasped the insect and pulled it out. He shook his hand, trying to dislodge the bug, ignoring Zira's yelped "Don't!" But it had somehow attached itself with sticky feet to his finger and clung on with determination.

"Don't tell me this is another pet?" he asked sarcastically, but wondered immediately after the words left his mouth, if it might be true. "These things don't bite, do they?"

Blowing a lock of hair from her eyes, Zira shot a look of annoyance at him. "No. And yes, they are often kept as pets, but that one is not mine."

"Oh." Examining the fat caterpillar, which was approximately the size of his forefinger in width and length, he couldn't see anything that would make it interesting as a pet. Fuzzy black hairs covered its underbelly and large black eyes stared back at him. An ugly white worm creature with black hairs. It made the yeep look like a jewel by comparison. "Do I dare ask why it is kept as a pet?"

Zira's aggravation had fled, replaced with a smile of delight. "Put out your hand, palm up."

After he did, she reached over and tickled the ezlor's sides, whereupon, it released its grip on his finger and rolled onto his palm, lying there on its back like the fat slug it was. Next, Xandor's lover started a lively humming. The caterpillar's body trembled and then it leapt into an upright position, stretched horizontally across his hand. Xandor's palm tickled, so he peered beneath the fat cylinder body and spied tiny feet. It shocked him. The feet looked very much like the cartoon feet of the ancient Mickey Mouse of Earth.

Astonishing him further, the little ezlor began to dance. Moving in rhythm to Zira's humming, its tiny stick legs and oblong feet jiggled up and down, tapping in time to the beat against his palm.

"Your mouth is open again."

Xandor shut his mouth, but then let loose with the laughter he'd been suppressing. "What an amazing insect." He couldn't keep the delight from his voice. Truly, this ugly bug had turned out to be even more entertaining then the clumsy Ak. "Can I keep him?"

"It."

"What?" he muttered, his attention on the insect.

"They're hermaphroditic."

"Oh, that's handy." He grinned, genuinely impressed.

"And, yes, you can keep it, as long as it doesn't bear the mark of an owner. Here." She flipped the now quiescent bug over on its back. She poked gently at its belly, causing it to stretch so that its underside was clearly visible. "No owner's mark. Guess you get to keep it."

"How are they marked?"

"The owner's initials are painted on." She pointed to its ugly, slug belly.

"Doesn't that hurt the ezlor?"

Shaking her head, she flipped the insect back on its feet. "It's a special harmless mixture that lasts for months."

"How…do I take care of it? What does it eat? Where should I keep it?"

They both noticed at the same time that Ak was crawling down Zira's arm toward Xandor's hand. "No!" Zira and Xandor screamed in unison.

Their shouts startled the yeep, who plunged over backwards. With a squawk and a ruffling of his leathery wings, he took off, giving them both angry looks.

"Frustrated?"

"Yes, but probably hungry this time." Tapping her cheek, she stared at him. "I guess you wouldn't have a box on you?"

"No, but I can whisk one up."

"That's right." Her eyes shone with interest when he conjured a small box.

He'd made it rectangular and about nine inches long. "Is this too little?"

"Should be just about right." She took it from him, examining it on all sides, as if a magical box must surely be special. Seemingly aware of his amused stare, Zira looked slightly embarrassed and set the box on the ground.

Scooping up handfuls of earth, she dumped them inside, pushing most of it to one side of the container. Next, she grabbed a bunch of the silvery-green grass underfoot and placed it in the cleared area of the box. "You can put it in now."

The caterpillar crawled slowly around the perimeter, seemed to sniff the grass, and then went to the humped dirt and began to burrow.

"It's making a nest."

"Hmmm, I thought so." Watching the fast-moving bug, he said, "You know, I can't keep calling it 'it'. I should name it."

Thinking and mulling, he couldn't seem to come up with anything original or charming. Finally he said, "I'll call it 'Worm'."

"Does that mean anything in your language?"

Flushing a dark pink, he answered, "It's a word for a creature that crawls on its belly and digs in the ground."

Laughing merrily and slapping her thighs, she exclaimed, "So, wizard, not everything you produce comes out magic."

He frowned, not sure if he appreciated her humor at his expense. She seemed to enjoy teasing him. But then, he realized he liked it too.

Setting the box down, he asked Zira if she'd ever owned an ezlor. After that, their conversation turned into an exchange of information about pets they'd owned. His dogs and cats, creatures she considered exotic, fascinated her — even though to him, next to a yeep or ezlor, they seemed pretty tame.

Soon, she seemed completely at ease, laying her head in his lap while they talked. And boy did they talk. At one point, he asked, "What did you want to be when you grew up?"

Zira's giggle delighted him.

"I wanted to explore space when I was little." She shrugged. "But then, I became interested in teaching young children."

"And are you a teacher?"

"Yes, at the local school for Sertosh children between three and five." She smiled. "Of course, I'm still in training."

"That's wonderful. Teachers are highly respected on all the planets I've visited."

Her lovely eyes sparkled at his compliment.

For hours they discussed their lives. He knew more about Zira at the end of the evening then he had ever known about any human companion.

It pleased him that they shared the same love for and interest in animals, that they both were concerned with preserving natural environments, and dearly loved long walks in shadowy forests. He seized that for an opportunity to tell her of the woods he'd discovered on other worlds. She gasped when he explained about the whispering willows of Sartus Ten, and her eyes grew larger after he described the deadly *aruztoo* trees, which were capable of wrapping limber branches around a person and choking them to death.

* * * * *

It had started to cool a bit and evening was fast approaching, but neither was ready to part company yet. Xandor materialized his cloak from his inn room, spreading it over them. Although it was only early fall and still comfortably warm in the daylight hours, the nights on Sertosh were quite chilly. Something fluttered overhead and they both glanced up. Surprise hit Xandor when Ak landed on his shoulder.

"That's odd."

"What?" Did she mean he or the yeep?

"He never takes to strangers."

Glancing toward the tiny dragon, Xandor was startled when it met his look, eye-to-eye. It hadn't fallen asleep immediately as seemed to be its nature. Turning back to her, he whispered, "Maybe he thinks if he makes nice with me, I'll give him the ezlor."

"Probably still mad at me."

He chuckled, sure she'd hit it on the head. The perching yeep on his shoulder was rather nice, and to be accepted by your lover's pet was important. But, he couldn't get a good look at the little fellow in this position.

Propping one hand on a bended knee, he stuck out his forefinger. "Ak, would you sit here?"

A ruffling against his hair told him the yeep intended to comply with his request, but he felt a painful tugging and Ak screeched loudly in his ear.

"Hold on." Zira laughed and knelt next to his side. "He's gotten tangled in your hair." After a minute of hair-pulling and yeep-grumbling, everyone resettled into their former positions, except the dragon, who now perched on Xandor's finger.

Unobtrusively he rubbed his thumb against the animal's lower belly. As he'd expected, the skin felt like fine leather. Ak purred, which he found delightful. Closing his other hand into a fist, he stuck it in front of the yeep's face. It drew the dragon's lively attention to his hand. Unfurling his fingers, Xandor watched with amusement when the dragon squawked happily and swooped to gulp up the *vaqi* Xandor had materialized from overhead into his palm.

After that, Ak really warmed up to him, eying his hand hopefully every few minutes. Xandor wanted to explore the yeep's language capacity, so ignored its greedy looks. He found by using simple two or three word phrases, he could carry on a crude conversation with the tiny creature. The yeep's mind was refreshingly uncluttered with the worries of humanoids.

By the time twilight began creeping through the trees around them, Xandor had laughed many times at the yeep's funny observations. In return, Ak seemed to eat up the attention Xandor gave him.

The yeep suddenly screeched in his ear and took off skyward. He circled another, smaller dragon, squawking in intermittent yeeps.

"That's his mate," Zira said with a chuckle.

"I take it that is his mating call." At her nod, he couldn't help but grin. *To each his own.*

Sighing loudly, Zira stated, "It's getting late. We should be going."

Chapter Eleven

"Of course." He sprang upward and pulled her up beside him. "Let me walk you home."

By the time they reached her cottage, it had already turned dark. He conjured a lantern and luckily Zira knew the way with confidence through the dense brush and overhanging trees.

"See you tomorrow?"

"Wild horses couldn't keep me away." He kissed her nose lightly.

"You have many strange sayings."

"You'll get used to them." The foreboding on her lovely face made him uncomfortable. Clearly, she still had not cemented her decision to go with him. Her features were drawn. "I'd better get going. You look tired."

Glancing at the heavy darkness of the woods, she said, "Perhaps I should have walked *you* home."

"No problem." Xandor snapped his fingers, calling down a huge lunar moth bigger than Ak, which landed on his hand. "Just give him the general directions."

She did, peering with wonder at the giant insect's attentive attitude, the way its antennae waved slowly while she talked.

After she finished her instructions, the moth flew with slow grace upward, circling overhead, waiting for him. Placing his arms about her, Xandor pulled her close, giving her a slow, soft kiss, one meant to express love, not passion. She looked perplexed when they parted, a mixture of both happiness and sadness.

With a backward wave, he followed the moth. The fact that the insect glowed in the dark made it easy to keep in view. On the lovely stroll to the inn, he had much to mull over.

Sex with Zira was wild and passionate. Better than he could have dreamed possible. But, during their long hours of talking today, he had also discovered he liked the petite blue woman. He'd never met a sweeter person. Her open attitude, and her wonder at the small discoveries he'd mentioned, invited more disclosures. It would be very satisfying to watch Zira while they explored the galaxies together, almost as if he were investigating them for the first time, too.

Surprisingly, he had found they thought along the same lines about many topics. They would need to discuss so many more in order to truly know one another, but he looked forward to the task. Xandor fingered the necklace nestled snugly under his vest. Truly, the piece had great power imbued into it, to lead him to a mate so perfect for him. The odds were astronomical and the mathematical calculations probably mind-blowing.

Later, as he prepared for bed, he realized one important fact—Zira liked him too. He could see it in her eyes and the easy way she responded to him. Acquaintances had told him of cases where they met someone and had instant rapport. He'd never experienced it, until now. It felt like they'd known each other for years. They *clicked*.

Having passed one Jekar, he was confident he could release two more body orgasms from his lovely mate to be. Now, if he could but calm her fears, her heart would speak the final truth between them. He had won her passion and friendship. Now he must win her love.

* * * * *

The next morning, he arrived at her cottage at ten, as they'd arranged the evening before. No crowd greeted him, which provided some relief. Zira and her father met him outside, and Wythoth gave the same short ceremonial speech as the previous day, then waved them on their way. Strolling in the garden, holding hands, he asked, "Where do we go for the Jekar?"

Shrugging she said, "Anywhere you want."

"We don't have to do it in your bedroom again?"

She giggled softly. "No, that was only for the first ceremonial Jekar."

"Great." Xandor rubbed his chin in thought. "Let's go to your most favorite place."

"Okay." Her face lit with delight.

Stopping her in mid-track by tugging her hand, he asked, "But how will your father or relatives know we attained the second Jekar?"

"Simple." She whistled and the yeep swept down from a branch overhead, making a skidding landing on her shoulder. "Ak will report to my father."

"He'll take a dragon's word?"

Nodding, she smiled. "Yeeps never lie."

"Uh huh." He examined the already blinking creature, wondering how Ak would stay awake long enough to report anything back.

It didn't take long before Zira parted some thickly-branched flowery bushes and stepped into a tiny clearing, no bigger than her cottage. Carpeted in the soft silvery green grass, the edges overflowed with purple, yellow and blue flowers. At one end, a miniature waterfall sprinkled clear blue water over layers of rock into a two-foot pool below. A perfect setting for a seduction.

Alas, they wouldn't be able to make love within the limits of the sparkling pond, but it would aid his magic. The explosion of leaves over their heads heralded Ak's arrival. Xandor didn't know if he liked the idea of a tiny dragon watching them, but having no choice, decided to ignore his presence.

"Are you sure we won't be interrupted?"

"Positive. This is my father's land and he never comes here anymore. And my fellow Sertoshians are very respectful of others' property and privacy."

Satisfied, Xandor clasped her within his arms, kissing her deeply. Her mouth was warm and inviting, her tongue honey flavored. He unlaced her dress and belt, sliding the tunic down her form slowly. He nuzzled her neck, enjoying the silken slide of her hair against him. Her skin smelled sweet, and he wanted to taste it. Kissing each exposed patch of flesh as the material slithered downward, his cock twitched as the velvety skin met his lips.

After stripping her bare and warming her body to a dark flushed hue with his attention, he stepped backwards. "Undress me," he commanded.

Breathing raggedly, she complied, taking her time as he had. Her hands grazed his skin, making shivers erupt wherever she touched. Then her tongue and lips set his flesh afire, licking and nipping while she uncovered it. His breathing was labored by the time he too was nude. When she gave his nipples flicks of her tongue, he ached for her to suckle them. And she did. His balls tightened. Her hot mouth felt so good.

"Now, close your eyes and trust me." She gave him a worried glance, but did like he asked. Concentrating briefly, Xandor poured power into his hands, and then using a lifting motion, levitated Zira into the air. Gently, he rotated her body backward, until she floated horizontally at his waist.

"What are you doing? I feel strange." Panic edged her voice.

"I am using my magic. Open your eyes, but remember to trust me."

She gasped and flounced. Quickly, he gained her side and smoothed the hair at her brow. All heat was gone from her eyes, replaced by fear.

"There's nothing to fear Zira. I am levitating your body, it is an experience I hope you will come to love."

Stretching her neck, she stared down at her body. "But, there is nothing beneath me."

Chuckling, he replied, "As there shouldn't be."

"Xandor, I cannot float in the air with nothing between me and the ground. Please, release me." Her eyes were glued to his, fear making them darker.

An idea struck him and with a wave of his hand, he materialized a cottony-looking substance beneath her. He gave it a soft consistency so she would feel its pressure beneath her flesh. It stuck out about a foot all around the edge of her body.

"Is that better?"

"Yes." Her voice still trembled, but just barely.

"I'm sorry if I frightened you, beloved. It was thoughtless of me. I have been a sorcerer so long, sometimes I forget not everyone is familiar with things I take for granted." He would have to slow down, make sure Zira accepted this magic before moving on.

She stared up at him, a tentative smile replacing the frozen grimace. "You are forgiven. You promise I won't fall?"

"Never, not as long as I stand here alive before you."

Sighing deeply, she closed her eyes. "Like this?"

Brushing the silken locks at her jaw line, he soothed her with soft love words. He was proud that she had remembered his instruction in spite of the traumatic experience he'd flung on her. Leaning down, he kissed her gently, the pressure as light as yesterday's feathers had been. Repeatedly, he kissed her lovely face, down to her swan neck and then back again to her lips. Just kissing her made him rock hard. Soon, she was relaxed; her body sagged into the downy substance beneath her.

"Open your eyes, I don't want you to be surprised by the magic I have planned for you."

Her curious stare stayed on him while he palmed his hands and centered his powers.

The water of the tiny pool started bubbling, something she couldn't see. Several clouds the size of watermelons erupted from the stew, bursting forth from the liquid as if they'd been bound by magic to the pool's essence. With a wave of his hand he sent one over each of Zira's lovely breasts, keeping the last off to the side for now.

"What?" She stared at the puffy confections.

"Shhh." He smiled. "Just ride the experience. Don't question the magic." Surely, she wouldn't be frightened of cute little rain clouds.

Not taking her eyes from the pale blue clouds, she still gasped when Xandor snapped his fingers and the tiny mass of moisture-laden air started raining on her breasts. "It's cold," she cried, jerking away.

"Sorry." *Lug-head.*

With a wave over her body, he changed the water to a most pleasant warmth.

"Better?"

"Oh, yes. Very nice." She couldn't keep the surprise from her voice. "Are you giving me a bath before we start?"

"No, I'm washing you in my magic."

Zira didn't understand what he was talking about, but concentrated on the pleasing shower, which hit her breasts and nipples like thousands of tiny massaging fingers. She didn't have to look down to know her nipples had hardened—not merely due to the water hitting them. Shards of aching desire flashed through her pebbled nipples. They had become quickly excited by the surprising magical shower.

The rain changed in rhythm, became harder in spots and lighter in others. The next minute, the drizzle shifted again, hitting her sensitized breasts in different areas. Glancing at Xandor, she saw him waving his hands at the clouds and directing their showering movements. *Like a music director.* She almost giggled at that thought, but her *flakora* ached too much for laughter.

She couldn't hold back a moan—the rain massaged her nipples into hard, aching nubs. They responded to the rain like a lover, thrusting skyward to offer better access. She fixed her eyes on her wizard. It was as if every time his strong hands made a movement directing the down-pouring liquid, he stroked her swollen breasts himself. Desire flashed through her. Keeping her eyes on him, she watched with heated interest as his *vunu* grew larger and more firm.

In confusion, she watched when his eyes left her body and flicked to the side. Turning her head, she spied another tiny cloud waiting on the sidelines. What did he plan on doing with a third?

It didn't take but seconds for her to find out.

Xandor directed the cloud over her body, settling it into position over her groin.

The cloud floated in position, no rain as yet pouring from its interior. Her lover used his magic to move her legs up and out, so she was splayed wide. Those invisible hands spreading her legs apart sent a shiver through her. Defenselessness heated her stomach and made her *flakora* clench. Never taking her eyes from his face, she watched the fierce heat washing over his handsome face.

He liked what he saw. She knew that from the sparks that seemed to erupt from his black eyes. She had seen them in his countenance the last time also, but there was something about the display of his hunger in broad daylight that made it more concrete and savage.

Her eyes went to his *vunu*. It was erect, hard. A pulse beat beneath the skin. A drop of moisture sat atop the head of his *vunu*. She licked her lower lip, wishing she could lick the droplet. Drawing his eyes from her body, Xandor turned his attention to the cloud.

At a snap of his fingers, the little rain cloud started its downpour over the highly sensitive, exposed flesh of her *flakora*. She groaned. The water temperature was just right.

"Xandor, what is this wondrous magic?" He didn't answer and she really didn't expect him to.

Squeezing her eyes tightly shut, she let the feeling of the intense massage flush through her nerve endings, as well as the swollen flesh of her *flakora*. Breathing became difficult. She couldn't seem to suck enough air into her lungs. Her nipples and *kora*, the nubbin of flesh being bombarded by dancing raindrops, throbbed, each setting up their own individual beats in time to the watery manipulation. It felt like Xandor flicked her *kora* softly in a seductive rhythm.

Electric tingles, like tiny shocks of lightning bolts shot throughout her whole body, centering in her aching *flakora*. Exploding into a huge orgasm that ripped through her body, she thrashed her head furiously against the soft substance beneath her while her hands dug into it. She squeezed and released the material as gasps fled her mouth. She wanted him inside her right this minute. Desired his hard flesh pressed against the softness of her inner walls.

Barely able to speak, she reached for him and rasped, "Come to me, now!"

Chapter Twelve

Xandor snapped his fingers. The three miniature rain clouds drifted swiftly to the pond, sinking into the liquid from whence they'd been born and dissolving slowly. Taking the few steps to close the distance to her spread legs, he gripped her thighs and teased the entrance of her *flakora* with his large *vunu*.

"Yes." She moaned, shifting her bottom toward him.

"Anything you desire," he whispered hoarsely, sliding into her inches at a time.

"Harder," she pleaded. And he did. Withdrawing and slamming into her, repeatedly, he satisfied her wish. Her *kora* throbbed and her nipples ached for his touch. As if reading her mind, he leaned down and sucked one nub into his hot mouth. The stabbing motions of his *vunu* matched the fierce suction of his mouth, bringing her closer to Jekar.

Rotating his hips, he swept his *vunu* against the walls of her karra again and again. Once more he matched the movement with his tongue in her mouth, flicking it in spherical motions that caused the ache to rip from her nipples to her *kora*. It felt as though a string attached the two and Xandor played upon it with knowledgeable hands.

The Jekar was building in her, threatening to burst through her body with the strength of ten huge orgasms rolled into one fiery ball. Desire, want, need, and lust vied for supremacy; a confusing mix, since they all were borne of the same beast. She shuddered and quaked. Her skin undulated with tiny quivers. Pleasure so intense it ripped through her system like pain pulled her into a frenzy. She screamed, her head pitching wildly upon the magical substance beneath her. Wildly, her hips bucked up to meet Xandor's savage thrusts.

The birds perched in trees around them, took off in flight, squawking in reaction to her cries.

Her body slowly sank down into the softness bracing her, drained of all energy and need. Her lover, too, looked sated, and a momentary guilt shot through her. She'd never even felt his seed pouring into her, because she was so wrapped up in the Jekar.

Thrusting his arms straight out from his body, Xandor lowered both hands slowly. At the same time, the substance beneath her drifted lazily to the ground. Once the material settled, Xandor crawled onto it as if it were a mattress, took her into his arms, kissed her brow, and then closed his eyes.

Light snores emitted from him but a minute later, and she had to suppress a giggle. He had done a spectacular job as a lover.

Zira was tired but didn't want to nap. Her mind tumbled with worried thoughts. Reaching a hand past the cottony substance, she called a vine to her, drawing on its energy to replace some of her lost zest. While the plant gave her succor, her mind ran round and round her problem.

Xandor.

He became dearer to her each time they met. She found this strange since they barely knew each other. But then, he was no ordinary man. He was a powerful sorcerer, a devilishly handsome man, and an astounding lover. How could she resist him?

She sighed. But she must. To give in to him would mean leaving this world and life she loved so much.

He was a magic-filled being, commanding and highly respected, while she was what—a simple maid, not even of his race. How could she hope to measure up to his needs as a mate?

She was afraid. Afraid if she agreed to follow him, the essence of Zira would be swallowed up by his overpowering influence.

It was silly. She acknowledged this to herself, yet she couldn't help feeling this way.

Finally, she drifted off to sleep, her mind still a stew of worry and doubt.

A tickle beneath her nose aroused her some time later. Her handsome wizard was looking at her, a soft expression in his eyes and a silly grin on his face. He held a feather in one hand, the one he'd tickled her with — probably magically created.

"Time to get up sleepy-head. We've got the rest of the day to enjoy."

"What do you wish to do?" She wouldn't mind another hour of lazy napping upon this wondrous magical mattress.

He laughed. "Since I know little of your world, I should be asking you that question." He paused and then said, "Why don't we do something you really love? Is there an activity or hobby you enjoy?"

Her brow knit and then her eyes slid up to his, turning mischievous. "There is something I love to do. Fly."

"Fly?" Laughter flitted across his sexy mouth.

"Yes." She smiled widely. "Not levitating as you do, but flying through the sky like a yeep. Are you game?"

"Sure." His expression was curious, though puzzled also.

Jumping up, she dressed quickly and waited impatiently for him to do the same. She grabbed his hand after he stood, then led him down another woodland trail. After an hour of walking, they came across a cottage sitting at the edge of a steep cliff. A pleasant Sertoshian male came out and Zira gave him a coin fished from her pocket, and then led Xandor to a large woven basket perched on the edge of the cliff. The top of the basket had thick loops; in between each ran a heavy rope.

"What's this?"

"Look." She pointed in the far distance. A huge mountain rose against the dark blue sky, its rugged sides softened by multitudes of the silver tipped willow trees.

He looked shocked.

"It'll take us there." She waved between the basket and the mountain range.

"Are you sure it's safe?" His voice caught in his throat.

Zira laughed. "The great wizard is afraid?"

A flush hit his cheeks. "No, I've just never ridden in such a contraption." He didn't wish to add he had a slight fear of heights.

Grabbing his hand again, she pulled him to the primitive sky lift. He stepped in gingerly. Spacious, it could have fit two more people easily. The intricately-woven basket seemed too delicate to serve its intended function. Swallowing his qualms, he knew he'd have to trust his companion. Trust that she knew what she was doing.

The owner waved at them cheerfully. He flipped a switch on a simple pulley machine, and with a jerk the sky lift started moving slowly upward.

Stamping down the anxiety that strove for his attention, Xandor decided to enjoy the ride as best he could.

And he did after a few minutes. The scenery was spectacular.

The land below was a wash of silver and creamy beige, intermixed with the silvery tipped lush green grass growing in wide stretches between the trees. Thankfully, the cool colors soothed his racing heart. And Zira's presence beside him, her delight when she pointed out wondrous views, pulled him from anxiety to wonder.

By the time they reached the mountain range, Xandor was enjoying the vista and Zira's stimulating company. She seemed as at home in the high elevations as a bird.

When the sky lift gently nudged against a large ledge, a young woman secured the ropes and greeted them warmly. Three Sertoshians waved and climbed into the basket for the return journey.

He watched when the trio took off, the lift looking even more precarious from this position. It swayed slowly as wind hit it.

Zira grabbed his hand and attention, pointing toward a rugged peak, one devoid of trees, composed of slate-like rock.

After about fifteen minutes of strenuous hiking, they gained the top. A large stretch of grass was strewn with what looked like huge kites. Several Sertoshians were engaged in lively discussions around different kites, while a few were being roped into the things.

"This is your method of flying?" At her enthusiastic nod, he added, "They look like hang gliders." Her giggle told him that once again she thought his words were funny.

"Well, what do you call them?"

Her face flushed a dark hue. "Yeepsters."

At his loud, abrupt eruption of laugher, she turned an even darker blue.

Annoyance shot through her eyes. "We'd better get started...*if* you can control yourself."

No problem there, he realized, as she led him to an empty glider. Just thinking about pitching himself off that cliff with only those frail-looking wings to hold him up, made him sweat. He had to admit the yeepster was pretty—the underside painted with a gaily-colored yeep, wings spread in flight. And it had an impressive wingspan of twenty feet.

Zira showed him the ropes and large rectangular cloth where his body would lie, explaining how everything was attached. Then she went into discussions of wind currents and errant birds slamming into the glider. Her dark blue eyes grew wide with excitement, but he had a hard time suppressing thoughts of his body crashing to the ground.

Interrupting her fast spiel, he asked, "Wouldn't an uninitiated person need to take lessons first?"

"Oh, yes. Usually about a dozen are recommended first, on lower levels, before one tries such a cliff as this one."

His forehead creased. "Then, why exactly am I doing this?" Was she a thrill seeker and hoped he was too? Or simply naïve?

She giggled, covering her mouth with one hand when she saw his concern. "Many young men on Sertosh, who wish to prove their bravery, take one lesson, and then fly from steep cliffs."

"A foolish endeavor." He wanted to point out he wasn't a young Sertoshian male intent on proving his manhood and he hadn't had his one lesson, but she already knew that.

"Perhaps, but it shows their village they are men."

"Any survivors?" He couldn't keep the sarcasm from his voice.

"Oh, Xandor, of course there are. In fact, few crash to their deaths." She glanced skyward at a circling yeep. "We seem most adept at flying."

"And what makes you think I am?" He wasn't a bird!

She stepped closer and stroked his arm. "You are a powerful wizard." She stared up at him, as if that were enough and should close the subject. Apparently, noticing his wary look, she added, "Besides, you can levitate if you get into any difficulties."

He didn't want to throw a kink in her nicely-laid plans by telling her he needed to concentrate in order to tap into his powers of levitation. And, he didn't wish to appear a coward in front of her. Suddenly, it seemed to him he was being as foolish as the young men who came to prove their bravery.

Following her directions, he got into the holding contraption and tied the ropes securely into place. The wind rocked the kite and he nervously gripped it tight, afraid it would swoop up abruptly. Turning his head, he watched while Zira prepared herself in a similar looking glider. Every move was elegant and fearless. She took the lead afterwards, showing him how to jog swiftly toward the cliff's edge.

The glider was much heavier than it looked, perhaps fifty or so pounds. Putting a little more effort into it than he first estimated necessary, Xandor kept up with his future wife, running a safe distance behind her so they didn't become entangled. She dipped from his view for a few seconds and he'd plunged off the cliff before he realized they'd reached the end of the running lane.

Holding his breath, he felt his stomach pitch into his feet. He was going to die before he ever got a chance to consummate the Jekar. The next instant, the immense wings caught the light wind and lifted him upward. A dizzy sensation hit him before he adjusted his sight—he was floating gently away from the cliff edge. It was a powerful awareness, one akin to those produced when he worked a magic spell.

Zira glided by, laughing with pure joy, her kite moving with surprising elegance. She must be a master flyer, he thought, for he was having trouble merely keeping the wings balanced. His must surely look like the first flight of a wobbly young bird by comparison.

Following her prior instructions, he finally found his balance, although he had to constantly shift his weight to counter the light winds that assailed them, or to change directions in order to keep up with Zira. After he became more comfortable with the process, Xandor began to truly enjoy it. Such a sensation, of floating far above the earth, was unbelievably exhilarating.

Even more exciting than levitating. He forgot his fear of heights. It helped that they stayed high up, which seemed contradictory, but wasn't really. Being held up by the extensive wings and winds, on level with the mountain's reach, surprisingly frightened him not at all. He hovered. Strangely, he didn't feel like he was falling. Hence, in an odd counterbalance, it eliminated his phobia.

They must have flown for hours; he lost track of time. Pure joy rippled through his body. Flying was a very freeing sensation, as Zira had claimed. He had to chuckle whenever birds flew by, eying them like they were aliens—which he was.

Alien to this planet and an alien species to be flying far into the heavens.

The sky had been clear all through their flight, but just ahead, he spied a large cloud. A lovely, fluffy confection like blue cotton candy. He wondered how it would feel to fly in the center of such a mass, but didn't think it was a good idea, since he probably wouldn't be able to see.

Zira flew to the side, circling a large bird's nest against a tall tower like rock outcropping. She probably hadn't spotted the cloud. Dipping the wings, Xandor decided to fly beneath it. Once underneath, Xandor felt as though a giant hand reached down and yanked him upward. Suddenly, he was tangled in the mistiness of the cloud's belly. He kept his wings steady but had an odd sense of disorientation.

Was he flying horizontally? Sideways? Up? Down? Crazy thoughts, he knew, but he had no sense of direction whatsoever.

"Xandor?" Zira's voice cut through the weightless mass around him.

A flush of relief gripped him at the sound of her voice. It seemed far away. "I'm here, in the cloud," he yelled, not sure how well his voice would carry amongst the clinging wet particles.

"Are you holding steady?" This time her voice seemed nearer.

"Yes…but I can't tell what's up or down." Sweat broke out on his forehead, in spite of the coolness of the vapor surrounding his body.

"Spit."

"What?" *Did I hear her right?*

"Spit, then you'll know which direction is down."

"Oh." Made sense. Gathering all the scanty saliva he had in his mouth, he squirted it out and watched with satisfaction when it shot straight down. Good, at least he knew he was flying fairly straight.

Zira's voice came to him again, directing him to follow the sound of it. She began to sing and he made for the angelic voice that had guided him true across the galaxy. It got louder and louder. He was headed in the right direction. Finally, after what seemed an eternity, he erupted from the cloud's clinging vapors, almost running into Zira, who veered swiftly to the side.

"I think we've had enough excitement today." Her voice was kind and concerned. "Ready to call it quits?"

He nodded, too drained to answer.

By the time they made the crossing in the swaying sky lift, Xandor was ready to see the last of steep heights. He'd enjoyed flying with Zira, but the near disaster had cemented his feeling that once was enough for him.

After disembarking, they strolled down sunlight-dappled trails and finally stopped in a new place, a tiny park with benches and several tinkling fountains. It was a most soothing environment, one that his rattled nerves needed just now. They sat side-by-side on a bench, backs propped against one of the large gray-barked trees.

"Thanks for saving my life."

Her gaze slid sideways, coy and twinkling with mischief. "You're welcome. But, it really wasn't saving, just giving directions."

"Call it what you will." He picked up her petite hand and kissed it softly, and then laid it on his knee, his much larger hand covering it. Laying his head back against the tree, he almost drifted off to sleep.

The adrenaline rush was over, his body wanted to relax.

Chapter Thirteen

While Zira watched her wizard sink into a semi-sleep, she realized he was right. He could have easily died today. That thought caused a sick feeling to well in her stomach.

The world...the universe without Xandor.

It was a most unpleasant thought.

Cuddling up closer to his side, she laid her head softly against his arm, not wishing to rouse him. He muttered, but seemed to sense her and moved his arm, bringing it about her shoulders. She readjusted her head to lie against his hard chest. It was not the most comfortable position she could have chosen, but it felt very soothing nonetheless.

She listened to the rise and fall of his breathing, enjoying the movement of his chest beneath her temple. He was so strong, and he'd been brave too. Now she realized he had a fear of heights, but still had consented to go flying with her.

Again, pictures crowded into her mind of him plunging to the ground. Squeezing her eyes closed tightly, Zira held back the tears that threatened to fall. Why did she suddenly care so deeply? The next instant she answered back—because she had come to admire many aspects of this wonderful man in just two short days.

The mystery of her feelings went beyond her ken. The Jekar guaranteed a match of physical lust and pregnancy. But, couples who attained the three day Jekar still had to work on their marriages, build trust, friendship, and set common goals. Yet, from the first time she'd set eyes on the dark stranger, she was drawn to his power, beyond that explained by the passion of the Jekar.

She gently fingered the chain that secured the necklace beneath his vest. This soul matcher had drawn him to her across countless stars and two galaxies. Who was she to question such magical knowledge? But then, if she gave in to its influence, that would mean leaving this world.

Glancing up at his handsome face, she was totally confused. She wanted him. Desired him above any lovers she'd ever encountered. Yet, it was not just his commanding lovemaking she was drawn to, it was him.

He had so many mysteries about the universe yet to uncover and share with her. But she'd avoided his telling, not wishing to be enchanted by the power of his spoken words. Xandor had tried to share the wonders of his enchanted life and she'd buried her head in the comfort of home.

Did she dare ask him now?

Perhaps his answers would pull her outside her own comfort zone and make her desire to be a seeker of knowledge and stranger wonders beyond her own experience. Did she really want this? She just wasn't sure. But, she did know she had to give him that chance. If not, she'd always wonder if she'd made the right decision.

She sighed. One more Jekar to go and she would have to make a choice. Go or stay. But then, she really didn't think any of it would matter — his desire for her, his power, and the exotic mysteries he offered to share with her. How could she go when her very existence depended on the life force of her planet.

Just like that, Zira's mind was made up. She would ask him to share his knowledge and sorcerer's world, and then she would explain to him why she couldn't go with him. It would break her heart and probably his too, but sometimes things just weren't meant to be.

* * * * *

Xandor drifted in and out of sleep, but once fully awake, he stayed silent, watching his blue siren through barely-cracked eyelids. She appeared deep in thought, sometimes staring off in the distance, at others staring up at him in confusion. He guessed the flow of her worries. Did she dare leave her safe haven and venture out into the unknown with him?

She'd been an air goddess today, winning his admiration of her spirit as well as other qualities he already appreciated. Without a doubt, he knew she would love exploring other worlds with him, but he had to convince her of that fact first. Did he dare broach the subject of the dazzling planets he'd visited? Last time she'd fended off his efforts, changing the subject with verbal flare.

He wanted her to choose to go with him because she wished to, not because lust flashed between them in the Jekar, nor because his power thrilled her. Barely holding in a chuckle, he had to admit, she seemed impressed with his magic, but it did not make her run into his arms. When he first started on this venture, he'd been intent on finding his true love in order to return immediately and begin work on his fifth level of sorcery. He'd never stopped to consider a real woman would be involved in the equation or that his feelings might come in to play, as well as hers.

Now, all he seemed to think about was convincing Zira to return with him. He lusted after her body and the spectacular sex it was true. But, he also desired her unique spirit. He wanted her by his side from now on. He wanted to exchange thoughts and views with her bright, untainted mind. He wanted to hear her light, tinkling laughter and to be the one who caused it, often. He wanted to be the one who brought the sparkle to her lovely blue eyes, the one who deepened her sexual need.

The real clincher was, he had an answer she would desire to hear, one to which he was sure she'd answer, "Yes, I'll go with you." But it was the easy way out. He wanted her to want him with every fiber of her being, not to say yes because he provided an easy out for her attachment to her home planet.

Was this love? Xandor wasn't sure. But his emotions were certainly more intense then anything he'd ever felt about any other woman. The necklace rested warmly against his chest, reminding him of its properties. If he truly believed in his own and the Dragon Fire's magic, then it was true. Why did he continue to question himself and his destiny? Shaking his head at himself, he made up his mind to do just that; accept the Dragon Fire's guidance.

"Awake?" Her soft question broke into his thoughts.

"Uh huh." He smiled down at her tenderly, swiping a lock of silver hair behind one cute, pointed ear.

"Can...I ask you something?"

"Sure." Her hesitation made him wonder what had her worried now.

"Will you tell me of some worlds you visited and how you helped them?"

His breath caught in his throat, he couldn't help it. She asked that which he had wished, but didn't think she ever would. It was as if she read his mind.

Taking the hand that still rested on his knee, he rubbed the back gently. "Once I was asked to a small planet, one barely known in our galaxy."

"Why wasn't it known?" she interrupted.

"Because it held no riches others would seek. The planet was desolate and its people poor. They scraped a living from the earth with much effort, but it was their home. And even when they sent an emissary to Varzkar, only I and one other wizard agreed to hear their case."

"Why?" She sat up straighter, her eyes curious.

He smiled at her and she grinned back. Her enthusiasm bordered on a child's, a surprising and welcome change. "The coin they offered in exchange for a sorcerer's talent was small, pitiful compared to other planets."

At her wide-eyed stare, he continued, "The emissary had already taken all possessions collected and sold them offworld, turning them into the few gold coins he offered. The planet has a sparse population, but the people gave everything they claimed as valuable—jewelry, silverware, crystal glasses—treasured inherited pieces."

"Why did you choose to help them?"

Shrugging, he answered, "I had more than enough money by that time to last me several lifetimes. And their problem was a challenge." Should he add he'd felt pity for the people as depicted by the emissary?

"What was it?" She rubbed his knee.

"Simple, really—they'd had a drought going on six years. All their crops were dying, cattle barely hanging on."

"What about the other wizard?"

"Oh." He chuckled. "Lucky for me, unlucky for him, he caught a bad case of *Taluson* stomach virus."

She smiled. "I thought wizards didn't get sick?"

"Not often, but sometimes there's a bug out there that even we have problems controlling."

"So, how did you help these people?" She was truly interested and watched his face, as if gauging his expression as well as his words.

"I have some good friends who taught me how to search out water with the power in my hands and a few selected phrases." He stared down at his hands. "It took me months of walking the planet to find enough underground water sources...if I had been a fifth level wizard, I could have pinpointed all with a wave of my arms."

"That might be true, but you still helped those people. You used the talent that you had in a very caring way." She smiled gently, seeming impressed with his mission.

He blushed slightly. No need to add he'd slipped away from the planet, leaving the coins they'd paid him with a note instructing them to utilize the money for building wells. He didn't want Zira to think he was a martyr.

Feeling uncomfortable suddenly, he sidestepped the issue and asked, "Do you want to hear about my unusual friends — the ones who taught me how to find water?"

At her nod he told her about the fairies and their magical planet. "Their world is peopled with the Taweeg, tiny humanoids reminiscent of the fabled fairies of Earth."

"What are fairies?"

Xandor smiled. He forgot not every species knew of fairies or had myths about them. "Fairies are magical beings, legends on most planets. But, there are a few worlds where the natives are as true to the fairy mythology as the fairy tales imagine them."

He smiled and purposely looked at her ears. "One feature all stories incorporate, is that fairies have pointed ears."

Zira briefly touched one ear tip while he talked.

"Now, as far as the Taweeg, no wings mark their shoulders, nor can they fly, but in every other respect they fit the mold. Their lives were made up of merriment, mischief, and communing with woodland friends." He paused. "And they do have pointed ears."

Wide-eyed and attentive, Zira exclaimed, "Oh! How lovely!" when he shared the Taweegs charmed lives. Her face was as delighted as a child's.

When he finished, Zira shared a fairy tale from Sertosh. But his thoughts returned to the Taweeg and how they figured as an important part of his thought-searching. Other sorcerers scoffed and dismissed the Taweeg as useless magical beings, but he found them fascinating and made a habit of visiting every few weeks. Thus, he made friends through his mental contacts and gained knowledge no other wizard before him had. The Taweeg showed him how to whisper secret words in their language, words understood by the strange, wondrous animals inhabiting their land. He learned how to consolidate the powers in his hand and splay his fingers, using them to seek out sparse water sources.

Many other little tidbits came his way over the years, most probably would never benefit him. He sighed. Certainly, the attaining of the fifth level of sorcery had not grown any closer due to his Taweeg friendships, or other thought-searches either, but he knew now that he'd had to find Zira first.

Realizing that she'd finished her story, he focused on Zira and her excitement. "We can visit them one day, you know."

"We could?" Curiosity and anxiety seemed to fight for dominance in her dark blue orbs. "It would be most wonderful to see such a place."

"And many more." Xandor used the opening she'd given him and told her of other planets he'd explored simply for pleasure, or others where he'd provided services required.

* * * * *

By the time he ran out of steam, evening shadows were draping the leaves around them.

"Better walk you home," he said. She nodded and slipped her hand into his without thought, as if it were already an old habit.

"By the way, thanks for introducing me to the caterpillar. He…it's been a blast." At her curious look, he explained, "I sang a song last night, something with a wild beat and that little guy went nuts dancing up a storm. It was quite entertaining."

"Glad you are enjoying its company."

"I'd rather share yours." He squeezed her hand, eliciting a giggle.

They reached her cottage just before nightfall and made arrangements for the next day. *The big day.* Just thinking about it made him nervous, so he turned his mind to the activities they'd engaged in today. It'd been a time of discoveries for him and of solidifying his feelings for Zira. And he thought perhaps her feelings for him had grown stronger too. When they stopped at the door, he got a romantic idea and reached to the side, plucking a large pink blossom. With a flourish, he stuck it behind one pointed ear.

"What...what did you do?" Her voice was a screech while she fumbled with her ear and lowered her hand, the flower lying upon her palm.

"I wanted to give my special girl something pretty. What's wrong?"

Tears shimmered in her eyes, she sobbed and ran into the house.

Xandor was shocked. Had he stumbled into a horrible faux pas by picking the flower? Unsure what to do, nevertheless, he didn't wish to leave on this note. Knocking softly on the door, he had to wait a few seconds before Wythoth opened it, a grim expression across his normally cheerful countenance.

Ak chose that moment to fly straight in through the door, squawking "Jekar" twice when he passed Wythoth. It made for an awkward moment.

"Best you come back tomorrow, as arranged," Zira's father said in a low, solemn tone.

"I'm sorry if I did something offensive." *What did I do?*

Zira's father nodded and then eased the door shut.

He was left feeling like an idiot, as if his foot was still stuck in that door. Knowing he'd worn out his welcome, he headed for the inn.

Great. Worry laced his thoughts as he walked. Tomorrow would be a challenge as it was, but now he'd upped the difficulty scale.

He didn't know how, but he guessed tomorrow he'd find out.

Chapter Fourteen

The next day when he approached her cottage, he wondered what his reception would be. Would she see him? Slam the door in his face?

Or would she complete the Jekar with him? Would she turn her anger against him, so that achieving the final orgasm was impossible?

He'd really bungled things by presenting the flower to her — but how?

Zira answered his knock, wearing a bland expression. He couldn't tell what she was thinking or feeling. But he didn't read any anger in her body language.

Wythoth went through the short ceremony with them, his face as mild as his daughter's.

Clearing his throat, Xandor asked, "Where do you wish to go for the Jekar?"

Shrugging, she said, "Doesn't matter."

Her apathy didn't bode well for him. "How about your favorite spot?"

She nodded and took off down the trail. He had to stretch his legs to keep up with the rapid pace she set. His stomach was tense. She seemed determined to get to the Jekar as quickly as possible, and then just as quickly dismiss him from her life. At least, this is how he read her. Ak, who'd been perched on her shoulder, took off in the air, flying ahead of them.

Stopping abruptly in the middle of the pathway, he glanced around and saw they stood at the edge of the meadow where he'd first seen her. Since they'd paused, he thought maybe it'd be the right time to apologize.

"Zira, I'm sorry about the flower. I'm not sure what I did, but if I broke some law...whatever I did, I'd like to make up for it."

She looked at him with unblinking blue eyes, turned and waved one hand at the flowers growing profusely throughout the open field. "I'm going to show you why plucking that flower upset me so, and why I can't go with you." She walked a few steps and turned back, fixing him with a firm look. "Stay there, don't tread on the plants, and don't interfere in what you see."

Curious, he watched her stroll slowly between the blossoms and fronds, never stepping on one leaf or green vine. Gaining the center of the meadow, where a small area was clear of anything but the lush silver green grass, she quickly slipped her dress off. Then she stretched out on her back and spread her arms outward. She began to sing, a haunting melody, like a chant. The flower blossoms all around her trembled.

Xandor glanced at the leaves overhead. No. No wind disturbed the trees' foliage.

Looking again at Zira, he was shocked to see vine creepers and leafy branches begin crawling toward her. In less than a minute, he could barely see her tiny body. Flowers, leaves and vines covered the spot where she lay. He started forward, but then remembered her warning.

Reassurance hit him when he realized her singing chant still floated from beneath the plants covering her. The trembling had changed and become synchronized with her singing. Now the plants swayed back and forth in rhythm with her song.

Squinting, Xandor tried to zoom in on the activity beneath the verdant growth, but to no avail. Shaking his head at himself, Xandor whipped up a spell to give himself the sight of the famed Earth-eagle.

Ah. Now he could see vines wrapped around her legs and arms, leaves quivering upon her flesh, and flowers brushing her body with their bright heads. Some strange ritual.

Xandor watched with interest. Some thirty minutes later, Zira stopped singing and the plants withdrew to their previous positions.

When she arose and walked toward him, he was astonished. She looked so refreshed. As if she just returned from a wonderful vacation. Her skin glowed, her eyes sparkled, and there was a spring in her step that hadn't been there this morning. On the way back to him, she picked up the dress and slid it on.

"Please, tell me what just happened?"

She stopped and faced him. "We replenish ourselves through the plants, and in return they gather nourishment from us."

"I don't understand."

"We don't eat as you do, except for slices of fruit and the nectar drink. Our needs are given to us by the plant life using transference through our pores."

"And, what do they get from you?"

"They extract all the wastes from our system."

"Really?" What a bizarre but beautiful process.

"Yes, we have no…anus as you humans do."

"Interesting." He rubbed his chin, suddenly intrigued with the prospect of examining her lovely butt. "But that doesn't give you an excuse for not going with me."

"What?" Placing both hands on her hips, her expression was annoyed. "I just told you we depend on our plants for nourishment and to cleanse our bodies."

"That's right. But plants can be potted and taken aboard spaceships. Many ships have nurseries onboard; in fact, most do, in order to supply extra oxygen to the ships air flow system."

"What about once we reach Varzkar? They would have to be transplanted."

"Most soil is easy to replicate. I can take a sample and recreate the mix once we reach the school. We have a very lively horticultural area, since we wizards grow most of our own herbs. Many exotic species are garnered from across the galaxies."

"I see. You have an easy answer to all my problems." She sounded annoyed.

"No. Please don't be this way Zira." He took her hands. "I'm sorry about the flower yesterday. Now I understand their importance to you." He paused. "When I came to Sertosh, my deepest wish was to secure my true mate and return immediately to Varzkar to further my studies."

He looked into her troubled eyes. "But now, I wish only for you to return with me, not because of the fifth level, but because I want you."

"You want me? Is that all?" The annoyance in her voice had eased a bit.

Tucking a strand of her hair behind one ear, he said, "I desire you. I want you by my side as my wife. I believe I love you, but to be honest, I'm not even sure what love is."

Her eyes flitted to his chest, as if she could see the necklace beneath. "I admit...I'm not sure what true love is either." That lovely dark gaze came back up to his face. "I have feelings for you...I felt like a part of my heart would be torn from me if you'd died yesterday. Is that love? I don't know, but I do think it is a beginning."

"Just as I cannot picture returning to Varzkar without you." Why did that thought make his stomach knot?

"But, I cannot tell you what my answer will be if we get through the last Jekar." She turned and stared into the distance. "My emotions are torn. Can you understand?"

"Yes." Without another word, he offered his hand and she placed hers within it. It was a silent commitment between the two of them, to at least see the Jekar through to the end.

Zira's secret sanctuary was lovely beyond words, even more so than the other day. The flower blossoms were fully open to the sun, their unusual fragrances saturating the air with a delightful mix. A light wind ruffled the leaves overhead and lent the air a pleasant crispness, while a flock of *ruhuris* birds, perched in trees around the perimeter chirping haunting love songs to their mates. The small waterfall tinkled cheerfully in the background, completing the natural symphony. Unexpectedly, an irritating squawk interrupted the idyllic scene when Ak landed clumsily in a large tree near the tiny pool.

Xandor stopped in the grassy area where he'd played upon Zira's body the last time. He wanted to do things differently for the last Jekar, to use only his own body parts and skills in lovemaking to push her into a full body orgasm. He first whisked a large blanket onto the grass, then doing a quick conjuring spell, materialized the mattress from her bedroom. He set it square in the center of the open space, over the blanket to keep grassy stains from clinging to it. Next, he manifested a *crituun* fur, big enough to cover the surface of the bed.

Zira watched in silent curiosity. It seemed strange that he conjured her mattress here in the middle of the woods, but it would be most comfortable for the Jekar. She guessed that meant she wouldn't be floating in the air this time.

She couldn't hold back the smile that tugged her lips at that thought. What magic did he have in mind?

He approached her slowly, a sweet smile on his rugged face. Just the look in his eyes made her stomach clench in anticipation. Placing both hands on either side of her face, he began gently, covering her flesh with tender kisses. He switched tactics, turning from tender to conquering. His lips were demanding and hot. He pressed hard into her lower lip — so hard she knew tomorrow it would be swollen.

Only after her whole face had been loved by his masculine lips, did he truly concentrate on her mouth. She sighed, taken once again with the expertise of his tongue and lips. He smelled so good too. Not like her people — not flowery. His odor was slightly spicy with an undercurrent of something indescribable. She thought the mystery scent might be his magical essence.

Giving in return with her tongue, she enjoyed hearing his rough groans and loved catching them in her mouth. The strokes of her tongue became bolder while the heat in her mid-section spread outward. Sometime during their intense kisses her arms had circled his neck, while his brawny arms had pulled her to him in a fierce grip. She pressed her breasts into his unyielding chest, enjoying the prickling in her nipples as they hardened.

One calloused hand caressed her shoulder and then slid her tunic down. His hand trailed across her exposed breast, causing the nipple to pucker immediately. Those long fingers, their magic sheathed today, rolled her nipple and tweaked it gently. Cupping the mound, he kneaded it over and over, until it expanded, filling his hand. His caresses made her breasts ache. She wanted him to squeeze them harder, to suck on her nipples until her body melted beneath his lips.

She thrust her breasts into his hands and he complied by kneading them with rougher strokes. "Oh, yes." She moaned.

"Your breasts seem to desire my kisses."

Zira ignored the teasing humor in his statement. "You're so right, my wizard." She rubbed his male nipples, felt them pucker beneath the leather. The heat in his eyes told her he liked her caresses.

His head descended as he trailed kisses down her neck, setting her blood on fire when his tongue dragged across the tender flesh. "Mmm, just so."

He laved her breast, round and round, coming near, but never touching her aching nipple. Groaning in frustration and arousal, she shoved her nipple toward his tongue. He chuckled, and then drew it into the wet heat of his mouth. The suckling caused searing heat to lance from her sensitive nub to her *kora*, which throbbed with excitement. She had a sudden urge for him to bury his *vunu* deep inside her. His intense attention to her breasts made her wonder what it would feel like if he sucked on her *kora* as he did her nipple?

His hand brushed the second strap down exposing her other breast to his attention. Soon, it too had plumped up. Withdrawing for a few seconds, Xandor held each breast in his hands, staring at them, until his fiery stare made them swell even more.

"Beautiful," he whispered, bringing his eyes up to hers so she could see the desire shining within his dark orbs. Her lover definitely appreciated that her breasts swelled to at least twice their normal size during sexual arousal, sometimes more if she had grown very excited, as she had now—for her breasts more than filled his two large hands.

Leaning down, he renewed his assault on her breasts, lavishing attention on each in turn. His long hair brushed over her sensitive mounds. It both tickled and excited her further, especially when it slid like silk over her hardened nipples. When he briefly returned to kiss her mouth, she undid the clasps on his vest then slowly slid it from his muscular biceps and let it fall to the ground.

Pressing her swollen breasts into his rigid chest threw her body further into feverish heat. The sensation of softness against unyielding hardness sent a flood of moisture to her *flakora*. He moaned softly into her mouth gratifying her that it affected him as well. Delighted, she kissed her way down his chest. When she licked one nipple and flayed it into a hard nub, his whole body jerked. Xandor groaned and gripped her hair.

She moved back up his chest, licking her way to his mouth again. He untied her belt while they continued the exchange of sensual kisses. The dress slithered off, pooling at her feet. The cool air brushing her skin, as she stepped out of the dress, felt delicious.

Rough, manly hands stroked her sides, slid in hard caresses up and down her butt. It tingled and sent pleasurable shocks all the way to her toes. His kisses once again trailed down her chest and he gave her breasts new caresses and licks. His hand slid from her breasts and repositioned on her bottom, gripping her cheeks and kneading them while he suckled one nipple. She gripped his shoulders, head flung backward while her *kora* pulsed unmercifully.

Unexpectedly, he stopped and picked her up in his arms, placing her gently on the luxurious fur throw. Zira stretched upon it lush pile, enjoying the sensual pleasure it aroused, and watched while Xandor slowly stripped out of his clinging leather pants. She licked her lower lip when his *vunu* bounced free. It was most majestic in its length and width, much larger than those of the men of her planet. She loved the feel of it stretching her and filling her.

She'd examined him briefly the other afternoon as he'd directed the sensual shower, but now she took the time to really give his powerful *vunu* the attention it deserved. Its shape was the same as a Sertoshian *vunu*, something that brought a sense of comfort to her. The dark pink color seemed shocking compared to the normal blue of the Sertoshian males. But, it also excited her. The head puffed out, larger than the shaft. She suddenly wanted to stroke it, to caress the softness laid over its steely strength.

He crawled onto the mattress, rubbing his body against hers. Her breath hitched for a second, feeling his muscular length brush her whole front. He gave her a quick kiss then trailed his lips and tongue over her breasts. She arched up for his attention, but he kept moving down her belly. Why?

Chapter Fifteen

He nibbled her abdomen and swirled his tongue into her belly button. At first she giggled, but she moaned the next instant. Soft, silken hair stroked her hips. Surprising her, his mouth moved to her hipbones. He sucked on each gently, strangely evoking sensations in her *flakora*.

Positioning himself between her splayed thighs, he ruffled the curls at her groin. Startled, she sucked in her lower lip. He parted her nether lips just as he had the last time, setting off a fire in her belly. Lifting her gently, he ran one hand down her slit all the way to the crease of her butt.

"All smooth," he whispered. His hand caressed the crease in her derriere.

She giggled. It seemed hard for him to accept the proof that she had no anus.

Her giggle was cut short by the contact of something warm and wet flicking her *kora*. Glancing down, Zira was shocked to see Xandor's nose and mouth between her lips. Sodden warmth swiped her whole *flakora* from bottom to the top and she groaned. She had never heard of such a thing, this licking of genitals.

Her whole *flakora* ached. Her *kora* throbbed madly.

Conceding to this wondrous experience, she lay her head back down and gave herself up to the new sensations. Xandor's tongue licked up and down her *flakora*, over and over, until she squirmed and fidgeted restlessly. Her *kora* jumped in some crazy rhythm of its own and she desperately wanted him to flick it again, but he avoided it, teasing her with his maddening genital kisses. His tongue slid around and around her whole *flakora*. Her *kora* was hard, felt ready to explode, if he'd only caress it with his wet tongue.

When she was sure she would die from his torments, that marvelous appendage of his slipped into her karra, not filling it as had his *vunu*, but her inner flesh quivered nonetheless.

His tongue moved in and out, imitating the action of his *vunu*, and she groaned over and over. "Oh...oh, Xandor...that feels so good. But...I want...I want something...I need your *vunu*." But at the same time, it made her desire his male organ in place of his soft tongue. She wanted something hard to stroke her inner walls instead of pliable flesh.

But then, oh then, his tongue caressed its way upward, licking her *kora* as she'd desired all along. His movements changed constantly—from licking to swirls, to suctioning of his lips, and then quick flicks of his tongue. The slurping sounds made her hitch her bottom upward. That sound connected with something deep inside her, something that set fire to her blood. She thrust her hips upward again, gaining a deeper contact between his tongue and her *kora*. She felt close to a precipice.

"Oh, Xandor, yes. Don't stop!" Zira panted and then grabbed his hair and shoved his head at her aching flesh.

"Yes, Zira." Xandor released himself for a few seconds to speak against her mons.

The humming sensation of his voice sent a different excitement through her *flakora*, yet she still groaned in happy abandon when he reattached his head to her *kora*. She felt it coming, a huge orgasm. It gripped her abdomen and clenched the muscles of her lower legs. Zira screamed.

It was not the Jekar, but so close.

* * * * *

Xandor had been totally shocked by her taste once his tongue dipped into her pussy. *The same wild flower flavor as her luscious nipples.*

It floored him when she climaxed and a slow stream of nectar dripped from her *kora*. He'd suckled madly once he got a taste, enchanted by the ambrosia-like liquid. He was gratified by her very reactive orgasm, even though it was not the one he ultimately sought.

After her breathing slowed, he rolled her onto her stomach and directed her into the doggie position. He'd been shocked when he got his first good look at her luscious bottom, in spite of his foreknowledge about Zira's lack of an anus. But he wanted to explore this phenomenon a bit further.

Her lovely, rounded cheeks were displayed nicely. As he edged his cock into the opening of her vagina, he kneaded her buttocks and ran one finger up and down the crease of her ass, fascinated with its smoothness. Her slick juices caressed his cock as he pressed into her. Satisfied by her feminine moans, he slid slowly inside and circled gently. Then he shoved hard, all in one stroke. When he withdrew completely and teased her by rubbing his cock against her clit, Zira groaned. Her hips rotated in circular motions, and then she bucked backward, coordinating her actions with his, creating even more intense excitement. His balls slapped against her shapely ass when he increased the tempo of his thrusts.

Zira's groans told him she was close to orgasm again. Whether it was the Jekar or a normal climax, he wanted to see her beautiful face while she found release. Slipping out, he turned her over and repositioned himself missionary style, but with her legs raised. Leaning down, he thrust his tongue into her mouth at the same time as he plunged into her pussy. She moaned against his mouth, driving him wild with excitement.

A loud racket overhead caused them both to glance upward. A huge flock of those strange, noisy purple birds was flying by, screeching. It took at least half a minute for the group to pass.

When Xandor glanced down at Zira afterwards, her distracted look disturbed him. The heat of desire barely flickered in the blue depths of her eyes.

Squeezing her breasts gently, he again took up his thrusting movements. Her expression warmed, but not nearly enough.

Cursing silently, he searched his mind for a method to lash her desire back up to the level it'd been before the birds had thrown ice on their sensual haze. She had been so close. He needed to whip her into a sexual frenzy again before the feeling was lost altogether.

An idea came to him. It would take magic. But still, it would be his body that would throw her into Jekar, if it was fated to happen.

Continuing to thrust into her wet warmth, he reared back until he was nearly vertical. Creating a quick spell, he stuck out his tongue and lowered one hand in a flowing motion.

With that one wave, his tongue increased a foot in length. Xandor made a few more fluid motions of his wrist, until his tongue hung down to Zira's pussy. With a swift adjustment of his hand, it was able to easily reach her clit.

His blue siren had been watching him the whole time, her eyes getting wider at each flip of his wrist. Adjusting to the length of his immense appendage called for a control spell; he didn't have the time to learn how to direct its movements. He cast the spell quickly and when he lapped his newly grown tongue over her clit for the first time, she gasped loudly.

Rubbing his tongue up and down on her excited nub, he continued to fuck her at the same time, giving her the double pleasure of his cock and tongue. God, she tasted delicious. Flowers mixed with nectar. Her honey flowed over his tongue as he stroked her swollen *kora*.

Her arousal came back swiftly and fiercely. Her inner walls gripped him hard, squeezing in spasms. Zira's face flushed to a dark hue, her nipples hardened, jutting upward. Stepping up the pace, he flicked his tongue in rapid strokes up and down her *kora*, while plunging into her pussy with deeper, harder thrusts of his cock.

An orgasm overcame her within a few strokes. The scream that erupted from her throat was long and drawn out. Her whole body went rigid and then quivers erupted beneath her soft skin. Her face and breasts turned almost navy blue. His balls tensed and his cock swelled, so hard it hurt. The blood rushed to his cock as he continued to drive into her grasping slickness. Her vagina spasmed around him painfully and he let his orgasm flow into her.

Her climax ended with a small sigh of exhalation. It pleased him to no end. They'd achieved the last Jekar.

The birds perched in the branches burst from the trees, chirping in alarm when Ak flew among them screaming "Jekar".

Withdrawing his tongue to its normal size, he sank onto the mattress and took Zira into his arms, falling immediately asleep.

* * * * *

Some time later, he awoke to her blue eyes examining his face.

"I've been thinking," she said with no preamble.

He nodded, he knew where her thoughts lay, but was almost afraid to hear her pronouncement. What would he do if she refused to go with him?

"I will be your wife."

Xandor let out the breath he'd been holding. "What changed your mind?"

"It was not changed...I have been trying to ignore my feelings." She stroked his cheek. "I do love you. I knew it after I realized you could have been killed yesterday."

He started to question this statement; she'd told him after the gliding incident, that she thought she loved him, but wasn't sure. Now she was. But then, he realized he felt the same way, that he'd been holding back his true emotions from them both, in case he didn't win her through the Jekar.

"I love you too." He stroked one finger down her upturned nose.

"You are sure?"

Her eyes twinkled. Were those tears of happiness shimmering in their dark depths?

"Yes, I am. I have felt such an attraction for you from the first time we mind-touched. Perhaps it was love at first sight. Then, yesterday when you said you didn't know if you'd come with me...I didn't want to think about returning to Varzkar without you."

He stared off in the distance. "Maybe it is fate. Or the fact that our souls are matched as the necklace indicates."

He looked back at her, liking her sweet expression. Picking up one petite hand, he kissed it softly. "Being a wizard has many compensations — respect, money, power. But it also makes for a lonely existence, one I never thought much about until I met you."

Smiling, she caressed his jaw. "Am I to be a salve against loneliness?"

"No." He placed her hand over his heart. "You make me feel whole in a way I'd never thought possible."

"Oh, Xandor."

"And now, I can tell you something I've wanted to share all along." At her curious look, he said, "Once I attain the fifth level of wizardry, I will be able to cast a spell to transport us wherever we desire in the universe."

"What?" She propped up on one elbow. "Even Sertosh?"

"Yes. We can live anywhere we choose and travel to Sertosh whenever we want, and also to any planet where my services are needed."

"Why didn't you tell me this before?" She sounded frustrated.

"Because I didn't want to influence your decision."

Those lush lips drew up in a smile. "I understand." She fingered the curls on his chest and said softly, "I wish we could make Sertosh our home."

"You read my mind." He kissed her nose. "I love Sertosh. We can move here after I attain the fifth level."

Her sweet breath fanned his face and he couldn't resist capturing her lips in a kiss. Soon, their loving exchange turned into something deeper and they again made love; this time in a slow, gentle manner, one that befitted their mood. They spent the rest of the day talking, truly getting to know each other, and sporadically engaging in rousing sessions of sex. It was an enchanted day, full of discoveries and a different sort of magic.

* * * * *

Ak made a screeching announcement of their return to her cottage later by screaming "Jekar" three times while flapping his wings furiously in front of Wythoth's face. The man simply raised his eyes heavenward and patted his shoulder for the yeep to perch.

Parting was difficult, but Zira had a busy day planned for the morrow and several days following. She must make arrangements for the marriage ceremony.

He was to return three days hence to the cottage. The groom was not allowed near the bride beforehand, so he cooled his heels at the inn, soaking up the local culture and exploring knowledge from their small library.

He'd decided one thing for certain while he waited. He would love to make Sertosh his home once his training was completed. And he didn't wish that only to please Zira. The people were cheerful, friendly souls and they were the healthiest species he'd ever run across. He put that down to their natural exchange with the plant life. The environment was clean, the air fresh and sparkling, thanks to the lack of major industries. Sertosh's only products sold offworld were the delicious vegetables and fruit grown in this paradise. And, hands down, this was the most visually gorgeous world he'd visited. To call it home would be an honor.

* * * * *

Approaching the cottage on the fourth day, Xandor was met by a stream of people coming and going, more than the last time her relatives had gathered. Greetings and questions about his sorcery went on for well over an hour before three men with strange instruments began playing a charming melody. Wythoth pulled him into position in the middle of flowering bushes taller than he was. So, he couldn't see but a dozen feet where the plants parted for a winding trail. Leaves rustled, and Zira appeared, walking slowly toward him.

His dream girl. Her slim form was draped Grecian style in a shimmering silver toga, her long locks melding perfectly with the material. *A goddess, albeit an alien one.*

She stopped. Turning, she faced him and Wythoth went through a ceremony only a bit longer than the announcement of the Jekar each day. Instead of kissing at the end, though, Zira rubbed her nose against his and he followed her lead.

He thought it strange that the ceremony was peformed in such a secluded setting, but once the three of them reappeared from the overgrown bushes, the guests cheered loudly. Clearly, they had overheard the words spoken. He and Zira were grabbed by the hand by two cherubs and guided to seats bedecked in flowery vines. Xandor noted that the vines grew next to the chairs and trailed up the sides and back of each. The seat and where their backs would rest were clear of plant life, though. He idly wondered if the vines were "trained" or if some type of inherent intelligence guided their growth.

The tiny blue children, as lovely as any elf-like child he'd ever encountered, joined a flock of small bodies gathered in front of them. They wore a variety of colors, almost as if they represented the flowers on Sertosh. For that's what they seemed to resemble to him.

The musicians sitting on the sidelines started up a merry tune and the children danced around in abandonment. Their movements seemed to have no particular pattern, merely that of joy and happiness. Several guests started clapping in rhythm to the music and soon he and Zira joined in. Giggling laughter melded with the music as the children flowed back and forth in the cleared space in front of their chairs.

After this performance, Xandor remembered little of the festivities that followed. He got too drunk with his wife's beauty and the thought of their many heated nights to come.

Long after the sun set, people started leaving, including Wythoth, who was staying the night with relatives, leaving them to enjoy the cottage in solitude. That night, their passion ran as hot as any previous encounters, but Zira experienced multiple orgasms within the normal range. He already had studied all he could find in the library concerning the Jekar and knew that one full body climax a day was the limit. Poor Zira was exhausted by the time sleep claimed them.

* * * * *

It took a week of checking with the one pod spaceport before they secured berth on a large freighter. During that time, he and Zira potted samples of the many varieties of plant life that she deemed necessary to her survival. Though Xandor wondered by the time they were through if she hadn't slipped a few in simply because she loved their beauty so much. Then there was Ak, his food needs, and his mate. After all, the yeep need companionship, just as they did. And he had to take a long terrarium, big enough to nourish the caterpillar for the trip. They had quite a load to place aboard ship, but fortunately it could accommodate them.

Xandor admittedly liked Ak's mate, a more petite version of him, who acted slightly less goofy. At least she seemed to keep her perch without falling into an instant snooze. She looked very pretty perched on Zira's shoulder actually. But, unfortunately, that meant Ak took up the habit of making a sliding landing onto his own shoulder. Xandor spent more time then he thought he should, straightening up the sleeping yeep who had fallen upside down against his vest. In reality, the yeep had taken a shine to him immediately after the Jekar had ended and had already insisted on perching on his shoulder constantly. It set Zira off into giggles.

Saying goodbye to her father, relatives, and friends, was a sad affair for his wife. Many tears and hugs passed around before they entered the small metal door of the spaceship. He spent a good part of the night comforting her, not bad for him, but miserable for her.

At first, it seemed their trip back would be made in record time; they knew exactly where they wanted to go and the ships in this trading route certainly knew where Varzkar was located. Problems arose when they sought new accommodations in order to keep on track. Some ships were simply too small for Zira's plant collection. Hence, it'd taken longer to reach Varzkar then he first estimated.

But the many weeks it took to find the right ship were hardly an annoyance. Zira's joy at exploring new planets was delightful and contagious. Xandor rediscovered his own delight of strange, alien wonders.

They were one day from landing on Varzkar when they made a discovery that would change their perception of the yeep forever.

Chapter Sixteen

Returning to their small cabin after supper one evening, a sudden loud sneeze drew their attention to the yeeps, who were clinging side-by-side to the perch Xandor had made for them at the end of the bed.

"Poor Ak, he's been doing a lot of sneezing since this morning."

"I know. He must be allergic to something." He walked over and petted the yeep, who squawked.

Zira came and stood next to him. "Maybe we should —"

Her words were interrupted by another extremely loud sneeze. A scarf draped on a chair in front of the perch whooshed into flames.

"What the —?" Xandor stared at the charred remains of the scarf.

He was staring at Ak when another sneeze gripped the yeep's small body. A small fiery ball erupted into the air in front of the tiny dragon's face. Turning to Zira in shock, he asked, "Did you know he could do that?"

Surprise painted Zira's lovely face. She shook her head slowly, then whispered, "No yeep has ever spit fire."

Pulling up the chair to the side, so he would not be directly in front of the perch, Xandor examined the yeeps. They, or rather, one of them suddenly showed signs of magic? Most mysterious. He rubbed his chin. Or was the fireball magic at all?

He had to test this phenomenon. "Ak, can you spit more fire?" The dragon stared at him sleepily, on the verge of falling into one of his deep sleeps.

"Great," he mumbled, then had a thought. Snapping his fingers, he materialized pepper from a table in the dining hall. Pouring a few grains onto his palm, he blew it into the yeep's face. The dragons' cheeks puffed out and both sneezed, but only Ak blew out a fireball. Xandor caught the sphere with a spell, holding it between his outstretched hands.

"Better." Ak squawked, "Pain gone," then fell into an instant sleep, his mate right behind him.

Maintaining the ball with one hand, Xandor waved the other, materializing a cylinder into his palm. He asked Zira to lift the glass, then directed the ball inside and sealed it. Carrying the cylinder carefully, he set it down on the tiny corner desk.

It was as he'd guessed. The fiery orb gravitated to the top of the glass. The ball reminded him of the Dragon Fire, except it was only about three inches across, and the color was predominantly yellow with swirls of red lacing through it. What this meant, he had no idea, but intended to ask Master Talorg as soon as he could. In the meantime, he studied the fire and tried to read its magical emanations, for it certainly had some inklings of enchantment within its flames.

* * * * *

He felt fortunate the next day when Master Talorg came to the spaceport. He'd been expecting a shipment of valuable crystals and was delighted to see Xandor and meet Zira and the yeeps.

Talorg could tell him no more about the fireball than he knew himself. But, the dragon and tiny ball of fire were taken under study by the Master himself, several fifth level sorcerers, and Xandor. Were the yeep distant relatives of the highly revered Varzkar dragons? It seemed unlikely, but that was one theory being batted about by the intellectuals.

Whatever the outcome, Xandor enjoyed the silly yeeps, once he got used to their frequent habit of falling asleep in the blink of an eye. Now that the rumor about the dragons had gotten around the institution, it didn't matter if Ak fell into an undignified heap upon his chest. The wizards smiled and shook their heads, as if this were but a part of the magic embedded in the tiny blue body.

Life fell into a rhythm that he came to look forward to and his training each day progressed quickly. He loved that Zira awaited his arrival in their apartment every day, ready with a sweet smile and stimulating conversation. Or sexually sizzling encounter — whatever met their mood that particular evening.

* * * * *

Six Months Later…

Xandor kissed Zira's nose and patted her stomach after he entered their apartment. She seemed to notice the distracted expression on his face.

"Is everything all right?" Concern laced her voice.

"Yes." His eyes came down to her blue ones; the faraway look gone. "It's just that today Master Talorg said I've made astounding growth toward completing the fifth level."

"Really?"

Her excitement made him smile. Clasping her in his arms, he gave her a deep kiss, enjoying the softness of her lush lips beneath his. Drawing back, he said, "In fact, he said at this rate, I might be through in another six months."

"Oh, Xandor." She squeezed him around the waist.

"We can move to Sertosh just after our son is born." He rubbed her prominent belly, which looked rather odd upon her otherwise still slim figure. But he still thought she was the most beautiful woman ever born.

She sighed and laid her head against his chest. "You have made me the happiest woman in the galaxy."

"Just the galaxy?" he teased, caressing the soft hair at her temple.

When she raised her head, her dark blue eyes twinkled. "In the universe, then, great wizard."

"I'll settle for that." He chuckled.

"And it all came about because of this marvelous necklace." She fished beneath his vest and pulled it to lie against the leather.

She stared at it, her eyes becoming glazed in thought. "Xandor, do you think we should share such a wondrous object with others?"

Shaking his head, he said musingly, "You have read my mind again...we have achieved happiness because of its charm, perhaps another could benefit also."

"You have someone in mind." She peered up at him, curiosity flitting across her face.

Nodding, he answered, "I was thinking of Thorras. He's only a third level sorcerer and he's been having some problems lately in his attempts toward the fourth." He paused. "Do you think we should gift him with the necklace?"

"Oh, yes. I like Thorras. He's so funny and charming. Will you tell him of its magic?"

"No, I can't. I can inform him it will find his true love, if he's interested, then it'll be up to him if he follows through."

She hugged him tight. "This is so exciting."

"Hmmm, but you know what's more exciting?" He lowered his voice.

Zira giggled and then her hand went to his belt and fumbled with it. "I don't know, let me see if I can find out." With that she slid his pants down.

By the time she'd tugged them to his feet and he'd kicked out of them, his cock was stiff and bobbed against her bent head. She rubbed her silken hair against his shaft. It jerked under the soft caress.

Kneeling awkwardly, she continued her erotic play. Her head rotated playfully several times, and then her lips made contact with the head of his cock. One hand held him steady, while her lovely eyes stared up at him. At first, she tortured him by simply giving him soft kisses all up and down his shaft, coming back to press her full lips against the sensitive head. Next, her tongue flicked out and lapped up a drop of semen shining on top and he groaned.

For a woman who had known nothing of oral sex before their marriage, Zira had learned wonderful skills in six months. When her lips closed over him, he shut his eyes and soaked up the erotic sensation. Wet warmth wrapped completely around him; her tongue slid against the head inside the heated cavern of her mouth. He moaned when she started moving her head up and down, sucking at the same time. The sultry, heady odor of exotic flowers wafted to his nose, tickling and enticing him. He thought it was the scent of her arousal. Opening his eyes, he watched her head bob and then how she removed her mouth briefly.

"Zira." He groaned. She stared up at him while she licked the head, her pale blue tongue flicking rapidly. Her wet tongue slid all the way down his shaft, then she gently sucked one testicle into her moist mouth. His thighs clenched as she let it plop out, and then nuzzled the other, laving it as she looked up at him.

It was too much. His balls tightened and Xandor gripped her head, driving into her waiting mouth, pumping his hips in rhythm with her bobbing head. His seed spurted into her warmth, and he groaned again while he watched her swallow.

With a flick of her dark tongue, she licked the last drop from his cock. She smiled sweetly, pleased that she had pleased him.

He knew she got turned on by sucking him off, but she needed her release also. Their lovemaking was less frequent lately; he had to be considerate of her sensitized body during her pregnancy, but oral sex was no problem at all and much welcomed by them both.

Laying her gently down upon the *crituun* fur, he slipped her tunic off. He kissed her full lips until they felt swollen. Then went straight to the already excited nub nestled in her sweet pussy. Her hands clutched his hair. The pain excited him still further. Her clit was hard and when he laid his tongue against it for a few seconds, he could actually feel it throbbing. He stroked around and around the nub and only when she wriggled upon the fur did he draw her clit into his mouth. Her heated flowery scent filled his nose. He breathed in deeply, loving her smell.

He kneaded her butt cheeks firmly. Loosing a hand, he gently slipped one finger into her vagina, waiting until it became slick with her juices before sliding it in and out. Then he returned to her clit and licked it swiftly while he finger-fucked her in a slow rhythm. Zira moaned loudly. Her hips began thrusting upward to meet his tongue.

It only took a few more licks and swirls and she climaxed, her thighs tightening on each side of his head while she moaned little "ohs".

He couldn't wait for the child to be born. There were so many delicious and naughty things he wanted to do with his lovely wife. But for today, he was more than content. He gathered Zira into his arms and they discussed mundane married things like baby names and their upcoming move to Sertosh.

* * * * *

It was only a month later that Thorras came to say goodbye. He was on his way to Earth to look for his soulmate. During a meditation spell, he'd gotten the distinct impression his future wife was an Earthling. As they waved bye to the enthusiastic young wizard, Xandor could only hope his protégé had as much luck as he had in finding his true love.

Epilogue

They'd just returned from the bazaar and Zira spun around the room, delighted with the blue dangle earrings he'd purchased for her. The silver metal matched her hair, while the dark sapphire blue reflected her eye coloring. She was a charming picture.

His knees buckled under. Confusing, powerful images shot through his head.

Lights flashing, alarms shrilling, sickening, intense spiraling motion, and then inky blackness.

Zira knelt beside him and he heard her "What's wrong?" as if from a far distance.

Taking a few deep breaths, he took control of the sharp mind-touch, which had thrown his system into chaos. Thorras was at the other end of the link.

He was in trouble and had reached out to his mentor.

While the young wizard's mind temporarily floated in shock within the arms of blackness, Xandor told Zira of the mind-touch. Settling his body into a more comfortable position, he meditated, waiting for Thorras to reach out again.

This time the image was stronger, less fuzzy—as if the young wizard looked out a view plate and related the pictures to Xandor's mind.

Thorras's ship erupted from the bowels of a black hole and plunged toward the planet below.

Earth.

"I wish I could see what's happening," Zira whispered.

Without breaking contact or losing concentration, he placed one hand over her two hands, which clutched the material of her tunic. He made mental contact with her and Zira's gasp told him she now saw what he did. Earth's blue oceans, topped with layers of cottony clouds were breathtaking. But not to the people aboard the ship. The out-of-control vessel plunged through those lovely clouds, its hull burning a fiery red when it entered the atmosphere too swiftly.

The spaceship broke through the lowest level of clouds and spun toward the ground. Xandor maintained only the slightest contact the next few seconds. Water surrounded the ship— they'd landed in a lake, river or the ocean.

Thorras made it through the shredded metal, swimming away from the chaos. Rain poured down in painful sheets upon the luckless individuals trying to survive the savage conditions of their crash landing. Visibility was almost negligible. The ship suddenly upended and sank swiftly from sight, sucking down floundering people with its powerful death.

A huge wave washed over the young wizard after the spaceship sank into oblivion. He was sucked under for a few seconds, flipped over and over, but then he managed to swim to the surface. Thorras's gaze sought something, which floated on top of the raging waters—the necklace. It had been ripped from his neck by the rushing water and was being swept away from him at a fierce pace.

Gallantly, he swam after it, but its lighter weight and his exhaustion played against him. Paddling to keep his head above the waves, he watched the direction the waves were moving the necklace. It was headed toward shore, which could be seen now, since fortunately, the rain had slackened some.

Visibility was still poor, but through Thorras's eyes, Xandor saw reddish-brown earth where the waves slashed against the shoreline. Several tall trees, with fringe-like branches only at the top, waved madly in the whipping winds. Towering, rugged mountains ripped upward in the background. The whole setting was surreal. It looked savage and untouched. Thorras swam toward shore, the necklace far outpacing him. He abruptly lost the connection with his apprentice.

Xandor came out of his meditation trance and found Zira's worried face right in front of his.

"What happened to Thorras?"

"From the images I received, I think the ship may have been sucked into a black hole."

"But...wasn't that Earth?"

"Yes. For some reason I think the ship was pulled into a time warp."

"Is he all right?'

He nodded. "He was swimming toward shore when I lost contact. He'll be fine."

She smiled, her eyes staring behind him. "I'll pray to the mother goddess every day for his safe return."

Hugging her to his body, he whispered in her cute ear, "You're my goddess."

Giggling, she shoved back from him and stared into his eyes and asked, "What do you think will happen to the necklace?"

He shrugged. "Maybe some lucky person will find it swept up a riverbank."

"Will they be able to use it...I mean, will the magic work for them?" Zira's expression had turned excited.

"It should. I put a powerful spell on it." Now he was the one who stared at the wall. "Although..."

"What?"

"Hmmm." His distracted thoughts came back to his luscious wife, who cuddled in his lap in a most distracting manner. "I was just thinking...if someone with psychic or magical abilities gets their hands on it..." He frowned. "Who knows what may happen?"

"Like what?" Her hands had stopped stroking his chest and she stared up at him with curiosity.

"The necklace may take that power and do different things than was intended for it." At her persistent look, he said, "For example, if a telekinetic person held it and concentrated their power, they might be able to more easily move objects."

"Oh, I see, but not likely to happen." She wiggled into a more comfortable position and stared up at him adoringly. "But, the power of love will continue, whether the necklace is there to help out or not."

"That's right." He tightened his arms about her waist. "Our love continues, and grows everyday."

She giggled, that girlish, tinkling sound that always caused a responding thump in his chest.

"Just think. Creating the necklace helped continue the Dragon Fire legacy."

"Huh?" She furrowed her brow.

"The Dragon Fire was used to make the necklace...remember me telling you the story?" At her nod, he continued, "The magic will live on somewhere else now, perhaps behave in new ways. Help people in ways we cannot imagine, take on new legends. At the very least it will help fated lovers find one another."

Laughing, she twisted a handful of his hair and brought him down for a sultry kiss. "And you will continue to torture me with your magic, wizard?"

"Always."

He sealed his promise with a fierce, possessive kiss. Pulling back, he caressed the soft hair on either side of her elfin face. "You have brought more magic into my life by your love, than I could ever hope to create."

"Oh, Xandor, tell me more. Your poetry affects me more than your sorcery."

He didn't think that likely when he recalled her sexual reactions to his magical foreplay. But if words were what she desired, perhaps he could create a few sonnets, even if he had to borrow some wisdom from such greats as Shakespeare. But first, he thought he'd remind her of the magic between the two of them.

It didn't take long to stoke the fires within the blue depths of her lovely eyes. He knew that for as long as they both existed in this world, their love would sizzle, an eternal flame as bright and mystical as the Dragon Fire.

About the author:

Myra Nour grew up reading s/f, fantasy, and romance, so she was really thrilled when these elements were combined in Futuristic Romances. She enjoys writing within all these elements, whether the hero is a handsome man from another planet, or a tiny fairy from another dimension. Myra's background is in counseling, and she likes using her knowledge to create believable characters. She also enjoys lively dialogue and, of course, using her imagination to create other worlds with lots of action/adventure, as well as romance. She uses her handsome husband as inspiration for her heroes - he is a body builder, a soldier, and has a black belt in Tae Kwon Do.

Myra welcomes mail from readers. You can write to her c/o Ellora's Cave Publishing at 1056 Home Avenue, Akron OH 44310-3502.

Also by Myra Nour:

Vampire Fangs and Venom
Future Lost A Mermaids Longing
As You Wish
Sex Kitten

Visions

Sahara Kelly

Chapter One

She was taking as much of his cock as she could deep into her body and it still wasn't enough.

He thrust harder into her channel, which welcomed him with hot and plentiful honey and caressed his rock hard cock with ripples and flutters. His balls slapped against her buttocks and he spread her thighs apart even further so that he could drive himself in as deeply as he could go.

Pounding roughly against her clit, sweat fell from his face and dribbled down his body, melding with her juices and pooling on the ground below. His shoulders ached, his vision blurred and he felt a tightening across his buttocks.

Moaning and writhing beneath him, she was nearing her peak, clasping him with inner muscles that were starting to tremble. He lowered his head and suckled harshly at her pebbled nipple, pulling it into his mouth and rolling it between his teeth.

She screamed as her body released its tension in a series of violent shudders. The inner massage against his arousal was enough. He quickly withdrew and spurted his seed across her golden thighs.

Long moments passed as he caught his breath and waited for his heart to slow down.

Rolling onto his back, he watched birds fly past, startled no doubt by the loud yell she'd loosened on the deserted field. He turned his head and looked at her. She was asleep on the damp grass that had thirstily drunk the rains from last night's storm.

Good. Now it didn't matter so much if he couldn't remember her name.

Rising to his feet, Nerin of Kushuk stretched his arms to the sky, enjoying the feel of the sun on his naked skin. He felt sated, but not pleasured, and consequently a little irritated with himself.

Oh not because he'd forced her—such an act was not his style. The maid had been willing enough. She'd been sending out signals for several weeks now and he was only human after all.

He turned away from the sleeping woman and headed for the riverbank. He needed a cool dip in the waters of the blessed river. Perhaps that would restore his equilibrium and cleanse his spirit at the same time.

As he walked he proudly surveyed his land. As far as he could see was *his land*.

Rolling fields of young barley, orchards with ripening oranges, date palms, all had their place in his well-ordered world.

He'd worked hard for the last ten years to bring his father's dream to life, and here it was, glowing before his eyes in the bright afternoon sun.

Why, then, was he feeling so strange? As if he was waiting for something to happen. His ordinary activities had ceased to occupy all of his thoughts, and when he had tried fucking a few more women than usual, it had still not solved his problem.

It had, however, left a number of satisfied smiles in its wake. Nerin prided himself on leaving no maiden unhappy. Or pregnant. He was scrupulous in withdrawing before the moment of bliss arrived. He'd had a few close calls, but come to think of it, he couldn't remember their names either.

His slow stroll had brought him to the edge of the wide river that was the foundation of much of his wealth. Were it not for the annual floods that brought rich mud to his fields each year, he would have poor crops and little yield to show for his hard work.

Now, thanks to the River Goddess, his farm was expanding, his workers content, and he himself had enough time for the occasional fuck outdoors in the sunshine. A pleasure indeed. If he kept telling himself that, maybe he'd believe it.

He moved forward a few feet, allowing the cool water to swirl around his legs. This was a particularly shallow area, the bend in the course of the river providing a sandy outcropping where many a child had learned to swim. None were here today, however, and it was very quiet.

A few more steps and he was almost deep enough. A smile crossed his face as he dove headfirst into the smooth waters and swam for several minutes like an otter playing in a stream.

His head burst through the surface and he tossed his long dark hair away from his eyes. The distinctive gold streak was muted by the water that streamed from his head, but his face had cleared and he looked and felt refreshed.

Lost in his thoughts, Nerin almost missed the glitter that flashed from a patch of nearby reeds.

There it was again—a sparkle of some sort.

Heedless of his nakedness, Nerin walked through the ripples to find out what was causing such a reflection. He thought it was probably just the flash of sunlight on water.

But he was wrong.

White limbs lay tangled in the reeds at the edge of the river. She was naked and unconscious.

Nerin quickly pulled her to the bank and stretched her in the sun, touching her neck and feeling for a pulse. A steady throb beneath his fingers reassured him and he sat back on his heels to survey his catch.

She was a beauty. Her skin was milky and smooth, and her jet black hair hung in wet splashes across her shoulders and breasts. Her nipples were large and dusky brown, and topped a perfect pair of well-formed mounds. Her waist was slender, her belly softly curved.

Where her thighs met, an abundant crop of black curls hid her woman's secrets, but Nerin could imagine them, pink and moist, peeking from their shadowed depths.

His cock stirred.

Then he saw the mark on her ankle. Shaped like a shepherd's crook, it was branded into the skin.

She was an Akkadian slave.

Suddenly she moaned and her eyes flickered open.

Deep blue pools of fear gazed at him as he squatted naked next to her. She shoved her hand behind her back and inched away from him.

"Who...who are you? Where am I?"

Nerin's mouth hardened.

"More to the point, who are you? And is your master looking for you even now?" Nerin closed the distance between them and in a lightning move grabbed her arm. "And what is it that you attempt to hide so badly?"

He wrenched her hand out from behind her and twisted her arm until she gasped. Her fingers opened and something glittery dropped on the grass.

"Aha. Stolen something, I see. Typical of Akkadian slaves. Untrustworthy to the end."

"I am not an Akkadian slave." She pulled herself up onto her knees and stared at him. Pride radiated from every pore and surprised him with its intensity.

"Then explain your ankle brand, slave," he sneered.

"I...I cannot," she muttered.

Nerin paid no attention. He reached down and picked up the article she'd tried so hard to conceal.

It was some kind of necklace, he guessed, but very unusual in design. He had never seen its like. The pendant was made of an oval stone, which featured the painting of an eye, but no ordinary eye. It was a delicate shade of blue, like those of the northern tribes whose members occasionally traded in Sumer.

The most arresting feature was the one perfect teardrop that fell from the corner of the eye. A delicate chain with gold and red stones held it in place.

"That is mine. Please return it immediately." Her voice was authoritative, although shaking with fear.

"I don't think so, slave."

"My name is Karrina Ishalla of Agade. I am not a slave. I am second only to the Priestess of Zagros."

Nerin laughed out loud. "And I am the Shepherd of Sumer."

The woman's eyes narrowed. "I demand the return of my necklace. It was given to me by my brother —"

"Stolen from one of the Akkadian ladies, more like," sniffed Nerin, unimpressed by the slave's statements. "I'll have to find out more about this piece." He weighed it in his hand. "It is very unusual, and could be worth a lot."

With a screech, she launched herself at him, heedless of her nakedness, and Nerin found himself tumbling backwards with his arms full of biting, scratching, kicking wildcat.

He sighed. Pulling back his arm he landed a neat punch to her jaw.

She dropped like a stone, and once again he hauled her out of the river.

Clasping the necklace firmly in one hand, he turned and walked away from the silent body lying next to the water. A few minutes later he spied a woman walking through one of the fields.

"Daria? Hey…Daria?" He called and waved at the older woman who came quickly through the field to his side.

"Been at the women again, Nerin? I thought I heard some screaming a little while ago." She chuckled, eyeing his manhood, which lay comfortably between his legs enjoying the sunshine.

"Jealous, old woman?" he teased.

"I've had better, and you'll never have as good as me," she quipped back.

"My loss, I'm sure." He grinned at her. "Listen, some woman has washed ashore down by the river. I need a couple of men to go get her and take her down to the main house. She probably won't like it, so tell them to do whatever it takes to get her there and shut her up. I have to ask around about her before I decide what to do."

"Since when have you had to ask before doing?" Daria's wrinkled eyes narrowed against the sun.

"She says she's from Akkad, and her brand says she's a slave."

The woman hissed air into her mouth through the gaps where teeth used to be. "That changes things. Go on, find out what you can. I'll take care of her and see that she gets to the house."

"My thanks, Daria." He turned and walked down the lane to where a pile of clothes marked his earlier rendezvous with whatever her name was.

"And Jana has a big smile on her face too…" yelled Daria after him.

Jana, yes. That was her name. He promptly forgot it again.

But, he couldn't forget the fear that had shone from a pair of deep blue eyes.

* * * * *

The streets of Kushuk were buzzing with their usual blend of sales pitches, gossip, laughter and noise. Nerin strode along, eyes watchful, noting the bargaining between merchants, the latest shipment of gold from the mountain craftspeople and the current price of barley.

He grunted when he saw that it had risen slightly, knowing that his profits would reflect the increase most satisfactorily.

Today there was an extra edge to the noise, however, as the citizens of the small Sumerian town discussed the great storm of the day before.

It had been the Festival of the New Year, and although storms were common, this one had been of extraordinary strength. It had flooded the landscape with lightning beyond anyone's recollection, and the fields had been inundated as the River Goddess had shed her tears and filled her streams to overflowing.

Many were speaking of the damage done, the produce lost to the driving rain and the fact that the High Priest of the Sun God had disappeared, taking the High Priestess of the Moon Goddess along with him.

Although fascinating, the latter subject came in a distant third to the first two. Gods and goddesses functioned on their own timetable and had their own plans. Damaged crops and flooded fields were everybody's business.

For himself, Nerin couldn't give a camel's fart for gods, goddesses, or their representatives in Sumer. As long as the law was fair, administered judicially over the populace and didn't get in his way, he was happy leaving all that nonsense alone.

He supposed that Ronnil would now take over as High Priest of the Sun God. He had some passing knowledge of the man, and thought it a fair choice. He probably wouldn't have much to do with him anyway.

His steps took him to the temple of the Moon Goddess, however, as there was one person inside he needed to see. He was quite sure he'd receive a warm welcome, since the last time they had parted, she was flat on her face in front of him and panting from the extraordinary climax he'd just given her.

Remembering Lilianna's cheeks as they parted in welcome and offered him the snuggest little ass he'd had in a long time brought a flush of heat to his face, and he relished the cool shadows of the temple's interior as he stepped inside.

A handmaiden noted his arrival and saluted him with a bow.

"Greetings, Nerin of Kushuk. May the Moon Goddess shine brightly upon your nights."

Nerin responded with a polite bow of his own.

"Thank you. I seek audience with Priestess Lilianna."

The handmaiden nodded and beckoned him to follow, leading him through several passages and out into the sunshine of the temple's private garden.

A woman sat beneath a strangely shaped awning.

She smiled as she saw Nerin's eyebrow rise at the contraption. "One of our High Priestess's creations. She had such fair skin she needed protection from the rays of the Sun God. We have discovered its shade to be pleasant enough here." She crossed to Nerin and looked up into his stern face.

"Greetings, Lilianna," he said quietly.

She sighed. "I take it you are not here to explore your pleasure today, Nerin." A note of wistfulness crept into her voice.

Nerin gazed at her. "Some other day, perhaps, we may share such pleasure again. Today I need your wisdom on another matter."

The woman waved gracefully to a stone bench in the shade of the awning and seated herself, folding her hands and awaiting his words.

He removed a small pouch from his belt before he took his seat and held it out to her.

Carefully, she pulled the ties free and allowed the contents to tumble into her hand.

She froze.

Nerin moved not a muscle, but observed her unnatural stillness.

"Where did you get this?" she breathed, not touching the necklace that had fallen into her lap.

"From a runaway slave who ended up on my lands today. I would guess she rode the river down from Akkad because she wears the brand of an Akkadian slave." He tilted his head towards the necklace. "She was hanging on to this and certainly didn't want to part from it. I knew you had spent time in Akkad and wondered if you might be able to tell me something about who she stole it from?"

Lilianna closed her eyes for a moment, and Nerin had the strangest feeling that a shadow passed across the broad planes of his back. The hair on his forearms stirred slightly, and he had to force himself to dismiss such absurd feelings. He should have had a better meal to begin the day. He must be experiencing hunger pangs that were making him lightheaded.

"I have never seen this before..." Lilianna's voice broke through his discomfort. "But I have heard tales of such a thing." She poked at it hesitantly, then gently picked it up and put it back into the pouch, tying it tightly and handing it back to Nerin as if in a hurry to get rid of it.

"And what might those tales be, Lady?" encouraged Nerin.

"Are you sure you wish to know?"

Chapter Two

Karrina Ishalla of Agarde regained consciousness on the floor of a small room. It was so familiar to her that for a moment she felt she was back in her cell. Then she remembered.

A giant with a lock of gold in his hair. He'd stolen her necklace and he'd…he'd…she raised her hand to her chin and winced as she felt the bruise. He'd knocked her out cold.

Squirming onto her knees she peered around her.

The room was small, but clean, and light poured in through the small opening high on one of the dark stone walls. It was warm enough but not stifling, and there was even a pallet with clean straw and a light blanket on it along one wall. She struggled to her feet and made her way over to the pallet, sinking down onto it with a sigh of relief as her stiff muscles began to relax.

A clinking rattle drew her attention and she looked at her feet. One ankle was manacled to a chain, which was fastened to a massive ring in the marble floor.

Not only did she wear the brand of a slave on one ankle, now she wore the mark of a prisoner on the other.

She dropped her head and allowed scalding tears of anger, pain and frustration to pour down her cheeks.

Was this to be the end of the House of Ishalla? Would her mother's plans finally succeed?

Karrina sadly acknowledged that it was quite likely she was about to die. She knew well that runaway slaves were treated harshly, if not brutally, and had no illusions about what her fate would be.

If she were found guilty of stealing the necklace she'd be immediately put to death.

If she was found to be a runaway slave—and with her brand how could it *not* happen—she would be turned over to the authorities. That meant working in one of the lowest and most menial jobs the city could find, and being used by most of the men who supervised them. She'd seen it before.

She remembered a group of soldiers who had taken their pleasure with an unfortunate slave who'd tried to escape. The woman had stopped screaming after the fourth man, and her moans had faded long before the rest of them had finished. Her mother had not let her look away, knowing it would be a lesson to Karrina. To disobey the Utta of Ishalla was to die.

Karrina had disobeyed the Utta of Ishalla.

* * * * *

She was asleep.

Nerin stood in the doorway of the small storeroom he'd converted into a holding cell for security purposes.

Someone had given her a blanket and she'd obviously tried to cover herself with it, because it was wrapped around her from breast to thigh. A glimpse of dark hair between her legs taunted him as she moaned and turned on the straw pallet.

A twinge of guilt crossed his conscience as he saw the bruise on her chin, but he hardened his heart when his gaze traveled down her leg to that brand on her ankle. She was a runaway slave. That was all she could possibly be.

Yet as the darkness crept across the sky of Sumer and light in the small room faded, Nerin of Kushuk could swear that for one instant he could see Karrina lying there, not on a humble pile of straw, but on silken pillows and with gold and jewels in her lustrous black hair.

Her skin was pale in contrast to the deep colors of the fabrics beneath her and she turned her head to him and smiled in welcome.

His cock leapt to attention.

He blinked and the vision cleared. She was still sleeping.

He turned and left, angry with himself for such thoughts, and not willing to admit that his earlier conversation with Priestess Lilianna had shaken him.

"Jana!" His voice roared through his large home, sending servants scurrying.

"Where's Jana?" he shouted his question as he strode to his chamber.

"Here, Lord..." She appeared breathless and flushed, as if interrupted in the middle of something.

Nerin couldn't care less. She was his servant, there to serve him. And serve him she would.

He ripped off his clothing and gestured at his hard cock.

"Attend me."

Jana's eyes glittered. "As you will, my Lord. On the bed?"

"Here, woman. Take me in your mouth. I need release."

Jana willingly knelt between his legs. Her hand rose to clasp his cock and she licked her lips as she stared at the hardness in front of her.

"Well, get on with it," he snarled, widening his stance slightly.

Jana bent to her task, sliding her mouth around his head and moistening his rigid flesh with her tongue.

He closed his eyes as her touch found his sensitive areas and her hand began to fondle his balls in a way he particularly enjoyed.

Dropping a hand, he grabbed her hair and encouraged her head into a rhythm that was particularly pleasing. Prepared to surrender to his pleasure, Nerin found an unbidden image cross before his eyes.

He saw *her*, on her knees before him. It was *her* mouth that was sucking him, *her* tongue flickering over his cock, *her* hands caressing his balls. It was *her* black hair that slid between his fingers, and as his mind looked down, it was *her* blue eyes that filled with desire and took him even deeper into her mouth.

He hardened, carried away by the images he saw. Hanging on to his sanity by a thread, he managed to stop himself from thrusting too far into her throat, but as it was she was taking him much further than usual.

He watched her face as she sucked and licked and kissed his erection, then drew it past full and red lips back into the recesses of her mouth.

He knew he was going to come.

"I'm going to…" he grunted.

"Mmm," a voice encouraged.

His sight cleared and he climaxed, pumping himself into Jana's willing throat. She sucked him dry, licking her lips in obvious enjoyment.

For once in his life, Nerin could not find the right words. He'd climaxed all right, and Jana had indeed attended to his needs. For that, he supposed she should be thanked.

"Here." He tossed her a small coin.

Jana's eyes flashed greedily and she pounced on the gold. "May I serve you further, Lord?"

"Go. I'm done with you for tonight."

Jana left silently, clutching her coin and smiling.

Nerin wished that he could feel as satisfied. He'd come, and he'd rewarded her, but something was still gnawing at his guts.

He crossed to his sleeping chamber and tumbled onto his bed. He reached for the necklace that lay on the table beside him. It was strangely warm in his hands. Could the woman, Karrina, have been telling the truth?

Was Lilianna's story a simple tale told by travelers to gain enough coins for an evening meal?

He closed his eyes as he recollected her words.

It had been the tone of her voice that had first disturbed Nerin as he had listened to Lilianna relate her tale earlier that afternoon.

The sounds of the town and the birds faded to a distant hum and for Nerin there was nothing but Lilianna's deep brown eyes gazing at him and her soft voice.

"My family is originally from Akkad. And yes, you are right, I spent time there. Several years, in fact, before my dedication here to the service of the Moon Goddess. I was able to stay with my grandmother, and it was a wonderful time for us both."

A smile crossed her elegant lips. "Nona was an amazing lady with interesting views. It was she who 'enlightened' me about many areas of a woman's life, and I shall be forever grateful to her." A small blush chased across her cheeks. "As should you."

Nerin shifted uncomfortably as he caught her inference.

"But to get back to the point, she told me many tales of Akkad, and Sumer, and at the time I thought they were just stories to wile away the evenings. But now, after seeing that," she gestured to the leather pouch," I'm not so sure."

Nerin contained his impatience, simply continuing to gaze at Lilianna and wait for the rest of her tale. He was very good at waiting.

"One night, my grandmother told me the story of a special pendant. One that showed the picture of an eye. An eye which cried a single magical tear."

Nerin sat forward now, resting his strong arms on his knees.

"She told me it was rumored that this tear had been formed from the tears of the Gods for their people. It was their tears of joy and sadness, of pleasure and pain, of all their emotions wrapped into one single tear."

Lilianna's eyes slid back again to the little pouch, like those of a frightened animal confronted by its predator. "It is said that this tear will disappear from this pendant if...if..."

"If?" Nerin's voice throbbed in the silence.

Lilianna drew a ragged breath. "If true love exists between whoever holds the pendant and whoever is in their arms."

Nerin leaned back and snorted his disbelief.

"You are jesting, surely, Lilianna. True love? A young maid's dream. And I have yet to see any painted decorations disappear and reappear of their own free will. It is far more likely that this tale was concocted by the jeweler who made this so as to increase his price for the trinket once it was on his stall."

"'Tis also said," interrupted Lilianna abruptly, "that this necklace is in the possession of the rulers of Akkad. That the one who holds the pendant holds the heart of the kingdom."

That made Nerin pause. He sucked in air and blew it out through his teeth.

"This sheds a different light on things," he muttered.

"You must find out who she really is, Nerin," urged Lilianna. "Bring her here if you need to, but do it quietly. If she is anything but the slave you believe her to be, there could be trouble ahead for you both."

* * * * *

The dream crept up on Karrina and slid softly into her jumbled thoughts. She was cold. Her body was shivering, and yet the air around her was warm.

She was standing in a room that glittered with highly polished marble. Walls, floors, columns, all marble veined with something that sparkled so brightly it almost hurt to look at it.

Her hands were tied before her, crossed wrist over wrist and yet she was not afraid. Just cold.

She turned and saw him.

He was as naked as she, huge and bronzed, with that gold lock of hair tumbling around his expressionless face.

In one hand he held a whip.

Somehow, Karrina knew what to do.

She gazed into his eyes trying to pick some isolated spark of emotion from their depths, but there was nothing. Just the blank stare of a man who was used to hiding his soul.

Turning, she crossed to a column. A little above her head was a protruding carving, and she hooked her wrists over it.

Her back was to him, and she turned her head, looking over her shoulder in invitation. Some part of her screamed at the surrender, but another was encouraging her to submit to this man.

At last a gleam crossed his face and his harsh mouth curved. "You agree?"

"I agree. You will give it to me when you are done?"

"Perhaps."

The conversation made no sense, but neither did the situation.

Karrina found part of herself watching the scene unfold, yet she was standing in front of that column and shivering as she awaited his next move.

The man neared her and raised the whip. With an odd little whistle it fell, landing near her thigh with a crack.

She jumped.

"It is not too late to refuse."

"I have my honor, if not my skin, to consider."

Karrina was proud of herself for her answer.

The whip whistled softly and flicked her buttock, raising a red weal. She flinched as the pain became not a pain but a pleasure, spreading tendrils of warmth over her chilled flesh.

Her nipples hardened and she spread her legs a little to firm up her stance. She was ready.

So, apparently, was he.

From her other vantage point, watching the whole drama, Karrina could see his cock, jerking as he moved, hard and with a tiny tear emerging from its head.

Another lash, another welt, and the sweat started beading on his forehead. As if in pain, he spared a second to stroke his cock, clenching his teeth at his own touch.

Looking across at herself, Karrina was astonished to see that she had turned within her bonds and was now facing the man.

He licked his lips.

Karrina raised her chin and stared into his eyes.

He flexed his arm and flicked the whip, just grazing the side of her breast. She moaned.

Another lash, another writhing response. The scent of Karrina's arousal was permeating the chamber and she could feel herself dripping hot juices from her aching cunt.

The next lash caught her nipple and she cried out, squirming in her need to answer the pain with passion.

The man was rigid, sweat darkening the gold lock. He wiped his palms down his thighs and flicked the bead of moisture away from the head of his cock. He stared at her swollen tissues, exposed as she spread her legs wide in frustration.

A subtle twist of the wrist and the tip of the lash stopped within a breath of her clit. She sobbed and fought against her own restraints.

Dream Karrina was so painfully aroused that each breath was becoming torture.

The observer in Karrina knew she couldn't last under this treatment. She'd have to come or pass out.

Luckily, the man seemed to understand. He'd neared her aching body and was breathing heavily, as if scenting her readiness. The whip was tossed aside, rough hands grasped her thighs and pulled them wide.

His cock was huge and dark and it was the work of a second for him to raise her up slightly and ram it deep inside her cunt.

Karrina screamed.

She woke on her pallet to find a large body bending over her. A lock of gold hair tumbled around his face.

She screamed again.

Chapter Three

Nerin jerked back as the woman screamed at him.

"Quiet, you'll wake the entire household," he muttered irritably. "I'm not here to hurt you."

She pulled as far away from him as she could, eyes blindly trying to focus in the low light cast by the oil lamp he'd brought.

"What do you want?" she rasped, dry throat desperately trying to make the words sound brave.

Silently he offered her a drinking vessel.

She looked at him for a moment then accepted with a nod. The water was cool and fresh, and she felt her senses return as she awoke fully. She couldn't resist a quick glance at her breast, though. The whipping had seemed so real. But there were no welts. It had only been a dream.

As she returned the vessel her eyes caught sight of his chest. He was wearing her pendant.

She drew in her breath on a gasp of horror. "Take that off. It's mine."

She spat the words at him as her hand came up and pointed accusingly at the pendant.

"You're a slave. How can you own something like this?"

"I am not a slave. I am Karrina of Ishalla."

"You are a lying slut."

Karrina sucked in her breath. "You are a thick brained idiot. I should have expected no less of a Sumerian. And a stupid farmer to boot."

"I am Nerin of Kushuk. Yes, I farm. So you could accurately call me a farmer. Stupid, however, I am not. You are lying."

Karrina gritted her teeth. "Just because I have a mark on my ankle, you immediately jump to conclusions."

"No jumping involved. That is a slave brand. Only slaves are branded. Now, I ask again, where did you get this pendant?"

"Did it ever cross your dense mind that perhaps others could be branded as slaves as well?"

"No."

Karrina was starting to sweat with fury. What would it take to get through to this thickheaded, irritating, block? "You are wearing my pendant. It belongs to me. I am not a slave, Nerin of Kushuk. I am Karrina, house of Ishalla, and you have my property around your neck."

Nerin leaned his considerable bulk against the wall and crossed his arms patiently over his massive chest.

Karrina tried her hardest not to notice how damned good looking he was in a solid, ziggurat sort of way.

"Very well. You would ask me to believe that the naked woman I found washed up on the riverbank clutching a priceless jewel and branded as a slave, is actually a highborn Akkadian woman."

"That is correct."

"You really do think I'm stupid, don't you?"

Karrina growled.

"And you smell. Come on…"

Nerin produced something from behind him and approached her pallet making her retreat to the wall.

"I am not going to hurt you. I am merely going to attempt to rid you of that disgusting stench that comes from too few baths and too much heat. I'm not sure if you are familiar with the concept of bathing, but it's painless."

Karrina snorted, sparing a thought for the luxurious bathing chamber in her mother's palace.

"A bath would be most welcome." The words were spat out between clenched teeth.

Her eyes widened as Nerin swiftly placed a leather collar around her neck and wrapped the small chain that fell from it around his fist. With his other hand he released the manacle from her ankle.

She was free to walk around at last, providing she went where he led. Suppressing a snarl of fury, she ground her teeth and followed his tug, hoping that the opportunity for escape and possibly murder might arise very, very soon.

* * * * *

Nerin cursed himself for not wrapping some kind of robe around his body before he'd indulged his need to visit his prisoner. At least with her leashed behind him she'd not see his rock-hard erection, which was pointing the way to the bathing chamber.

He could hear her nervous breathing as she followed him down cool passageways to the underground chamber where his personal retreat waited for them.

She couldn't know that she was the first woman he'd brought here, but he needed privacy and knew this would be as good a place as any.

He smiled to himself as she gasped when they crossed the threshold.

The room was dimly illuminated by several oil lamps he'd lit earlier. The air was warm as the gentle sandstone walls radiated back the heat they'd gathered during the day. The huge sunken bath that dominated the room reflected the moonlight that streamed in through the one open wall. Beyond was a small courtyard where plants of all kinds grew abundantly in great pottery urns.

It was a little bit of heaven and a private indulgence for Nerin. Few people even knew of its existence.

"This is…this is…splendid," whispered the woman behind him.

Nerin permitted himself a small smile. "Never seen anything like this, eh slave girl?"

A tug on her leash served to remind her of where she was and her eyes frowned at him.

"I have seen much better bathing chambers, you peasant. The Temple in Agade possesses a much greater facility. At least twelve can bathe in *that* room."

She snorted and pointed her nose in the air.

Nerin punctured her pride with a sharp tug on the leash. She stumbled and fell on her knees before him.

"Right now, you are here, not in some imaginary Akkadian temple. Do not forget who holds your leash, slave."

"Or who has stolen my possession, *farmer*," she hissed back.

Nerin's teeth clenched as he looked down into her deep blue eyes. They were filled with distrust, suspicion, and a healthy dose of temper. Just seeing her that close to his aroused cock was making him frantic. A quick glimpse of his earlier vision made his senses swim and he hurriedly turned, pulling her to the water's edge.

"Get in."

He gave her no choice. As he pushed, she fell, pulling the leash taut around her neck.

But Nerin followed her, allowing her enough slack to sink to her shoulders in the warm water.

She settled herself on a ledge beneath the surface and he heard her sigh as the heat soothed her.

Nerin did much the same, but kept an iron grip on the leash. "Feel better?"

"Mmmm...much."

A muscle flickered in his cheek as her little moan danced through his body and played around his still-rock hard arousal.

"It would be even better if you had cleansing cloths."

The comment surprised him. Slaves were lucky to get a weekly dunking in the river. Soaps were not everyday features of their lives.

He reached behind him thoughtfully and passed her a soft fragrant cloth.

He was surprised again as she used it to thoroughly cleanse her body, as if unaware of his presence.

He was hard pressed to restrain his own moan as she delicately washed her breasts, and he thanked the gods for the dark waters when she dipped her hand beneath the surface and washed other places.

Finally she dunked her whole head and spent considerable time cleaning her hair.

Nerin watched, judging her actions, noting her familiarity with the entire process. That told him a story that he was slowly beginning to believe. But she would not know that. At least, not yet.

"I am clean. Oh you have no idea how good it feels." Karrina smiled and raised her hands, letting water trickle down her arms and splash back around her.

Meeting Nerin's eyes, her smile died.

"Perhaps now you have cleaned your body, you will be ready to clean your conscience and tell me the truth."

"Will you return my necklace if I tell you the truth?"

"Why should I?"

"Because it belongs to me."

"And you belong to me."

"I do not. I am a free woman. I am Karrina—"

"Of Ishalla. You've already said that."

"Then why don't you believe me?"

"You are branded. I am not a fool. Akkadians brand slaves. No one else."

"How I wish you were right." Her voice was low and she gazed out onto the moonlit courtyard as she said it.

"Then convince me."

Her eyes flashed to his face. "Convince you? I cannot convince you of anything, it seems. If I told you that the sun was light, you'd say I was lying. I have told you the truth and you refuse to accept it. Would you have me swear on my father's grave? On my brother's love? How would you have me convince you, Nerin?"

Nerin studied her, his thoughts shielded behind years of control. How could she convince him? Not by swearing on any family attachments, that was for sure. They were too fragile to withstand the weight of such an oath. He knew that all too well.

"Be honest with me. Tell me how you washed ashore on my riverbank. Tell me the truth about the brand on your ankle. If you are a slave I will do my best to protect you. All I ask, all I have ever asked, is honesty. It's all there is."

* * * * *

"Very well."

Karrina's words shattered the silence that had fallen and she felt her heartbeat pounding as she stared at the big man who shared her bath so casually. Something inside her was telling her to pour her troubles out onto his shoulders—the gods knew they were broad enough to take the weight.

But her lifetime of caution was nagging her to be careful. Very careful.

She opened her mouth to begin the story of Karrina of Ishalla when a tug on the leash interrupted her.

"Not like that. Move over here."

Nerin pulled her to the shallow end of the bath and sat her down on the carved bench that rose a little above the water's surface. The warm stone cushioned her back, the night air swirled softly around her damp body and the moonlight flooded the area with silver rays.

Nerin sat opposite on a matching bench, the leash still firmly in his grasp.

Karrina opened her mouth again.

"Wait."

Her teeth snapped together in irritation. "For *what*? I thought you were going to let me tell you my side of the story?"

"I am going to let you tell me the *truth*. Lie and I shall not be pleased. Open your legs."

"What?" Karrina gasped.

"You heard me. Open your legs. I want to see you spread before me like the slave you are."

Karrina was stunned. "I have told you, I am not a slave."

"You have told me, but not convinced me. Open your legs. Wide. I am within my rights to do a lot worse and you know it. Comply with this and I will listen."

His face was blank as he made the demand, and if it hadn't been for the fact that his cock was jutting out like a carving towards her, Karrina might have believed him totally unaffected.

She stared at him, realizing that he was quite serious. "I...I..."

"Open. Now."

Karrina felt the tug on the leash punctuate his words. Helplessly she spread her thighs.

"Wider."

Swallowing, she obeyed.

The moonlight shone brightly on her body, and she knew he could probably see just about everything there was to see. His eyes had dropped and lost their blank coldness. For once she swore she could see fire in their depths. Then he raised them to look at her again and the fire was gone.

"Now begin."

Awkwardly, Karrina started her narrative, remembering her brother's wry sentiment, that when lying always stick to the truth if possible. Having the night air wash around her personal and private parts was distracting, but she refused to allow this perverted Sumerian to stop her from telling her tale.

"I am, in truth, Karrina of Ishalla. My father was the Magad of Ishalla. He died a little more than four years ago." Her voice faded for a moment as she allowed the pain of his loss to traverse her heart.

"We have extensive holdings in the foothills of the mountains and our wool is prized for its texture. My family has held Ishalla for many generations. Until now."

She spared a glance at the man seated opposite. His eyes darted to her exposed mound and back to her face. No expression marred the harsh planes of his features. He gazed blankly back. Waiting, always waiting. She was coming to realize that he was very good at waiting.

"My mother became Utta of Ishalla when my father died. In the regular course of things, my brother, who is younger than me, would have become Magad a year and a day after my father's death."

She paused and shifted slightly.

"Open wider and touch yourself."

Wrenched from her story, Karrina jumped.

"What?"

"You heard me."

"I can't...do...I can't..."

"Are you a virgin? Did all this apparent luxury you grew up in not permit you to enjoy a woman's pleasure?"

Karrina's jaw hung wide as she stared in disbelief at Nerin.

"Well? It's not a complex question. Are you a virgin?"

A blush spread its fiery tendrils across her creamy skin, turning her bright pink from breast to hairline.

"I'll take that as a no. Spread your legs wider and touch yourself. Find the place that feels most pleasant."

"No!" Outraged, Karrina spat the negative across the small expanse of water that separated them.

A savage pull on the leash and she was underwater, scraping herself on the bottom of the pool.

She surfaced, coughing, spitting out water and pushing her hair out of her eyes.

"Defy me again and it will be worse."

There was no emotion behind the words, and Karrina shivered as she realized Nerin was very serious. He intended her to submit to his every whim or pay the price. She wasn't sure if she wanted to find out what the price was.

Glowering at him she resumed her seat. Defiantly she spread her thighs wide and slid her hand to her mound.

"Is this satisfactory, *Lord*?" she inquired, giving her words a sarcastic bite.

"Better. Move your hand and pleasure yourself as you speak."

Sighing, Karrina obeyed, finding that her body was already sensitive and her juices flowing. It seemed this man could reach some hidden places deep inside her just by his presence.

The light caught on the pendant and reminded her of her goal.

"Now continue."

"My brother disappeared within weeks of my father's death. My mother put it about that he had been killed while hunting in the high lands, but I knew better…"

Nerin watched as her hand slicked through her juices and rubbed around her swollen cunt. He was in pain, but his suffering was nothing compared to what she would endure if she lied to him. He had to get at the truth and making her speak while she was at her most vulnerable seemed to be a sensible way of finding it.

Of course, his cock might blow up before she'd finished. It was a risk he'd gladly take.

He manhandled his brain back to focus on her words.

"My mother spread the story of my brother's death so cleverly that it was accepted as truth very quickly. She presented herself as the grieving widow struggling to cope with the loss of her son. The townspeople cried for her and sobbed with her, never knowing the woman whose pain they apparently shared."

Nerin noted the bitter edge to Karrina's voice, but said nothing. He watched her hand as she stroked around her clit, and legs widened a little to give herself better access. She'd all but forgotten that he was watching. Which was exactly the way he wanted it.

Or thought he did.

"In fact, my brother had run away. He'd told me not long after our father's funeral that he was afraid of our mother and what she would do. We both knew she wanted all the power. She'd made no secret of the fact that we represented the fulfillment of her duty to her husband. We'd never been anything but a nuisance to her, and occasionally a pawn in her greedy games. But with my father's death everything changed."

Absently, Karrina's hand slid up to her breast and passed gently over her nipple.

Nerin's muscles tightened and his cock throbbed, but he was not going to move if it killed him. He wanted to hear the story to its end.

"Now the Utta realized that my brother was more than a nuisance, he was a threat. He was young, healthy and everyone expected him to take over the duties of our father. That would have finished her hopes for control. She arranged to have him killed, I'm sure of it. Somehow he found out and a few nights before his scheduled hunting trip he came to my chamber, and said goodbye. He…that's when he gave me the necklace…"

Her hand trembled within her curls. "I can't…I can't go on." She sobbed out a sigh.

"You can and you will."

Nerin pulled on the leash and tugged her across the water to his body, catching her in his arms. He held her tight, keeping her locked in one arm while the other roughly pushed her legs apart. She was sprawled on his lap, open to his gaze.

"Go on. Your brother left you...what happened next?"

Nerin's hand took over where she had left off, and began caressing her clit with a light touch.

She squirmed, sending bolts of lightning through Nerin's cock.

She fought for breath, lungs rasping in his hold.

"My...my mother announced my marriage. She was going to sell me off to a neighboring landowner whose water rights she coveted. Aaaahhh..."

Nerin continued his stroking, neither varying the speed nor the pressure. She was writhing beneath his touch like a wanton.

"And you did not want this marriage?"

"He was old, he had children older than me. It was for political reasons and was something that my Father promised would never happen to me. I couldn't stand it. So I...I ran away..."

"And ended up on my riverbank."

"No, no." She gasped out the words as his finger relentlessly drove her into an upward spiral of arousal.

"That was the first time. She caught me that first time. That's when she branded me."

For a second, his finger paused. "Your mother had you branded as a slave?"

Karrina sobbed out another breath and bent backwards in his arms, thrusting her breasts upwards.

"No—she didn't *have* me branded. She branded me *herself*."

Chapter Four

Karrina was beside herself. She didn't know whether to sob or scream or beg for release. His fingers were driving her insane and if he didn't touch her breasts soon she'd break free and kill him. Right after she'd fucked him.

As if he sensed her distress, Nerin lowered his head and fastened his mouth around her pebbled nipple.

She sighed in ecstasy.

He released it and she muttered a curse.

"Your story, Karrina. Continue with your story. I must know the truth of your situation."

"Put your mouth back where it was and I'll continue," she hissed, beyond shame, beyond awareness, just trembling on the edge of a sexual precipice and itching to jump off.

She missed the quick curve of Nerin's lips as he bent to her breast.

"After the branding, my mother locked me in one of the holding cells in the palace. I was a prisoner in my own home for several months. She didn't know my old friend had smuggled food and clothing to me, or that my brother had entrusted me with the pendant. He said that if things got very bad, I should take it to one of the Agade elders. They'd know what to do with it."

She sighed as his lips moved to her other breast, leaving the first one wet and sensitive. Her legs were parted willingly now, and she knew her juices had soaked him. His hand was firm and she craved his touch. She was close but he refused to allow her to get closer. It was frustrating and wonderful and amazing and she couldn't think straight.

"Continue." The air from his mouth washed over her wet nipple like a tongue of flame and she shivered.

"Well, that brings me to last night...the huge storm. The guards were celebrating the festival and most of them were three parts drunk. My friend Domara managed to slip away from her family and open the cell door. I ran out into the storm."

She was really having trouble breathing now, as his fingers started to penetrate her slick heat. She could feel his cock digging into her and wanted nothing more than to grab it and bury it deep inside her.

"Yes...the storm..." His voice seemed less calm now, too.

"It was a big one. The lightning...so bright...I couldn't see...I fell..."

Her voice faded away and she moaned, body on fire beneath his touch.

"Nerin..."

"I know." His words rattled from his throat as he raised her before him and sat her on his knees.

She straddled him willingly, hands on his shoulders.

"Nerin...please..."

His hands searched out her secrets in the darkness. With a simple move he found her.

She cried out in pleasure as she felt his cock nudge her cunt.

"Yessss...oh gods..." Her head fell back, hair brushing his legs, and finally...finally she had what she wanted.

Nerin thrust his full length into her body, pulling her down onto his hardness and filling her silk channel with his rigid cock.

Their bodies meshed, blended, adjusted.

They stilled for a moment, and blue eyes met brown. No longer an unemotional void, Nerin's eyes were burning. Lids heavy and face flushed, he looked as if he could devour her, all his passion focused in his gaze.

Her own eyes widened at the glimpse of the man beneath the facade. He was a force to be reckoned with, a seething cauldron that could warm or burn.

Then he moved, and the heavens fell.

Rubbing, touching, soothing and stroking, Nerin's cock slid easily from Karrina's body, only to bury itself again in the welcoming warmth.

His fingers found her clit as she grasped his chest and flicked his flat nipple with her nails.

He responded by pressing her breasts to his face and latching on to one with an almost cruel suction.

It was what she needed. The combined assault on her body was pushing her to her goal, and with a scream she felt herself fly apart.

Never had she imagined her whole being could pulsate in time with her release. Never had she realized that she could be so aware of the cock inside her as she gripped it with her inner muscles in a rhythmic spasm of delight.

And when his cock let go and his groan told her of his own climax, she was astounded that the feel of his cum flooding her womb brought her to the peak and tipped her over once again.

Sobbing with exhaustion, she collapsed on his chest, feeling the shape of the necklace beneath her hand.

Slowly she leaned her head back against his shoulder and turned to look at him.

The necklace caught a stray moonbeam and for a moment shone brightly.

The tear was gone.

* * * * *

What had he done?

Nerin's mind was frozen in a mix of joy and horror. He'd lost all touch with himself, his beliefs, his guidelines for his life.

She'd brought him to the point of complete and utter insanity.

He'd come inside her.

And now she was staring at him with some nameless fear in her eyes.

He glanced down, following her gaze and the hairs on his body rose in concert.

The necklace around his neck still featured one beautiful eye, but the tear that had trembled in such a lifelike fashion at the corner was gone.

The image was clear. And the legend was apparently true. The tear could indeed appear and disappear. But true love?

Nerin roared his anger.

"You trickster bitch. What kind of foolery is this?"

Karrina's head snapped up and her eyes flashed blue fire at him.

"It's no trickery of mine, you…you…savage!"

"Water. The water washed it off. Of course. Some special kind of dyes that are removed by water. Pah. Fakery and superstition. All of it."

With those words Nerin grasped the necklace, ripping it from his neck. He flung it across the pool where it hit the wall with a little chink and fell to a glittering heap on the ground.

Karrina's gasp of anger echoed after it.

"You…you…animal. That's mine!" Still clasping his relaxed cock inside her, Karrina pulled back her shoulder and punched Nerin with all the force she could muster.

His teeth clacked and his neck bones jarred as her fist connected with his cheekbone.

Angrily he thrust her away, ignoring the sense of loss he felt when her body released his cock. "You slave bitch. Get away from me. You and your stupid stories of magic. All you wanted was a fuck. Well you got one. We're done."

Heedless of his nakedness or her juices still coating his body, he stood, tugging harshly on the leash.

"I will get my necklace." She ground the words out between furiously clenched teeth, standing rigid against his pull. "You will have to drown me otherwise."

"Don't tempt me."

"The necklace is my property. I will get my necklace." Resistance was evident in every muscle of her body. Her nipples were hard still and her dark curls gleamed where their bodies had joined and caressed each other.

Nerin was horrified to feel the need for her building again.

"Very well. Fetch the damned thing."

He breathed easier as she turned away, almost stumbling in her eagerness to reach her pendant.

Parts of his mind were still numb from the orgasm he'd had inside her, and he fought the urge to bend her over the wall and take her again. Often. All night long.

His anger built with his desire. What was she doing to his ordered world? What kind of witchcraft was she using to make him want her like this?

He couldn't wait to lock her back in her cell and get away from her, before he did something really stupid like lay her down and fuck her again. And again. In several different ways.

Damn, he was hard again.

Savagely he pulled at her. "Enough foolishness. Follow me."

"As if I had a choice." The mutter followed him. He paid no attention to it as he led her back to her cell, and rechained her ankle to the manacle.

He ignored his arousal and the fact that he could smell himself on her. Their combined fragrances were making him dizzy and he had great difficulty unlocking the catch on her collar to remove the leash.

He couldn't help noticing her nipples were hard. She was as aroused as he was, even though they had just shared a shattering climax.

Then he noticed her hands. They were clasped around her pendant in a death grip, the knuckles white with the force of her hold.

"You have your pendant. I hope this will keep you quiet."

"It's a start. Now free me and I'll go away. You need never see me again."

"Out of the question." The words popped out of his mouth before he even considered them. Again, he was shocked to find himself quite out of character. Nerin never spoke before giving thought to his words.

"Free me, Nerin of Kushuk. You have had your fill of me. You have returned my property. You have no reason to hold me here."

"You are, for all intents and purposes, a runaway slave. You were found on my property. I have every right to do with you as I please. There will be no more discussions on this subject."

Nerin stepped hastily away from her as his cock brushed past her shoulder and throbbed with need.

"So you'll rape me again?"

"That was *not* rape, and you know it." Nerin's words hissed at her, and he fought the urge to prove his statement by taking her again and making her melt and beg and scream out her desire for him.

She sighed. "I know. That was wrong of me, and I apologize. I'm just tired."

"So sleep. I'll not bother you further."

He turned and left the cell abruptly as Karrina lay back on her bed, holding fast to her pendant.

"I'm afraid you'll always bother me, Nerin of Kushuk…"

The low-pitched murmur followed Nerin, but the words were indistinguishable to his ears.

He strode away from his house, away from his servants and away from the woman who had cracked the facade that was his ordered existence.

He walked on through his fields until he came to the river, his favorite spot, where the grass grew soft and the murmur of the water could soothe many ills.

He lay down and crossed his arms behind his head, allowing the night to calm his troubled thoughts.

He needed to find his center again. Tonight it had come close to being knocked askew by one slender blue-eyed slave.

* * * * *

Nerin became slowly aware that his surroundings were changing. Part of his mind reassured him it was only a dream, but another part felt a chill of fear as a bright light enveloped him.

"Nerin of Kushuk…" a voice whispered in his ear.

He turned his head to see who had spoken and looked into a pair of dark blue eyes, smiling and widening in anticipation.

She was there.

She couldn't be there.

But she was, and she was beckoning him. He rose and gave her his hand, feeling a tingle as their skin touched.

She led him behind her, dark hair rippling to buttocks gleaming naked in the light.

They came to a high place, where the land was spread out beneath them—but what a land.

It was like no place Nerin had ever seen. Smoke grayed the horizon, and noise filled his ears.

Nerin's eyes opened wide as he saw strange vehicles flying through the air. There were many people walking the streets, dressed in strange clothing. There were more people than he'd imagined existed. And they showed their bodies by wrapping them tightly, not by leaving them bare.

He jumped as he saw a strange wagon pass along a road beneath them. No horse or mule drew this noisy contraption.

His heart sped up as he realized this was no land that he knew. He must be dead.

His companion tugged gently on his hand. *"Look up, Nerin of Kushuk…"*

Obediently he raised his head to the skies.

He gasped.

Faces of wise men appeared like paintings on a veil of silk as the sky darkened to night. A woman stood naked on a strange world, surrounded by a blue haze.

He blinked and the images were gone, the land empty and his hand free.

He was definitely dead.

"You are not dead, Nerin of Kushuk…"

She was behind him, lying on soft grass, one knee raised, gazing at him with blue eyes full of passion.

He went to her, unable to resist the call of those eyes. Their skin met in a searing touch as he lay beside her.

"Give it to me, Nerin of Kushuk…"

Nerin opened his mouth to ask her what she wanted, but before the words could escape she pulled his head down and stopped him with her mouth.

Her lips pressed against his and her tongue demanded entrance. He opened and allowed her access to his warmth, sucking her deep and stroking her tongue with his.

He knew he was hard for her and the added press of her breasts rising to graze his chest sent a shot of sensation from his head to his knees.

She rolled him onto his back and bent over him, her hair swinging free and laying on his stomach in a silken cloud. He could feel every single strand as it slicked over his skin.

She smiled and bent to his chest, grasping his wrists and easing his hands apart.

He willingly let her move him as she pleased.

She lowered her head and sought out his flat nipple. Her tongue teased at it, bringing sighs of pleasure to his throat. Her teeth nipped at it, making him squirm and clench his jaw against a groan. With a final caress of her tongue she moved away, leaving him bereft. But not for long.

She whipped her hair over her shoulder to gently lash his chest as she moved down his body, trailing a hot, flickering tongue. When she reached his navel she paused, nibbling, licking, biting, teasing, driving him insane with need. He'd no idea his navel was such a hotbed of sensation. He'd no idea it was directly linked to his cock.

After paying homage to his belly, she moved further, allowing him to push her hair aside so that he could watch her face as she explored him. Intent on her task, she looked focused and excited, ready to find his next point of pleasure and tease it into awareness. She found it.

The skin above his groin was rich with nerve endings, and a quick stroke of her tongue sent shivering flutters across his abdomen. She followed this with the sharp scrape of her fingernails, tossing a light dose of harsh sensation into the mix.

Nerin was losing his mind. How he kept himself flat beneath her was a mystery to him. His cock was distended, leaking fluids in its pleasure at her movements, and he was afraid he was about to burst in an almighty explosion of cum that would rival the greatest waterfalls of Sumer.

She apparently was not about to let that happen quite yet.

"You have taken something from me, Nerin of Kushuk." Her dark blue eyes were staring at him from the region of his cock.

He wanted to scream at her that he didn't know what she meant. That if she stopped doing what she was doing he was going to die—that is if he really wasn't dead already.

Her hand slid through his wiry curls and grasped his cock firmly. *"It was mine to give, not yours to take..."* The voice sighed over him like a wind from the western deserts. *"But what's done is done..."*

To his dismay he could not speak, only watch as she moved her head over the tip of his cock. Her mouth opened and her eyes slid to his face.

His jaw dropped in symphony with hers, as if encouraging her to go ahead, suck him, for the sake of all the gods, before he either crossed over into the next world or embarrassed himself beyond belief by spurting his seed up her nose.

She lowered her head, eyes fixed on his. Eons passed.

Finally, at long last, she took him into her mouth. He couldn't help it, he moaned with pleasure.

Her tongue teased as her lips pulled, and she worshipped him with her mouth, tracing each little ridge and valley and paying homage to the delicate tissues beneath the head.

He felt the tingles of a climax begin as his buttocks hardened beneath him. He nearly cried when she pulled her head back.

A smile crossed her face as she inched upward between his thighs. Her breasts brushed his balls in a moment of exquisite torture, and she snuggled herself into his body.

His eyes widened as she pressed her breasts together around his cock. It was amazing, unbelievable, arousing to the point of insanity, and Nerin knew he was a lost man.

She rubbed her chin lightly over the tip of his penis and urged him to move within the warm prison she'd created for his rigid length.

He needed no further encouragement.

Their eyes locked as his hips thrust into her. She tightened her pressure on him, nipples hard and pointing out from her breasts as they pillowed his cock.

"Is this what you want me to give you, Nerin of Kushuk?"

He was helpless, no words would come.

"What will you give me in return?"

Words might not come, but he could. Teeth gritted, lips curling back, a ferocious orgasm swept through him, sending his muscles into knots and streams of cum over her flesh.

She pressed him even tighter, milking the last of his seed with gentle movements of her body.

He ached, his balls, his cock, his toes, even his hair ached with the intensity of it.

"You have given me your essence, Nerin of Kushuk. Now give me what I must have from you."

"What do you want?" The words passed his lips, waking him from his dream.

Back at his house a light flickered in the early dawn light. A woman tossed and turned, gripping a necklace so tight that the beads left an imprint on her fingers. She was dreaming too, and at the very moment Nerin managed to speak to his alluring companion, words left her lips in a soft scream.

"Your heart."

* * * * *

Karrina woke as the first rays of the sun flickered over the walls of her cell. She relaxed the grasp of her hand and looked down for her necklace. She should have put it on last night, but she'd been too tired.

The marks of the beads were still on her fingers, but the necklace itself was gone.

Chapter Five

The sound of a woman screaming in fury brought servants running. Daria was the first to reach the cell.

"What on earth...stop that noise this instant. This is a respectable house."

She stood frowning at Karrina, hands on her hips.

"He *took* it!! He *stole* it. Once again he proves himself to be a faithless lying worm..."

Karrina paced and ranted as best she could, her frustration growing as the length of the chain around her ankle brought her up short.

"Who took what? You're not making any sense. Sit. Down." The sharp tones penetrated Karrina's rage and she took several deep breaths as the older woman pointed at the bed.

Daria dismissed the other servants who were watching with awe as this captured slave indulged in a splendid fit of hysterics. "Now tell me what all this fuss and bother is about. And don't try any games with me, they won't work. You've been nothing but trouble ever since Nerin pulled you out of that river. He probably would have been a lot better off if he'd left you to drown."

Karrina couldn't help herself. Her eyes filled with tears at the harsh words from this woman. No one, it seemed, had any use for her. Not anymore.

"You're right. He should have." Her shoulders slumped as her anger drained away, leaving only despair in its place.

"Oh come on, it can't be that bad." She crossed to the bed, sitting next to Karrina and putting an arm around her shoulders in a motherly gesture.

"He'd never leave anyone for dead. He's an honorable man, is our master. Now supposing you tell Daria what all this is about, eh?"

Karrina sniffed. "He's not honorable. He stole my necklace again."

Daria sighed. "How can he steal something 'again'? If it's his in the first place it's not stolen, is it? And if it's yours, it's his. Same thing."

Karrina closed her eyes and prayed for patience.

"Daria. Listen to me. I am not a slave, I am Karrina of Ishalla. I escaped from a terrible situation in Akkad to seek refuge here and make my way to Ur. That necklace belongs to me. He...he gave it back last night. Then he came and took it away again."

Daria clicked her tongue at Karrina. "Now, now. Everyone knows that brand on your ankle is the slave brand, young lady. Don't go trying to fool us with pretty tales and fancy stories. And Nerin couldn't have taken your necklace last night. He's been gone. His bed wasn't slept in at all."

Karrina couldn't refrain from pointing out that Nerin could well have slept in someone else's bed. Like hers, for instance.

She snorted. "Just because he didn't use his own bed, doesn't mean—"

"Oh yes it does. You stop right there, Karrina or whatever your name really is." Daria gripped Karrina's shoulders and turned her roughly around to face her. "Nerin of Kushuk is a good and honest man. He's harsh, yes. He has to be. This is the biggest farm in the area and if it has problems, people can starve. Do you understand that kind of responsibility?"

Karrina nodded, knowing only too well what *that* kind of responsibility entailed.

"He has a code, a set of values he lives by. And one of them is that he never, ever, sleeps anywhere else but in his own bed when here in his own home. Yes, he may summon someone to join him, but even then, he never leaves his seed. Never. He's always been careful that way and his women respect it."

"Never?" Karrina couldn't help the question, it slid between her lips before she'd had chance to think about it.

"Never. A cock like his gets plenty of work, you can bet the gods' balls on that. But he's never left a woman with child, because he knows to always spurt his seed to the gods not the woman he's with. That's an honorable man, in my opinion, and I'll not have him scorned by some runaway slave who knows no better."

Karrina bit her lip. "I'm sorry Daria, I meant no insult. But I had the necklace last night...look." She held her hand out to the woman sitting beside her and showed the indentations of the design that were only now fading from her palm and fingers. "I slept with it tight in my hand. My brother gave it to me and it's all that I have—"

"Then why won't the damn thing stay with you?"

The rough voice from the doorway made both women jump.

"I did *not* take it. By all the Gods I swear I did not take this accursed thing from your hands during the night."

Both Daria and Karrina noticed Nerin's pallor and the dark shadows beneath his eyes.

"So would one of you explain to me how it ended up here?"

He gestured to his chest, where the pendant hung, glittering in the morning light.

* * * * *

Two pairs of eyes widened as they gazed at him, and two mouths fell open in surprise. If it hadn't been such an uncanny situation, he'd have laughed at the sight.

He strode to the bed and seized Karrina's hand. Sure enough, the imprint of the necklace was still visible. He shivered in spite of the warmth in the room.

"Daria, take her. Feed her, wash her, do whatever you want with her. Don't let her escape, though. It's time I went back into town and checked on a few things."

His fingers scrabbled at the chain as he tried to unfasten it. With an oath he gave up.

"Master Nerin." Daria's voice could have been any mother from twenty to seventy. "You'll not use language like that around my ears. Come here and bend down."

Obediently, Nerin bent to Daria's side and she unfastened the necklace for him.

He felt the chain slip slowly away from his neck. He was free of the accursed thing. Then why did a sharp stab of discomfort prick at his mind?

He shook his head and watched as Karrina folded it into her hands once more.

"Why do you not wear it?" The question fell from his lips without thought.

"If I wore it I'd be dead and long gone. You believe me to be a slave, a runaway slave at that. Slaves are killed for bread in some places, Nerin of Kushuk. Can you imagine what my fate would have been, had someone seen me with this?" She raised her hand and leveled a blunt look at him.

Nerin nodded.

Karrina ran her fingers over the smooth surface, brushing the golden edge gently. "It doesn't feel right, holding it like this. Something's wrong." She frowned down at her hands. "I can't wear it, I can't hold it…it won't stay in my hands…what's the matter with me?"

She looked back up at Nerin. "You will have to keep it for me."

Words of refusal sputtered from Nerin's lips.

"It's not my choice. It's the necklace. It is telling me that you are the one who must guard it while I'm in this place. I know it as sure as I know the sun will rise tomorrow."

She held out her hand and Nerin reluctantly took back the pendant. The two ends fastened around his neck with a satisfied click.

He tried to ignore his own feeling of relief as the necklace settled on his chest, and the sigh that hissed from Karrina.

"Daria, she's in your care. I shall return later."

He turned on his heel, anxious to be away and put some distance between him and a pair of dark blue eyes that sang strange songs to places in his body where there had been no feeling in the past.

He didn't think he liked it.

He knew it bothered him.

By the gods, she fucked like a dream though.

He left his home before his cock could signal its agreement by raising itself up for a "Yea" vote.

* * * * *

Kushuk was busy as always, recovering from storms, festivals, and strange happenings in the temples of the gods. Life went on for its residents, who loved, married, raised families, and eventually passed beyond regardless of outside occurrences.

Few who saw Nerin make his way through the crowds would have guessed that a chill was creeping around his belly and fear was lurking somewhere behind his ribs.

Nerin was not a superstitious man. He was practical, prided himself on his common sense, and felt that most legends were mumbo jumbo thought up by priests under the influence of *Huk Gil.* He'd attended one ceremony where the incense had been made from the juice of this poppy, and had not enjoyed the experience. He liked his self-control too much to surrender it to some strange smelling fumes.

He needed to talk to Ronnil, High Priest of the Sun God. Another practical man, with a streak of scientific knowledge learned from his predecessor, Ronnil might be able to help him shed light on what was happening.

Also, Ronnil would know of any news from Akkad that might back up Karrina's story. If she were really an escaped noblewoman, would there not be a hue and cry for her return?

The Temple of the Sun God welcomed him with its warm stone facade and he was shown into Ronnil's chambers without delay.

"Greetings, Nerin. Good to see you." Ronnil rose with a pleased smile on his face.

"Thank you for seeing me, High Priest."

Ronnil waved his hand in dismissal of the title, and led Nerin over to a small balcony where drinking vessels were laid out next to a couple of chairs. The walls shaded the spot and the breezes were most pleasant.

"You have had some trouble?"

Nerin looked at Ronnil with a questioning frown.

"I have never known you to get into a tavern brawl, so must assume you had trouble." He gestured to Nerin's cheek where a bluish bruise was quite visible.

Nerin blushed. He'd completely forgotten that the conniving slave bitch had come very close to blackening his eye. His teeth gritted.

Ronnil coughed and turned away. "Well, I'm glad you sustained no other injury. Now, how may I help you?"

He took a swig from his vessel and smacked his lips together in appreciation. "By the gods, Ishkar's brews get better all the time, don't you think?"

Nerin nodded absently, wiping a little foam from his lip. He put the vessel carefully back down on the table. "I need information, Ronnil. I am faced with a problem that I do not know how to handle."

Ronnil paused, looking at his friend. "Tell me."

Nerin closed his eyes and began to speak.

He told Ronnil everything. Well, almost everything. He skipped the incident in the bathing chamber because Ronnil didn't need to know that. It was not really relevant to the matter at hand. Or shouldn't have been.

Ronnil listened quietly until Nerin reached the end of his story.

"So what do I do? Do I release her? That brand is tantamount to a death sentence if anyone catches her, and the necklace will certainly disappear forever. Do I send her back to Akkad? What if she is telling the truth? That would have the same results. Or worse. She'd end up married to some old disgusting lecher who'd use her body for his own pleasures, taking her soft thighs and spreading—"

"Ahem." Ronnil cleared his throat and did his very best to bite back his grin. Poor Nerin. Caught at last. Remembering his own lust filled and frustrating days before Enshilla had succumbed to his passion, he felt a pang of sympathy for Nerin.

"Yes. Well. You can see why I need advice," muttered Nerin, burying his embarrassment in his drinking vessel.

"Indeed. An interesting situation." Ronnil rose and paced the room. "I don't usually discuss this sort of business with you, Nerin, but I agree that these are unusual circumstances." He turned and faced Nerin. "I will allow you into my confidence for this, because I believe you to be a man of honor."

Nerin lowered his head in a gesture of appreciation.

"Messengers have been traveling between Sumer and Akkad for some time now. We have pretty good channels of communication, and we feel that it is important for most Sumerian towns that lie between the borders of Akkad and the city of Ur to be aware of the current political situation."

Ronnil trusted Nerin enough to openly imply that the tentative peace agreement between the two lands was far from reliable and Nerin nodded in agreement. Both men knew that Ur would be a juicy and tempting target for invaders.

"My latest information contains nothing of any dispute between a House Ishalla, nor does it speak of a lost son or daughter. There is, however, talk that the Queen, whose husband died in the not too distant past, has taken the throne illegally. Apparently the Crown Prince, he who would have ruled Akkad, has disappeared."

Nerin's jaw dropped.

"Her other child, a daughter, has been reported as dead."

Nerin tried to swallow and started choking. Ronnil slapped him on the back and helped him take a breath.

"Is it possible that you harbor a princess of the Akkadian royal blood in your house? Or is it merely her slave who escaped from the Queen and her wickedness, and stole a necklace along the way?"

"I don't know." The whisper was more like a cry for help.

"I must go to the Moon Goddess's temple for a ceremony, Nerin. Walk with me and let us take counsel from the High Priestess. I have come to rely upon her wisdom and her insights." *And her sweet mouth, not to mention her white thighs and welcoming cunt.* That thought was not for Nerin's ears.

The two men left the ziggurat, one anxious to see his woman, the other staggered by the information he'd just received.

Ronnil was also trying not to be too amused at the fact that his friend might just have fucked a princess last night.

Chapter Six

Karrina leaned back from the table and licked the last of the date juice from her lips. "That was wonderful, Daria."

The older woman smiled. "It is good that you have an appetite, at least. With all this strangeness going on, it's a wonder anybody can eat anything." Daria had also apparently managed to convince her appetite that mysteries shouldn't interfere with the enjoyment of good food. She polished off her fourth piece of *bappir*, enjoying the fresh Sumerian barley bread.

"Well, you're clean, you're fed, and you have your necklace. What am I going to do with you now?"

"Unchain my ankle?"

Daria snorted. "I don't think so."

"Well, it was worth a try." Karrina smiled at the woman, sensing warmth beneath her crusty attitude. "Talk to me, Daria. If you have no other duties that require your attention, of course."

Daria tilted her head. "What would you have me talk about?" Her lips curled. "Wait...no need to answer that. You'll want to know about Nerin, won't you?"

Helpless to prevent it, Karrina squirmed as a blush spread across her creamy skin.

"Oh don't bother coloring up, you won't be the first to find him appealing and I'm damn sure you won't be the last. He's a fine, fine man. Hung like a bull too..."

Karrina turned an even deeper shade of red.

"I certainly wish I had a lot less moons behind me. I'd give all you young things a run for Nerin and I'd take him every which way I could. Get him all hot and bothered and then finish him off with my tight ass. That's the way to keep a man. Never let him become complaisant. Keep him on his toes and not sure what he's going to find when he comes to your bed..." Daria smiled at her own words, obviously reminiscing.

Karrina's eyes were wide.

"You...you'd let a man...I mean...*there*?"

"Of course. You mean you haven't ever allowed a man to take the back door into the ziggurat?"

Karrina shook her head, tongue glued to the roof of a suddenly dry mouth.

"Good way to not get with child, too," added Daria, nodding her head for emphasis.

"Yes, but doesn't it hurt?"

Daria chuckled. "With Nerin, yes, it probably would. Not every man has been blessed with his inches. More's the pity."

Karrina's jaw had fallen and she was staring at Daria with a combination of fascination and disbelief.

"Oh, don't give me those big eyes of yours. You're no virgin, I'll wager. Life is short. Pleasure should be taken wherever you find it and you should grab it with both hands. And with Nerin you'd need both hands, too." She chuckled at her own joke.

Karrina chewed her lip as she pondered Daria's blunt words. A question crossed her mind. "Daria, why is he...like he is? You know, silent, unemotional...it's like he's made of stone."

Daria ran a finger around the edge of her drinking vessel as she considered her answer. "Nerin is not made of stone, Karrina. Never make the mistake of assuming he does not feel. He'll be angry with me for talking about him..." She put the cup back on the table and shrugged. "But you'd hear it from others anyway."

Karrina leaned forward, anxious not to miss a word.

"Nerin's family has farmed this land for generations. His parents were hard workers and Nerin and his brothers and sister all pitched in and helped, not because it was expected of them, but because they wanted to."

"He has brothers and sisters?"

"Had. Two brothers, one sister. Nerin was the oldest."

"Where are they now?"

"Gone." The tone of Daria's voice sent a fleeting chill down Karrina's spine. "There was a great flood. Oh there are always floods, but this one came without warning and well before the flood season. It took almost all this land and washed it clean. It also took Nerin's family."

"And Nerin?"

"Nerin wasn't here that night. He'd just discovered what his cock was for and had spent the night fucking a couple of girls up on the hillside away from town. He never knew the extent of the disaster until he came home the next afternoon and found his whole family gone."

Karrina was stunned. She couldn't begin to imagine what must have gone through that young mind when he learned of his loss — and his own survival.

"It was as if part of him shut down," continued Daria. "He turned from a carefree young lad searching for his next fuck, to a dedicated farmer and businessman. It was like he was doing penance for surviving. This farm had to be as good as, if not better, than it was when his father was alive."

Karrina nodded. Parts of the puzzle that was Nerin of Kushuk were clicking into place like the stones in a temple foundation. "He was rebuilding what was left of his family, wasn't he?"

Daria gazed approvingly at the young woman. "Yes he was. But the one thing he couldn't rebuild was the love they'd all shared. That was gone with the waters of the River Goddess."

"So now, he has everything the way he wants it. This farm is a monument to his family, proof that his survival was worthwhile."

"He doesn't have everything, Karrina. Nerin has never allowed himself to feel love. Not for anyone or anything. The closest he comes to it is a look in his eyes when he walks his fields."

"Never? No one?"

"No. I think he's afraid."

"Afraid of what?" asked Karrina.

"Afraid that if he loves someone he'll lose them again."

Karrina thought about that. "It makes sense, doesn't it? The fact that he never risks a woman bearing his child."

Daria nodded again. "Exactly. He's a successful, rich, handsome man. Who cannot love."

Karrina breathed out through her teeth. "We all have stories, don't we?" she mumbled, brain trying to sort out this latest tale.

"So are you going to tell me yours? The real one, not the one you've been regaling Nerin with."

Karrina flashed a quick glance at Daria whose eyes wrinkled as she grinned back. "I'm no fool, child. You're no more a slave than the Goddess Inanna. So how *did* you get that brand on your ankle?"

* * * * *

With each step they took to the Temple of the Moon Goddess, Nerin got angrier. She'd lied.

The bitch had lied to him.

All he'd asked was honesty. There was no other discourse between people that could endure. She couldn't tell the truth. From the beginning she'd invented her story about a forced marriage to gain his sympathy. She was obviously a slave who'd stolen her mistress's jewelry. It would account for her knowledge of well-born ways. A slave in a royal palace would learn quickly to ape her betters.

His temper grew, coiling within his gut like a hungry snake.

"Nerin, I would counsel prudence right now," cautioned Ronnil as they mounted the steps of the temple. "We still do not know yet if she is the missing princess or a slave. Whichever she turns out to be, she has knowledge of Akkad and the situation in the palace that might be useful."

Nerin nodded, agreeing with Ronnil's assessment and putting a lid on his fury. It remained where it was, however, fires banked, but still hot.

The Temple was busy preparing for the latest ceremony. Nerin realized it was the last day of the New Year Festival, one that bade a somber farewell to the preceding year.

It would be marked with offerings of flowers, ringing of bells to tell those in the afterlife that their relatives still missed them, and at sunset, those who wished could take their pleasure with another, trying to achieve climax at the moment the sun slipped below the horizon. That way their cries would travel with the Sun God to the afterlife where he spent each night.

Nerin knew his household would have the flowers ready, the bells would be rung, and if he chose not to shout his climax to the departing Sun God, well that was no one's business but his.

The Temple of the Moon Goddess celebrated in its own unique way.

As Ronnil and Nerin entered, they were greeted and led immediately to Enshilla's office. She stood with a welcoming smile, her eyes lighting up as Ronnil crossed to place a quick kiss on her lips.

"I did not expect you till later, Ronnil." She grinned.

"Couldn't wait." He smiled back. "Our shouts will be the loudest, never fear."

Nerin coughed, feeling like he was seeing something he shouldn't be watching.

Ronnil turned apologetically. "Sorry, Nerin. Enshilla, we have a problem and need some advice."

Enshilla turned and welcomed Nerin, seating them all comfortably. She listened silently as the tale was told again.

"So there you have it. What does Nerin do with this woman? Would Lilianna recognize her, do you think? Could she possibly be a princess? Or is it more likely that she is what she appears, a runaway slave?"

Nerin sat with arms folded, in his usual stoic position, eyes betraying nothing. Neither Ronnil nor Enshilla could have guessed that he was mentally flaying himself for fucking the bitch last night.

So what if her cunt had been the softest and tightest he'd ever slid into? So what if she'd tasted like honey and smelt even sweeter?

She was a liar. He could not forgive that. Nor could he forgive her for making him lose control. Gods' balls, he'd come *inside* her.

Enshilla stared at the pendant on Nerin's chest. The tear trembled from the eye, just as it had the first time Nerin had held it. He had no idea when it had returned.

"That seems to be the key, doesn't it?" mused Enshilla. "That necklace. It brought you to her, it keeps her in your home, and it seems to travel between you two at the whim of the gods."

Nerin snorted. "Trickery and magic, Enshilla. I do not believe in such foolishness."

"Ah. Then the necklace returned to your chest from her hands—how?"

Nerin had the grace to look embarrassed. "I have not yet worked that out. Probably she arranged for it to be brought to me as I slept near the river."

"Ah. So she has coerced someone from your household to act on her behalf?"

Nerin raised his chin defiantly. "I don't know. You may be sure I shall find out."

"Well, my counsel would be much the same as Ronnil's, I believe. Caution and prudence. Until we can verify her identity, I believe she would be safest with you. There have been no rumors about her arrival; fortunately a runaway slave does not occasion much gossip. If you can keep any mention of a magical necklace from reaching hungry ears, so much the better."

Enshilla and Ronnil exchanged glances. "I don't think we should involve Lilianna any further—she was young when she left and probably wouldn't recognize a princess from a slave. I do have a priestess traveling to and from Akkad within a few days."

Nerin's ears pricked up. This was unusual.

"Again, this information is not for public consumption, Nerin. We are placing our trust in you. The political situation is always fragile, you are not naive and this is surely not a surprise."

Nerin nodded in agreement.

"Our priestesses often travel quietly between Kushuk and Akkad, where there is also a thriving temple to the Moon Goddess. Such cooperation results in greater understanding between our peoples. Ronnil believes, as do I, that this will benefit both our lands."

Ronnil absently played with a lock of Enshilla's hair. "They do not spy, Nerin, but they do report on the latest news. Where better to learn what is happening in a country than in its temples?"

"A wise course, High Priest. Lady." Nerin agreed with both of them, realizing that there was more to being a "High" anything than simply participating in rituals and ceremonies. His respect for this couple grew.

"If you can keep her out of sight for a few days we may be able to offer better insight into her story. Such a necklace must have been mentioned somewhere, and perhaps news of its disappearance will lead to the truth of her identity."

Nerin sighed. It was a wise course of action, but did nothing to ease his anger at the woman who had lied to his face.

Enshilla rose. "Forgive me, gentlemen, but I must leave you — it is time for the Rites of Farewell."

"You'll stay, of course, Nerin?" Ronnil raised an eyebrow at the other man.

"Yes, indeed, please stay. Would you care to participate? I'm sure any one of my Priestesses would be honored to partner you in the rite." Enshilla added her voice to Ronnil's.

Nerin bowed his head slightly in acknowledgement of the honor. "My gratitude Lady, for the offer. I have not readied myself, however. I believe it would be best for me not to celebrate this ritual today."

"As you choose, Nerin. Ronnil and I shall, of course, be leading the ceremony. So our balcony will be available for your use."

Again Nerin bowed, knowing he would have to stay, but wishing he could get home where he could get his hands on a certain blue-eyed liar.

* * * * *

The bells rang in a steady tone as a line of priestesses walked slowly down the length of a huge chamber in the temple of the Moon Goddess. They were all wearing loose skirts of dark blue, the color of the sky as the Moon rises. It was a daunting sight as they marched in time with the bells and the drums that sounded a slow rhythm for their bare feet.

Behind them came an equal number of men, also wearing blue. A long wide length of silk had been tossed over their heads and secured with a band. It fell over their naked bodies like a cloak of darkness, leaving their chests and groins nude.

The pageant rolled out beneath Nerin's eyes as he sat in the seat reserved for the High Priest. It was a place of honor but he wasn't feeling terribly honored at this moment. He was feeling seriously angry.

He was also feeling seriously needy. Watching the swaying breasts and swinging cocks of the celebrants as they passed beneath him was making his balls ache, and try as he might he couldn't rid his thoughts of the image of Karrina as she rode him last night.

Nor could he forget the sight of her with her breasts squeezing his cock to climax.

A loud roll of the drums recalled his attention and he tried to focus on the scene below. It didn't help.

The priestesses had dropped their robes and were now taking up a position in front of each of the columns that lined the hall. They held flowers in their hands, which they raised to place on the ledge below the statue that topped each pillar. All the statues represented the Moon Goddess in her many incarnations.

She must be one busy goddess, thought Nerin, as he realized that there must be at least fifteen or twenty priestesses nakedly embracing the columns. Enshilla and Ronnil were all the way down at the front of the line.

Nerin offered a prayer of thanks for that. Watching two people he'd just spent an hour with as they celebrated this rite might have been a bit much even for him.

The beat of the drums picked up, and the bells tolled more loudly. Each man moved in behind a priestess.

Nerin knew that many of the men had spent the last twelve hours in prayer and meditation, denying themselves any pleasures in preparation for this ritual. He wondered if Ronnil and Enshilla had also observed any of these preparations. After what he'd seen flash between them, he doubted it.

A part of him envied them that connection, but the rest of him scorned it. After all, why risk the pain of loss for a few moments of pleasure?

The priestesses spread their legs wide and the men closed in. At this point, the blue silks of the cloaks hid the bodies of the celebrants from public view. But Nerin knew from experience what the men were seeing.

They were looking at the luscious naked ass of the priestess in front of them as she spread her cheeks and offered her tight entrance for their pleasure.

He felt his cock jump as his mind envisioned Karrina spreading her buttocks and presenting herself to him.

There were a few cries and sighs from the halls, but all the priestesses were experienced in this technique. No one was forced to participate, only encouraged. In fact, many were excited about the prospect, and there was always a greater number of celebrants than actual roles to play.

Nerin watched absently as the hips of the men began to move slightly. The drums kept pace, timing the movements and Nerin was pleased to see the men make a point of reaching beneath the women to ensure their pleasure as well.

It was not a long ceremony. Clearly twelve hours of deprivation during the New Year's Festival got a man ready for action very quickly.

Within a few minutes of the first penetration, men started falling by the wayside.

First one of the youngest shouted his orgasm, only to have his hand grabbed by the priestess in front of him. Obviously he'd neglected to finish her too. Blushing, he attended to her needs and she sobbed beneath his touch.

This started the sequence of orgasms that rippled through the hall. Sex was in the air and Nerin was getting increasingly frustrated. He didn't want a priestess's ass, no matter how tight and appealing.

He wanted blue eyes, black hair, white thighs and a cunt running with juices sweeter than his date honey.

He wanted Karrina.

And the fact that he did made him even more furious.

Chapter Seven

"So what do I do, Daria?" Karrina raised her deep blue eyes to the older woman who was watching her with a mixture of awe and disbelief.

Daria's words froze on her lips as a bellow shook the very walls of the house.

"Gods' balls, what's got into him?"

Karrina paled as she realized that Nerin had returned. It was his voice that roared through the chambers.

A girl rushed into the room. "Mistress Daria? It's the Lord Nerin. He's very-very—"

"I can hear that, Jana." Daria's lips curled in a small smile.

"Where is she?" The shout echoed through the room.

Daria turned to her. "Trust him, Karrina. He may be angry, and he may be harsh, but you can trust him. With your life if necessary."

He burst into the room, black eyes on fire.

"There you are, you lying..."

She shrank back, unable to stop herself. His face was flushed and his mouth a hard line.

He grabbed for her ankle chain, freed it and pulled, yanking her off her chair. But before she could hit the floor, he had her tossed over his shoulder like a sack of grain.

Her scared eyes met Daria's in silent entreaty.

"Believe me, Karrina, I'm right." Daria smiled encouragingly.

"Mistress Daria?" The scared voice of the servant interrupted her.

"Jana, I think you've lost your playmate."

The two women watched as Nerin struggled through the narrow door with his burden.

"Well, I can't say as I'm too sorry after watching *that*," shivered Jana. She turned to Daria in time to hear Karrina's head crack as it hit the jamb.

"You're smiling."

"I am." Daria's grin broadened. "He hasn't lost his temper since the flood."

* * * * *

Karrina winced at the pain that rocketed through her head.

The man carrying her grunted in acknowledgement but didn't let up his pace.

"Where are you taking me?" She panted out the words, hanging upside down over his shoulder.

"Quiet, you lying slut."

She wriggled. "How *dare* you call me that?" She freed one hand and pounded on his firm backside.

He responded with a far harsher slap to her buttocks, which were conveniently placed for his punishment.

"Ow!"

"Be silent. I'll have no discourse with liars."

Karrina huffed as he carried her down a set of stairs and out across the courtyard to the threshing barn.

She muttered oaths as his shoulder dug into her soft abdomen and got another slap across her backside. Her cheeks began to tingle and the feel of his hand grasping high up on her thigh was starting to become seductive.

She squirmed more.

He slapped her again, this time moving her skirts aside and making sure he got bare flesh.

The sound rang through the empty barn.

The harvest was over, the new plants readied and almost everyone was celebrating the New Year Festival in one way or another. They had the place to themselves.

"Maybe I should have done this when I found you," hissed Nerin.

"Done what, you brute. Beaten me?"

Nerin slid her off his shoulder and ripped her skirt away, leaving her nude before his gaze. He quickly wrapped the free length of ankle chain around both her wrists, holding her tight and ignoring her efforts to free herself.

"Yes."

He turned her and bent her over the table. Her buttocks shone white against the dark wood that generations of workers had polished to a soft glow.

His hand fell again, a sharp blow that brought the blood to the surface and stung.

She gasped, not sure if it was from the pain or the feel of his hand.

"Why are you doing this?" she cried, struggling against the chain.

"Be still." His hand fell, but this time it caressed her tingling skin with a delicate touch. She gasped again, but this time in no doubt of the cause.

Her bottom was hot, the cheeks so sensitive that the merest touch of air was like a slap. His hand felt like leather, all rough textures and smooth places, and her clit began to respond.

She knew she was becoming aroused. It was beyond her control.

His touch firmed and she braced herself for another blow.

Instead, he bent and freed her ankle, keeping her hands chained together. Gently, he eased her arms from beneath her body and fastened the chain to one of the hooks on the wall. She was stretched over the threshing table, feet on the floor, arms held tight, breasts pressing into the smooth wood.

She was as vulnerable as it was possible to be.

And she was running with hot juices, aroused, ready for whatever he would do to her.

To her astonishment, she suddenly knew she trusted him. He wouldn't hurt her. Daria, bless her heart, had been right.

She was stunned to feel the glancing blow of a lash across her buttocks.

"What the...what are you doing?" Her voice rose on a shriek as the sting of the lash bit deep.

"Trying to get the truth out of you. Trying to teach you how we deal with liars here in Kushuk. Attempting to explain to you that lying is not an option with me. And most of all, punishing you for lying to me in the first place."

Once again the lash fell, stinging, yet not hurting as badly as she'd expected. The touch was hard but fast, bringing warmth and a sharp burn to her flesh but leaving it sensitized and making her heart beat faster.

"I didn't lie," she snarled, refusing to weaken before him.

"Hah. And are you *really* Karrina of Ishalla? Is there even such a house at all?" Nerin punctuated his words with touches of the lash, some hard, some soft, some barely there at all.

Karrina's anger was mounting along with her arousal.

"How dare you? Yes, I *am* Karrina of Ishalla. My house is an ancient one. Our lineage goes back to—" She bit off the words as another blow fell. This one she really felt.

"Your lineage? What lineage would that be? Slaves have no lineage." A blow fell lightly across her shoulders this time, making her jump. Her buttocks were on fire, her clit burning, and her thighs were probably running like the great river. She could smell her own arousal.

"I am not a slave." She bit out the words as a light touch seared her buttocks. She no longer knew nor cared what he was touching her with, only that he would keep the sensations going. Sweat was pouring off her face.

"What are you, then, Karrina? A high born lady?"

Warmth neared her flesh, which was now so sensitive she could sense the heat radiating from him as he stood behind her.

"I have told you who and what I am," she hissed.

Something hard and smooth touched her, rubbing its way across her hot cheeks and down the cleft between.

She gasped as her breasts pressed tight nipples to the wood beneath her and involuntarily she opened her legs wide in invitation.

"You've told me nothing but lies. Why should I believe such wild tales, fit for little but stories to keep children in their beds."

Once again she felt the touch of that hot skin to her tingling flesh.

She sobbed out a breath. "I am not a slave."

A drop of moisture splashed onto one burning buttock. He was sweating too.

"If you are not a slave, and I don't believe you to be the daughter of some minor nobleman, then could you be a princess?"

She froze as his cock nudged its way between her cheeks and pressed forcefully against her ring of tight muscles.

"I...I..." She couldn't answer. She couldn't even think. All her attention was on her anus and the pressure it was receiving. Was he going to thrust his way in? She tensed, and readied herself for the invasion.

Suddenly the pressure eased and his cock slid lower, bathing itself in her moisture.

"Why do you ask about a princess?"

"Just a wild thought," he answered, his voice rough now and the lash forgotten next to her on the table.

His cock slid around her cunt, spreading slick honey and teasing the swollen flesh.

"Ahhh, Nerin..." she moaned.

"What have you done to me, Karrina," he breathed, stroking her tingling cheeks delicately with his hand. "I can think of nothing but sinking deep into you and fucking you, night and day. I want to feel your body holding my cock. I want your lips around it and my tongue inside you. I don't want to feel like this, but I do. You're nothing but a runaway slave from some remote palace who has stolen her mistress's necklace. And yet when I'm inside you..." He slid his cock into her cunt and pressed his flesh against her. His balls brushed the tops of her thighs and she gasped out a breath of sheer joy.

"When I'm inside you, nothing else matters. The world goes away and there's only this..."

He moved, pulling back and thrusting forwards again, wringing a moan of pleasure from her throat.

She met him, thrust for thrust, her cunt aching for his possession, knowing that finally she had found her mate.

She spread her legs wider in wanton need.

He met that need with a blazing passion of his own. He bent over, strong enough to hold the position while he slid a hand beneath her and fondled her clit.

The warmth and sweat of his body surrounded Karrina as she sprawled beneath him, welcoming his pounding cock into her body.

His grunts kept time with her moans and the pleasure of his movements took her places she'd never dreamed existed.

She sobbed, she writhed, she pushed back against him, trying to get more of his wonderful cock inside her.

He responded to her, pushing himself as deep as he'd ever been inside a woman. Still she demanded more.

She knew he could feel her womb touching him, so deep was he within her silky folds. They were both slick and slippery now, his hand drenched with her moisture, his cock leaking his seed to mingle with her honey.

The sounds of their lovemaking added to their arousal.

Karrina was beside herself. She knew that an orgasm was building inside her, but it was nothing like she'd ever experienced before. His cock was now pressing hard within her, growing impossibly huge and touching places that felt like liquid fire. Places she never knew existed.

Her buttocks tightened almost painfully, and she knew he could feel her tension mount. He answered with all the power he had.

She was pounded, harshly, savagely, by the huge dark haired man with the golden streak of hair.

She couldn't get enough.

But yet she could, and inevitably her orgasm neared.

"Nerin…" she sobbed.

"I know," he grunted, without a break in his rhythm.

"Nerin…" she screamed. *"Nerin…NOW…"*

The world trembled around her and Karrina felt every muscle and bone in her body vibrate in time with her orgasm. Stars burst in her vision, she went completely deaf, and for a frightening few moments she thought she would die.

Only Nerin's shout of fulfillment pulled her back from the brink.

She realized his cock was exploding within her and the feel of his cum squirting her tissues made her shudder all over again.

It was many minutes before either of them could move.

Karrina's head lay on the table and she had closed her eyes. She knew she was trying to shut out the truth.

The man lying on top of her in a panting, sweaty lump was her mate. Her soul was his. She loved him.

And it was the worst thing that could possibly have happened to her.

* * * * *

He still didn't know the truth. Her body was still clasping his, his cock so deep that even though it was relaxing now, it was still buried inside her. Even after this, she still had not told him what he needed to hear. The truth.

He withdrew, pulling quickly back from her and ignoring her little sound of protest.

She lay prone in front of him, thighs wet from their mating, cheeks reddened and blotchy from his punishment.

He felt a pain somewhere inside him, like something was breaking. It made him angry, and he refused to accept that his anger masked a fear.

Tamping down the emotions that were turning his mind inside out, he coolly unclasped her chains and helped her stand.

Her eyes opened slowly, still dazed and unfocused as her body pulled itself back from the sexual whirlpool she'd experienced.

"Nerin…" she breathed, swaying towards him.

His hands grasped her upper arms and he steadied her.

His rough hold snapped her trance and her eyes reflected surprise, bewilderment and even a little hurt.

"I must know the truth Karrina. I must know who you are and what you are doing here."

It was enough to make her turn her head away from his blank stare. She bit her lip but not fast enough to hide the slight tremble.

He wanted to hold her tight, pull her to his chest and imprint her scent on his body forever. Nerin cursed himself for his weakness.

"Come on…" He reached out and took her hand firmly in his, leading her back out into the sunlight.

"Nerin, I'm…I'm in need of a wash," she muttered, looking down at herself.

"You shall have one."

Silently he led her through the shadowed corridors of his home and back to the bathing chamber she'd visited so recently.

It seemed like a lifetime ago.

Nerin watched as she slid beneath the water's warmth and closed her eyes. He had spared a glance for the pendant, and knew that the tear had, for the moment, disappeared. He'd like to take it off and throw it as far as he could, but was frankly scared to do so. Besides, it really was not his. A well-developed sense of honor forbade him to do as he really wanted, throw the damn thing away and pretend it never existed.

"I can't tell you more than I have."

The words startled Nerin, coming as they did out of complete silence. "Why?" He snapped back the question before her words had faded.

"It is not a matter of my silly escapades. It's a matter that concerns others. A matter that could lead to tragedy, or worse."

"You are over dramatizing. Or being evasive."

Karrina opened her eyes and stared at Nerin, a dull pain dampening the deep blue to the murky shade of the River Goddess when it rained.

"Nerin of Kushuk. I swear by my father's spirit, I swear on that pendant you wear, I swear by whatever gods you hold precious, that I cannot tell you more than I have because other lives are involved."

Nerin watched her, saying nothing. Her eyes begged for his understanding. He wanted desperately to give it, but trust did not come easily, and he knew that if he surrendered his trust, then other things might also need to be faced. He wasn't ready.

"Let us compromise. You tell me whose lives are in danger, and I will do all that I can to protect them."

Karrina leaned wearily back against the tiles of the bath. "Nerin, I am who I say I am. I have escaped from Akkad. My mother branded me as a slave in the hopes that just this situation would arise. Should I manage to free myself, no one would ever believe my story. Not with this on my ankle."

She raised her foot and gestured towards the small mark that flared against her white skin.

Nerin caught her foot in his hand, tracing the brand with gentle fingers. He couldn't help it. He raised her foot to his lips and kissed the mark.

Her gasp echoed over the waters and around the silent chamber.

Nerin moved his lips gently around her ankle, pressing light kisses on the delicate skin inside her leg. His hands caressed her heel, and rubbed softly down towards the ball of her foot as he raised it even higher.

She slid down a little in the water, allowing it to lap around her chin.

He licked her big toe.

She moaned.

He assumed it was a good moan, because her foot shivered in his grasp and he could feel the movement of her calf muscle beneath his other hand.

He slid his lips over her middle toe and sucked gently, rubbing his tongue over its sensitive surface.

A gasp came from the woman opposite him, followed by a gurgle and a cough as water slid into her open mouth.

He allowed himself a small smile as he continued to lick, suck, stroke and feather his way over and under and between all her toes.

Judging from the sounds she was making, he was doing the right thing. His cock was certainly agreeing with her.

He bit down softly on her little toe, soothing the nip with his tongue.

"Nerin," she groaned. "What are you doing to me?"

"I don't know," he muttered, absorbed in his self-imposed task. "But I like it."

"So do I," she whispered, eyes fixed on his mouth.

"Other foot." His hand waited above the water line as he lowered the first one back down.

Obediently she placed her other heel in the palm of his strong hand.

Following his instincts, Nerin treated her second foot to the same loving attention, noticing her reaction to each thing he tried. She squirmed when he separated her toes and nibbled on the web of skin stretched between them, and sighed when his tongue swirled around and around as he slid his mouth back and forward over each toe in turn.

The heat between them was palpable, her breasts bobbing gently in the water, their hardened nipples breaking little ripples as she moved her body in response to his mouth.

His cock was hard again. He knew he was a reasonably sexual man, but this was beyond anything he'd experienced. It was as if he'd never taken her in the threshing barn. His need was as fresh and urgent as it had been since the moment he'd first set eyes on her.

"Come."

He tugged her from the water and led her out into the small, sun-warmed courtyard.

"What...?" She blinked in the light.

He rubbed her gently with soft towels and ran his fingers through the thick mat of her hair, spreading it out and letting the sun dry it to tousled silk.

He leaned over and licked her shoulder with a hungry tongue.

"I need to finish my meal."

She made no sound as he laid her gently onto the pillows his servants had placed around the courtyard.

Settling himself between her thighs, he spread her legs and feasted his eyes on her swollen tissues.

She found her voice at last. "Oh my...Nerin...what are you doing? You're *looking* at me."

"Yes."

"Why?"

"Because I need to." Nerin's conscience twinged. It wasn't exactly a lie, but *need* was such an inadequate word for what he was actually feeling.

He couldn't tell her that he wanted to learn every little nook and cranny until all he had to do was close his eyes to see her cunt shining at him. He couldn't tell her that he wanted to bury his nose deep into her softness and inhale her very essence until all he could smell for the rest of his life was her desire for him.

He couldn't tell her that for the first time in his life he'd found a place his cock could call home. A mate for his body, and the missing piece of his soul.

He couldn't even tell *that* to himself.

He slid his hands beneath her thighs and raised her from the pillows.

Lips burning and eager, he lifted her to his mouth.

Chapter Eight

Karrina awoke by slow degrees. It was dark and she felt disoriented, unable to remember for a moment where she was or why.

A snuffle behind her startled her and she realized she was being held tight by two solid arms.

Nerin.

The memories flooded back and she closed her eyes on a shiver of desire.

He'd touched her in ways she could never have imagined.

No virgin, she hadn't been a stranger to the act of love, but Nerin had done things to her with his mouth that had astonished and aroused her. Just remembering the feel of his tongue as it teased her clit and then plunged into her depths started her juices flowing.

She'd climaxed around his tongue, crying out in amazement as the waves of sensation rolled over her body.

Then he'd risen onto his hands and plunged himself deep, following the crest of her orgasm and keeping it alive, building it again and again until she'd been sobbing with passion and need.

Once again he had found his release inside her and filled her with his seed. His final explosion had been magnificent and she'd been able to keep her eyes open long enough to see his face as he let go of his emotions and pumped himself into her willing body.

He'd thrown his head back, neck cording and taut, eyes closed. His gold streak had caught the sunlight and almost blinded her as his throat contracted into a sound that was neither shout nor moan but was the sweetest music to her ears.

They'd collapsed together, exhausted and sated, and the last thing she could remember was the warmth of his arms as the shadows spread across them, chilling their sweaty flesh.

It would seem they hadn't moved. His arms were still there, although a light blanket now covered their bodies.

She realized it was the first time she'd slept without some kind of a restraint in a long time, and gave a long stretch, enjoying the freedom it gave her.

And yet, the restraints were still there. Oh not chains or manacles this time, but the restraints of Nerin's arms. His hold on her was complete.

He must never know that he held not only her body, but also her heart and her very being. If he knew that, he'd insist on knowing the rest and that would put his life in danger too. She could not risk that. He was too precious to her.

Her stretching had separated their skin briefly, and as if reacting to the loss, Nerin stirred.

Or rather, his cock stirred.

Karrina turned in his arms to see dark eyes gazing sleepily at her.

She was astounded when a slow smile spread across his lips. Her heart turned over as she relished this rare moment.

"Hello." He was unguarded, vulnerable, gentle—all the things she'd never have associated with Nerin of Kushuk. For this special moment, he was Nerin, her lover. Fearing the time would be all too short, Karrina took advantage.

Shamelessly, she slid her hand down his flat stomach to his groin and through his curly pubic hair. His cock was already stirring.

She grasped it gently. "Hello to you."

Within her hand, Nerin stiffened.

She smiled and moved her hand, slowly learning his secrets. Ridges and valleys emerged as he grew harder beneath her touch.

"I find that I have awoken with a hunger, Nerin," she breathed, moving over him and sweeping his body with her hair.

She heard him swallow harshly.

"I find I must feed this hunger…" Bending over, her lips trailed down his abdomen, making his skin flutter.

She felt him jump, but couldn't know that Nerin was remembering his dream. She noticed his hand flash to the pendant, however.

"It's still there, Nerin." She reached his cock with her tongue and felt his hand push her hair aside so that he could watch her face as she bent to him.

"The pendant is still around your neck, and the tear is gone." She punctuated her words with licks of her tongue. "Do you know what that means, Nerin?"

There was no response, just a lot of harsh breathing as she licked her lips and delicately placed them around the very tip of his cock.

"Do you like this, Nerin?" She sucked gently, only touching the very tip.

He moaned his approval, muscles tight beneath her hands.

"The tear only disappears under certain…circumstances…" Lots of licking and sucking was taking place and Nerin's silence was being broken now by little sounds of pleasure.

Karrina took more of him in her mouth. She hummed.

He jumped and shuddered. "Karrina…"

"Nerin, the tear has disappeared because there is something special between us…and I'm not talking about this…" She licked him from base to tip and wiped the bubble of liquid away from the tiny slit with a flick of her tongue.

"Karrina…" he said again, apparently unable to speak more than one word at a time.

She chuckled to herself, loving the power she had to turn this solid, silent giant of a man into a squirming heap of speechless lust.

"Karrina, I can't hold out much more." His words were rough, grating across her ears.

"I don't want you to." Her mouth was busy now, pulling, sucking, teasing, every which way she could imagine. She let her hand drop beneath and cup his balls, gently rolling them across her fingers.

"I want you to come. I want to taste you, to learn how you feel when your seed leaves your body. I want to feel you on my tongue, in my throat, I want to suck down your spirit and hold your manhood while it spurts…"

Her words inflamed Nerin and his buttocks hardened. His cock filled her mouth and she sucked him as far back into her throat as she could.

His hand tightened in her hair to the point of pain and he pushed her head down even more as he let out a yell.

She sucked him dry.

He lay helpless beneath her hands, her mouth, her body.

He'd given her something of himself at that moment, she knew. And just as instinctively she knew that to deny him the truth would be to deny what lay between them.

Dangerous or not, he now had the right to know. To make a choice about his next move.

"Nerin, the truth."

She sat against his hip and laid her hand on his chest, feeling his heart slowing beneath her palm.

"I am Karrina, house of Ishalla, and my mother is Utta. Utta, in Akkadian, is another word for Queen."

* * * * *

Nerin stared blankly at the woman stroking his chest. *Now* she decided to tell him the truth.

She'd just about sucked his brains out through his cock and now she expected him to be conscious enough to absorb all the important secrets she was about to share.

Damn her.

He struggled through a lingering sexual fog and grabbed his mind with both hands.

"Your mother is Queen of Akkad?"

"Well, it is more accurate to say that my father was King."

Nerin saw tears flood the blue eyes and her hand stilled.

"I'm still not sure why he fell ill so quickly and I have horrible suspicions. My brother did too. That's why he left, Nerin. We were both convinced she'd kill him too. She thinks he's dead. She hopes I'm dead. If she finds out she's wrong on both counts, my life is worth nothing. That is not as important as the fact that my brother's life is also in danger."

Her hand clenched on his chest and he felt her intensity down through his ribs to his spine.

"Nerin, my brother is the rightful king. He's a good young man with a solid head on his shoulders. He'll be a good ruler, fair and just, like my father was. He must have the chance to find allies and return to take his place on the throne. His life must not be jeopardized by anything I do. If our mother should find out that we live..."

Nerin shook his head. "What kind of mother could kill her children like that?"

"Truthfully, I do not know. My father seemed happy enough with her, but in later years, she changed. She saw plots and conspiracies where there were none. She dismissed servants who'd been with her for most of their lives because she said they were untrustworthy." Karrina tossed her hair back out of her eyes.

"I know she didn't love us, my brother and I. She never did. But that was all right, we had others who cared for us, and raised us, and our father was always there for us, in spite of his duties."

Nerin's hand covered Karrina's as it lay on his body.

She looked straight into his eyes. "Nerin, I am afraid. Afraid that she will come after me, and find you. Afraid that you will pay the price for sheltering me. If she knew how I felt about you..."

Karrina bit her lip.

"And how do you feel about me, Karrina?" He couldn't stop himself from asking the question, the words fell from his mouth like pebbles in an avalanche. The force of his heart drove them into the silence that had fallen.

Her hand stirred beneath his, lifting them both to the pendant.

"This has already told you. Accept its truth, Nerin. We cannot deny it."

Nerin struggled.

Struggled with the need to fold her into his heart, and struggled with the fear that loving her would only mean losing her. He closed his eyes as shards of remembered pain pierced his thoughts. He'd never survive that again.

"I can't." He bit the words off, expecting to see hurt in her eyes.

"I know." She smiled, surprising him. "And your heart knows, too. It's all right, Nerin."

Trustingly, she lay down beside him and snuggled close, allowing him to pull her half on top of him.

"Tell me about the necklace," he said quietly.

"It's a mystery to all of us," she answered, wriggling a little to get herself more comfortable. "The story goes that some ancestor of ours found it in the high mountains of Zagros while he was journeying to find his gods. We never knew if he actually found any gods, but apparently he did bring the pendant back with him from his travels."

Her hand caressed the soft whorls of hair that speckled his chest.

"He was about to wed, he'd taken a woman from a neighboring town as his bride, but wasn't sure if it was the right thing to do. Even then there were political pressures on marriages, and he was being urged to consider a bride from a more distant town that had better resources."

She sniffed her disdain.

Nerin restrained a wry smile.

"Well, the story goes that he went to his original choice of bride and told her that he was not going to be able to marry her after all, but that he'd like to give her the pendant as a token of his sadness at their parting. They embraced and found that the tear had gone."

She stilled within his arms, heart beating against his body, her breasts squashed softly between them.

"My ancestor believed it to be a sign from the gods. He accepted that the magic was sending him a message, telling him that his love was greater than the need for political improvement. They married, raised eight sons and five daughters, and lived together in joy and happiness for several generations. Since that time, the pendant has always shown when true love is present."

She stopped, as if waiting for a comment from Nerin.

He said nothing. He could not. His heart was tumbling about somewhere up in his throat and the darn necklace felt like it was burning a hole in his flesh.

"Eventually, of course, it passed into family history as more of a legend than a fact, and was lost for many years. I could only wish it had been around when my father met my mother. But it wasn't until a few years ago that my brother stumbled across it while helping some workers dig a new well. He brought it to me before he left and told me he'd kept it safe, and that I should do the same."

Karrina brushed her fingers across the pendant, perhaps reassuring herself that it was still there.

"Whatever happens, Nerin, know this. I have told you more than I should have, and probably placed your life in danger now, as well as my own. But this cannot lie." She pressed on the pendant, digging the beads into his skin. "It tells of what is between us with some kind of magic ability. I do not question it. Neither should you. I trust it, and now, I trust you."

She sighed and slid her arm all the way around his chest as far as she could.

"And I'm sorry if the telling upsets you, but you have something else along with my trust. You have my heart."

* * * * *

Karrina listened to the silence that followed her words, and allowed the fear of rejection to sweep over her. She knew Nerin loved her, the pendant said so, and her heart said so. But would Nerin say so?

Did he even know?

His hand slid down her body to her thigh and his fingers stroked small circles on her smooth flesh.

"Karrina..." he breathed, pressing her as close to him as he could. "You ask so much of me."

"I ask nothing, Nerin."

"Yes you do. By giving me your love, you ask that I return something. Something I don't know if I still have left to give."

"I ask nothing of you Nerin. Except perhaps your caution from now on. I have laid my most dangerous secrets on your shoulders. It may have been wrong, but you must realize that we are in the middle of a difficult and risky situation. I have probably brought great trouble with me."

"That you have." He sighed, running his fingers around her thigh and making her fidget. "You've brought enormous troubles. More than I ever imagined I could deal with."

He slithered around her as she frowned at his words.

"You've turned me into a lustful idiot, unable to think of anything but you, your eyes, your soft skin, your scent…"

He trailed his mouth down over her stomach, nibbling and licking as he went.

"I'm not content unless you're here beside me, beneath me, around me…"

He moved between her legs and she knew her juices were starting to flow. She writhed as he spread her thighs and raised her legs to his shoulders.

"Nerin…by the Goddess…" she gasped.

"I am not happy unless I have you like this, wet, hot, waiting for my mouth, my cock, my fingers…"

He licked slowly across her swollen tissues, running his tongue through the ruffled folds that glistened for him.

"Aaaahhh…" she breathed, so amazed by the touch that her heart stopped beating for what seemed like hours.

"Is that love? I do not know. Am I afraid? Yes. But not of any threats from Akkad or its Queen."

His words punctuated his movements and his breath whiffled through the black curls on her mound. The scent of her arousal was strong between them and she moaned as he inhaled deeply.

"I am afraid that I shall never be complete without you, Karrina. Afraid that you have found a place inside me that I didn't know was there. Afraid that if you leave me the emptiness that will remain will consume me. I cannot face that emptiness. It will surely kill me."

His head ducked between her thighs and he eagerly sought her most sensitive spots. His tongue pressed up under her clit and sent a lightning bolt of sensation to her breasts and her womb.

She cried out in pleasure.

He teased, learning her likes and her secrets. He pressed one side, then the other, and then delved deep into her cunt, only to withdraw and slide his fingers in where his tongue had been.

Kisses rained down on her clit, and Karrina knew if it was possible to die from pleasure, it would be happening to her any minute now.

He nipped at her, gentling his touch with his tongue and she could feel an orgasm beginning to throb deep inside her.

"Aaahh, Nerin..." she sobbed.

"Come for me, Karrina. Spill your release into my mouth, my soul...share it with me now..."

She was helpless under the attack of his tongue and his words. Her hands clenched at the blanket beneath her as the muscles in her buttocks thrust her upwards towards his ever-moving mouth.

He fastened on to her clit and sucked, hard, flicking her with his tongue as he did.

It pushed her over the edge, off the other side and down into the longest orgasm she could ever remember having. Her body shivered and shook for endless hours, or perhaps moments, she didn't know.

In fact, she probably lost consciousness for a few moments, because the next thing she knew, a hard cock was sliding through her trembling cunt and burying itself next to her womb.

Nerin had come home.

Chapter Nine

The town of Kushuk woke at dawn, ready to face a new year. The ceremonies, rites and festivities of the season had passed, and it was time to get back to the rather mundane business of living.

In two of the temples, however, life was anything but mundane.

"Are you sure?"

Enshilla had summoned Ronnil before first light, as soon as her Priestess had arrived, tired and dusty, from her trip to Akkad. Ronnil, who had spent a rather miserable night in his own temple thanks to a late meeting with some visiting traders, had come at a run.

Enshilla nodded her answer to Ronnil's question. "She came directly to me not an hour ago. She saw the boats being prepared and the servants loading up the supplies. It's definite. The Utta of Akkad is on the move and on the river."

Ronnil chewed his lip, thinking rapidly, but said nothing.

"It can only mean she's heard something, Ronnil. I doubt that she's headed out for a pleasure cruise, not at this time of year. In fact, she'd have to be pretty desperate to brave going *anywhere* on the river at this time of year."

"Agreed. We'll have to assume she's headed here. If your Priestess left yesterday morning, that gives us hours, at most a day, before her barge arrives."

Ronnil whirled and strode from the chamber, Enshilla right behind him.

"And we are going to do what?"

Ronnil slowed his steps.

"Warn Nerin at once. Then, it's time to make a few plans of our own. I don't think I like this Queen very much. I'll be willing to wager her people don't, either. Perhaps that will come in handy..."

* * * * *

The hubbub outside the house of Nerin of Kushuk woke those inside just as daylight began to chase the shadows of night from the fields.

Karrina, held safe and warm against a strongly beating heart, ignored it. She cuddled into a hard chest, and enjoyed the softness of his bed beneath them. She couldn't remember when he'd carried her inside, so tired was she from their loving. There was no need for her to move, or to think, or to worry. For once, she was going to simply enjoy the moment of waking next to her lover, clasped tight to his body, and with his cock lengthening against her buttocks.

She grinned. He was awake too.

With a smile on her lips she turned in his arms. "Good day to you, Nerin of Kushuk." She slid her hand down his abdomen to his stiffening erection. "And greetings to your friend here, too."

His eyelids opened a fraction, and she could see the lazy glitter of brown eyes as his face tensed with desire.

He allowed her to fondle him, breathing a little more rapidly as she traced her way delicately around his balls and between his legs.

"It would appear that we need to celebrate each morning with our own fertility ritual..." His words hissed through taut lips and before she knew it he'd flipped her onto her back.

She spread her legs in welcome and sighed with pleasure as he slid deep into her sleepy warm cunt. Their loving the night before had left her pliant and sticky, and she relished the gentle friction his cock was generating on her sensitive inner flesh.

Scarcely daring to breathe, she watched as his head dropped, he took his weight on his hands and stared at their joining, watching the slippery satin of their flesh part and meet and part again.

She watched too, fascinated at the play of the morning light on their bodies, noticing how his muscles flexed as he raised and lowered himself to her cunt, and the intense concentration on his face.

By all the gods, how could she have known it was possible to love a man this much?

Aroused, needy, her body responded to Nerin's warmly passionate strokes, tightening in preparation for yet another orgasm from his amazing cock.

She could feel him tense too, balls hard now against her flesh.

Someone tapped at the door.

"Not. Now." The roar from Nerin took her by surprise and she opened her eyes to see him rear back as his climax took him.

Hers was unstoppable. Watching him clamp his mouth down on his yell of completion, she felt it travel back from his throat, down past his lungs and into his cock. The tremendous jolt he gave her needy flesh tipped her over into her own orgasm, but she didn't have enough control to restrain herself.

"Nerin..." Her scream echoed through the silence that had fallen outside the door.

They collapsed into a sweaty heap as the tapping on the door recommenced.

"What?"

Nerin snapped out the words, still trying to pull out of Karrina and cover her with a blanket at the same time. It was as if he didn't want another looking at her body. She smiled at this sign of possession.

"Lord, there is a messenger from the Temple of the Sun God. He says it is extremely urgent he speak with you."

The respectful tones sounded within the chamber, and the servant, whose eyes were firmly glued to the ceiling, waited for a response.

"Damn." Heedless of his own nakedness, or the shine of Karrina's juices still moistening his cock, Nerin left the bed.

"I will see him in the main chamber. Give me a few moments to dress."

The servant nodded and left, happy in the knowledge that this tale would get him an extra measure of Ishkar's fine beer that night if he was very lucky.

"Nerin?"

He turned to her, crossing to the bed and kissing her firmly on the lips. "I don't know what it is, but it must be important for Ronnil to send word at this hour." He kissed her again, lingeringly. "Damn, I want you again. I had planned to spend the day in bed with you, and forget all about work." He flashed her a quick grin that softened his features and melted her heart.

"Stay there. I'll be back as soon as I can."

Another quick kiss followed, then Nerin left the room.

Karrina rolled over, heart still thumping from his lovemaking and his kisses. She was happy, scared, sated and aroused all at once, and wondered why she didn't have a headache to go along with all these emotions rioting through her.

Closing her eyes, she offered up a small prayer to the gods. She prayed that she could make Nerin happy and whole again, unafraid to love. She prayed that they would be able to find a way out of the tangle they were in, and spend many long years enjoying each other.

And she prayed that he'd get back soon, so that she could fuck him some more.

Her last prayer was answered before too many minutes had passed, but the expression on his face as he came back into the chamber told her that fucking probably wasn't on the list of things that lay ahead that morning.

"Bad news. The Utta of Akkad is on the river."

Karrina sat up, face ashen. "She has found me."

"It looks possible. I'm sorry. Ronnil is preparing for her arrival as we speak. He will greet her, as High Priest of the Sun God. We will have to see what she says. Will you come with me? Shall we confront her together?"

Karrina gazed into his dark brown eyes, reading his worries for her there. She knew her own were reflecting her heart as she answered. "Yes, together, Nerin. Always together."

* * * * *

"Nerin has sent this for you to wear, Karrina."

Daria had entered the chamber as Karrina finished her bath. Soft blue folds of silk spilled over her arms and the glitter of gold flashed beneath.

"He asks that you honor him by wearing the robes of his future wife."

She gasped.

Daria's smile almost split her face in two, and dropping her bundle on the mussed bed, she rushed over to hug Karrina tightly.

"Oh, my dear girl, I couldn't be more excited. I had despaired of Nerin ever being happy. Yet here he is sending you the finest silks and even smiling at one of the field workers this morning. The whole house is abuzz."

Karrina stared at Daria, still tongue-tied.

"I...he...future..." she stuttered incoherently.

Daria chuckled. "Come on, now. Let's make you gorgeous for him. I understand there's some important people visiting and he wants you to make a good impression."

A shiver ran down Karrina's spine as the reality of her situation tumbled back onto her shoulders.

"Oh my. Well, then, yes. Let's get on with it."

She slipped into the silk skirt and placed the matching belt low on her hips. A long length of the same fabric was draped across one shoulder and tucked neatly back upon itself, covering most of her breasts as was customary for a woman chosen as mate.

Her nipples hardened and protruded through the silk as she thought of what being Nerin's mate entailed. She wriggled as Daria was brushing her hair.

"Now, now, none of that. Keep your honey in its pot for the time being."

Karrina blushed.

Daria grinned. "The whole house is also buzzing about the sounds that woke them several times during the night."

Karrina didn't know whether she was supposed to be embarrassed or proud. She settled for mildly humiliated and closed her eyes.

A tug on a braid made her open them again.

"No need to feel uncomfortable. Our Nerin is a lusty man. You are the woman who has caught his cock in your pussy. We're all very happy that the sounds of joy are finally echoing through these rooms. And that Nerin is taking you anywhere and everywhere, too. That's another of his rules gone down the river. And by the way, how was the threshing barn yesterday?"

"Daria." Karrina was beet red.

"Never mind, child. What happens between two people who love each other should never be a cause for embarrassment. A cause for pride and boastfulness, yes. A cause for sighs and yearnings, that too. But when two people join their bodies for pleasure and desire and fulfillment—aah, that's the best moment of all."

"Love? Nerin has not said he loves me, Daria…" The words slipped out, trembling in the air between the two women.

Daria snorted. "Take it from me, Karrina. I have known Nerin since he was a wee one. He's head over ziggurat in love with you. He can see no other woman, think of nothing but your sweet cunt, trips over his words and shuffles his hard cock beneath his robes when he thinks nobody's watching."

Karrina gurgled with laughter at Daria's blunt assessment. "Really?"

"Really. He's never even been able to remember a woman's name for more than a day after he's fucked her. Now, all of a sudden, it's 'do you think Karrina would like this?' or 'I cannot spend more time on this matter, I have other things needing my attention'. And seeing as he was hard as a rock at the time, it was pretty obvious what those 'other things' might be."

Karrina winced slightly as a gold decoration caught in her hair. "I hope you're right, Daria. My heart tells me you are, but my mind would feel better if I heard the words from his lips."

Daria paused in her work. "Sometimes, Karrina, a man will tell you things with words, other times with actions. Someone like Nerin, a man who has been so badly hurt in the past, and who is so scared of ever feeling that pain again, might never use the words. But what he does will speak for him. Don't forget that in your desire to hear him say how he feels."

Karrina nodded. "Daria, you are a wise woman. Thank you." She smiled up at the older woman, whose eyes misted over with affection.

"You're good for him, and in that respect you're good for us too. Make us proud of both of you?"

She put down the brush she'd been holding and stepped back, indicating that she was done.

Karrina stood, taking a deep breath. Today would be the test of her strength, her courage and her newfound love for Nerin.

She prayed that she would pass the test.

Chapter Ten

The Queen of Akkad arrived in Kushuk early that afternoon.

Nerin had spent most of the morning talking with Ronnil and Enshilla, going over the laws and customs of both Sumerians and Akkadians, finding common ground, areas where there might be problems, and pondering the advisability of sending to Ur for help from their trained diplomats.

"It would probably be the best idea, Ronnil," encouraged Enshilla, worried that Ronnil would bear the burden for these events.

"If we had time, I wouldn't hesitate." He squeezed her hand. "But we don't have time. And perhaps our simple ways will lure this woman into overstepping her authority. Making a mistake. Underestimating us."

Nerin nodded. "The High Priest has a point, Lady Enshilla. What we have to do is keep Karrina out of her hands, but do it within the laws that govern both our countries. It will not be easy defying a queen, but both Akkad and Sumer have made a point of saying the law applies to all. This is our chance to prove what we stand for."

"And we're not above a little delicate footwork to achieve our goals, either," grinned Ronnil, thinking over some of the strategies they'd discussed.

"Our greatest strength is our desire for peace between our lands." Nerin had wholeheartedly agreed with Ronnil on this point. "If she does not support this goal, then she will be going against both sets of leaders, of priests, of politicians and diplomats. I doubt she would be that foolish."

Enshilla gave a little shiver. "I cannot tell. From Karrina's tale, she could well be that foolish, and stubborn as well. She sounded a little mad to me. Any woman who could treat a daughter like that..."

Enshilla's gaze dropped and her hand moved in a slight gesture to her belly. Her robes were full, the midnight blue of the Moon Goddess, and folded softly around her.

Nerin flashed a quick glance at Ronnil, unable to mistake the look on Enshilla's face.

Ronnil's eyes gleamed. "Yes, my friend. We have been blessed. But we have not told anyone as yet. May I ask you to keep our confidence?"

A rare smile curved across Nerin's mouth. "I rejoice for you both. May I hope that I too will receive your best wishes before too much longer? Karrina will be my wife before this day is out if I have my way, and she'll be carrying my child before the next harvest."

Enshilla smiled back at Nerin.

"If I have to work night and day to get the job done."

Ronnil let out a crack of laughter and Enshilla blushed as she too grinned. "We have much to be happy about, let's hope that the end of this day will find us all able to enjoy it."

They parted, knowing that their next meeting would be an eventful one.

* * * * *

The water was flowing rapidly today, Nerin realized, as he stood quietly on the bank at the head of a small entourage.

Several times he'd had to step back as a splash threatened to wash over the small pier on which he stood, slightly behind Ronnil. The rains of the past few weeks had doubtless fallen as snow in the far off mountains, and before too long they could expect the floods that would prepare their fields for another fine year of crops.

It was the natural order of things, this flood and growth cycle, and was a part of Nerin's very being. Yet he could not help the fanciful feeling that today the river was irritated, anxious, driven to reach its goals by a pounding and swelling somewhere upstream.

Even the pendant on his chest was cool to his touch. He'd hoped Karrina would wear it, but she'd refused, saying it was her gift to him and belonged on his chest this day. It was all she had to give.

He clenched his jaw against the emotions that welled up inside him. She'd given him everything. The gods had better make sure he had chance to return the favor. This time, he would not lose her. If the worst came to pass, he would follow her into the afterlife, for there would be no life left for him here without her.

He folded his arms and stared implacably upstream.

Ronnil was engaged in low conversation with another of his priests and Nerin felt the pier rock as the man raised an arm and pointed.

The dim sunshine was glinting off something, something that was moving toward them.

It was a flotilla of barges.

The Queen of Akkad had arrived.

There were six impressive barges. The first carried the Queen's Guard, a dozen huge men armed to the teeth with bows and shining daggers. Their shields hung along the sides of the barge reflecting rainbows into the eyes of the watchers.

This was followed by a line, three abreast, with the Queen's barge in the center.

A figure stood alone on the prow, shining with gold from head to foot.

Nerin snorted at the vision she intended to present.

Dark hair swirled down her back past her buttocks, and was the one feature she'd probably shared with Karrina. Now, streaks of gray threaded from her temples down to her shoulders, and the luster that shone from his Karrina's head was no longer present in her mother.

As the barges neared, Nerin could see the Queen's eyes. Blue like her daughter, yes, but that was all. These eyes were an odd mixture of cold assessment and burning anger.

The hairs on his forearms stood up as he felt her gaze rest on the pendant. Within seconds warmth radiated from the jewel around his neck, as if it was fighting her stare with powers of its own.

She was clad in a gown of gold. A great collar covered her shoulders and swept over her breasts to end in a point just above her navel. It must have weighed as much as a sack of barley, thought Nerin, amazed that a woman would choose to wear such a burden. The intertwined reed and bulrush emblem of the upper lands of Akkad circled her head and she stood straight and unmoving as the barge was guided near the pier where the welcoming committee stood at respectful attention.

"Welcome to Kushuk, Queen of Akkad. We are honored by your presence."

Ronnil bowed formally, voicing the traditional words of welcome.

"The Queen of Akkad accepts the welcome of the people of Kushuk. She regrets any inconvenience her unannounced arrival has caused."

A courtier spoke from the barge beside the Queen, his accent slight, but distinct.

"It is never an inconvenience to greet visitors from the great land of Akkad, especially when it is their Queen," Ronnil responded respectfully.

"Get on with it," hissed Nerin, trying not to fidget.

"Ssshh…"

"The Queen is here on a matter of personal business rather than Akkad interests, High Priest."

"How may we be of service to Her Majesty?"

"It has come to her attention that a slave recently stole a valuable artifact from the treasury of the House Ishalla. Word that the artifact has been seen here in Kushuk made its way to the Queen's ears."

The Queen's face registered no expression whatsoever. Neither did her gaze betray by one flicker that the "artifact" was resting comfortably on the chest of the largest man present.

"She looks with disfavor on any who betray her trust and that of the people of Akkad. Like you, we pride ourselves on our fair and equitable laws and their enforcement. The Queen asks that the runaway slave be returned to her along with her property."

"Are you sure that the slave was reported to be in the Kushuk vicinity?"

Ronnil was clearly playing for time. The Queen's request had been placed in polite terms and was going to be difficult to counter.

"Our information is reliable. Yes, we are sure that the slave is in this vicinity."

"And you say this artifact was stolen from the House Ishalla?"

The Queen moved slightly, turning her vicious gaze on Ronnil. Her courtier continued for her. "It was stolen from my Lady herself."

"So this slave was in service to your Queen?"

"That is correct. Would you bring the slave here that we may return her to face the charges and pay the price for her crimes?"

"What penalty do you impose?"

"She stole from the Queen. That is cause for a lifetime of servitude in the Zagros mines. But she also escaped. For that there is only one punishment. She will be executed."

Nerin's jaw worked fiercely as he bit back his anger at this golden queen with a heart of stone.

Then he heard a mutter, and the barges rocked slightly as all aboard watched a small procession of women nearing the bank of the river.

At their head was Enshilla, elegant in her robes of the High Priestess of the Moon Goddess.

At her side was Karrina.

"My apologies, gracious lady, High Priest. We were unavoidably detained." Enshilla's elegant tones slid across the water and echoed into the silence that had fallen over the barges.

Karrina felt naked, exposed, and scared to death. She drew strength from the man who stood in front of her. He'd not turned to watch her, but she knew he was aware of her presence.

Enshilla moved to stand next to Ronnil and as she did, Nerin extended his arm and hand behind him.

The invitation was unmistakable.

With a lift of her chin, Karrina stepped forward and took his hand in hers. He drew her to his side, where she belonged.

Together, they faced the Queen.

"The High Priestess of the Moon Goddess, your Majesty. Here to do you honor..." Ronnil gestured at Enshilla who bowed her head respectfully. "And allow me the privilege of making known to you one of our leading citizens, Nerin of Kushuk. And his wife, Karrina."

A murmur flew through the ranks of the Queen's servants and handmaidens.

At last a sound was surprised from her lips and she hissed as she met the blank gaze of Nerin and the cautious blue eyes of his wife, her daughter Karrina.

She stepped down from the dais and moved to the edge of her barge.

"I am surprised, High Priest, that you permit your citizens to marry indiscriminately."

Her voice was harsh, not in keeping with her dignified appearance.

"Our citizens, Lady, are *permitted* to marry where they will."

The Queen's eyes raked Karrina's face and body, observing the elegant silks that swathed her slender form and the gold jewels dangling from her black tresses. One young breast was bared to the light, and she stood proud and tall like the princess she knew she was.

"We have more care of our bloodlines than you do, obviously. Letting a leading citizen fuck a whore like that would be punishable by torture in my court. Let alone marrying her and possibly getting a child off her."

The Sumerians gasped and Karrina flinched, but steadied as Nerin's hand pressed her tight to his strength.

They knew it was going to be hard. She just didn't know how hard it would be to hear her own mother vilify her to the man she loved.

"The Lady Karrina is Nerin's choice as bride. We have welcomed her to Kushuk as is our right." Ronnil's voice had toughened and he was no longer the polite diplomat. Now he was a man defending his people and a woman maligned wrongly. Enshilla took a step closer to him, as if trying to bolster his courage with her own.

"Strange." The word echoed from the Queen's lips. A slight tremble made the gold decorations on her gown shiver. It was the only outward sign that she was experiencing any kind of emotion.

"Your lady Karrina strongly resembles the slave that stole from me and then escaped. Is this marriage of recent date?"

"It is, Lady," Nerin answered, his voice ringing strong and clear across the water.

"Then perhaps she came to you under false pretenses. Perhaps she still bears the mark of a slave. Should we request that she show us her ankle? Surely there will be no harm in such a gesture?"

Nerin's hand tightened on Karrina's, but she squeezed back.

"I am honored to receive the attention of such a gracious queen," said Karrina calmly. "Unfortunately, an error has been made and your informers brought you news that is false. I am no runaway slave. I am the wife of Nerin of Kushuk."

"Prove it." The Queen spat the command at Karrina.

"I see no reason for me to prove any such thing."

"Because I *demand*...because I *request* your cooperation." The Queen caught her anger before it betrayed her. "As a representative of a neighboring land, we must work together to achieve our goals, must we not?"

Karrina faltered, intimidated by her mother's vitriolic stare as much as her words. But the warmth of Nerin's body next to hers renewed her strength. "I must consult with my husband, Lady."

She half turned away from the Queen's barge under the pretext of speaking to Nerin.

"You. High Priest." The Queen's tone was sharp. "Tell this bitc...woman to obey me."

"Our citizens are free, Lady. Kushuk has no slaves, only those who are willing to work at a variety of jobs for a fair wage. We can ask, we can suggest, and we can certainly enforce our laws. None of which require our citizens to bare portions of their body at another's request. Even if she is a queen."

Rebuked, the Queen's gaze hardened and she shed her diplomacy like a dirty glove.

"It is her, you idiot. You think I don't know my own..."

"Your own what, Lady?"

The Queen paled, realizing her temper had brought her to within inches of revealing herself.

"A slave from my own palace. She is the slave who stole from me. That wanton bitch sliding over the great idiot's body. She's the one. There's no doubt."

Nerin straightened away from Karrina and turned to see the archers from the Queen's guard readying their bows and aiming them at Karrina. He stepped in front of her.

She stepped out and stood next to him.

"Get behind me, dammit."

"No."

"Karrina…"

"We said we'd face this together. And we shall. Don't argue with me on this Nerin. I love you too much to let you do this alone."

Nerin looked down at Karrina, brown eyes meeting blue. Her love for him was pulsing through her like a chime from a gong.

"I love you too."

His words stunned her, and she wanted nothing more than to jump on him, and bury him deep inside her. And fuck him over and over again, making him say those words endlessly.

With a smothered gulp, she turned back to the river. "You pick the damnedesttime to tell me things like that," she hissed out of the side of her mouth. "Wait 'til I get you alone."

"All right, but make it quick…" The fact that there was a laugh underlying the answering whisper gave Karrina all the courage she needed. That and the fact that she could detect a solid bulge taking shape under Nerin's formal robe.

She addressed the Queen. "I consider myself under no obligation to you, Lady, although I recognize your rank and pay homage to it. I'm sure your country and your *family* recognize their good fortune in having you as their head." Karrina couldn't resist the little dig.

The Queen's eyes narrowed.

"However, as a gesture of goodwill, I am happy to present my ankles for your inspection."

She raised the hem of her sky blue silk skirt and twirled around making them fly around her calves.

There was no mark on her creamy skin.

The Queen gasped.

"You…you…bitch. Trickery. It is you. That hulking mountain next to you wears my jewel, you whore."

The Queen's rage shook the barge and the sun dimmed as clouds scudded across the sky. A chill wind stirred the robes of those standing on the bank and the barges rocked as the water roughened.

"This woman is your slave? How can that be?" Ronnil asked the question innocently enough, but clearly with the intent of distracting her attention.

"I have many slaves. But this one I remember. She's the one who stole that pendant. She has hidden the brand, I don't know how, but she has. I demand you return her to me. Or let her pay the price, here and now."

Her hand gestured to her archers who strung their bows and aimed their arrows at Karrina.

"Lady, realize this. If your guards kill the wife of Nerin of Kushuk, it may well be interpreted as an attack upon our citizens. Such an action would not be viewed lightly in Ur."

The Queen froze.

Ronnil had been absolutely right, realized Karrina. Would she go so far as to precipitate war between the two lands over something as silly as a girl and a necklace?

Then the Queen's eyes narrowed. "You are wise, High Priest." She turned and her archers lowered their bows. One approached his mistress at her command.

"My guards must not be used in this matter. It is personal, and as such I must take responsibility for my actions."

Before the stunned gaze of her entourage, the citizens of Kushuk standing on the banks, and the assembled Priests and Priestesses, the Queen reached down to the waist of the guard and grabbed hold of the ornate dagger he wore at his belt.

Without a second thought she flung it with all her strength at Karrina.

Chapter Eleven

"Nooooo…"

The scream had scarcely left Enshilla's mouth when events began to blur for Karrina.

She could see the dagger shining as it flew towards her breast, but then her vision was blocked as she was roughly pushed aside.

She shouted as she realized that Nerin had thrust himself into the path of the knife with a speed that was beyond belief.

There was an odd clunking sound, and she waited, heart pounding, for Nerin to fall. He could not possibly have escaped the lethal blade.

But he stood, silent, and she carefully regained her feet, scared to look at him, afraid she'd see his life's blood pouring down his chest.

He didn't move, so she finally touched his arm. It was still warm. Tense, taut and rigid with emotion, but warm.

Cautiously she moved in front of him, noting the silence that had fallen.

He was staring at the pendant on his chest. A small dent had appeared in the gold tracery around the central jewel.

"It bounced off," he said, dazed. "The dagger hit the pendant and just…bounced…off…"

His eyes met Karrina's and she saw his love for her come swimming to the surface. He'd offered his life for her.

"Don't *ever* do that again," she sobbed, losing her composure.

Strong arms pulled her close, binding her to him with a grip of stone.

"Don't worry, I won't," he muttered, head buried in her hair.

"I think it is time you left my town, *Lady...*" bit out Ronnil, angrier than he had ever been in his entire life. "You nearly killed one of our most prominent citizens. The penalty for murder is severe. It does not distinguish rank. Leave now, or I will impose that penalty myself. With pleasure."

Enshilla stepped to his side, silently adding her voice to his.

Thus confronted, the Queen backed down, shaking with rage but defeated.

She turned to order her slaves to move the barges when a voice sounded from across the river.

"Hold."

Heads turned and people muttered, trying to see who had spoken.

A young man emerged from the reeds, accompanied by two large warriors and an aged priest.

"Rabi..." The breath seemed to drain from Karrina's lungs only to return in a huge gasp. "*Rabi...*"

She wrenched her hand from Nerin's and ran to the very edge of the river, dancing around to avoid the rough waves that were now splashing the very top of the bank.

"Rabi...I'm here..."

The young man waved and grinned and shouted her name. "Karrina, love. Yes, it's me."

Nerin's face had paled and those around him stepped prudently back a pace or two. But within seconds a smile lit his eyes. The black hair and blue eyes of the stranger were a giveaway. This was her brother.

This was the new King of Akkad.

A growl from the river brought everyone's attention back to the Queen. Her lips were puckered, her face frowning and her whole body shaking.

She watched as one of her barges quickly ferried the young man across the river and into the welcoming arms of his sister.

"Rabi," sobbed Karrina, beside herself with emotion. "I thought you might be dead, I dared not hope…"

"Ssshh…I'm alive, we're alive. Karrina, hush. It's going to be all right now."

She felt his arms hugging her tight, so tight she thought her ribs were about to crack and gasped out a laugh through her tears.

"It won't be if you break a bone."

He released her and looked at Nerin. "Suppose you introduce me to your husband?"

Karrina looked a little self-conscious. "Ah, yes. Nerin of Kushuk, this is my brother, Rabi."

Nerin bowed his head politely. "I think you mean the King of Akkad, Karrina," he corrected.

"Ooops. Sorry, Rabi. Yes, I do mean the King of Akkad. But to me, he's still Rabi, my brother."

"As you are always my sister. Greetings to you, Nerin of Kushuk. I saw you take that blade for Karrina. If I had had any questions about my sister's choice of a mate they would all have been answered in that moment."

With his arm still around Karrina, Rabi turned to the river where the Queen's Guard was now looking hesitantly around. Who was their true leader? To whom should they be looking to for allegiance?

The Queen had turned a mottled shade of red, rage and caution fighting in her expression.

Rabi straightened his shoulders and stared at the guard. As one, they fell to their knees and bowed before him.

Rabi had truly become the King. Karrina rejoiced, although the knowledge would add to his burdens and keep them apart.

His companions behind him, his sister and her husband on one side, and what was now *his* guard on their knees before him, Rabi finally looked at his mother.

"Queen of Akkad."

Her eyes fixed on him, but Karrina couldn't even tell if she saw him. Some kind of madness was upon her, turning her face gaunt and her mouth to a pinched line of flesh.

"You have behaved disgracefully and dishonored the House of Ishalla, not to mention threatened the entire land of Akkad. Our father..." His voice caught for a moment, then strengthened. "Our father was ever a wise man. It was he who placed my life in the care of these companions, and he who is responsible for my safety. The man you buried not so long ago and professed to mourn suspected your motives. If you did, as I believe, hasten his journey to the next world, then know this. He's laughing at you now."

She remained rigid and unmoving, letting her son's words wash over her with all the fury of the waters surging beneath her barge.

"You are henceforth disgraced and banished. I cannot, in all fairness, have the Queen of Akkad executed, even though I think there may be some who would be only too willing to draw the bow. You are spared with your life. You may take no courtiers, servants or slaves. You may have two companions if you can find someone who wishes to accompany you."

The ex-Queen of Akkad shuddered once. "Do you expect me to starve?"

"I do not care."

"Rabi..." Karrina's voice came softly over the wind. "We are better than she is, Rabi. Let's remember that."

Nerin pressed her close to his side in comfort.

"I have a suggestion, if you will agree." She reached to Nerin's neck and undid the clasp on the pendant. She handed it to Rabi. "This brought Nerin and I together and helped us find love. Perhaps the good it can do will rub off on her. Let her take it. It has served its purpose."

"Will your brother not need it?" Nerin's brows drew together slightly, as if he hated to see it go.

Rabi chuckled. "I have a feeling my true love won't be influenced by a pendant. Rubbishy story, anyway."

Nerin and Karrina exchanged glances. She couldn't tell Rabi how well it worked. Some things were not meant for brother and sister to share.

"Very well." Rabi turned to the barge where the woman waited his verdict. "You shall leave disgraced and forbidden to ever return to these lands. But you shall not leave completely destitute. Here…"

He flung the necklace out over the roiling waters towards the ex-Queen of Akkad.

His aim was true, but the necklace apparently had other ideas.

It arced into a beam of sunlight, then suddenly dipped and twisted, out of the grasp of the woman whose hand had greedily reached out to catch it.

She snarled and grabbed at the chain.

A large surge of water rocked the boat just at that same moment.

Her balance was shifted, her foot slipped, and the dark haired woman who had wanted nothing but power became nothing but a ripple in the fast running river as she toppled in with a shout and a splash, the necklace grasped in her flailing hand.

The massive gold collar dragged her down into the depths of the fast running water and acted as a magnet for the strong current.

Before the horrified eyes of the crowd on the bank, her body was pushed downriver, picking up speed as the flood waters continued to rise. Mere seconds passed and she was nothing more than a glint of gold as the River Goddess tossed her victim around and then pulled her beneath the surface once again.

She never reappeared.

The necklace had claimed its just revenge.

Stunned, Karrina reached for Nerin's hand. "By the gods..." she breathed, still watching the river as it widened and took her mother's lifeless body with it.

"Karrina..." Nerin pulled her close against him.

"I feel sad, isn't that funny? After everything she did, the people she killed, the fact that she would have killed Rabi and me...I still feel sad."

Rabi looked at his sister. "It's not funny, Karri, it's human. You're human. She...well, I don't think there was very much humanity in her. Ever."

Nerin glanced at the young King with approving eyes, noticing much the same expression in Ronnil's as he and Enshilla approached the small group.

"Lord, I don't know what to say."

Rabi extended his hand. "Say 'Welcome', High Priest. I would stay here for a little time, with your permission. Messengers must be sent back to Akkad with news of what happened here today. And I must get ready to assume my place there. But for a couple of days let me stay, please? Let me get to know you and your citizens, and this man my sister seems to be attached to..."

Karrina blushed at her brother's teasing, and thrilled that Ronnil was shaking his hand and introducing Enshilla.

She knew her instincts had served her well—her brother was going to make a great king.

"And perhaps attend our marriage?" Nerin's voice cut quietly through the babble.

"You aren't...I thought you said..."

Karrina giggled. "A little distraction, brother mine. We anticipated the event by a few hours, that's all."

"Which reminds me, soon-to-be-mate, how did you remove the brand?"

"I didn't." Karrina laughed again at the puzzled looks on the faces of those around her. "Thank Daria, Jana and some of your kitchen servants, Nerin."

She held up what looked from a distance to be a pristine ankle.

Close up, however, a slightly bumpy patch was evident. "A little honey, some barley meal, and the juice of a pomegranate or two, and we had a very nice soft paste. It looked just close enough to my skin color to cover the mark. At least from a distance anyway. And it worked."

She put her foot back on the ground and grinned cheerfully at them. "In fact, Daria was rather excited at the possibilities. Last I saw she was off to the marketplace with a pot full, muttering about stretched bellies and mating rituals."

A general laugh greeted this statement and Ronnil politely ushered Rabi toward the path to Kushuk.

"So, may I call you your Majesty? How would you like to be introduced?"

"For now, please just call me Rabi. I'll be stuck with my royal title for the rest of my life so I'd like to just be plain Rabi for as long as I can." The engaging young man smiled, his grin embracing both Ronnil and Enshilla.

"King Rabi," mused Enshilla. "It is an unusual name for a king."

"Well, yes, but I'll probably have to use my full name. Rabi is the nickname Karrina gave me when we were children."

"And so you will be…" prompted Ronnil.

"Hammurabi. King Hammurabi. Awful mouthful, isn't it?"

"Oh I don't know," considered Ronnil thoughtfully as they walked away. "It has a good ring to it."

* * * * *

Nerin pulled Karrina aside when she would have followed the crowd back to town. The barges were dispersing, some back to Akkad with news, the rest tying up alongside the piers to accompany their new King during his last few days of freedom.

"Now, woman, we have something to settle between us."

His cock was rising hard against her belly, giving her a pretty good idea of what was between them.

She audaciously reached down and grabbed his length through the silks of his robe.

"Does this have anything to do with it?" She dragged the silk over him, slowly, teasingly.

He gritted his teeth. "It will do, in about two seconds. But first, I just want to hear from your own lips that you will pledge your life to mine. You'll have to give up being a royal princess..."

Did she realize how much those words cost him? To ask her to be with him forever, rather than insist? To take the chance, however remote, that she would say no and once again smash his life to shards of pain?

Her eyes told him she understood.

"Nerin, from the moment you dragged me onto the riverbank, my life has been yours. Your touch reached my heart even as your fist whacked my chin..."

He caressed her cheek, running his fingers over her jaw and dropping kisses where he'd bruised her.

She arched nearer. "I cannot imagine living as a royal princess. I don't want to live as a royal princess. I want only to live as your woman. Your mate. I want my life and your life to become one life. I want your children, I want your thoughts. I want your cock. Soon. In fact, this very minute would be just about right."

Her hand tightened on him and his lips peeled back from his teeth as she squeezed.

He dragged her off the path and behind a large bank of wild grasses. The voices faded in the distance and within moments there was no sound but the calling of the river birds and the rush of the waters.

Within seconds her clothes were gone and his but a memory. Seconds later and he was buried to the hilt inside her.

"Did I hurt you?"

"How could you hurt me? I wanted you so badly all I could think about was if you'd been killed I'd never know *this* again."

She raised her hips and took him even deeper, and his heart hammered as he felt the head of his cock snug up to her womb. It was a heady experience and he could tell she was aware of it.

Their eyes locked as he moved, pulling back then sinking deep again. The grasses tickled their bodies and the sun broke through the clouds to shine down on their naked skin.

Her slick body gripped and slid over his cock, caressing, loving, holding and releasing in an internal dance that sent lights flashing through his brain.

"Mine, Karrina. Mine…" His words pounded with his hips, erupting on a gust of breath forced from his heaving lungs.

"Always, Nerin. Always and forever…" She held his gaze, refusing to miss a moment of this experience.

He rolled suddenly, taking her with him, and looked up, seeing her black hair flying and her face blushing pink against the deep blue of the sky above her.

His heart swelled at the beauty and the love hanging over him.

He felt his body shudder and tightened his grip on Karrina's hips as she too began to come.

Their shouts mingled, their juices blended into one. Nerin spurted deeper into Karrina then he had imagined possible, and her cunt milked him for more.

Finally, she toppled onto his chest with an exhausted grunt, holding his softening cock tight with internal muscles that asserted their ownership of his body.

"I love you, Nerin of Kushuk." Soft lips dropped a kiss on his.

"I love you too, Karrina of Kushuk."

Epilogue

"And the wicked queen was never seen again, right Father?"

The young voice excitedly finished the story as his mother sat quietly in the sunshine.

"That is absolutely correct, young Kyall," said Ronnil, grinning at his son.

"But what about her gold collar, and the magic necklace?"

Enshilla raised her eyebrows. "Ah the greed of the young..."

Ronnil chuckled. "The large gold collar was washed up several miles downstream of here, a couple of years ago. It was returned to Akkad, where your Uncle Rabi put it in the Royal Treasury. No one wears it now."

"Not even Uncle Rabi?"

"No. Not even Uncle Rabi."

"And the magic necklace?"

"Ah yes, the magic necklace. That has never been found, Kyall. Some say the wicked queen took it to the afterlife with her. It is more likely to have been washed a long way downstream. Maybe even to the mighty sea that ends our lands."

Wide eyes listened to the end of the tale, heedless of the fact that another man had entered. Then a cough distracted the child.

"Uncle Rabi...Uncle Rabi..."

King Hammurabi of Akkad grinned and pounced on his nephew-by-choice. "Hello, young Kyall. Are you being a good fellow for your poor parents?"

He tossed the squealing child upside down and tickled him, bringing gales of laughter from Kyall and smiles to the lips of his parents.

"No, Enshilla, don't get up. I'm here informally today. It seems I can't get enough of your husband's wise ideas. After a play with this young man here, I need to pick his brains on that irrigation project we were discussing last month."

Enshilla nodded, easing her bulk back down onto her seat. Carrying a third child was wearing, and she'd determined this would be their last. But how she loved them. Well, maybe one more.

A wail from the corner alerted her to the fact that little Annilin was ready for her meal.

She rose again and watched as her son followed the two men from the room.

"Are you going to build a new dam, Uncle Rabi?"

"It's one of your father's ideas that we're discussing, Kyall."

"I 'spect he got it from that special Priest of the Sun God," said Kyall wisely. "Did Father ever tell you about him, and his white haired woman…?"

About the author:

Born and raised in England not far from Jane Austen's home, reading historical romances came naturally to Ms. Kelly, followed by writing them under the name of Sarah Fairchilde. Previously published by Zebra/Kensington, Ms. Kelly found a new love - romanticas! Happily married for almost twenty years, Sahara is thrilled to be part of the Ellora's Cave family of talented writers. She notes that her husband and teenage son are a bit stunned at her latest endeavor, but are learning to co-exist with the rather unusual assortment of reference books and sites!

Sahara welcomes mail from readers. You can write to her c/o Ellora's Cave Publishing at 1056 Home Avenue, Akron OH 44310-3502.

Also by Sahara Kelly:

Zayed's Gift

Ann Jacobs

Prologue

"We'll be landing at Andrews at thirteen hundred hours, Captain Shearer." Like all the noncoms who'd regarded him as though he were a sideshow freak in the week since he'd begun his trip back to official life from "killed in action," the steward on this sleek VIP-outfitted T-43 treated Brian with a kind of distant respect. The deferential attitude didn't sit right with him.

Hell, they'd just pinned captain's bars on his shoulders yesterday at Ramstein. And handed him dress blues for the dog-and-pony show that apparently awaited him at Andrews.

Hail the conquering hero.

Only Brian didn't feel very heroic. After all, he'd gotten himself shot out of his airplane and captured, and he owed his escape after eleven long years not to any cleverness of his own but to his fellow prisoner's ingenuity and an old man's dead-eye shooting in the desert firefight that had followed the escape.

Zayed.

Brian would never forget the venerable Marsh Arab who'd died the first night of their deliverance from the Butcher of Baghdad. Brian pulled out the hauntingly beautiful pendant that had been Zayed's dying legacy and studied it as the plane began its final approach.

It was a unique piece of Middle Eastern art—of history, he supposed. His only souvenir of his eleven-year vacation in hell, unless he wanted to count scars, which he didn't. The sky-blue, hauntingly beautiful eye stared up at him from its ornate, exotic-looking setting.

It was then he noticed th flaw. Glistening almost like a diamond in the pearl-like white of the eye, what looked like a tear held his attention.

Had it always been there for him to notice only now, when he was moments away from giving the necklace to his beloved Diane?

Or was the tear an optical illusion?

He had a sinking feeling that it wasn't when he stepped off the plane and didn't see her there.

* * * * *

The damn necklace somehow had foretold Brian's pain.

His anguish when he'd stepped off that plane. Heartbreak he'd had to hide while shaking the President's hand and accepting greetings from a long line of military brass whose faces all blurred into his sea of despair.

The final blow had come when the reception finally was over and a sad-faced Air Force chaplain had sat him down and broken the news. His bride, the woman he'd struggled to come back to for eleven agonizing years, had married another man two years after the Air Force had declared him dead. She had the children they'd once planned with a husband and father who wasn't him. And she'd apparently decided it would be too painful to see him now.

He lay on a lonely king-size bed in the bridal suite a five-star Washington hotel had provided him for his first night home—and he wondered how the hell he'd manage to go on. The agony, the torture. All he'd endured had been for nothing.

Brian Shearer was alive, but at the moment he wished he were dead. Because he no longer had the home and family he'd struggled to survive for so he could return.

* * * * *

Zayed was dead, but his ghost shed a tear for the young American pilot who had tried so valiantly to save his life and now was wondering whether he should end his own existence on earth.

The ghost's instinctual assessment as he'd lain there dying had been right. His young friend had yet to find his true soulmate.

At that moment, the ghost had vowed to forego the joys awaiting him in paradise until he'd imparted the secret of the pendant Brian now held and stared at as though it embodied his lost dreams...his despair...a future that no longer gave him incentive to live. Now he would have to stay earthbound until he was satisfied that his young friend would survive and find the one woman whose love would make him celebrate life again.

Chapter One

Galveston, Texas, a few weeks later

The incoming tide swept gently off the Gulf of Mexico, lapping at Brian's bare feet while he strolled on the deserted barrier island, along the same beach where he and Diane had first made love. Strange, that memory that had sustained him during his long imprisonment now seemed a lifetime ago.

He stared beyond the breakwater toward the rustic cottage on shore where he'd grown to manhood. His home, the place he'd returned to a thousand times in his lonely dreams.

No, it wasn't home. Not any more.

Damn it, he didn't have a home. Or a life worth living, either.

A pelican dived into the foaming water and came up with its fishy meal. Gulls flapped their wings overhead, in perpetual motion yet going nowhere.

Not unlike himself.

Beyond the island lay the two massive offshore rigs Jake Green had told Brian to look for when he came home. Those were the rigs he'd looked forward to working on when he'd still thought of Galveston as home. When he'd thought Diane would be waiting here for him.

Diane. He'd come here intending to confront her, to demand...hell, he didn't know what. One last tumble between the sheets for old times' sake?

For starters, he guessed. And a few minutes ago he'd been on the way to confront her and get that farewell fuck when he saw her from half a block away, a baby in her arms. She'd been waving goodbye to a smiling little girl while the kid clambered onto a school bus.

Brian had realized then that he couldn't disrupt that laughing child's life even if Diane were willing.

Seeing her with the children she'd made with another man had hammered home the fact that for her, life had gone on and left him far behind.

And that knowledge tore at him worse than the torture and deprivation he'd suffered at the hands of his Iraqi captors.

He paused, staring out at the aqua sea that had once been his source of peace. With a certain detachment, he recalled the hours he'd spent here as a kid, dreaming of soaring high above the water in a jet like the one he spied flying overhead.

Back then he'd wanted Diane. And he'd wanted to be a jet jock. Craved the excitement of flying his high-tech bird in combat while liberating the victims of a crazed dictator.

And later he'd thought he had it all.

Until a heat-seeking missile had found his F-15 and shot it out of the sky.

Shot him down into a hell that had no end.

A lone seagull landed at Brian's feet, its feathers damp with mist. It looked up, as if assessing him with beady eyes and finding no threat, no cause for caution.

He imagined it sensed that he was nothing but an empty shell. Impotent. As of the moment yesterday when he'd signed his discharge papers, he no longer even had the Air Force as an anchor.

"I could walk out into the Gulf and not come back," he said to his silent companion.

If he did there would be no one to miss him. Not Diane and her new family, and not his parents who'd died not long after his plane had gone down — according to their neighbors, because of their grief at losing him.

Fate had cheated Brian of grieving for them. Now was too long after the loss for that comforting ritual.

He soothed his pain by telling himself that if there was the heaven his preacher dad had promised in his sermons of long ago, he would join him and Mom there.

Or maybe not. *Only God can call us home*, he recalled Dad having said while condemning one of his flock who'd decided to join her husband of fifty years in death by swallowing a bottle of sleeping pills.

But what the fuck kind of god would have let him rot in prison for eleven years? And then resurrected him so he could watch his wife living happily with another man?

Damn. Brian's faith, once so strong, seemed to have deserted him. Strange, he thought, that it had survived the Iraqis' torture only to succumb to the bitter blows life had dealt him on his return.

A chilly wind came up suddenly from the south, cooling the air and churning the surf to a foamy froth.

Slowly, step by step, Brian moved into the surf. One step at a time.

Another step closer to the oblivion he sought.

Until a surreal presence grabbed his shoulders and dragged him back onto the dry, packed sand.

"You will find your paradise on earth, my young friend."

Whirling around at the sound of the eerie, heavily accented voice, Brian saw Zayed.

Or Zayed's ghost.

The old man's eyes glittered, black as night against the translucent paleness of his once-swarthy skin. His bright white desert robe and *ghutra* reflected the blinding rays of a noonday sun.

Brian blinked, then looked again. Was he hallucinating?

Or seeing a guardian angel? Certainly no angel he recalled seeing in the illustrated Bible stories of his youth looked like the wizened Marsh Arab.

Brian could not break the old man's hold, though he could not feel the weight of the hands that held him so securely.

"Let me go," he said.

"I cannot. You are the keeper of the necklace. I cannot allow its legend to drown with you in a foreign sea. Take it to its home, and it will lead you to your destiny."

"Home?" Surely the ghost didn't mean he should return to —

"Not to prison. To the land of our deliverance."

Kuwait? The ghost had to be insane. Brian tried to snap the chain that held the pendant around his neck but the fragile gold seemed to have developed the strength of tempered steel. "Here. Take your damn necklace. I don't want it," he said, lifting his hands behind his head and groping for the delicate clasp.

The ghost's bony fingers caught his arms, held him fast. "Let me go."

"You've survived to live, not die alone in an unforgiving sea. Come. I will tell you about the magic of the gift you would bury along with your future."

Drawn by a phantasmagoric power stronger than his own will, Brian let the apparition drag him to a deserted pavilion and shove him onto a wooden bench along its edge. The seagull followed, perching on the rough-hewn rail and staring at him with its beady eyes.

And as Zayed's ghost hovered before him, holding Brian's gaze despite his desperate need to look away, the pendant grew warm against his bare chest, almost as though it had taken on a life of its own.

"It is fitting that we talk here at the water's edge, for it was at the convergence of two ancient rivers that I found the necklace when I was a lad, younger than you are now. At first I thought it to be a costly trinket. I'd planned to sell it and buy rich possessions beyond my wildest dreams. But then, ere I could arrange transportation to Al Basrah to sell the piece, a wizened soothsayer came to me as if by magic

and told me how Fate had chosen me to hold and guard the ancient treasure.

"To partake of its magic and pass it along at the hour of my death to a man worthy of caring for it and passing along its legend. A legacy that began far off in another dimension before the necklace was brought to earth in ancient Sumeria only to be swept away centuries later in a great springtime flood of the Tigris and Euphrates Rivers. For a thousand years or more the great rivers held their prize until one day the chain became tangled in the rushes where the rivers converge and form the Shatt al Arab. Fate sent me fishing where I spied it covered with silt but for a bit of its bright gold chain that caught my eye.

"I never regretted the loss of what riches the necklace might have brought me, for it gave me something of far greater value. Years later, after my third wife had died leaving me with a newborn infant and my two young sons, I thought my grief would have no end. Fate had taken away three women I had loved. Sadly, I took a fourth wife, Fatima, for my children needed a mother.

"When months later I finally took Fatima to my couch and we shared a lover's embrace, the soothsayer's prediction came to pass. As he had said would happen when I embraced my true love, the tear in the eye of the necklace had faded away. I had found my soulmate, the woman with whom I shared the next fifty years in joy and passion."

When Brian glanced down at Zayed's gift, he saw the tear glistening against the creamy white of the eye. "I see the tear now," he said, reluctant to buy into the old man's incredible story.

"And there it will remain until you meet the woman who is your soulmate," said the ghost, hunkering down to meet Brian's gaze. *"At that time, when you embrace her with perfect, committed love in your heart, the tear will fade away only to return when the soul link between the two of you is broken by death. Contrary to what you believe now, this woman is in your future, not your past."*

* * * * *

By the time Brian traveled to Houston the following day to explain to his new employer that he couldn't take an assignment based out of Galveston, he was reconciled to living. Suicide had never been an option, aside from those few minutes before the ghost of the old Marsh Arab had materialized and drawn him back.

He'd have changed his mind anyway, he decided, trying as he did to convince himself that Zayed's ghost had been nothing but a figment of his imagination—a conscience, as it were, conjured up in his mind to convince him his life still had meaning. That he still had a future.

But Brian wasn't sure. Reaching into the open neck of his polo shirt, he pulled out Zayed's supposedly magical gift, felt its warmth on his palm. When he glanced at the sky-blue eye, he still saw the tear, sparkling like a diamond in the brilliant Texas sun.

The old man's words rang in Brian's ears. *The tear will go away when you embrace your soulmate.*

"Yeah, right." He tucked the pendant inside his collar as he pulled his rental car onto the street where Jake Green lived.

Texas royalty. That's what he'd heard Jake's family called since he was a kid. But the high-rise condo where Jake lived in Houston seemed pretty ordinary, except for the collection of high-priced foreign sports cars in the covered garage that took up the first two floors of the building. When Brian knocked on the door, he was greeted not by some servant but by Kate, Jake's pretty, pregnant wife whom he'd met during his brief stay in Kuwait.

"Come on in. You're just in time for lunch," she said, her soft drawl sounding more southern than Texan now that he'd become re-acclimated to the way Americans talked.

She looked puzzled, Brian thought as he followed her into a wide-open living area that reminded him a lot of the living room at the Washington hotel suite where the Air Force brass had put him up a couple of weeks earlier.

"Is something wrong?" he asked, wondering if he should have let *them know exactly when he'd be arriving from Galveston.*

"Of course not. I was hoping you'd have brought Diane along."

"I'd have had a hard time doing that. When they told her I was dead, Diane found herself another husband." Brian tried to soften the bitter words with a grin. "So I guess you'll have to settle for just me."

Jake stepped into the room and laid a hand on his wife's shoulder. "Sorry, man. I didn't think to tell Kate about the welcome-home surprise your wife sprung on you," he said, his jaw tight. Brian imagined Jake was itching to repeat the diatribe on faithless women that he'd delivered when they'd talked yesterday about a possible change of Brian's work assignment. "Come on, let's have lunch."

"Women. They're more trouble than they're worth. Present company excepted," Jake commented a little later, reaching over to stroke Kate's knee. "I understand you wanting to get the hell away from here and all the lousy memories. How about I send you back to Kuwait?"

"I'd appreciate it. No way can I—"

Jake held up a hand. "No need to explain. I've been pretty much where you are now. Trust me, the desert's not a bad place to come to grips with things. Besides, the manager of Jamil al Hassan's oilfield wants to come home now, and Jamil and Leila will be in the States for at least six more months while the docs revise her scars. If you'll go there, you'll save me from having to reshuffle a bunch of engineers."

Two beers, a huge meatball sub, and several phone calls later, Jake had reassigned Brian to replace the engineer in charge of maintaining wells in Jamil's oilfield.

"The field's between *Mina Su'ud* and *Al Wafrah*, near the Saudi and Iraqi borders," Jake explained when he pointed out the location on a large map he'd unrolled on the low table in front of the sofa. "Pretty isolated. But it should be fairly safe unless we go to war and Saddam decides to rain missiles down on every target within reach."

Brian couldn't care less where he was going or whether it was likely to be safe, as long as he could run from the memories he knew would eventually destroy him if he stayed in Texas. "I appreciate this, Jake."

"No problem. You're doing me a favor, if you want the truth. I need to bring Joe home, and I couldn't do it until I found an engineer who speaks passable Arabic. A lot of the workers in this field don't speak English."

"When do you want me there?"

Jake looked up from the map. "How soon can you go?"

"Sooner the better." Brian had nothing keeping him here. Nothing at all.

"If you mean that literally, you can leave tonight. There's an El Rashid Oil Company jet loading drilling equipment at Hobby Airport as we speak. It's outfitted for passengers as well as freight, and you're welcome to hitch a ride. If you can leave tonight."

"El Rashid?"

"Bear's family's company. GreenTex works with El Rashid on a lot of projects in the Middle East. And our big jet is out at Boeing for a major overhaul. You may as well enjoy the trip in solitary luxury instead of flying commercial." Jake rolled up the map, looked at Brian, and shot him a grin. "And I do mean luxury. Kate and I flew home on it last week."

* * * * *

Jake hadn't been joking, Brian thought a couple of hours later when he was stowing his duffel bag in one of the bedrooms in a Boeing 737. From what he'd seen, he guessed the aft part of the cabin had been modified to haul cargo. The remaining space, which would have held at least fifty passengers if it had seats like a commercial airliner, had been outfitted for a handful of guests to travel while enjoying all the comforts of a very luxurious home.

A smiling cabin attendant had inquired about his preferences in food and drink, and he'd seen two pilots board and disappear into the cockpit during their short conversation. Soon after the attendant asked him to buckle up for takeoff, he felt the vibration of the plane's engines. Moments later they were airborne.

Brian watched the darkening sky through a porthole, saying a silent farewell to Texas and the home he'd kept in his dreams for the years of his imprisonment. Maybe he'd take the attendant up on his offer of dinner later, but at the moment he wanted a nap.

Obviously the attendant had been busy since the plane lifted off, Brian thought when he saw the bed covers had been turned back to reveal fat pillows monogrammed with the same ornate burgundy-colored logo he'd noticed on the side of the plane before boarding.

Fragrant steam wafted upward from a silver carafe on the bedside table. Coffee, he guessed from the familiar smell. But he smelled something else, too. Something sweet and spicy.

Brian poured some of the sweet, dark brew and sipped it while he stripped off his clothes. Its heat warmed his insides, making him drowsy.

Naked now, he sat on the edge of the bed and finished his drink before lifting the covers and sliding between the silkiest sheets that had ever touched his skin. Pressing the remote control panel in the wall above the bed, he shut off the overhead light, leaving the room in darkness.

For the first time since he'd come home, he shut his eyes and didn't visualize Diane. Instead he saw the old Marsh Arab, as clearly as if his eyes were open and Zayed was still alive. Maybe, he thought, the old man's spirit was watching out for him.

* * * * *

Exotic music suggestive of some foreign land played from somewhere in the distance while the plane's gentle vibration lulled Brian to a peaceful slumber.

Soft at first, the sounds grew louder as he fell deeper into sleep. Thin melodies from reedy instruments and the erotic cadence of the muffled drums reminded Brian of the faraway land where he was going. The familiar smell of coffee mingled with something musky, sweet—a woman's perfume, dark and as sensuous as the music that resounded in his ears.

Arousing sensations, the haunting notes and drumbeats now seemed to be coming closer, punctuated by rhythmical clicking of what sounded like tiny metallic cymbals. Arousing smells surrounded him, drew him into exciting but unfamiliar territory.

Brian's balls tightened and his cock rose, tenting the silky sheet and reminding him he'd denied it satisfaction for much too long. Half expecting the bite of a prisoner's chains, he moved one hand to his crotch and wrapped his fingers around the base of his erection, ignoring the small voice inside his head that tried to remind him he'd been taught self-gratification was wrong.

As if by magic, the sheet slid off his body, but the air felt hot, not cold.

"Open your eyes, American."

The voice was husky, feminine, and heavily accented. But Brian got the message loud and clear. As though drugged, he did as the voice had commanded—and glanced up at the most erotic, exotic female he'd ever seen.

Her jet-black hair rippled, its wavy ends brushing her rounded ass as she swayed to the rhythm of the unseen instruments. Her dark eyes flashed with unabashed desire, and full, red lips promised forbidden pleasures.

Brian's hand tightened around his cock, as if that could stem the flow of lubrication that glistened at its head. His mouth watered when he got a glimpse beneath the tiny sleeveless thing she wore on top and got an up-close look at plump breasts tipped with reddened, jutting nipples.

I want to taste them.

He shouldn't be ogling this beautiful stranger, but no force on earth could stop him. Her long, shapely legs were bare but for see-through pants that billowed out around her legs and were gathered at her ankles with winking jeweled bands. A matching jeweled belt hugged her undulating hips.

She wore a huge incandescent pearl in her navel, what looked like a diamond just above it. The jewels caught the dim light, winking at him as she danced for his pleasure.

When she moved closer Brian saw the harem pants she wore were open at the crotch. He choked back an oath as his mouth went suddenly dry.

God help him. Her pussy was bare. Completely hairless. Pale pink and satiny looking, lighter than her torso. He gripped his cock harder still, jerking on it as though by sheer force he could will it into submission.

That had the opposite effect. His balls felt as though they were about to explode when more blood surged into them. And his erection kept growing. Good thing he was lying in bed, because his head felt fuzzy. If he'd tried to stand, he just might have keeled over.

No wonder, he thought when he glanced down and looked at the pulsating beast that the woman had tempted from its slumber with her sensual dance. He'd never seen his cock get so big or so hard.

Out of control now, he advanced and retreated to the rhythm of the drum, his movements awkward when he compared them with the smooth gyrations of the woman's slender belly.

The music slowed and faded, and so did the sensual motion of the woman's hips. She moved closer, so close he felt her heat and smelled the heady musk of her desire. Strands of her long silky hair fell over one shoulder and cascaded down her body, almost to her naked mound.

He wanted to lick off the drops of moisture sparkling on her bare pink pussy lips when her hips rolled forward, stopping well within the reach of his free hand.

No force on earth could have stopped him from sitting up and touching her. Satiny smooth and slickly wet, her outer lips were softer than anything he'd ever felt before. But jutting out from within those folds, her clit poked at his fingers, barely the size of his little fingernail but as hard as his cock.

When he let go of his cock and swung around to face her, she moved closer still, enveloping his knees and lower thighs in the gauzy see-through stuff that ballooned around her legs. When she bent forward, her bolero opened, giving him a mouth-watering view of the firm orbs of her breasts and puckered nipples the color of ripe berries. She'd painted them, he realized when he took a closer look.

Incredibly arousing that she'd enhanced her body for his pleasure, he thought, his tongue tingling at the prospect of tasting those exotically colored nubs.

With hands almost as silky as the lips of her pussy, she lifted his head. "Kiss me," she said as she took his mouth and forced her tongue inside.

She tasted sweet, like honey and spice. And Brian wanted to devour her. Opening his mouth wider, he tangled their tongues. And he slipped his hands under that little bolero and filled them with her luscious breasts.

Her slick juices dripped onto his straining cock, and the smells of exotic spices and aroused woman made him dizzy with the need to bury himself inside her and pump her full of cum until the well was dry.

Then slowly, as though entranced, she lowered herself onto his cock, enveloping him in her tight, wet heat. Inch by inch she took him, squeezing and teasing and coaxing him to respond, though God knew not much encouragement was needed to set his long-denied libido on fire.

Her warm, smooth pussy lips cradled his balls with moist, satiny softness. Her pussy twitched around his cock. And her nipples hardened into throbbing nubs that stabbed into his palms.

Damn. She was moving on him now, riding him with a slow and sensual rhythm, squeezing his cock when she rose off him and letting up when she sank onto him again. The suckling, slapping sounds of sex had him tensing up, trying to prolong the pleasure as long as he could.

She increased the pace, as though she realized his control was slipping fast. Her pussy milked his cock as if she wanted his cum now, and her tongue slid in and out of his mouth, stealing his breath and his sanity.

He was coming. Wave after wave of pleasure rolled over him as he took over the movement, straining with every burst of his hot seed into her womb. Her breathy scream hinted that she was coming, too.

Knowing that enhanced his pleasure. Another sexual rush coursed though his body. His nerves still thrummed for a long time after he'd spent. Vaguely his mind registered when his partner slid off his cock and faded away, leaving him alone.

It was all right, he told himself. He'd rest a little, then give back to his sexy *houri* all she'd given him.

But when he woke up hours later, the plane was on the ground in Lisbon to refuel and he was alone with his memories and his cum.

His dream lover had been just that—a highly erotic dream straight out of *The Arabian Nights*.

Chapter Two

"By Allah, you're a princess, not some *houri* straight out of *The Arabian Nights*," Sheikh Dahoud El Rashid yelled at his sister Alina shortly after her arrival from Kuwait City at his seaside villa near *Mina Su'ud*.

"What, Dahoud? You have no proper welcome for your precious little sister?" Alina's ears still stung from the harsh dressing down her father had delivered hours ago, before sentencing her to vegetate in *Mina Su'ud* while the scandal blew over.

"It's past time you started behaving yourself. I have better things to do than defend you to our father and threaten the lover you've scandalized so that hopefully he will keep the knowledge of your disgrace to himself."

"You? You've been defending me? To whom?" Alina couldn't recall ever having seen her usually affable older brother so angry.

"I just now spoke with Sharif al Mohammed, suggesting he make no further remarks about your virtue or lack thereof if he wishes to keep his tongue."

"I could cut out his tongue myself, but that would do him a great disservice. I hold out no hope that his puny *lingam* can pleasure any woman, but perhaps if he learned to use his—"

"Cease, Alina. I would not have my children or my servants hear you disgrace yourself further."

Alina planted her hands on her hips and tilted her head so she could stare Dahoud down. "Disgrace? That's rich coming from you. Even now the servants talk about you setting up a harem and then marrying one of the *houris* who pleasured you there. Not to mention the sly whispers about how you and

Shana still act like cats in heat. You're a fine one to preach to me about denying myself my right to be pleasured."

"By Allah, I'm a man. A man, I remind you, who has been faithful to his wife for twelve years. You're a woman. A young woman whose parents expect you to settle into a respectable marriage, not sleep with every live, warm prospect who catches your eye and then critique his performance in bed."

"I didn't sleep with 'every live warm prospect who caught my eye'– only the one I was considering marrying. How can I marry a man unless I knew whether he can satisfy me?"

"We all have more or less the same equipment, little sister," Dahoud said, his sardonic grin infuriating Alina further.

"Don't be condescending. It doesn't become you. And don't forget I went to medical school." Alina paused, wanting her next pronouncement to have maximum effect. "In case you're interested, this problem started when I learned that what Sharif has can only be described as less. And he knew not how to make the best of it."

When Dahoud's face turned red, Alina didn't even try to hide her satisfaction. "A fact which I shared with him after turning down his halfhearted offer of marriage."

"Saying that was undoubtedly what triggered Sharif's loud and very public complaint that he had been so foolish as to consider marrying a whore. By Allah, what are we to do with you?"

This whole affair had turned out to be a disaster. How could Alina have known the serious, skilled young man she had thought might make her a suitable husband would have switched from Dr. Modern Kuwaiti Surgeon to Sheikh Primitive al Suppressionist the minute she shared his couch?

Not only had Sharif been highly vocal about her lack of virginity, he'd been a clumsy, inconsiderate lover. And the *lingam* he'd been so proud of would barely have done justice to a pre-pubescent boy.

"You could let me be my own woman, not expect me to follow some archaic rules made by men," she said, determined to make her brother understand.

"Or Father could marry you off to an old-fashioned desert chieftain who still keeps a harem. After this escapade, even that might prove impossible. Sheikhs of the old school tend to expect all their wives to be virgins."

Alina hadn't expected Dahoud to understand, but neither had she expected him to become a younger and slightly less chauvinistic version of their father, who yesterday had sworn he would direct all his energies toward finding her a husband and keeper. After all, Dahoud was only ten years her senior—and he'd married an American he'd met while attending college in the States. She was still thinking of a suitable comeback to that when Shana joined them, shaking her pretty head at Alina when she stopped behind Dahoud and wrapped her arms around his waist.

"What's all the commotion about?" she asked.

Dahoud laid his hands over Shana's. "Alina has insulted a lover and disgraced our family, according to our father," he said in English, his belligerence seemingly disappearing with the appearance of his beautiful, sexy wife. "Father has sent her here until gossip in Kuwait City over her latest escapade quiets down. I've just had the futile task of trying to appease Sharif el Mohammed, whose male attributes apparently don't meet my little sister's exacting standards."

"Now, Bear. I wouldn't have married you if your...male attributes...hadn't lived up to your advance press," Shana said, one hand sliding down almost, but not quite, low enough to tweak his crotch with one long, perfectly manicured fingernail. "Don't you think you should let up a little on Alina?"

"No. Particularly not since she's going to be our responsibility for a while. She's going to be staying here and working at the hospital in *Mina Su'ud*, where hopefully she will keep her nose clean. I've suggested to her that Father might give her to some desert sheikh who doesn't know the meaning of women's rights."

"Welcome, Alina," Shana said, grinning at her over Dahoud's shoulder. "I'm sure you know Bear's bark is louder than his bite."

Alina sensed she'd find an ally in her beautiful sister-in-law who'd stolen her brother's heart back when they were both students in Texas. Oh, if she could only have the freedom Shana must have enjoyed back then—and find a love as strong and sensual as what she apparently had with Dahoud now, after twelve years of marriage and three children!

"I was just talking to Jake. He's got Brian Shearer coming to take Joe's place managing Jamil's oilfield. I told him it was okay for Brian to hitch a ride on your company's plane," Shana said, as if to explain why she'd barged in on Dahoud's sanctimonious lecture.

"Good. I was hoping he'd find another engineer to replace Joe until Jamil comes home. I'll fly up to Kuwait City tomorrow and bring him back. I need to collect more of Alina's things, anyhow."

"Hmmm. He's the American who escaped that Iraqi prison with Jamil, isn't he?" Western men were so much more...understanding about women's needs, Alina thought. Pity she'd not encountered many since returning to Kuwait after completing her surgical residency in Houston.

"Don't even think about it," Dahoud told Alina, his expression fierce. "This guy's been through hell. Last thing he needs is for you to go sniffing around him like a mare in heat. Besides, you promised Father you would marry a Kuwaiti."

Shana squeezed Dahoud harder, tipped her head back, and spoke softly in his ear—yet clearly enough for Alina to hear. "Hush, Bear. Maybe Alina is exactly what Brian does need. After all, he spent years in an Iraqi prison, then found out his wife had dumped him while he was gone—I imagine he could use a little tender loving care."

"Not from my sister, love." Dahoud reached around and pulled Shana to his side. "Father has ordered me to make her behave herself while he attempts to find her a suitable husband. Finding a Kuwaiti man who's not insistent on having a virgin bride and who's willing to risk having his ego shredded by her sharp little tongue will not, I'm certain, be an easy task."

Behave herself? Alina stopped herself in time to keep from stomping a sandal-clad foot on the gold-flecked white marble floor. Dahoud might think he could rein her in, but she had a mind of her own — and a life she was determined to live her own way.

* * * * *

This was traveling at its finest, Brian decided as he hefted his duffel bag and prepared to deplane after the seventeen-hour flight that had left him clean, rested, sexually appeased, and looking forward to immersing himself in the job of keeping Jamil al Hassan's oilfield running smoothly.

As he took one last look around the luxuriously appointed cabin, he listened to the haunting sounds of muffled drums and exotic reed instruments that echoed softly around his head. He traced the sounds to speakers over which a pilot had just announced in halting English that they had landed in Kuwait City and would stop momentarily.

Brian glanced around, half expecting to see the exotic woman who'd pleasured him in his dreams. But she wasn't there, though he thought he got a whiff of her elusive scent as he moved from the bedroom to the plush salon.

Just as well. Dream lovers didn't break hearts.

A few minutes later he stepped onto the tarmac and headed for the hangar with the same distinctive logo as the big plane. Glancing around, he noticed that a twin-engine Cessna taxiing to a halt not far from the Boeing 757 also bore the El Rashid Oil Company insignia.

As soon as its pilot stuck his head out the door, Brian recognized him. Bear el Rashid, at least six-six and still as muscular as he'd been when he played inside linebacker for the University of Texas years ago when Brian was still in high school, was hard to miss.

"We'll head down to *Mina Su'ud* in a few minutes," Bear said once they were off the tarmac and settled in a small office inside the hangar. "Do you have everything you need?"

"Jake said I'd find everything I might need at the oilfield — and that this is likely to be a pretty routine assignment."

Bear nodded. "GreenTex has done a good job repairing the damage the Iraqis did during the Gulf War. Jamil's oilfields were hit hard, but there are only two or three wells that still are out of commission, and one new one that's being drilled. El Rashid completed a pipeline from the oilfield to our refinery last year, so transportation of the oil is not a problem. Do you have clothes for the desert?"

"Jeans and khakis and shirts." Brian adjusted his baseball cap. "I wouldn't want to offend anybody, but I'd probably be more comfortable wearing desert robes to work. The Iraqis put us in them to work in the oilfields..."

"No one will think anything of it. When in Rome, they say...anyhow, you'll find plenty of robes and headgear in the GreenTex trailer out at the oilfield. Jake found out first time he came over here to work that Western clothes get damnably hot under the desert sun." Bear sipped the coke he'd gotten from the machine in the corner. "We're waiting for my sister's belongings to arrive," he said, glancing at the big clock on the wall.

"I don't believe I met her," Brian commented politely.

"No. Alina was here in Kuwait City when you and Jamil escaped from that Iraqi prison. She's staying with us now while she does some work at our little hospital."

"You must be proud of her."

Bear shrugged. "She's smart enough, for sure. An eye surgeon. She finished her training in Houston last year.

Unfortunately Alina's too smart for her own good. Living in the States for seven years got her used to...doing exactly what she pleases without thinking about the consequences. Father has charged me with watching over her until the scandal she caused here dies down."

"I've often wondered how women live in the Middle East, as restricted as they must be."

"They're not restricted at all, in my family at least. Of course, my mother's English and my wife's American, so it's logical some of their independence would have rubbed off on Alina. But she carried that independence too far this time." Bear shrugged, then looked toward the sky. "*Insha'Allah*, I will not have so many headaches when my own daughters start growing up."

Having met Bear's two gorgeous little girls, Brian imagined the big Kuwaiti sheikh would be in for plenty of trouble when they hit their late teens — unless, of course, their father's massive size intimidated their would-be boyfriends. "Good luck."

"Thank you." Bear glanced toward the tarmac, then turned back to Brian. "Let's go. Looks as though Alina's belongings have finally arrived."

* * * * *

"Daddy's plane just landed. Hello, Aunt Alina," eleven-year-old Yasmin said an hour later, her jet-black curls bouncing as she bounded inside the villa and screeched to a halt in front of Shana.

"Yasmin, you're covered with sand. Go wash up and change if you want to join us later." Shana waved the child away and turned to Alina. "How was your first day at the clinic?"

"Uneventful." Singularly unexciting compared with the bustling hospital where she'd worked in Kuwait City, although she could tell her services would be needed. She'd encountered several patients who needed eye surgery and were thrilled not to have to journey to the capital city.

"I know," Shana said, answering her sullen comment with an understanding smile. "You miss America. You're angry with your father and Bear. But think about it. Perhaps it's your destiny to be here instead of Kuwait City. And maybe Brian Shearer will be the man destined to capture your heart."

Alina thought that unlikely. Many men had tried, but none had succeeded. Not even the senior resident she'd lived with her last six months in the States, though she'd thought for a while that she was finally in love. She'd settle for a short, wild affair—that is, if the former pilot and Iraqi POW was half as hot in the flesh as he was in the pictures the newspapers in Kuwait City had run after he and Jamil had escaped.

When he and Bear strode through the door, she gasped.

Brian was hotter even than he'd looked in the photos she'd drooled over weeks earlier following his and Jamil's miraculous escape from what must have been the Iraqi version of hell.

Dark-blond hair, eyes bluer than the clear skies she remembered looking at so often over Houston, Texas—and a sad smile that wrenched at Alina's heart when Bear introduced them—the American was all his pictures had promised, and more. Almost as tall as Bear, he had big, square hands and muscles that rippled when he moved, despite his being thin almost to the point of gauntness.

And those fascinating, deep-set eyes focused on her, heated her, made her *yoni* wet and aching. It was as though he knew her and had feasted those eyes on her naked body in another place…another lifetime.

She wanted to fatten him up now and devour him piece by piece.

She yearned to chase away his sadness, fill his life with exquisite pleasure.

And she was going to do it, no matter what wiles it took.

"Alina, this is Brian Shearer. Brian, Alina," Bear said before bending to kiss Shana as though he'd been away from her for weeks, not mere hours.

In defiance of Kuwaiti custom, Alina held out her hand to Brian, enjoying the warm tingle that started in her fingers and shot through her body the moment skin touched callused skin. "Welcome back to *Mina Su'ud*," she said, ignoring her brother's fierce glare when she rose on tiptoes to brush a kiss across Brian's weathered cheek.

Chapter Three

That night, as he stood on the balcony outside the same bedroom he'd stayed in after his rescue and looked out at the ships' lights flickering in the distance atop the Persian Gulf, Brian tried to put his fantasy woman out of his mind.

But she haunted his memories. And her exotically beautiful face reminded him eerily of Alina el Rashid. Could she…?

No. It wasn't possible that Alina could have been on the plane when he'd enjoyed that sinfully erotic dream. Bear had said his sister had left Houston months before his arrival there — and that she'd been working at a hospital in Kuwait City up until the day before yesterday.

He had no trouble imagining the flirtatious young doctor stripping down and dancing with the same sort of abandon, though. The conservative skirt and blouse she'd worn tonight had done little to hide voluptuous womanly curves, and her dark eyes had flashed with the same passion for life as his dream lover's.

He was losing his mind. First Zayed's ghost. Then an elusive *houri* out of the *Arabian Nights*.

Brian needed to get to work, bury himself in something to take his mind off the sensual thoughts that threatened to consume him. Good thing he was heading out to Jamil's oilfield in the morning.

It was much later, while he lay between sheets even silkier than those he'd slept between on Bear's company plane, that he realized he'd gone for hours this evening without grieving for home. When he rubbed the smooth eye of the necklace Zayed had insisted had magical powers, he thought perhaps the old Marsh Arab had been right to suggest he make a new life for himself here.

* * * * *

While the living slept, Zayed's ghost hovered in the darkness outside the magnificent villa that belonged to one of his deliverers. America had its own beauty, he allowed, but he was glad to have returned to the homeland of his ancestors. Truth be told, though, this rugged coastline of southern Kuwait bore scant resemblance to the desert wasteland that the southeastern Iraqi Marshes had become.

Lights flickered on the waters of the Khalij, lights too bright to belong to little fishing vessels. No, they had to be from the great warships that carried airplanes and munitions. Insha'Allah, the Americans and their allies would soon free his countrymen from the scourge that was Saddam Hussein. His one regret was that he had died before seeing his beloved country liberated.

But Zayed might yet see it, he realized, for he had vowed to postpone the joys of paradise until the tear left the eye of the magic necklace. The necklace Brian Shearer might have buried in a faraway sea had he not interceded and persuaded the grief-stricken young man to live, not die.

Now he had only to help Brian find the woman who was his destiny.

* * * * *

The spicy scent of a thousand roses mingled with that of lush sweet jasmines that tumbled over the courtyard walls. Alina inhaled the lush smells, letting the gentle breeze caress her naked body as she lay alone in bed and wondered if Brian, too, had felt the heat that sprung up between them the moment their gazes had met.

Idly she slid a hand between her legs and stroked her clitoris. What would Brian's tongue feel like there? That thought triggered a gush of warm lubrication from her *yoni* that trickled down and tickled the sensitive flesh around her anus.

His big work-hardened hands would chafe her tender skin, but he would handle her with exquisite gentleness. His lips would feel soft, moist, soothing to flesh abraded by his callused fingertips. And oh! His big, hard *lingam* would brand her with its throbbing heat when he plunged it into her body.

Her nipples tightened, part of a chain reaction of sensation moving across synapses from one nerve to the next, heating and sensitizing her needy flesh. She altered the motion of the finger that stroked her clitoris, moving now in a slow, circular motion. Harder. With the other hand she pinched one nipple until the pleasure turned to pain.

The pain distracted her, left her mind empty but for the sensations of impending orgasm — the urgency, the congested feeling in her lower abdomen. As she had so many times since walking away from the American resident who'd sworn he loved her yet refused to come live and work with her in her country with even more fervor than she had declined to stay with him in Houston, Alina brought herself to a lonely climax.

She longed to come while her *yoni* clenched a man's hard *lingam*. To feel his weight, his strength. To share the pleasure...

Pleasure she'd realized too late that she'd never find with the likes of Sharif el Mohammed. And not only because of his puny attributes that she'd unwisely commented on after he whined that she'd not saved her hymen for him to break. Sharif had cared only for his own pleasure, had not even tried to arouse her before sticking his penis into her vagina and ejaculating with clinical efficiency.

Truth be known, she'd become more aroused while removing cataracts from old women's eyes than she'd been while they had sex — and she didn't consider performing surgery a sexual turn-on.

Not even the most starry-eyed romantic could term what Sharif had done making love. And Alina had a feeling no man her father chose for her would be much different from Sharif.

But she had a feeling Brian wanted her in spite of his attempts this evening to ignore her blatant flirting. She knew she intended to test her hypothesis that American men made considerate lovers—a hypothesis she had formed by comparing her former lover's performance with Sharif's.

* * * * *

On the other side of the villa, Bear lay back on the silken couch beside the balcony door in their room, stretching and moaning like a big contented tiger-cat while Shana massaged sweet-smelling oil onto his freshly depilated body. His fingers still tingled from stroking her silky pussy earlier, the way she stroked him now.

"You need to go easy on Alina," she said, scissoring her fingers and catching the tiny, hardened nubs of his nipples between them.

Reaching up, he caught one of her tiny gold nipple rings and gently tugged on it until she lay over him. "She needs to go easy on the male population of Kuwait."

"Yes, but she's your sister. You can't be surprised that she has a healthy appetite for sex." His huge cock rose to attention when she lifted it and oiled around its root. "Oooh, you're raring to go right now, aren't you?"

"Always, love." Flexing his hips, he ground his throbbing *lingam* into his wife's belly. "I fear Alina acquired a taste for Western men while training to become a doctor– and that Father has set himself an impossible task by declaring he will choose her husband. I could practically see her plotting to seduce Shearer under our very noses."

Shana's copious love juices bathed his belly, inflamed his senses. "Ride me," he said, trying without success to stifle the groan that followed when she raised her luscious ass and enveloped him in her hot, wet *yoni*.

Her motions were maddeningly slow, sensuous. Bear gripped her lush, firm flesh, as lithe now as when, nearly thirteen years ago, he'd brought her to the old villa here and set her up in a make-believe harem. What they had intended to be a week of erotic fantasy had morphed into years of sizzling reality that kept on getting better every day—and night.

Every time they fucked the sex seemed to get better. Bear flexed his hips, filled her fuller. Her muscles, strengthened by the ben-wei balls she wore a few hours every day, rippled around him, made him grow even harder inside her.

Her clit ring abraded his pubic bone when she sank on him all the way to his balls. Allah, but he loved being with her. In her.

Her skin felt like satin against his callused fingertips. The slight rise of her belly beneath his hand reminded him that in seven more months they would welcome their fourth child into the world. A world, he hoped, that would finally be free from the ever-present danger of Iraqi brutality.

"You are all right?" Though still as beautiful as she'd been at twenty-two, thirteen years had passed. And Bear sometimes worried because Shana was carrying his child again—a brother for Jamil, she'd said when she'd pitched her case for another pregnancy in spite of her age and the unstable world in which they lived.

He hadn't had the heart to tell her no.

Now he found the knowledge of her pregnancy incredibly frightening…yet incredibly arousing.

"I'm ecstatic. And healthy as a horse. I forbid you to worry. Now fuck me, my sexy, insatiable sheikh."

"Your wish is my command." Rolling her over, he held his body off hers, sparing her his weight while he did her bidding. Slowly, carefully, with all the love that was in his heart, he fed her passion and his own.

When she convulsed around him and uttered the sexy little whimpers of completion that he loved to hear, he let go of his iron control. Waves of pleasure washed over him with his climax—waves made sweeter because he shared them with the woman of his dreams.

Later he lay on the silken sleeping couch, a damp breeze off the *Khalij* cooling the backside of his spent body while Shana lay beside him, her silken back warming his chest and belly. He splayed his hand protectively over her still-slender abdomen, anticipating the day when he'd feel their baby move within her beautiful body one more time.

His mind drifted to Alina—to their father's fury at the disgrace she'd caused. And Bear realized he couldn't stand by and let his sister be doomed to live her life without the sort of joy he'd found because he'd listened to his heart and body.

Thirteen years ago he'd forced his parents to accept that he'd have Shana and no other. If need be, he would now help her persuade their father that she, too, deserved to have her heart's desire—whoever he might be.

* * * * *

The next morning Brian noticed that Bear seemed more relaxed than he'd been when they'd first arrived at his palatial villa—and that Alina seemed even more intent on inflaming his senses. Fortunately she'd left soon after his arrival downstairs to spend the day, she'd told him, seeing patients at a health clinic in *Mina Su'ud*.

During the helicopter ride to Jamil's oilfield forty miles or so east of Bear's villa, Brian watched the endless desert pass by. Acres of barren desert were punctuated with occasional date palms clustered together around small blue pools of precious water. At one oasis he noticed a band of nomads with their tents and camels.

Unable to converse with GreenTex's pilot over the noise of the rotors, Brian turned his gaze upward toward the hazy blue clouds. Trails from jet fighters lay high above them, making him think of long ago when all he'd dreamed of was joining those cowboys in the sky. And of the moment when he'd confidently strapped himself into the seat of an F-15 and begun what had ended up as a trip to hell.

His love for danger had died. It had withered during the hellish years he'd spent as a prisoner saved from the most brutal forms of torture his captors favored only because of his knowledge of oil wells and the equipment needed to drill and operate them.

Ironic. That same knowledge was now about to give him a new purpose in the life he had nearly decided to end—until the ghost of an old Iraqi had intervened and steered him here.

Was Zayed somewhere nearby, watching him? Brian found comfort in the ridiculous idea that the ghost might be his own personal guardian angel.

A weather-beaten trailer, its white and green paint job dulled by the regular sandblastings it had endured over the years when fierce winds whipped up the desert sand, sat next to the remaining walls of a crumbling building Brian imagined must have once been Jamil's home. Now, Brian noticed as the chopper was setting down, it was nothing but a burned-out shell.

A grim reminder of the havoc Saddam's army had wrought in January 1991 as they'd retreated ahead of the American tank units that had chased them back to Iraq.

After stowing his gear and watching the chopper take off again with Joe, his predecessor, Brian fired up the Jeep and toured the oilfield.

Pumpjacks moved up and down with mesmerizing regularity. And a dozen or more robed workers tended a metal derrick that sparkled in the brilliant sunshine. When one smiled and waved, Brian waved back.

There was a sameness about the desert, whether it was here, in Saudi Arabia, or in Iraq—endless sand, now piled in constantly shifting dunes as far as he could see. Sand occasionally whipped up into cutting whorls by a capricious wind.

A scene that was vast. Lonely. Lifeless but for the sparse vegetation and a few hardy creatures that had adapted to incredibly harsh conditions over many centuries.

The desert was lonely, stark. Much like Brian. He'd become that way since learning that the life he had endured eleven years of hell to return to was gone. A cruel dream that would never come true.

Stopping the jeep, Brian got out and headed for the derrick. Maybe a hard day's labor would cast out the emptiness inside him. With luck it would squelch other, more earthbound thoughts.

Futile, sensual images that plagued him and belied his emotional emptiness. Fantasies about an exotic, erotic lover who now had a name as well as a gorgeous body and flashing dark eyes that promised forbidden pleasures.

* * * * *

Work. That was Alina's prescription for sublimating the needs she hadn't yet managed to satisfy. And so far this afternoon it was working.

She picked up a chart, exchanged pleasantries with the nurse at the clinic's main desk, and flipped through it before stepping into the examining room to see her next patient.

At the sight of the old man whose cataracts she'd removed yesterday and his obviously anxious daughter, her facial muscles automatically flexed to produce a smile. Alina truly enjoyed using the skills she'd learned to help others, and she'd discovered there were as many needy patients here in the small facility in *Mina Su'ud* as had been sent her way in the big impersonal facility where she'd worked in Kuwait City.

More. And many like the elderly nomad whose eyes she was examining now. His cataracts would probably have gone untreated if he'd had to travel to the capital.

"I can see clearly," he said, his voice full of wonder. "A thousand thanks, pretty lady doctor. *Insha'Allah*, this miracle will not fade away as my vision had been doing for years."

"*Insha'Allah*," she repeated, smiling at him as she fitted dark glasses over his hawklike nose. "Preserve my handiwork, and wear these when you ride in the desert."

When she noticed the old man staring dubiously through the unfamiliar glasses, Alina turned to his daughter. "You will need to remind him to stay out of the sunlight, and to wear these glasses when he must venture outside."

The woman nodded, then babbled her effusive thanks before helping her father to his feet and ushering him out the door.

By afternoon, Alina was pleasantly tired, professionally fulfilled, and mildly interested in a discussion that was taking place in the employee lounge between two colleagues. Apparently, from the conversation she just overheard, she'd proven to them already that she was more than a dilettante princess seeking to amuse herself by playing doctor.

She loved her work, loved helping people to see all that surrounded them.

But work was not Alina's whole life. She wanted more. The pleasure...the satisfaction...the security of loving and being loved, of sharing all those emotions with joy and abandon in the arms of an eager and skilled lover.

And she would have it. Her mind drifted back to this morning, to the breakfast table where Brian's sapphire gaze had bored through her, made her *yoni* twitch and weep.

He'd wanted her. Of that she was certain. The yearning in his eyes and the potent male musk that mingled with the tangy aftershave he wore had told her as much about his desire as the swollen flesh that had strained impressively against the zipper of his snug jeans.

But Brian had demonstrated a stubborn determination to reject the mutual attraction—a reluctance as easy to read as an xray picture of a metal object embedded within an eye. She was certain that getting him to set aside his reservations would be a daunting task—but then Alina had always confronted challenges with skill and determination.

When, a week later, the opportunity arose for her to take a colleague's place and do a clinic for the nomadic tribesmen who camped out in the desert not far from her cousin Jamil's oilfield, Alina surprised the administrator of the clinic by jumping at the assignment. Little did he know it was a rugged blond American and not insanity that made the otherwise forbidding desert call out to her.

* * * * *

Was constant sexual frustration Brian's fate or his destiny?

After the twenty-four-hour ordeal of getting a massive gusher under control, he came back from the new oil well filthy, exhausted, starved...and horny, he added when he glanced inside the Health Services tent the workers had set up next to the GreenTex trailer and saw her.

Alina el Rashid. The beautiful, unattainable woman whose face had replaced the one of the nameless *houri* who'd visited him in his wildest fantasy and returned nightly in his dreams.

In her colorful traditional robe and veil, she reminded him of the Madonnas depicted in illustrated children's Bible stories. That made his sudden arousal seem very nearly obscene, but it didn't make it go away.

Desperate to escape his own lascivious thoughts, he waved at her then fled inside. As though cleaning his body would cleanse his mind, he stripped down and scrubbed off the layers of sand-encrusted oil and sweat.

Why had God made him lust after a woman with whom he could never share a life?

She's a princess, richer than the Greens and God. A Kuwaiti, Muslim princess. If that's not enough she's a doctor, with a brain at least twice as agile as yours.

And if he ever went after her, Brian had no doubt that her brother Bear would tear him limb from limb. Arabs tended to be possessive about their women.

When he finished bathing and telling himself God had sent Alina his way to punish him for some unknown sin, Brian was still in agony. His cock throbbed, and his balls throbbed as though he'd been kicked by a horse.

His guilty feelings multiplied exponentially when he strode to the tent late that afternoon, unable to keep on resisting temptation.

Chapter Four

There he was. Finally.

Looking fit and better fed than he had last week when they'd first met, Brian apparently had learned the traditional robes served better in the desert than Western work clothes. The stark white of the *dishdasha* and *ghutra* he had on framed a face that seemed more rugged now, baked anew as it had obviously been by long exposure to the fierce sun. And it made his brooding eyes look even bluer than before.

Desperate to have him to herself, Alina handed the screaming infant she'd just inoculated back to his mother and murmured a few parting words. Then she held out both her hands to Brian, mentally shrugging off the look of shock that action generated in the departing tribeswoman.

"Did I do something to upset her?" Brian asked, his gaze following the mother as she scurried away with her baby.

He had a lot to learn, she thought. "I did. I touched you."

"Huh?"

"Properly modest women here don't touch men who are not of their family," she told him as she tightened her grip on his callused fingers. "But no one has ever accused me of being proper. How are you adjusting to life in the desert?"

"Well. I didn't expect to see you again so soon."

"Nor I you." She hadn't, at least, until the chance to come here had more or less fallen into her hands.

"How long will you be here?"

Alina didn't delude herself into believing Brian was anxious for her to stay. His expression and tone made it clear that she couldn't leave soon enough to suit him.

"Not long. The clinic's helicopter should be coming for me momentarily."

Shifting his weight from one foot to the other, Brian held his hands stiffly at his sides. "The workers appreciate you coming," he said as if to fill the charged silence.

"I wanted to come." *Wanted to see you, seduce you, learn if you can pleasure a woman the way I want to be pleasured.* She took a deep breath, then let it out. "And I want to be with you."

A throaty roar came from the sky, obliterated Brian's reply and filled Alina's ears while the accompanying winds caused the sturdy walls of the clinic's tent to shudder.

"What the–"

"A *shamal*. A summer windstorm–"

Brian held up a hand as though to silence her. "I know what it is. Hot, dry wind that sweeps down from the north and creates dust that rises further than the eye can see. It's like nothing I've ever seen except here — and in Iraq. From the sound of it, this is a big one." He paused, looking out the tent flap at the swirling golden sand, then back at her. "No chopper's going to fly into this."

"No." Alina tried to stifle her fear — and her excitement.

"Trailer's tied down. We'll be safer there. We'd better make a run for it."

* * * * *

Gritty sand slid off their robes onto the linoleum floor of the trailer. Brian shook off the worst of it from his robe and *ghutra* before removing the headgear and looking over at a pale and obviously frightened Alina. The *shamal* whined and groaned, picking up dry sand with every angry gust and blasting the trailer so hard that it shook.

"Are we safe here?" Alina asked, her voice husky, provocative.

And very feminine, bringing out every protective instinct Brian had ever known. Huddled near the door, her Madonna-like garb twisted by the wind, she made him want to hold her, protect her—but also to sample her sweetness and the passion she projected like a beacon in the night.

Powerless to stop himself, he moved forward and gathered her against his chest. Her warm breath tickled the part of his neck and chest left bare by the slit-necked robe he wore.

"The trailer's tie-downs are built to withstand winds of up to a hundred miles an hour. We should be all right as long as we stay inside."

The tension he'd felt in her shoulders and back eased, as though all she'd waited for was his reassurance that they were in no great danger.

He should have let her go then, but he didn't. It was almost as though fate had decreed this, as if God in his wisdom had conjured up the sandstorm to force him together with this beautiful, sensual woman.

His cock rose against the softness of her belly, its only restraint the loose boxer shorts he'd put on beneath the loosely woven cotton robe. Alina didn't pull back, the way Diane had always done at such blatant hints of his arousal—even after they'd finally made love. Instead she angled her hips toward him, increased the exquisite pressure—and she tilted back her head in blatant invitation for him to mate their mouths.

God, but he wanted to do that and more. Much more. The subtle yet seductive fragrance that tickled his nose lured him, tempted him to slip his hands beneath the deep-red scarf and veil that hid her hair and tangle his fingers in the silky jet-black strands.

He lifted one hand to brush the satin softness of skin that looked surprisingly pale beside his own sun-bronzed fingers, slipped a finger beneath the concealing scarf.

Then he jerked the hand back.

He would not give in to temptation. Wouldn't succumb to pleasures of the flesh that he'd been taught since childhood were pathways that would take him straight to hell. The numbing, killing sort of anguish that loving Diane had brought him. The tempest in his head overshadowed the fierce storm going on outside, but he shelved his desire and pulled reluctantly away.

When he met her gaze he thought he saw the sheen of tears in her dark, seductive eyes.

"Are you all right?" he asked, not at all certain that he fared any better for having backed away.

Alina turned away, stared out the small window. It seemed she was mesmerized by the sand that twirled and swirled in eerie patterns, each tiny grain catching rays from the setting sun and creating a surrealistic golden aura.

"How long will this last?" she asked, turning back to Brian and biting her full lower lip.

He wanted to taste her, to use his lips and tongue to soothe the bruises she was making with her teeth.

He wanted to strip off the all-encompassing robe she wore, feast his eyes on the voluptuous curves he knew lay beneath it. His fingers itched to free her long, silky hair, to stroke every delectable inch of her gorgeous body before he took her.

And he sensed that she'd cooperate, all the way.

Clenching his fists, he struggled to contain a desire stronger than any he'd ever known.

"Brian?"

Startled, he looked over at her. "Sometimes they can last for days." Longer than he could, with her in such close proximity. God willing, the storm would play itself out ahead of him playing out his self-control. "You'll probably be more comfortable if you got out of those sandy clothes. You can put on one of my shirts if you'd like."

"Mmmm." The sound that came from deep in her throat was a feline sort of purr, as though she realized how much harder it would be for him to keep his hands off her when her long, silky legs were bared. "I will if you will," she said, and when she met his gaze he saw the blatant challenge in her eyes.

* * * * *

Brian's shirt came almost to Alina's knees, and she had to roll the sleeves over several times to free her hands. But the soft cotton felt good against skin chafed by the sand and wind. Warm and caring like its owner.

The man was an enigma, but that made her want him more, not less. And she knew the desire was mutual. She'd seen and felt his *lingam* swell and harden each time they came within yards of each other.

Still he wouldn't accept her blatant invitations. It was almost as though he were a reluctant virgin, afraid to sample the pleasures of a woman's body.

As she buttoned his shirt over her tingling breasts she shrugged off that hypothesis. After all, Brian had been married—though Shana had told her before his arrival that he had apparently remained faithful to the woman during the long years of his imprisonment, only to learn upon returning that she had married another man, thinking he was dead.

Alina understood his hurt but not his apparent determination to remain celibate even now, when his marriage was unquestionably over.

They'd shared sandwiches and fruit, and afterward they'd lingered at the small kitchen table while darkness enveloped them and talked about their respective lives. It was later, after Brian had turned off the lights to conserve power while the storm raged on outside, that he'd told her stories that gave her insight.

Stories about his childhood in Galveston as the only child of older parents—his father had apparently been a Christian minister of some conservative sect—had convinced Alina that his attitude had been shaped not as much by lingering, futile love for his wife as by the strict parents who'd taught him sex outside the marriage couch was sinful and wrong.

She would teach him otherwise.

Now.

In the vast blackness of night on the desert, with the *shamal* trapping them together and no avenue for escape.

But she'd not rob them of the gift of sight.

Slowly, silently rising from the couch where he'd told her she could sleep, Alina opened the buttons on his shirt one by one until it hung loosely off her shoulders, then lit the candle Brian had taken off the table and given to her before retiring to the spartan bedroom where she'd shed her sand-encrusted robes.

Her *yoni* wept, and her nipples puckered against the soft cotton of his shirt as she made her way to him.

The trailer creaked in the wind, masking her footfalls and the groan of the generator that provided electricity for the trailer. As she stepped inside his room the candle flickered, but its flame flared again when she set it on the little table beside the bed.

Clothed, Brian had attracted her with his ruggedly handsome face, his lean muscled masculinity—and the beautiful sapphire eyes that spoke silently of unimaginable suffering. Naked now, with his powerful legs tangled in bed linens he'd apparently kicked off in his sleep, he took her breath away.

His pale body hair caught the light from the candle, cast golden shadows over the angular leanness of his sculpted torso. Small copper-colored nipples puckered in the cool air, and the hint of a golden beard shadowed his strong jaw line. A jagged scar, white with age and probably a souvenir of his imprisonment, started beneath his right clavicle and snaked down that side of his body almost to his pelvis.

But it was his *lingam* that held her attention. It was as beautiful as she'd imagined. With a pale circumcised head crowning a rosy golden shaft and full, darker scrotum, his sex was large and thick even while he slept. It nested amid a tangle of light-brown hair and spilled over against his inner thigh. It would fill her to perfection.

She wanted to feel every delicious inch of that long, thick shaft buried deep inside her *yoni*. Stretching her, making her swell around him…bringing her to a shimmering, mind-stealing orgasm.

Suddenly she hated the faceless woman who had stolen his joy at attaining freedom after all those miserable years in one of Saddam's torture chambers. If she'd once had him but thought him dead, she doubted any man could have aroused her interest.

The *shamal* still roared outside, its rhythm stronger and louder than the beat of the *tabla* echoing in her head. Her sense of hearing heightened by the lack of light, she let those discordant drumbeats mingle with the quiet cadence of his breathing and her own.

She'd dance for him some other night. Tonight she would inflame his senses, indulge desires she'd been too long denied.

His magnificent body called out, and she lay beside him and answered with a feather-light exploration made by gentle fingertips. His hair, silky and limned in gold. The abrasive texture of his beard stubble, surprisingly dense and coarse for one with his coloring. His earlobe, soft as her little nephew's bottom, giving way to the rougher and warmer texture of the area on his neck that baked regularly under the fierce desert sun. Biceps and triceps developed to hard perfection by years of physical labor, flexed involuntarily where she touched them, even now while he slept.

Alina tangled her fingers in golden chest hair, so foreign in this land where men as well as women removed all body hair. It, too, felt silky soft, cool compared with the warm, dry skin that lay beneath it.

Unable to resist, she bent and tongued his nipples, first one and then the other. She slid her palm along the route that scar took, mentally calculating what vital organs had barely been spared. A deeper cut along that path could have destroyed his liver, taken out one lung and a kidney. Even the lightest slash that might have left such a scar could have caused his death by massive hemorrhage.

It had obviously been Allah's will for him to live.

It was her will that he should live the life he had been given to the fullest.

He shifted restlessly, murmured something unintelligible when she nipped his chest with her teeth.

When she sat up on the bed and wrapped one hand around his *lingam*, it was already growing and hardening though his chest still rose and fell in the slow, even rhythm of sleep.

She gave in to temptation, taking the ruby head of his penis between her lips and tasting the milky lubricant her touch had coaxed so easily from the slit at its tip. He tasted clean and slightly salty, very male and very, very sexy.

Apparently lost in a dream, he groaned and flexed his hips, pushing his *lingam* deeper into her mouth.

She swirled her tongue over his distended flesh, sampling the different textures: the silky-smooth hardness of his shaft, the rhythmic pulsations of veins pumping blood just below the skin, the fleshy ridge of his corona. The coarse texture of his pubic hair abraded her fingertips when she combed through it to cup his heavy testicles in her hands.

As if starved, he slid in and out of her mouth, pushing deeper then retreating, his anguished moans growing louder, more frequent. His breathing grew ragged, became more labored as passion pulled him inexorably from the sleep that had claimed him.

"Not...not like this," he ground out above the rumblings of the wind. His fingers tangled in her hair, and he pulled her off him.

With callused fingers he explored her much as she'd explored him earlier. Her earlobe heated when he stroked her there, and when he sank his fingers into her hair and gently massaged her scalp, sensations rushed through her, exciting her more. Every touch, each shy caress of her breasts and belly made her hotter and wetter.

Alina had been touched before with passion, but never with such tender wonder...as though Brian thought her precious, fragile. The slight trembling she detected in his hands, the pulsating pressure of his erection against her thigh, inexplicably aroused her more than her former lovers' practiced foreplay.

Her *yoni* throbbed, wept for his touch.

"Here." Catching one of his hands she dragged it between her legs, felt her *yoni* swell with anticipation when he cupped her there.

So hot. And so gentle, as though he were fondling a woman's sex for the first time and was afraid of hurting her. He made her feel cherished yet hotter than she'd ever felt before. Alina held her breath, savored the exquisite sensations that flowed from his fingers to her sex, sending waves of anticipation throughout her body.

He stroked her clit for what seemed like hours, until she was so hot with wanting him that she could barely keep from crying out. His warm breath tickled her belly where he'd lain his head.

She wanted his tongue on her, in her. But he made no move to assuage her need that way. Instead he slid between her outstretched legs.

In the flickering candlelight she saw passion in his eyes. Passion she returned in full measure.

"My *houri*," she thought she heard him say at the moment he flexed his hips and joined their bodies.

By Allah, this was the man she had waited for all her life. His *lingam* stretched and filled her like no other ever had. The heat, the wetness, the slapping sounds of his heavy scrotum against her vulva stole her breath when he plunged inside her all the way.

"God, yes. Take me deeper," he choked out when she wrapped her legs around his narrow waist and clamped down on his muscular buttocks with her heels.

The candle flickered out, leaving them in total darkness. But she didn't need to see his face. Joined with him in the most elemental way, she only needed to feel. To take his potent sexual energy, use it to feed her own, and give it back with every contraction of her *yoni* around his huge, rigid *lingam*.

Basic. Elemental. And beautiful. No pretense or posturing, no need to coax out his climax. He took her, and she took him, and when he stiffened above her and began shooting his hot, wet seed inside her, the full, tingling feeling in her *yoni* burst, sending waves of pleasure through her.

Pleasure so deep, so profound, that all she could do when it was over was lie in his arms, trembling with the afterglow, her fingers clutching the ornate chain she just now noticed he wore around his neck.

* * * * *

The next morning Brian woke up hard as stone, his cock tucked warmly between his body and...Alina's luscious ass cheeks.

Last night they'd had sex. It hadn't been just another highly erotic dream.

She'd played with his nipples and swallowed his cock. And then he'd fucked her. He'd come and come and come for what had seemed like hours. And he didn't think he'd even managed to ask her about protection.

Lord, he'd never been so careless. Not even when he'd been a horny teenager making it with Diane once he'd persuaded her they didn't need to wait for the preacher to say it was okay to make love.

Alina's jet-black hair draped over one of his arms, its texture as silky as he'd dreamed it would be. And the even rise and fall of her firm breasts registered against the other arm, which he'd draped across her torso as if he had every right to have her in his bed.

"Alina?"

"Hmmm?"

"Wake up." Part of him wanted to throttle her for threatening his resolve to concentrate on his job and let his emotions remain dead and buried. His cock, however, was telling him a different story.

From the way it was growing and throbbing, it wanted a repeat performance. Badly.

She stretched, arching her back like the lazy tiger cat his mother used to have and putting more delicious pressure on his erection with her firm, rounded ass. That made his balls draw up and sent more blood surging to his sex.

Catching his hand, she pulled it to her mouth and sucked a finger inside. The slick wetness of her tongue brought back memories of that tongue on his cock last night. Of the exquisite torture he'd experienced before, but only in his wildest dreams.

Not only was the woman whose ass was cradling his raging hard-on equally as unattainable this morning as she'd been last night, she was also out of his league sex-wise.

But he couldn't pull away. Her nipple puckered against his fingers as though she liked the way he was rubbing it between his thumb and forefinger, and the little moans coming from her sweet mouth had him losing whatever control he might otherwise have held onto.

Her baby-smooth pussy beckoned, and he cupped the silky mound in his other hand, wiggling his fingers against the hard little nub of her sex.

"Yesss."

Her little scream made him hotter, and he stroked her clit a little harder.

"Oh, Brian...Yesss. Don't stop." She covered his hand with her own, guided his movements. "Like that. Rub me. Make me hot and wet for you."

Seemed to him like she was sopping wet already, because her slick, fragrant juices had his hand slipping and sliding over her swollen pussy lips. His balls tightened painfully, and his cock bulged and throbbed. "I need you now," he croaked when she scooted her ass against his belly and lifted her top leg to give him more room.

"Take me, then," she told him, reaching between them and fondling his raging hard-on. "Please."

"Are you protected?" he asked, reason seeping through the foggy sexual haze that enveloped his brain.

"I take the Pill."

Surely that was relief he felt—not regret. "Then roll over and let's make love."

"Take me like this," she said, trapping his cock between firm, silky thighs.

From behind, with him on his side? Hell, he was ready to take her any way she wanted him. His cock didn't care. But he'd never fucked this way before. Maybe if he had her show him how? "Put me inside you then."

She rubbed his cockhead along the inside of her dripping pussy. "Yes. You're so big and hard. I want you in my *yoni*. Now." Shifting the slightest bit, she enveloped his cockhead in her hot, slick pussy. "*Nek ni*, Brian."

He knew enough Arabic to know that meant "Fuck me," and his cock was happy to oblige. But their position didn't make it easy. After a few frustrating thrusts he rolled on top of her, lifted her ass, and sank into her to his balls.

"Oh yesss. More."

He withdrew almost all the way and slammed back into her. The sucking, slurping sounds, the musky smell of sex, even the golden sunshine pouring through the window and gilding the satiny expanse of her ass and back worked together to drive him wild as he pounded over and over into her tight, slick hole.

She arched her back, took him so deep this time that he felt her hot little clit bore into his balls. "My nipples. Pull them. Help me come."

The tight nubs grew harder, longer when he caught one in each hand and tugged gently. Her pussy clamped down on his cock with every tug, so tight the friction on his cock was torturous.

He felt it coming. The pressure in his balls, spreading to his thighs. The feel of cum flooding his cock, demanding release. Her hot, wet pussy milking him, as tight as a fist around his shaft...

"Pull them harder. Yesss. Like that."

Her breasts seemed to swell against his hands when he did as she asked, so he gave each hard little nipple a gentle pinch.

And then her pussy spasmed around him, sucked him in. And when she shook all over and screamed out her pleasure, he let go and spurted out his cum in hard, hot bursts that left him helpless, drained.

Chapter Five

If the health service's chopper hadn't arrived moments after that tumultuous orgasm, Brian had no doubt they'd have done it again before crawling out of bed and getting on with their lives. He'd even felt another hard-on coming on when he hugged Alina goodbye as she was leaving.

Work distracted him during the coming days, but when all the sand-clogged equipment had been cleaned and put back in service, his mind drifted back to Alina and her undeniable skills at seduction.

Part of him wanted to follow her back to *Mina Su'ud* and gorge himself on the sex he'd missed out on for too long. But a voice in his head, a voice left over from his childhood, whispered that the mind-blowing kind of pleasure he'd found in Alina's gorgeous sexy body was wrong. Sinful.

Brian wasn't sure he believed that.

But he wasn't certain he didn't, either. After all, he'd loved Diane, and he'd never wanted to devour her. As he recalled — and he thought ruefully that his memory had probably faded after all these years — sex with her had been pleasant, even fun, in a plain-vanilla sort of way.

Sex with Alina was everything but plain-vanilla.

And he was having a hard time convincing himself anything that felt so good could be a sin. Or that the deeper feelings for her that threatened to churn from the depths of his mind could be anything but moral and right.

He'd even felt momentary disappointment when she'd said she was on the Pill, wished he might see her swelling with their child — before sanity returned and relief replaced his initial reaction.

Recalling Zayed's prediction that when he embraced his soulmate the tear in the eye of the pendant would disappear, he lifted it off his chest and took a look.

The tear was still there. Not as distinct as before, he thought, but that might easily have been his imagination.

"It goes away, then comes back after a time, until your hearts commit to each other for all time."

When he looked toward the sound of the eerie voice, there was the ghost hovering in the corner near the window. "How did you get in?"

"It is easy to move about when one has no substance."

"Are you always lurking?" Brian felt his cheeks growing hot when he imagined Zayed's ghost watching what he could only imagine had rivaled a triple-X porn show back in the States.

"No. I would never intrude upon another man's pleasure." Indignation rang in the old man's voice.

"What pleasures are permitted to Muslims?"

Zayed laughed. *"Any that bring a man and woman happiness."*

That made a compelling argument for harems, Brian thought, wondering at his unreasoning anger that Alina had done the things she'd shared with him last night before, with other men.

Zayed said something, but his words were drowned out by the scream of afterburners igniting overhead. Fighters. Brian recognized the familiar roar of their straining engines. Roaring toward Iraq, more today than yesterday, more yesterday than there had been the day before.

"War is imminent, is it not?" the old man asked. *"I see more of your American soldiers arriving each day."*

"It seems so." Brian hated that when war came, more decent human beings would sacrifice their lives to rid the world of Saddam Hussein.

"It is past time. Insha'Allah, I shall stay around to see it. You do not fly your bird this time?"

"No." Brian's passion for flying had died in an Iraqi prison. "The only airplanes I'll be flying are the ones GreenTex uses to ferry workers and supplies to and from its oilfields."

"My people will be freed. And the Butcher will finally get his due." With that solemn pronouncement Zayed's ghost faded away, leaving Brian with his conscience—and the fantasy that he might someday find this soulmate the old man insisted lurked somewhere in his future.

No way could Alina be that woman even though she filled his dreams and a good many of his waking fantasies.

* * * * *

She was back again, he noticed when he came in from the oilfield the following day.

Once he could understand. But twice in a week? Surely they had enough doctors and nurses at the clinic in *Mina Su'ud* that they didn't need to send an eye surgeon like Alina to inoculate the nomads and oilfield workers against the smallpox and anthrax germs the Kuwaiti government feared Saddam would unleash on their most vulnerable people.

"I volunteered to come," Alina said when he confronted her. "Are you not happy to see me?"

Ambivalence. That was the word for his emotions. Desire and fear. Gratitude to her for dragging his battered emotions back to life and resentment that she'd done it when he was just beginning to accept what fate had dealt him.

Desire won when she smiled and licked her lower lip as though she wanted to taste him again.

"Of course I'm glad." Checking to be sure no new patients had wandered into the tent, he bent and brushed a kiss across her delectable lips. "Could I interest you in a swim?"

"A swim?"

"More if you're inclined."

"I could be."

* * * * *

Palm fronds swayed in a gentle breeze, casting shadows over the crystal-clear oasis pond. Brian stripped down with careless efficiency and hung his *dishdasha* and *ghutra* over a shrub whose leaves had been blown off during last week's storm. Alina struggled to keep up, but by the time she'd removed her traditional robe and chemise, he'd already waded up to his waist in the water.

When she joined him he splayed his big hands over her buttocks and pulled her close. Her nipples brushed his chest, and his growing erection branded her belly, made her muscles clench in anticipation.

Water bubbled up around them from the underground spring, cooling and effervescent. A brilliant sun beamed down from its spot in the western sky, its waning rays baking their upper bodies in warmth—not that Alina needed more heat than was being generated within her naked body.

Heat...moisture...and a tingling need to wrap her legs around Brian and take his hard, pulsing *lingam* into her body.

He shuddered when she cupped her hands and splashed water over his massive shoulders. "Show me how to give you pleasure," he murmured, burying his face in her hair as though embarrassed to voice his lack of sexual experience—an innocence she found more arousing than the most practiced seduction.

Because he cared about pleasuring her.

Enjoying the feel of his incredibly soft hair between her fingers, she gently drew his head down to one breast. Then she whispered softly what she wanted him to do.

"Take my nipple in your mouth. Suck it and nibble it and flick it with your tongue until it's as hard as your huge, hot *lingam*."

He raised his head, shot her a quizzical look. "*Lingam*?"

"This," she said, slipping her free hand between them and stroking his hot, hard organ. "What do you call it?"

"My penis."

She found his obvious embarrassment endearing. "Really?"

"Or my cock," he said. "But not generally in front of a woman."

"You should feel free to use whatever language arouses you to the woman whose *yoni* you're filling with your cock, I think."

Slipping one big hand between her legs, he cupped her. "Then I guess you won't mind if I call this your pussy. Your bare, silky pussy that I love to fuck."

He was definitely a fast learner, she decided when he spread her legs and found her...pussy. And she found she liked thinking of sex with him in those blunt English terms.

"Or if I play with your pretty little clit while I suck you here." He drew a nipple into his mouth and flicked it the way she'd asked while drawing lazy circles around her swollen clit with one long finger. Then he switched to her other breast and gave it equal attention.

Allah, but he was good for a beginner. In no time he had her panting and gasping for breath, wanting his huge throbbing cock inside her spurting out its seed.

No. She wanted more of the sensual torture he was meting out. As much as she could take.

But she didn't last long, savoring the incredibly arousing foreplay.

Alina's pussy was on fire, demanding more. She wanted to feel his cock throbbing against her belly from the inside. Or in her mouth, tickling her throat with its big, blunt head while she swallowed his milky, slightly salty cum.

But she also wanted his face between her legs, needed to watch and feel him sucking and biting her throbbing clit and reaming her pussy with his tongue until she collapsed in a mindless heap of ecstasy.

"*Nek ni*. Please."

Brian hardly believed he'd reduced a princess to begging for his cock. Swollen almost to bursting already, her plea got him so hot he had to fight to hold onto the shreds of his control.

"Wrap your legs around my waist," he said as he lifted and impaled her.

Her pussy was so hot, so wet. So damn tight around his swollen cock. And her silky pussy lips cradled his aching balls. His lips closed over one reddened nipple, and he sucked it in.

She clamped her pussy down on him every time he withdrew, as though to hold him prisoner. And with every moan, each whimper, every murmured word of sex, of love, she drew him under a sensual spell he doubted he'd ever escape.

At the moment he didn't care. All he wanted was to make her come. And then let go and shoot his load.

"Oh, yesss. Brian, I'm coming."

Yes. God yes. Sucking her harder, fucking her deeper, he rode on the crest of her orgasm, let it carry him over the edge.

His ejaculation seemed to go on forever, each convulsive spurting sending a new wave of release throughout his body. And she was there to hold him, to support his weight when it was finally over.

He loved this beautiful, sensuous, genuinely caring woman who had made him want to live, not just exist. And because he did, he was going to have to let her go.

* * * * *

It was over. The last words Brian had said before she'd left the oilfield camp this afternoon had sounded final, though he'd worded them prettily. As far as he was concerned, any relationship they might have would be doomed to failure from the start. Alina blinked back tears, unable to keep her emotional turmoil hidden from Shana and Dahoud any longer, having managed to fool them through the entire ordeal of eating dinner.

She didn't want to face Dahoud, not after he'd had to smooth the bruised ego she'd given Sharif. So if she could keep her wits about her, until she got Shana alone...

"Why can't he see we can make it work?" Alina asked between sobs as soon as her brother left to spend his customary hour after dinner with his daughters. "You and Dahoud did."

Shana stretched out her legs and stared out at the ships' lights flickering over the *Khalij*. As though considering her answer carefully, she nibbled for a minute on a long, perfectly manicured nail, then spoke slowly. "In spite of Bear and me having different religious beliefs and being from different countries, our backgrounds aren't really all that incompatible. Wait, before you tell me those two items constituted awfully big hurdles. They did, particularly with our families—but think about it. Take away the cultural differences and you had two rich kids whose families had made their fortunes in the oil business. Two kids who had gone to the same college for four long years and wanted basically the same things in our lives. Not to mention the chemistry...

"The chemistry between us was just too strong to ignore. Still is, even after all these years," she said, her dark eyes sparkling. "Why did Brian say a relationship between you two wouldn't work?"

"It was almost as though he'd rehearsed his speech before I went out there. Our worlds are too different, he told me at first. And when I asked him to explain that, he ticked off reasons the way the chief of ophthalmology my first year out of medical school used to rattle off patients' symptoms. He's American, I'm Kuwaiti. He's Christian, I'm Muslim. He's average, I'm ultra-rich. On and on, down to the fact that I have a few more years' education than he."

Alina paused, then decided to unload what had been Brian's final, hurtful observation. "He even touched on the somewhat embarrassing conclusion he'd drawn that he's sexually conservative and I'm 'liberated', as he put it. Which I think means he believes I have the morals of a cat in heat."

Shana shook her head. "I can't argue that he's wrong about any of that. Except the cat in heat bit. And if he suggested your parents probably expect you to marry a Kuwaiti, he's right. They do, probably because Bear didn't. Sorry about that," she said with obvious insincerity.

"I don't want a Kuwaiti husband. I want Brian, and I don't even care if he doesn't want to marry me." Tears threatened to spill down Alina's cheeks, but she batted them back as Dahoud strode out onto the breezy patio where they'd eaten their dessert.

"What's wrong, little sister?" he asked as he poured iced fruit juice from a pitcher on the table and settled on the couch next to Shana. "The girls were watching the latest Harry Potter movie, so I thought I'd leave them to it and find out what has you acting as if you'd just lost your best friend."

"He doesn't want me," she said, gulping back the sob that threatened to tear itself from her throat.

"Shearer?"

"Yes."

"And how do you feel about him?"

"I—"

Dahoud held up a huge hand, silencing her. "Not so fast. Not, 'how do you like having his *lingam* in your *yoni*?' I assume his male parts meet your exacting standards or you wouldn't be mooning over him. How do you feel about Brian Shearer, the man? You've known him less than two weeks."

"I...I admire him for what he's gone through. I feel good when I'm with him. And, damn it, I want him as much as you apparently wanted Shana thirteen years ago and I will not apologize for that. If Father had wanted me to grow up a dutiful, passive woman he shouldn't have encouraged me to think for myself or sent me to the States for my medical education."

"No. He shouldn't have. If you want Shearer and he wants you, I'll run interference with him and Mother."

Although Dahoud's apparent change of heart since the day he'd had to speak with Sharif lifted Alina's spirits somewhat, it would do no good if she couldn't get Brian to change his mind.

She summarized what she'd just revealed to Shana. "You see," she concluded, "there is no cause to raise Father's blood pressure, since Brian has convinced himself any relationship between us is futile."

"Do you want me to talk with Brian, wield the figurative shotgun as they say in the States?" Dahoud asked.

Alina couldn't help laughing at the thought of her big brother chasing Brian down with a loaded gun. "No. If he is to be persuaded, it will be by me. My way. Thank you for listening. Both of you. I'll survive with or without the man of my dreams."

Shana stood and rubbed at the small of her back as though it pained her. "Are you sure?" she asked as Dahoud rose and took over the massage.

"I'm fine. Go on to bed. I think I will stay here a little longer and stare at the ships on the *Khalij*."

Dahoud came to her, bent his head to her ear, and gave her a bit of brotherly advice. "If you love him, little one, don't let him get away."

And as she stood at the edge of the patio surrounded by exotic fragrances mingled on the breeze, Alina began to plan her avenue of attack.

Chapter Six

Alone in the trailer after a hard day fighting malfunctioning oil well pumps damaged during the sandstorm, Brian mentally kicked himself for having accepted Bear's invitation to join his family for the coming weekend. It had been bad enough that he'd had to call Alina's brother for help locating replacement parts he needed to repair a pre-Gulf War pumpjack. But to have jumped on the chance to see Alina again…

Guilt rode him hard. He'd taken shameless advantage of the man's sister then sent her away the other day. And his cock still stood at attention every time he thought of her.

Yeah, he deserved the beating Bear would undoubtedly give him if he found out what had gone on out here when Alina had waited out the *shamal* in his bed. Not to mention the erotic hour they'd shared in the cool, clear waters of the oasis.

Thing was, something compelled Brian to see Alina again. Be with her. Maybe this time seeing her in her own privileged environment would reinforce his belief that they could have no future together, strengthen his resolve to walk away before their emotions got irreparably tangled up with the fierce sexual current that connected them.

Before she came to love him as he already loved her.

Brian stared out the window at an endless expanse of sand dunes, but he saw the blue waters of the Gulf where he'd grown up. And Diane, her sunny smile lighting her pretty face as she ran to him, arms outstretched. They'd been so young, so much in love. So sure of having a bright future together before the Air Force had sent him and his squadron of fighters to fight Saddam.

The last time he'd been on that beach he'd nearly ended his life. If not for Zayed's ghost who'd physically restrained him, his despair might have won over the lifelong belief that only God should decide between life and death. And if it had, he'd have been dead. Dead and quite possibly beyond hope for heaven — or paradise as the Muslims called it. He'd have taken the coward's way out.

You would never have returned here, never have discovered the exquisite pleasures to be found in the embrace of a beautiful, hot-blooded Arab princess.

Brian looked around, expecting Zayed to materialize. Then he realized the voice he'd heard had been inside his own head.

If Diane had waited for him, he'd have found those pleasures with her.

Or would he?

His eyes closed against the rays of a setting sun, Brian lay back on the couch and pushed the vision of his unattainable fantasy from his mind. For the first time since learning Diane had thought him dead and built a new life for herself that left no room for him, he traveled back in time twelve years — to his wedding night at a hotel on Corpus Christi Bay, a week before he'd shipped out.

Finally. They were married. No more furtive groping on the backseat of his car or shaking sand out of their clothes on a deserted stretch of beach.

While Diane was changing in the bathroom Brian stripped off the dress uniform he'd worn for their wedding, eager to explore every inch of his bride's petite body and have her explore him, too. Maybe...

His cock swelled and his balls tightened when he imagined her touching them. Taking them in her mouth. Stroking and squeezing and licking and sucking. The way he planned to pleasure her sweet pussy.

Of course he'd never let her hear words like that. Diane was a good girl. A little prissy, even.

But she was awfully pretty. With her light-brown hair, china-blue eyes, pink lips, and creamy pale skin that freckled in the sun, Brian had always thought all she'd need to be an angel would be wings. Or the silky white nightgown that billowed around her now, like a cloud.

"You're my angel."

"My lord, Brian. Didn't you bring any pajamas?"

He looked down at his cock, realizing that though she'd had it in her pussy she'd never seen it before. The way she stared at it reminded him of how she'd once gaped at a coiled rattler in the woods.

"I thought it would be a waste of time since I'd be taking them off anyhow. Come here," he told her, laughing to mask a sudden wave of self-consciousness. "You can get naked, too, if you want."

"Brian!"

"It's okay. We're married now."

"But still…"

Brian tried to shut off the memories that weren't as precious now as they'd been during all those lonely nights in a dank, dark cell.

But he couldn't. While he'd idealized the good things, romanticized his feelings then, now a voice inside him forced him to face those memories squarely.

Diane had shied away all that week from anything but under-the-covers missionary style fucking. And he recalled that he'd pushed pretty hard for more. But when they'd said goodbye, she'd had tears in her eyes. And he'd believed for twelve long years that once he got back she would be ready to get a little adventurous with their sex life.

Maybe she had—with the guy she'd married believing he was dead. Or maybe Diane just didn't have much interest in messing around in bed. He'd had a hard enough time coaxing her to let him fuck her before they'd married.

It didn't matter now.

Brian had told himself that before, but now he realized he meant it.

Because of Alina, who seemed determined to put joy back in his life.

Beautiful, exotic, Alina who deserved far more than an empty shell of a man who could breathe and fuck but who no longer was capable of more than the rawest of physical sensations. And emotions. Yeah, he loved her. But she needed a man who could love without fear or reservations. One who could look to a bright future, not struggle to cope with a troubled past.

Maybe…maybe he could change. After all, he'd decided to keep on breathing, to come here and do something useful with his existence.

But Brian doubted he could change that much.

Or that they could ever make a life together. Too large a gap separated their worlds.

And no way would he ask her to help him bridge that gap unless he could find a way to resolve his self-doubt.

And cast aside a few of the moral values he'd held all his life — but which he now strongly suspected were flawed.

* * * * *

"We've got him here. Now it's up to you."

Since hearing last night that Brian would be their guest at the villa this weekend, Alina's mind had churned with possible ways she could make him realize what they'd discovered together was precious — well, at least worth exploring much, much further. Home from the clinic early, she glanced out the window and saw a GreenTex helicopter settling onto the concrete pad beyond the wall.

She watched Brian climb down and head for the house, then ran down the stairs to greet him.

So little time, a weekend. Yet it might be all they would have — her request to return to the desert next week to inoculate the nomads she'd missed on her previous visit had been turned down by the clinic administrator. He'd told her venturing so close to the Iraqi border was too risky now, with the Kuwaiti army and its American allies moving in and gearing up to defend those borders—and rich oilfields like Jamil's.

"I almost didn't come," he told her when she opened the door.

That statement hurt, almost as much as his earlier pronouncement that their relationship had no future. "Welcome. I will show you to your rooms," she replied tightly.

Setting down his duffel bag, he drew her into his arms and held her as though she was, at least, desired. "But I couldn't stay away. Help me. Talk to me. You said the gaps between us are not so huge. Show me."

She tilted her head back, looked into his eyes. "Come with me."

"Shouldn't I say hello to your brother and his wife?" he asked as she practically dragged him across the central courtyard and up the stairs.

"They're resting. Shana is pregnant again, and Dahoud is insistent that she take care of herself. Yasmin and Selena are busy with their studies, and baby Jamil is napping under his nanny's watchful eye. We are quite alone," Alina said, lowering her voice to a suggestive purr. "And these are your rooms."

Larger and more ornately decorated than the room where he'd stayed before, the sitting room they entered featured a breathtaking view of the vast, blue Persian Gulf from wide, silk-draped floor-to-ceiling windows and a door that opened onto a vine-covered balcony.

"Do you like it?" Alina asked, throwing open the bathroom door to reveal a huge sunken marble tub filled to the brim with bubbling water and surrounded by plants with profuse, fragrant blossoms. Next to the wall stood a padded massage table stacked high with thick, luxurious-looking towels and robes. Beyond a pair of glass doors he glimpsed a toilet, a shower, and what looked like a cross between a toilet and a urinal.

Brian tried to keep his jaw from dropping open, but it wasn't easy. The bathroom was easily as large as the trailer he lived in—and it was small compared with the room where they now stood — a room he supposed was meant for sleeping as well as the sexual activities portrayed in graphic detail on exquisitely detailed murals along the inner walls.

"The towel racks and faucets are all gold," he muttered, stupefied.

But it was the mural on the wall beside him that had him practically speechless — a man on his knees beside what looked like the huge, silk-draped couch in the center of the room, his face buried between the legs of a voluptuous naked woman who sat on its edge, her head thrown back as if in ecstasy and her satiny legs draped over his shoulders.

His cheeks were burning, and his balls felt as though they might explode.

"Go on in. Take a good look." Alina practically dragged him into the bathroom. "This suite is what Dahoud and Shana call the sultan's chamber."

On the marble vanity next to the massage table were the most obscenely beautiful phallic symbols Brian had ever seen. Six sculpted cocks, perfect to the last circumcised detail, varied in size from a four-inch ebony penis set onto what looked like balls carved from gleaming mahogany, to a beautifully carved red one at least a foot high that sat on a delicate gold stand. And when he looked down he saw the biggest one of all, a four-foot-high wood carving resting in solitary magnificence on the floor beside a plant full of hot-pink flowers.

"My people believe in enjoying the pleasures of the flesh," she said while he gaped at the basket of dildos, cock rings, and other toys set out in plain sight — toys he'd seen before but only in pictures.

"After reading about how adult toys can enhance lovers' pleasure, I ordered some on the Internet," she said once she realized what had caught his attention. "We believe nothing that goes on between a man and a woman is sinful as long as it gives them both pleasure."

Brian really wanted to buy into that argument, and his flesh was getting anxious for her to pleasure it, but... "We need to talk, Alina."

"Later. Now I want to show you some of our roads to ecstasy."

His cock won the silent argument with his brain, hands down. "Later's good," he croaked.

How could he be strong against such potent temptation? He turned, led her toward the pillow-strewn couch—and couldn't help looking at that erotic picture again. Could he do that? And would she like feeling his beard stubble against her satin-smooth pussy?

"Alina?"

She followed his gaze, smiled. "Would you like to taste my *yoni*?

The mental picture he drew of tasting her juices, sampling the satiny textures of her pussy with his tongue...incredibly arousing. Maybe more so because he had the vague feeling it might be forbidden.

Nothing between a man and a woman that gives them both pleasure is wrong.

He liked that philosophy. A lot, he thought as he squeezed her hand. "Would you like for me to?"

"Oh, yes. Come here."

Scared yet throbbing with excitement, Brian let his gaze wander to the other paintings while Alina slowly removed her clothes and his. There were eight murals all told, each more erotic than the last one—or maybe it was just that he was getting more turned on with every touch of her hands, each brush of her soft, gentle fingers against his throbbing cock and balls.

The sweet-smelling candle she lit and set on a small gold table beside the couch reminded him of their first night, when the *shamal* had roared outside the trailer with less potency than the lust that had driven him to take her.

He kissed her lips, open-mouthed kisses that robbed the last shreds of his sanity. With both hands he cupped her breasts, rubbing his thumbs over the tight nubs of her nipples. Then he edged her toward the couch and went down on his knees.

When she sat down he spread her legs with his hands and just looked for a long time at her baby-soft mound, her pretty pink clit, and the glistening lips of her pussy. Her asshole reminded him of a tiny rose, round and puckered. He'd never seen anything so erotic, so perfect.

Bending his head, he took a tentative taste of her slick, wet juices. "You taste good. Sweet," he murmured, "and spicy."

"Go on. Taste some more."

Draping her legs over his shoulders, he leaned in and opened his mouth over her clit. Her pussy trickled its slick hot juices over his fingers where he used them to spread her open for his tongue.

"Yesss. Like that."

He felt her fingers tangling in his hair, pressing his head against her satiny slit. His cock twitched as if to remind him it wanted her attention too, but he did his best to ignore its insistent throbbing.

When he took her clit between his teeth and gave it a gentle nip, more of her slightly salty juices gushed onto his chin.

"More. Please Brian, I'm coming. Help me."

He sucked harder, ground his chin against her swollen inner lips. Not certain what more he could do, he slid a finger along her hot, wet slit until he found and filled her dripping hole.

She screamed out her pleasure, collapsing as she did onto the silk-draped couch.

His balls full to bursting, he stretched out beside her and tried to will away the painful erection he figured now would not be the time to satisfy. Still, loving her that way, getting her to come with just his hand and mouth, gave Brian a sense of power.

And he hardly felt a twinge of guilt, even before Alina rolled over and stroked his cock.

"Would you like to try duplicating another of the murals now?"

What Brian wanted now was a good old-fashioned fucking, and he told her so as he rolled her onto her back and plunged his cock into her.

The sensation was incredible. The walls of her tight, sopping pussy were still contracting, and now they were milking out his cum. "Oh, yeah," he muttered, dragging her legs around his waist before bending over her and fucking her mouth with his tongue.

"Yesss. Make me come again."

The sucking sounds of him pulling out and slamming back into her were driving him wild. Her moans and his, their labored breathing punctuated the silence until, as he sank into her one last time and let go of his cum, she clamped down on him even harder and screamed his name.

"Are you ready for another new experience now?" she asked later, *sliding her fingers into the tangle of hair around his balls and cupping them between her palms.*

She was killing him with her teasing touch. "What do you think?"

"I think you are ready to get the full experience of being an Arab sheikh. Come on, I need to do this in the bath."

Chapter Seven

A few minutes later Brian was lying on the massage table, his balls drawn up and cock pointed toward the swirling plaster patterns on the ceiling. If he hadn't just been fucked and sucked every way he'd ever imagined and then some, he'd have been embarrassed — but he doubted guys who gave head the way he'd done earlier let anything as bland as lying around naked in front of their lovers get to them.

He wouldn't either.

The warm sticky stuff Alina had rubbed into his arms, legs and torso was making his skin tingle, but it felt good. Relaxing. Exotic smells of almonds and apricots and some sort of spices filled his nostrils when swirls of steam blew his way from the bubbling tub, and the piped-in sounds of exotic instruments and muffled drums flooded his mind with fantasies of harem girls swaying for a sultan's entertainment.

"Alina?"

She looked down at him, smiled. "Yes?"

"How much longer?

She glanced at the gold-rimmed clock on the wall. "Ten minutes. Think how you're going to feel when I run my tongue over every inch of your silky-soft skin."

"Men aren't meant to be silky-soft," he complained even though the idea of getting rid of his body hair for her was a turn-on in itself. "I'll look like a damn girl."

She laughed, a tinkling sound that made his cock twitch with anticipation. "You aren't in any danger of being mistaken for a woman. Trust me. I'm a doctor."

"Sexier than any doctor I ever met before."

Suddenly Brian realized that more than anything, he wanted this fantasy to last. "The other day you said that if we try, we can build bridges. Do you really believe that?"

"Well, you're building one bridge now by sampling the ways Arab couples live. From your reaction so far, I'd say that bridge works quite well."

He couldn't argue with that, not when he was laid out, enjoying every minute of having her render him hairless. Or after they'd enjoyed several hours of mind-blowing sex in a sheikh's playroom.

"I'm no sheikh, Alina. I'm not even a rich oilman, just a scarred-up field engineer with a lot of lost years and no experience I can put on a resumé. I've only got the job I have, thanks to the generosity of your brother's in-laws. What happens if we get serious and your father doesn't think I'm good enough for his only daughter?"

"Dahoud approves of you."

"Does that mean your father would?"

She pursed her lips. "Not necessarily, but it will help."

Brian caught her change of tense, as if that hypothetical confrontation with her parents was a given. "Will?"

"Yes. It will. I love you, Brian Shearer, and I intend to keep you. I believe you'd love me, too, if you'd just get it through your head that you're a wonderful man. A fine catch. Worthy of any woman on earth, including an aging Kuwaiti princess whose father considers her an albatross to be passed along to the first willing Kuwaiti sheikh."

"Yeah. I think I love you, too. I know I love loving you the way you like it. But like I said, I'm no sheikh, Kuwaiti or otherwise."

* * * * *

Alina had Brian where she wanted him. Silky smooth, stark naked, and willing to admit he was close to loving her. Now she was ready to bring out the big guns. But not until they initiated the heated bath…and tried out some of the more interesting postures depicted on her brother's playroom wall.

In the shower where she'd just rinsed away the paste, she went to her knees and sucked his velvety sac into her mouth. With gentle fingers she stroked the sensitive skin at the base of his huge, hard *lingam*.

His cock. She mentally tried out the English colloquialism, liked it. It had a strong, stark sound that matched the man. Her man.

The warmth of his long fingers threading through her hair inflamed her senses. But she wasn't ready yet to move into the bath, stroke him head to toe while the effervescent bubbles burst around them.

No, Alina wanted to savor every moment, each sensation. She rolled his testicles around their sac with her tongue, then released them to give equal attention to his huge, hard…cock. Tracing the throbbing vein on the underside of the long, thick shaft, she circled the fleshy corona before licking off a drop of pre-cum that mingled with drops of water on the pale, blunt head.

"You have a beautiful body. A beautiful cock."

She had no time to take him in her mouth. No time to think. Brian had her up against the shower wall and impaled on the cock she'd been admiring, before she realized he'd tired of his passive posture.

"And you, lady, have a delicious pussy I can't wait any longer for. *Nek ni*," he demanded, using her first language as though to be certain she could not misunderstand.

It was fast. Explosive. A fucking by a man who knew what he wanted and had no problem taking it.

The most exciting fucking she'd ever had. When she felt his cum shooting in fast, hard bursts into her womb, her *yoni* clenched around him as wave after wave of pleasure flowed to every cell in her body. A long time later he let her slide onto her feet, steadying her against his big, muscular body when she started to stumble.

* * * * *

And when they woke the following morning and Brian lifted Zayed's pendant to slip the chain on over his head, he saw that the tear was gone. Gone. Not faint, but completely gone. The painted eye stared at him, as blue and clear as ever, and the faceted red stones below the eye winked in the sunlight that streamed through the open balcony door—but the diamond-like tear had disappeared.

"What's that?" Alina asked as she sat up and wrapped her arms around Brian's waist.

He handed her the pendant, noticing that it seemed to glow when he laid it in her hand. "Zayed, the old Marsh Arab who escaped with Jamil and me, gave it to me before he died."

"It's beautifully crafted. And probably valuable. I noticed it before, when we made love at the oasis." Alina turned it over, as though checking for a jeweler's mark. "At first I thought it was an evil eye."

"Several of the workers have said that. Some acted downright terrified when they first saw it. But Zayed said the pendant held magic, that when I found my soulmate, the tear in the eye would disappear."

Alina came up on her knees and lifted the chain over Brian's head. "I don't see a tear," she said, her smile full of promise for a future he'd have sworn yesterday could never be.

"That's because I've found my soulmate. You. Are you ready to fight dragons with me, persuade your family we can build those bridges, make ourselves a happily-ever-after sort of life?"

Alina's delighted scream gave Brian the answer he needed to hear.

Later they'd make the compromises, placate her parents, and build the bridges they'd talked about last night. Right now Brian was about to pleasure the woman he loved.

Epilogue

Three months later

Zayed's ghost looked on with satisfaction while his young American friend married his Kuwaiti princess. The eye in the pendant, he noticed, sparkled in the noonday sun, its blue iris making it stand out clearly against the creamy white of Brian's traditional dishdasha.

There had been no sign of the tear since the day the lovers had agreed to find a way to mold their very different worlds into one– and he knew now it would not return as long as Brian and his beautiful Alina were together.

Paradise. This was what Zayed thought it must look like. Flowers, sunshine, and lovers. The sweet smell of the jasmines and more exotic blooms filled the courtyard where the ceremony had just taken place. And now a group of colorfully garbed musicians began to play their haunting tunes.

He saw many lovers in this man-made paradise. The bride and groom were only two of many who had the look of soulmates.

Jamil and Leila, who had flown in from America for the wedding, looked radiantly happy as they stood at the edge of the crowd and spoke with the gray-haired parents of the bride about their stay in America– and their plan to return so Leila could complete the series of surgeries needed to lessen her scars.

And Zayed's rescuers, Dahoud and his American brother-in-law, could not have been any more solicitous than they were of their beautiful pregnant wives before and during Brian and Alina's exchange of vows.

Where were Dahoud and Jake now? Both men had stood up with Brian at the marriage ceremony a few hours earlier. But now they were gone. Zayed saw Dahoud's wife and daughters mingling in the crowd...

There they were– and they were stepping up onto the raised platform where the musicians were playing. What…?

Dahoud held up his hand, and silence followed.

"We have been twice blessed by Allah this day, first with a new brother and now a new nephew," he said. "Join me in congratulating Shana's brother Jake. His wife, Kate, has just presented him with a healthy son. The first grandson to bear the Green name for my father-by-marriage," he added, smiling broadly at the attractive older couple standing next to Shana.

Life begins, and life begins anew.

Zayed watched the joy spread, watched guests hugging and crying and laughing among themselves while their host repeated his announcement in English.

Suddenly anxious to reunite with Fatima and see long-gone friends from his youth, Zayed faded away, bound for a paradise of his own. Brian had his soulmate to watch over him.

Keeper of the pendant…guardian of lovers…

The ghost of the old Marsh Arab faded away, content now to embrace Paradise now that he felt assured that the magic of the pendant would live on.

About the author:

First published in 1996, Ann Jacobs has sold more than thirty-five books and novellas. A CPA and former hospital financial manager, she now writes full-time except, of course, for the hours she devotes to being a wife and mother to seven kids. A transplanted Midwesterner, she's lived in west-central Florida all her adult life.

Ann loves writing Romantica--to her, it's the perfect blend of sex, sensuality, and happily-ever-after commitment between one man and one woman.

Ann welcomes mail from readers. You can write to her c/o Ellora's Cave Publishing at 1056 Home Avenue, Akron OH 44310-3502.

Also by Ann Jacobs:

Love Magic

Black Gold: Love Slave

Black Gold: Firestorm

Captured

Colors of Magic

A Mutual Favor

Lawyers in Love: In His Own Defense

Awakening

Lords of Pleasure: He Calls Her Jasmine

Black Gold: Another Love

Lawyers in Love: Bittersweet Homecoming

Enchained

Black Gold: Dallas Heat

Lawyers in Love: Getting It On

Gates of Hell

Gold Frankincense and Myrrh

Storm Warning

Dark Side of the Moon

Colors of Love

Tip of the Iceberg

Enjoy this excerpt from
As You Wish
© Copyright Myra Nour, 2004

Once upon a time, long ago in a land far, far away, there was born a girl of extraordinary beauty. Her parents named her Amira, meaning Queen, because she was so lovely and they hoped her future would shine as brightly as her physical appearance.

Fate was not as kind to the fair maiden as her parents had prayed. Her silken, gold hair, delicate face, and slender form drew the attention of not only those who truly loved her, but the unwanted attention of a powerful, evil sorcerer. The wizard Bakr desired the fair maiden and wooed Amira with words plucked from a dead poet's heart, and the finest silk woven by spiders, creatures created with his magic. His final gift was a breathtakingly beautiful rose carved by trolls from blood-red rubies dug from the Earth's belly.

Alas, the fair maiden was in love with a handsome youth named Omar. Being kind in spirit, Amira turned Bakr down gently, but a scorned sorcerer is not to be reckoned with, and the earth trembled as the wizard's anger spewed forth violently.

Bakr strove to create a unique and cruel punishment for the fair Amira, turning her into one of the djinn. She would not be an ordinary djinn, like those who granted three wishes of a new Master, moving on to a new owner each time they were fulfilled. Amira would be forever condemned to stay with a Master throughout his lifetime, fulfilling his or her deepest, darkest sexual desires.

Every djinn is governed by rules, set forth by the Master djinn, Hadji. A powerful sorcerer may succeed in changing the edicts slightly, as Bakr did, adding one specifically tortuous command. Amira was compelled to watch the fulfillment of her Masters' sexual desires while she was forever denied physical release, unless it came by her own hand.

Throughout the endless centuries, Amira lived alone in her lamp, serving countless self-centered Masters, and long ago sickened by their lustful, selfish fantasies. Oftentimes, sorrow overcame her and she dared to dream of the day a caring Master would release her from eternal imprisonment. The fair maiden wept through the centuries and millennia, her tears sparkling like splintering diamonds dropped from a dragon's eye. Would any Master ever fulfill her wish?

"So...you grant me three wishes?"

"No," she shook her head, sending her silken ponytail swishing back and forth. "I grant your wishes as long as you are my Master."

"Really." Nick rubbed his chin. "This is starting to look up." Staring at her lush curves, his thoughts flew here and there. "All right, I wish for a million dollars." He tapped the palm of one hand. "Right here."

"Oh, I'm sorry, Master. I can only grant certain kinds of wishes."

"Wait a minute, you're setting conditions. I thought I was the Master," he chuckled.

"You are." She executed a graceful bow of her head and upper body. "But I am restricted by rules."

Folding his arms, Nick stared at her. "This sounds fishy, but go ahead, give me the bad news. You're probably going to tell me I can only use my wishes for the good of mankind, or maybe I can't wish for things like material gains."

The genie sighed softly. "I wish that were so, Master. I can only grant your sexual desires."

"My sexual wishes?" Nick stared hard at her. Was she serious?

"Yes." Her lovely face was totally serious.

As he leaned back into the couch, Nick's arms gripped his body tight in a self-hug. Congratulatory. She could grant a life-long dream come true? "You're not kidding, are you?"

She shook her head in the negative.

"Anything I wish sexually?"

"Yes," she whispered.

Man, how many of his hot dreams as a youth had been filled with imagining a genie at his disposal? Lots.

Nick's mind was a whirl of possibilities. Any sexual desire? He had so many. He had already managed to fulfill sexual fantasies many men only dreamed of, but still, there had to be some that were out of even his reach. His thoughts latched onto the potential. Finally, his mind was spinning with so many erotic images he had to take a break.

Shaking himself mentally, Nick zoomed in on the very bizarre reality of a genie standing patiently, awaiting his sexual desires. He realized she was the most beautiful woman he'd ever laid eyes on, and he'd known plenty. Those amber eyes matched perfectly with the golden hair that caressed the slender waist. Even her skin matched, with its golden-brown glow. She was a golden goddess.

Suddenly, he knew what he wanted. He wanted to see his genie naked. See if the curls covering her pussy were as golden as the rest of her. He wanted her.

Going up and down her form with his eyes, he could find no fault with the firm, round breasts that were exposed above the low cut bodice of the pearl-trimmed harem top. Her curving waist flared into womanly hips, and he bet her butt was as inviting as her breasts.

Finally his eyes came up to her golden ones. "My wish is to fuck you."

Enjoy this excerpt from

A Kink in her Tails

© Copyright Sahara Kelly, 2003

Chapter One

It was Saturday morning. Nobody abused a doorbell at eight thirty on a Saturday morning. Nobody Eve Bentley knew, anyway.

Brrrriiiinnnggg.

"Goddammit. I'm coming, I'm coming."

Eve sleepily dragged herself from her warm bed, slipped most of her body into her old chenille robe and tied the belt haphazardly round her waist.

She ran a hand through her spiky brown hair and stifled a yawn as she stumbled to the door before it made that disgustingly intrusive sound one more time.

She eased the door open a crack and tried to focus on whoever was disturbing her slumber so rudely.

"What?" she asked.

"Hello?"

She blinked and opened the door a smidgen more.

Oh lord.

He was delicious. Better than coffee. Her sore eyes relished the sight of him. Six foot-and-then-some of delectably masculine attributes. Shoulders that were just perfect for cuddling up to topped a broad chest and tapered down to a huggable waist. It was a package that cried out to be explored, all while being held close by a pair of muscular arms.

"Sorry to bother you…"

Eve shut her mouth with a snap, realizing her saliva had dried to dust and she couldn't swallow. She also realized she looked like death on a bad hair day and wished she could slam the door, go change, and start again.

Given that changing would involve a facial, a hair appointment and possibly some liposuction, she supposed it wasn't an option.

"I woke you, didn't I?"

Swell. Obviously the man was also an Einstein.

"Um, well, I was just going to...actually..."

"Here."

He thrust a package at her.

"This is so sudden. We hardly know each other." Eve couldn't stop the words from slipping out of her mouth.

His lips twitched. "It was delivered to my door this morning and I took it inside and opened it without realizing it. I am awfully sorry, but you know how it is before you've had coffee."

"Oh, do I ever."

She took the package from him and looked at it.

"It doesn't bite, you know. And I already opened it, so I can guarantee it doesn't explode."

"Yeah."

"So, it would probably be okay if you opened it and looked inside?"

"Think so?"

"Mmm hmm."

Eve looked at him again. Her hormones slapped her upside the head—hard. She could swear she heard her dear departed mother's voice someplace, yelling at her. *Eve, find a nice man, for God's sake. You're not getting any younger.*

"So, uh, did you have your coffee yet? I guess I'm just about to make some."

He tilted his head while he considered her contorted statement.

He grinned. "Hey, I'd love to. Can't do anything on just one cup, can you?"

"No. I mean yeah, I guess so. Or not. Or whatever. Why don't you come on in?"

"Thanks."

"Oh. One question."

"Sure."

"Who the hell are you?"

"Simon Austen. Nice to meet you."

He held out his hand, willing her to take it, wanting to touch the rumpled warmth he felt radiating from this enchanting woman.

"Eve Bentley, Ma…" she bit off the response as she shook his hand.

"Ma…? That would be the sheep Bentleys?"

"Sorry." She chuckled as she led the way into the kitchen. "That would be Eve Bentley, Marketing Design, which is how I usually introduce myself when shaking hands. Force of habit I guess." She glanced down at herself. "I remembered just in time that this wasn't a formal moment."

She made a half-hearted attempt to straighten her robe, which failed miserably, bringing a mental cheer to Simon's libido. From where she'd seated him at her small breakfast bar, he had an excellent view of the curve of her lovely breasts beneath her nightgown as she bent to the coffee machine.

She was delightfully mussed, warmly sleepy, and he was finding it hard to resist the urge to pick her up and carry her back to wherever it was she'd just gotten up from. He'd like to muss her some more.

A lot more.

His pants started to hurt.

"So you live here in the building, Mr. Austen?"

"Please, call me Simon. Yes, been here about two weeks, I guess, but what with trying to unpack and also meet a major deadline for a job, well…I really haven't been anywhere for the last ten days but my desk."

"Deadline?"

Simon had a feeling the question was probably more polite than interested. Damn, how long would it take this woman to wake up? To realize that from the first moment he'd set eyes on her, he'd developed a major case of lust, which was probably showing in his gaze and his pants?

"Yes. I'm an architect."

"Oh. How nice."

What she meant, of course, was oh, how boring. For the fifteen hundredth time in his life he wished he was a bullfighter, or a rodeo rider, or a NASCAR driver. Something that would get women's attention more than an architect.

"Would I know anything you've built?"

"Westgate Mall?"

"Don't shop there."

"How about Treetorn Towers?"

"Too high priced for me. But nice windows."

"Thank you. I picked them out myself."

She glanced up and grinned, doing severe damage to his brain cells. That grin of hers was seriously dangerous. It went all the way down his spine and settled comfortably somewhere over his crotch. He could have sworn it hummed when it got there.

"Cute," she answered.

"Aren't I?"

"No, I didn't mean that. I meant your windows crack."

"No they don't. And if they did, they wouldn't be cute." His rapid quip was out of his mouth before he'd really thought much about it. Something about her seemed to bring out his best lines.

There was a distinct moment of silence, when most everything paused. Even the coffee pot held its breath.

"Talking to you is like talking to a snake. Somehow the conversation winds back on itself and ends up biting its own ass."

"I haven't bitten your ass yet, have I?"

One mobile eyebrow flew up toward her serious bed hair. "You are getting quite fresh."

"No, no. You misunderstand. I'm already fresh. It's you who's slightly wilted. But I expect the coffee will put the starch back in your stem."

She shook her head slowly, and poured a large mug of coffee, adding cream and stirring it.

"May I have one too?"

"Oh sh—Oops." She blushed. She'd almost said shit and she actually blushed. Simon promptly fell in love.

"I guess so. That's why I invited you in, wasn't it?"

"I was hoping you were overcome with serious morning lust and wanted to get me naked in order to slake your wicked desires, but this will have to do, I guess…" He gave her his best impish grin while patting himself on the back for his amazing ability to tell the truth no matter what the circumstances.

"Well, in the absence of any desire slaking, how about I open this?" She waved her hand at the package she'd set down on the countertop.

"Mmm. Do." Simon, who already knew what was inside, restrained his urge to snicker.

She peered at the label. "That's odd. No name and no return address. Just the apartment number, which is a bit smeared I must admit. Are you sure it's not for you?"

"Absolutely."

"Oh well, I guess that could be a "B". And you're in…what, 4D?"

"Yep."

She was spreading the tissue aside as she spoke, delicately parting the folds in a way that Simon, for some reason, was beginning to find rather erotically stimulating.

He'd like to part her folds that way, he mused. She'd be pink, too, like the tissue, rippled and ready for him. But she'd be slippery and shiny and hot, not crackly and...her gasp interrupted his rather charming fantasy.

"Good God. It's a dead critter."

Simon burst out laughing. "No it's not," he huffed, gasping for breath at her horrified expression.

"Eeeeuww."

"Oh for Pete's sake, come on, look closely."

Simon picked up the box and tipped it sideways so that the contents fell out onto the tissue between them.

Eve poked at the mass of fur. "It's too small for a mink coat. And it's real fur so that lets out any of my past boyfriends. Never had one that would spring for the genuine article."

"How about present ones?"

"Don't have any."

Simon mentally cheered.

"It's not moving." Eve stared at the tangle on the tissue.

"No it's not. And it won't until you pick it up."

Why an electronic book?

We live in the Information Age—an exciting time in the history of human civilization in which technology rules supreme and continues to progress in leaps and bounds every minute of every hour of every day. For a multitude of reasons, more and more avid literary fans are opting to purchase e-books instead of paperbacks. The question to those not yet initiated to the world of electronic reading is simply: *why?*

1. *Price.* An electronic title at Ellora's Cave Publishing and Cerridwen Press runs anywhere from 40-75% less than the cover price of the <u>exact same title</u> in paperback format. Why? Cold mathematics. It is less expensive to publish an e-book than it is to publish a paperback, so the savings are passed along to the consumer.

2. *Space.* Running out of room to house your paperback books? That is one worry you will never have with electronic novels. For a low one-time cost, you can purchase a handheld computer designed specifically for e-reading purposes. Many e-readers are larger than the average handheld, giving you plenty of screen room. Better yet, hundreds of titles can be stored within your new library—a single microchip. (Please note that Ellora's Cave and Cerridwen Press does not endorse any specific brands. You can check our website at www.ellorascave.com or

www.cerridwenpress.com for customer recommendations we make available to new consumers.)

3. *Mobility.* Because your new library now consists of only a microchip, your entire cache of books can be taken with you wherever you go.

4. *Personal preferences are accounted for.* Are the words you are currently reading too small? Too large? Too...**ANNOYING**? Paperback books cannot be modified according to personal preferences, but e-books can.

5. *Instant gratification.* Is it the middle of the night and all the bookstores are closed? Are you tired of waiting days—sometimes weeks—for online and offline bookstores to ship the novels you bought? Ellora's Cave Publishing sells instantaneous downloads 24 hours a day, 7 days a week, 365 days a year. Our e-book delivery system is 100% automated, meaning your order is filled as soon as you pay for it.

Those are a few of the top reasons why electronic novels are displacing paperbacks for many an avid reader. As always, Ellora's Cave and Cerridwen Press welcomes your questions and comments. We invite you to email us at service@ellorascave.com, service@cerridwenpress.com or write to us directly at: 1056 Home Ave. Akron OH 44310-3502.

NEED A MORE EXCITING
WAY TO PLAN YOUR DAY?

ELLORA'S
CAVEMEN
2006 CALENDAR

COMING THIS FALL

THE
ELLORA'S CAVE
LIBRARY

Stay up to date with Ellora's Cave Titles
in Print with our Quarterly Catalog.

Discover for yourself why readers can't get enough of the multiple award-winning publisher Ellora's Cave. Whether you prefer e-books or paperbacks, be sure to visit EC on the web at www.ellorascave.com for an erotic reading experience that will leave you breathless.

www.ellorascave.com

Printed in the United States
45992LVS00001B/91-123